WHEN DOCTORS FINALLY SAID NO

ROB TENERY, M.D.

Best wishes!
Rob Tenery MD
[illegible] '13

ARCHWAY PUBLISHING

This is a work of fiction. All of the characters, names, incidents, organizations, and dialogue in this novel are either the products of the author's imagination or are used fictitiously.

Archway Publishing books may be ordered through booksellers or by contacting:

Archway Publishing
1663 Liberty Drive
Bloomington, IN 47403
www.archwaypublishing.com
1 (888) 242-5904

ISBN: 978-1-4808-7468-8 (sc)
ISBN: 978-1-4808-7469-5 (hc)
ISBN: 978-1-4808-7487-9 (e)

Library of Congress Control Number: 2019901564

Print information available on the last page.

Archway Publishing rev. date: 2/19/2019

DEDICATION

WITHOUT THE SUPPORT of my wife, Janet, this book, chronicling the travails facing this noble profession would have not have come to fruition. Also I dedicate it to my father, Dr. Mayo, who taught me that caring about his patients was equally as important as caring for them.

LIST OF CHARACTERS IN ORDER OF APPEARANCE

Lou Bosser—EMT
Randy Sanchez—EMT
Jordan Springer, MD—intensivist, Methodist Hospital
John Terrell, MD—radiologist
Allison Terrell—John's wife
Lucy Salverino—patient, new mother
Manny Salverino—father
Rayborn Carlisle—United States senator
Leonard O'Bannon, MD—representative of AMA
Dorothy Peoples—Allison's mother
Lane Foster—Senator Carlisle's chief medical advisor
Mr. Files—patient in the emergency room
Mr. Mancuso—lobbyist for Allied American
Dr. Sidney Frances—physician at Metropolitan
Duke Dandridge—president, Horizon Data Systems
Art Bywaters—pharmaceutical representative
Dave Streeter, MD—physician at county society meeting
Ned Townsend, MD—physician at county society meeting
Hannabel Kornwall—witness at Senate Committee hearing
Jerald Todd, MD—Unified Medical Association
Mandy Jefferson—Dr. Broyle's assistant
Gene Broyle, MD—internist at Methodist, Unified Medical Association

Lori Anderson, MD—Dorothy's internist
Bailey Forman—majority leader of the Senate
Holland Moore—president of the United States
Arlen Roberts, MD—John Terrell's neighbor
Dr. Kinder—Allison's obstetrician
Jeffrey Woodlands—son of dying mother
Dolly—waitress in Longview
Seldon Rogoff, MD—physician in Longview
Stretch Daily—orderly at Methodist Hospital
Lucille Beating—emergency room nurse at Methodist
Mr. Morris—patient in the emergency room
Britt Barkley—chief executive officer, Methodist
Marvin Breedlove, MD—physician at Methodist
Ramon Zamora, MD—radiologist at Methodist
Sylvia Veller—billing secretary for Methodist
Maynard Dunn—senator from Wyoming
Rebecca (RJ) Talkington—AMA staff
Martin Bohannon—administrator, Crosstown Medical Center
Darnell—administrator, Mercy Hospital
Jimmie Fouts, MD—physician in the Texas Valley
Carlos Rodriguez—young girl's father
Dr. Atkins—director, Emergency Medicine, Parkland
Solomon—computer geek
Maggie—emergency room nurse at Irving Central
Barton—computer expert at Horizon
Jeffrey Schooner, MD—cardiologist at Irving Central
Stokley—US attorney general
Arlene Tragus, MD—American College of Surgeons
Lawrence Raven, MD—American College of Physicians
Traci Simms—reporter from the *Dallas Morning News*

PROLOGUE

"WATCH OUT!" LOU Bosser's plea was almost drowned out by the wail of the siren. "Another corner like that, and you're going to throw her off the gurney."

As the ambulance sped into the night, the driver fumbled through the purse of the patient they had just picked up after an anonymous call. They found the patient, a Caucasian in her fifties, unconscious, her limp body draped over the steering wheel of her still-idling car. According to the police officer who was first on the scene, there appeared to be no signs of foul play. The police had already made the identification by the time the EMTs arrived, but a telephone call to her residence had gone unanswered. A quick check of her vital signs revealed nothing alarming, but the fact she was unresponsive even to painful stimulation was reason for concern. After stabilizing her neck, she was loaded into the ambulance for the quick trip to the nearest emergency room.

"I've got it," Randy Sanchez said. "Her insurance card says that her coverage is by Allied American."

Bosser jerked his head around, a look of disgust on his face. "Shit! That's the one almost nobody takes." He looked down at his still comatose patient. "You'd better call ahead and see what to do."

Picking up his phone, Sanchez quickly scrolled through the list of hospital numbers, then punched the automatic redial button. Within seconds, he was on the line with someone from Lewisville General. After a few brief comments, he hung up. "They don't participate with that plan and want me to take her on to Parkland," he said, his tone frustrated. "That's going to be another twenty minutes. How's she doing?"

"Her vitals are stable. It must be something going on inside her head, probably a stro—" Bosser's comments were cut short.

Suddenly, the patient jerked as if trying to sit up. The surprised EMT reached over to restrain her, only to be hit in the face with a warm, slimy liquid as vomit shot from her mouth. He recoiled back, pawing at the putrid material that was now obstructing his vision. The previously lifeless patient struggled again, this time letting out a deafening scream, only to be followed by a gurgling gasp as she lapsed back into a coma.

Reaching for a towel, Bosser fought to regain some semblance of control, still reeling from the patient's unexpected outburst. His gaze darted back to the motionless patient, only to find a totally different situation. He quickly recognized the almost bluish color that now covered her face as she unsuccessfully struggled to bring air into her oxygen-starved lungs. "She's aspirated!" he called out while reaching for the portable suction tubing that hung precariously on the wall just above the patient's head.

It was an EMT's worst nightmare—the sudden loss of an airway. Without oxygen, all the medications and intravenous fluids were useless. There was no way she would survive a trip, even to the closest hospital, unless her obstruction was quickly eliminated. Bosser struggled to get the plastic aspirator tip between her tightly clenched teeth. "Call ahead to Parkland and get me a doctor on the phone—STAT!"

Within thirty seconds, Sanchez answered his request. "They're on diversion; the ICUs are overflowing. They directed us on to Methodist."

"Didn't you tell them this lady is going to die on us if we don't get some help now?" Bosser said, struggling to force oxygen into the patient's lungs with the Ambu bag tightly clamped across her mouth.

"We got cut off before I could say anything. You know how Friday nights are. That place is a zoo," Sanchez answered, looking at his struggling partner. "It looks like you're going to have to tube her."

A horn blared out as Sanchez spun back around to see he had drifted over into the lane of oncoming traffic. His years of training paid off as he jerked the steering wheel sharply to the right, just in time to miss a giant 18-wheeler heading straight at him.

Bosser looked up, grabbing onto the stretcher to keep from being thrown against the wall. "Some days, I wonder why you didn't take up some other line of work."

Sanchez didn't respond, apparently still trying to figure out his next move. Looking up at the street sign overhead, he picked up the phone again and scrolled down to Methodist Medical Center. "This is an emergency!" he barked out. "We've got a patient in respiratory distress. You're our closest hospital, but by my calculations, we're still a good five to six minutes away. Unless we can get her intubated, that will be too late. Can you patch me through to your doctor on duty?"

The ashen color of impending death was quickly setting in as the patient lay motionless, no longer able to call upon the strength to even try to breathe. Bosser abandoned the Ambu bag, instead grabbing for his tool kit with the intubation equipment. Moving quickly, he removed the plastic tube that would restore lifesaving oxygen to the patient's lungs and laid it on the gurney. He would have only one chance before his efforts wouldn't matter. Picking up the battery-powered handpiece, he slipped on the blade, moving it up to check the light. Nothing! Bosser nervously repeated the movement several times. Still no light! He held up the bulb. It looked fine. Desperately, he grabbed the kit again, his eyes scanning rapidly as he groped for the backup hand-piece and blade, only to find neither present. With the recent budget cuts, the EMT system had been forced to curtail their purchases of new equipment, even borrowing from one unit to meet the needs of another. A knot formed in Bosser's stomach; there was no way he was going to be able to intubate his dying patient.

"I've got him on the line!" Sanchez called out, handing the telephone back to his partner. This time, he made sure he kept his eyes on the road.

Bosser grabbed the telephone and quickly relayed his patient's desperate situation to the person on the other end of the line. "I can't see to put the tube in, dammit! They gave me a kit with only one laryngoscope, and it doesn't even work."

"Have you ever done a tracheotomy before?" Dr. Jordan Springer asked, his voice calm, paced.

"In my training, but that was on a mannequin," Bosser said, his breathing hurried. "And on a dog when I got my certification."

The anxious EMT heard muffled sounds over the line, and then the doctor spoke again. "It looks like you're going to have to do another one now. Do you have a scalpel blade in your kit?"

Bosser rustled through his box of supplies. He knew one was supposed to be there, but so was the backup laryngoscope. This time, his luck held out as he held up the scalpel, tightly wrapped in sterile plastic. "I've got it," he said, his hands shaking.

"Good! Now make sure your patient is flat on her back," the Methodist ICU doctor continued. "Feel for her Adam's apple, then stick the blade in just below it. Start with the point horizontal; it goes in easier. Then turn the handle back vertical to keep it open."

Bosser felt a wave of panic flood over him. He had been in scary situations before, but to stab somebody in the neck, even to save her life, well … "I can't," he muttered.

"Can't hell!" Springer yelled. "It's her only chance. Give the driver back the phone and do it."

He handed the telephone back to Sanchez, who was pulling over to the side of the highway to offer assistance, and quickly removed the cellophane wrapper. "Here goes."

With that, Bosser plunged the sharp blade into the patient's throat, just as the doctor had directed. Blood oozed from the wound, and then there was a rushing sound as air entered her lungs for the first time in several minutes. Bosser sat paralyzed, unable to move, the knife still protruding from her exposed neck.

"He's in," Sanchez said over the telephone. "What do we do next?"

Sanchez listened intently as Dr. Springer gave further instructions. Then he turned to Bosser. "He said cut the nose piece off the oxygen tube and stick it in the hole."

"Did he say anything else?" Bosser asked, his pulse slowly returning to normal.

Sanchez put the ambulance in drive and quickly pulled back on the highway. "He said to get the hell over to the emergency room."

1

"DR. TERRELL, YOUR wife is on line three," the receptionist said over the paging system as the radiologist sat hunched over a set of tomograms of an unknown lung lesion picked up on a screening exam the week before.

His concentration broken, Terrell reached for the receiver. "What's going on—"

Allison interrupted. "John, they say it's not covered," she said, her voice uneven, troubled. "The MR283. I went in to get my prescription refilled, and the druggist hands me a bill for $650."

His head spinning, Terrell said, "But they paid for it last month?"

"The pharmacist gave me some vague explanation about the medicine not being on the insurance company's formulary—that they still consider it experimental and would no longer pay for it."

"What did you do?"

"Put it on our credit card ... like everything else," she said. "John, I have to have my medicine. Dr. Toney said I'll need it for the rest of my life."

Allison was right, and Terrell knew it. The very advances that had allowed her a second chance at life now held her captive. Take the medicine that blocked her body's immune system from a dreaded rejection or face the possibility of a recurrence of her myelodysplasia. There was no choice. "Those bastards!"

"They offered me a generic substitute," Allison said, her voice weak, defensive.

"There is no substitute," John shot back. Once again, he was reminded what it was like to be a patient. As the feeling of helplessness welled up, his chest tightened in frustration.

Their conversation was suddenly interrupted as the voice clicked over the intercom. "Dr. Terrell, they are waiting for you in fluoroscopy."

. . .

"You've sure got one pretty baby there, Mrs. Salverino," the nurse said, not looking up as she stuffed the patient's personal belongings into a large plastic bag labeled Methodist Medical Center. "I told your husband to pull around to the emergency entrance. It's more private. We want only the best for our new mothers."

Lucy Salverino was still exhausted from her ordeal. The sixteen-hour labor that ended close to midnight had used up every ounce of strength she had. After the exhilaration, she was finally able to fall asleep. But it must have been around two o'clock by then. They didn't wake her until seven, the time for her baby's first feeding. She was awakened by the familiar screams of a cranky newborn whose only interest was getting her needs fulfilled. That was more than two hours ago. It was almost time for another feeding, but it would have to wait until they arrived home.

While she waited in the wheelchair, the nurse scurried around the room, gathering Lucy's last belongings. With her prolonged labor, Lucy had almost passed her approved length of stay. "Honey, I know you're still tired, but since there were no complications, your insurance company won't allow you to stay," the nurse said, a hint of remorse in her voice. "Any longer, and it's out of your pocket."

Lucy nodded weakly, gently cuddling her baby. "Oh no," she said. "With my husband working two jobs and me out of work, we can barely afford the insurance now, much less pay for more." She began to shiver as the chill of exhaustion coursed throughout her body.

"You'll be all right. You're young and strong," the nurse said with a smile, taking a blanket from the bed and wrapping it around her. "That's why God made younger women have the babies."

"If you say so," Lucy answered, unsure about almost everything at this point.

With the plastic bag precariously balanced in one hand and the handle of the wheelchair in the other, the nurse and her two patients were off. No sooner had the door closed to Lucy's room than a call went out to Environmental Services. They had thirty minutes to clean it up before the next patient arrived.

"That's him over there, isn't it, honey?" the nurse questioned, pointing to the dented red Dodge pickup idling by the dock at the emergency entrance.

Lucy smiled as she recognized her husband's handlebar mustache through the broken windshield, his white teeth glistening in the glaring Texas sun. Manny Salverino moved the beaten-up vehicle to the loading dock.

"Here you go," the nurse said, handing the bags over to the waiting husband. "You know you have to drive real carefully now that you have such precious cargo."

He grinned shyly, looking over at his wife and new daughter. "Yes, ma'am, I will. Don't you think they need to stay here a little longer, being that she just delivered last night and this is our first baby?" he asked hesitantly.

"It's not what I think, Mr. Salverino," the nurse said sharply. "It's the insurance companies. They make all the decisions around here. I know she'll do fine. Now, let's get her loaded up, so you can get home. Your daughter is going to need to eat soon."

Lucy winced as she stretched out her leg, climbing into the pickup. She was not unfamiliar to pain and hard times, being the oldest of six siblings in a family with no father and a mother who frequently didn't come home from work until after dark. She was strong—maybe not physically at this point but mentally. If she had to go home and take care of her baby that was what she would do. After all, her mother and countless generations before her had done the same thing.

Failing to notice the spots of fresh blood on the truck's running board, the nurse gently laid Lucy's new daughter in her lap and closed the door. "You take care of her and bring me a picture from her first birthday party."

Manny gave a quick wave as the old truck moved out onto the busy street. The blanket still tightly wrapped around her shoulders, Lucy clung to her baby as if to protect her from the new world she was entering for the first time. Home for the Salverinos was a good fifteen minutes away from Methodist even during the best of traffic. Today, it was stop-and-go. Manny's old truck moaned loudly as it inched along the crowded thoroughfare, the needle on the temperature gauge moving precariously close to the hot mark.

Manny was preoccupied, one eye on the traffic and one on the temperature, when he heard the sickening thud as his newborn daughter tumbled on to the littered floor below. He spun around just in time to see Lucy's unprotected face fall forward, crashing into the dashboard. Blood oozed down her pale cheek as a large gash opened just above her left eye. Lucy's lifeless body then collapsed, obliterating Manny's view of his screaming baby.

"Oh Jesus!" he screamed in horror, reflexively slamming on the brakes. As Manny's truck rapidly ground to a halt, now blocking two lanes of traffic, he jumped out and waved his hands in desperation. "Somebody help me! Please! Anybody!"

. . .

"Doctor, I believe you have the floor," Senator Rayborn Carlisle said into the microphone, his tone harsh.

The Senate hearing room was packed. Representatives from the medical industry and the media filled the chamber, trying to hear the debate on what could be the most important legislation to affect health care delivery since the advent of Medicare in the 1960s.

"Mr. Chairman," Dr. Leonard O'Bannon answered, clearing his throat, "as the spokesman for the largest medical organization in this country, I can only say that if Senate Bill 4215 is enacted into law, it will have devastating effects on the level of health care. Our patients enjoy the best medicine anywhere because we have had the freedoms and financial incentives to develop better drugs and better treatments. Your proposed legislation to convert to a single-payer system will not only stifle growth but—"

"Doctor, I must interrupt you." Carlisle shifted uneasily in his chair. "This hearing is not about what *was*. It's about facing the reality that there's no longer enough money to take care of all our citizens with the level of health care you brag about." The senator gazed around the crowded room and then slowly looked back at O'Bannon. "So, Doctor, please share with me and the twenty-plus million men, women, and children in this country without health insurance what you and your fellow physicians suggest we do to address the needs of our people."

Sweat glistened off his forehead as O'Bannon fumbled nervously through his notes. "Senator, the problem will not be solved by more government intervention but less. With all due respect, sir, before the Affordable Care Act—Obamacare—the system belonged to the patients in this country. It's time you give it back to them."

. . .

The ambulance backed up quickly to the loading dock at Methodist Hospital's emergency entrance. Following closely behind was Manny Salverino's pickup. "We've got a sick one here!" the attendant called out anxiously as he pushed the gurney through the electric doors.

"Take the patient into room 1," the nurse said, a look of surprise on her face from the sudden intrusion. "What can you tell me?"

"We picked her up on the freeway. Looks like shock from blood loss," the EMT answered quickly, continuing to move the patient in the direction of the trauma room. "According to the husband, she was discharged from your maternity service less than an hour ago. We got an IV started with lactated Ringer's, but her blood pressure is still less than sixty systolic."

The nurse spun around and flicked on the paging system. "Dr. Springer, STAT to trauma 1. Dr. Springer, STAT to trauma 1!"

Suddenly, the curtain flew open at the far end of the emergency department as Dr. Jordan Springer, head of Methodist's ICU and called in on double duty to also staff the emergency room, emerged from one of the cubicles and headed quickly toward room 1. "What is it?" he called out, his voice measured in the confusion.

"Evidently, she's one of our OB patients," the nurse answered. "They think she's in hemorrhagic shock. According to the EMT on the scene, she didn't even make it home."

Springer rolled his eyes in disgust. "I'll bet she's one of those drive-through deliveries," he said as he followed the nurse into the room. "Tell the lab to set up two units of uncross-matched blood while I check her over. Also, put in a call to her obstetrician."

Dr. Springer quickly completed his evaluation of Lucy Salverino, calling for two of the four units of blood. The bleeding from the scalp wound had already been controlled by the EMTs when they first picked her up and was not the problem. He would suture that up later after she was stable. The blood was coming from her uterus. He hung a Pitocin drip, hoping the drug would make her uterus contract while waiting for the blood to arrive, and had the nurse start a massage on her lower abdomen to stem the bleeding.

Within three minutes, the blood arrived. Another five, and the first unit was in. "Her blood pressure is up to ninety over sixty," the nurse called out as a look of relief came over her face. "Do you still want me to hang the other unit?"

Springer nodded as he leafed through her discharge papers. "Who knows anything about the baby?"

An aide standing by the door spoke up. "She's with the father in the waiting room and seems to be all right."

Springer started to leave, then stopped and turned around. "Check her blood pressure one more time," he said, his voice relieved but hesitant. "I want to tell her that her mommy is going to be okay. If the powers that be don't do something about quick discharges after delivery, some of these kids are going to grow up without a mother."

. . .

The envelope stamped Confidential had arrived unexpectedly on John Terrell's desk earlier that morning. There was no postage mark, since the correspondence came from somewhere in his own department.

John looked at his watch as he sat down to grab a bite and go through the day's mail. He had only twenty minutes left until he was supposed to be back in the procedures room. Most of the correspondence was the typical brochures from the pharmaceutical companies or a once-in-a-lifetime solicitation that people of moderate success get so often through the mail. Not interested in either, John picked up the envelope and tore it open. He laid down what was left of his sandwich. A look of disbelief slowly crossed his face as he read the contents of the letter:

> Dear Dr. Terrell,
>
> I regret to inform you that Radiology Enterprises has been unable to successfully negotiate a contract

> with Landry Medical Center for the coming year … as the corporation will no longer be able to operate in its present configuration, I suggest you begin to look for another position that would coincide with the termination of our contract with the hospital.
>
> The staff and I will help you in any way possible as we face this difficult transition period.
>
> Sincerely Yours,
> Taylor Chapman, MD
> President, Radiology Enterprises

John's hand went limp; the letter fell to the desk. He and Allison had arrived in Dallas barely two years ago with promises that he would make full partner within three years. The first year had been rough. Not only was his starting salary significantly below other offers he had received; there was also the twelve-month preexisting clause, which meant that during the first year, none of Allison's medical or drug bills were covered. Since Radiology Enterprises was one of the most successful physician groups in North Texas, John had considered the sacrifices worth it. Now, his dream was shattered because some bureaucrat at the hospital had decided to go with another group of radiologists. John knew the decision had nothing to do with quality care. It was the hospital's bottom line that mattered. What about the lives that were affected? Was everything in medicine turning into a business?

He slammed his fist against the desktop, knocking over his almost-empty cup of coffee. "Bastards!" His head was spinning at the thought of the problems he would have to face in the coming months. Radiology's recent popularity had produced an oversupply, at least in the desirable positions. Would they have to move again? And Dorothy Peoples, Allison's mother, just sold her home in St.

Louis and moved into a condominium not a mile away. What would happen to her if they had to relocate?

John was snapped back to reality with a blast from the hospital paging system. "Dr. Terrell, room 4."

. . .

"Is anyone here with Lucy Salverino?" Dr. Jordan Springer called out in the busy waiting area, just off the emergency room.

Initially, there was no response. Springer started to repeat his request when a reply came from across the crowd of people. "Yes," Manny Salverino said loudly, hanging up the telephone and quickly moving across the room in his direction. "How's my wife?" he asked, his voice cracking and agitated, the crying baby tucked awkwardly under one arm.

"Your wife is going to be okay," Springer said, trying to project a look of assurance. "She lost a lot of blood, so we had to give her two units. I put in a call to her obstetrician."

A look of relief came across Manny's face as he nervously shifted the baby to his other side. "Can I see her, Doc?"

"Not quite yet," Springer answered hesitantly, knowing it would not be good for Mr. Salverino to see his wife in her present condition. "Give us a few more minutes. Then we'll move her into a more private area where you can be with her. Let me ask you, Mr. Salverino, has your wife had any trouble with bleeding problems before?"

Suddenly, a look of anger flashed across Salverino's face. "Not until she came here," he said sharply. "My wife was always healthy until you doctors got hold of her."

Springer was stunned. The husband's comment had caught him out of the blue. "Mr. Salverino, unfortunately, complications happen." His mind raced trying to find just the right words to say. "Medicine is not an exact science where it's always predictable. We do everything we can to avoid problems like your wife experienced. The important thing is your wife is going to be all right."

"That's not what my lawyer said. He—" Manny Salverino stopped. He broke eye contact with Springer as he looked back across the crowded waiting area.

With the revelation that Mr. Salverino had contacted his attorney, Springer stiffened, and a pall now fell over their relationship. The quick discharges after most surgical procedures had bothered him from the start. But it wasn't the doctors' fault or even the hospitals'. It all started with Medicare and their rules; then the private insurers rapidly followed suit. In fact, even the patients were somewhat to blame with the thinking that they were no longer responsible for their own medical bills. That part was being left to the doctors and the insurers to work out. He was not about to get into that conversation. Not at this time. He had to get back to his patients, though not before notifying the hospital's attorney. "Mr. Salverino, the nurse will let you know when you can see your wife." Springer abruptly turned and walked away, feeling guilty that he had taken on the role of an adversary.

Tears began to roll down Manny Salverino's troubled face as he called out, "Doctor, I just want to see my wife."

2

AT FIRST, SHE tried to pass it off as indigestion. Being from St. Louis, Dorothy Peoples had not yet grown accustomed to the spicy Texas cuisine. But over the last week, the gnawing feeling in the pit of her stomach kept tugging at her. She wouldn't quite classify it as a pain, just a feeling of uneasiness, tightness. Antacids seemed to give her some relief, but they were only temporary. With growing concern, Dorothy finally decided the problem had gone on long enough. She would get professional help. Being her son-in-law and a physician, John Terrell should have been the logical place to start, since she had not yet established a relationship since moving to Texas to be near her daughter. But she had made a vow not to be a burden to her family unless she was desperate. So far, her problem was not to that point. Instead, she relied on the advice of a friend she had come to know through church.

"I'd like to make an appointment to see the doctor," Dorothy said, shifting the telephone to the other ear and picking up a pencil so she could write down the time. "My stomach's been bothering me for about a week, and I must tell you, I'm getting concerned."

"First, let me get some information from you, Mrs. Peoples," the receptionist answered. "Have you seen our doctor before?"

"No," Dorothy answered hesitantly.

"How did you get Dr. Howard's name?" The conversation was interrupted by a telephone ringing in the background. "Excuse me. Could you please hold while I get the other line?" Without waiting for Dorothy to respond, the familiar sounds of elevator music came floating through the receiver.

Dorothy fumbled nervously with the receiver cord as seconds turned into minutes. The so-called soothing background music was becoming an irritant.

Just as abruptly as she left, the receptionist was back. "Now, what did you say your problem was?" Without waiting for a response, she went on. "Oh, I remember. You're the one with the stomach problem. It gets so busy around here it's hard to keep everything straight. Everyone wants to see Dr. Howard. Now, how did you get his name?"

"Donna Stamps gave it to me," Dorothy said, growing irritated that the receptionist seemed more interested in how she got the doctor's name than why she called. "She's a friend from church. Now, I just want to know when I can get an appointment."

"You said Donna Stamps. Is that spelled with one P or two? We've just put in this new computer here, and it all has to go in just so."

Barely able to hold back her frustration, Dorothy answered, "One P."

"Now that we have that settled, give me your full name, followed by your Social Security number and your insurance."

Dorothy fumbled for her purse, reaching across the desktop. "You'll have to wait a minute. I don't normally have that information right with me … Oh, here it is." Dorothy carefully spelled out her name, hoping to avoid the previous confusion. She continued with her Social Security and Medicare numbers.

"Did you say Medicare?" the receptionist blurted out, her voice lathered in contempt. "Dr. Howard doesn't take Medicare. I'm afraid you'll have to call someone else."

Dorothy was in shock at the receptionist's abrupt response. "But my friend has Medicare, and he sees her."

"I don't know about that. Probably she was a patient here before she was eligible for Medicare, and Dr. Howard just agreed to keep seeing her." There was a long, uncomfortable pause before the receptionist continued. "It's nothing personal, Mrs. Peoples. The doctor sees his old Medicare patients, but he won't take any new ones. He can't afford to do it any other way."

. . .

"It seems like everyone wants to see you now, Senator," Lane Foster said, a cocky smile showing through his newly laminated front teeth. "Since they think you are about to take their golden egg away from them."

Rayborn Carlisle didn't acknowledge Foster's remark, continuing to rifle through the briefing papers scattered on the desk before him. "Where did you put the Allied American file?" The senator's tone was abrupt and to the point. Carlisle had hired Foster fresh out of University of Maryland law school. With the upcoming proposed legislation to convert the country to a government-run single-payer health care delivery system, the senator knew he needed the best minds around him money could buy. Graduating at the top in his class with an extra year in health law, Lane Foster was the logical choice. What he lacked in experience he made up for in connections. It just so happened that Lane's father was CEO of Norcross Health Care Delivery System—owners of over one hundred proprietary hospitals throughout the United States. Whenever Lane needed advice, it was only a touchtone away.

Foster jumped up, quickly scanning the papers he had laid on the senator's desk. "Here it is," he replied proudly. "My father said Allied American are real assholes. The insurance of last resort—mostly for the poor souls that make too much to be eligible for

Medicaid and can't get coverage by the better carriers because they are too high risk. In my opinion, they're almost better off without anything, since most of the health care institutions don't participate with them anyway, even my father's shitty hospitals."

The senator rolled his eyes at Foster's remarks—full of underlying meaning directed toward both Lane's father and what he stood for in the field of corporate medicine and his own rejection from medical school. It was a blot on the young man's career that even the senator was reluctant to discuss, one that would haunt him forever. "Lane, as chairman of the Senate Committee, I have a responsibility to see them all—bad or good. Look what happened to Hillary Clinton when she took the administration's proposed health care plan behind closed doors. Then Obamacare was supposed to be the fix, but the escalating premiums ultimately did it in. I'm not going to let that happen here. This country's health care system is slowly imploding on itself. It's too expensive, it's too inefficient, and worst of all, millions of people don't have access to it except through emergency rooms. Granted, some of them by choice. We here in Washington were given almost twenty years to solve these problems, and you can see the results."

Foster shuffled uneasily as he slowly headed toward the door to meet the people from Allied American. "Senator, it's like the military when it comes to public good. The private sector can't fight wars, and it doesn't look like they can run the health care delivery system either."

Carlisle looked up. Sadness filled his eyes. "I wish I knew the answer. I really wish I did. Why don't you show them in?"

. . .

"John, I tried not to bother you, but after my experience this morning, I don't have any choice," Dorothy Peoples said, her voice strained. "My stomach's been bothering me for about a week now.

Nothing terrible, but it's not getting better. In fact, I think it's worse."

Terrell could sense his mother-in-law's concern. Even though she had moved to Dallas to be closer to them, Dorothy had taken on an independent role, relying on her new church family for most of her day-to-day needs. They saw each other and communicated often but never to the point where John felt smothered. So, when she called asking for help, he knew it was important. "Let me get you a doctor."

"It may not be that easy," she continued, relating to him her experience with her friend's internist. "I just don't understand. People work all their lives for a little security, and when we finally get to that point, we're treated like second-class citizens. They made me feel as if having Medicare was a curse."

. . .

Surprised at Dorothy's story as well as her apparent resentment, Terrell agreed to see what he could do. He placed a call to the large internal medicine group at Landry Medical Center.

"You have reached Metropolitan Health Care Associates. If you are a patient wanting to make an appointment, dial one at this time. If you are a—"

Terrell tried to interrupt and then realized he was talking to an automated answering machine. He would just have to go along.

"If this is an emergency, dial 911 or go to your nearest emergency room. For all other inquires, an operator will be with you shortly."

It must have been close to five minutes by the time Terrell first heard a real voice. "I'm John Terrell, and I would like to make an appointment for my mother-in-law. She has some stomach trouble and needs to get in as soon as possible."

"Has she seen one of our doctors before, Mr. Terrell?"

"No, it's Dr. Terrell," he shot back, feeling defensive as if he were asking for a favor. "She just moved here from St. Louis to be near my wife. I'm a radiologist here at Landry."

"Why didn't you say so?" the receptionist questioned. "You know we always take care of our own."

Terrell decided a response to her last remark was not appropriate under the circumstances. He did wonder what happened to those who were not part of the hospital's family.

"Do you have a particular doctor you want your mother-in-law to see?"

"It really doesn't matter; I've heard they're all good," Terrell said, trying to be politically correct even though his tenure at Landry was apparently growing short.

There was a brief pause as she put John on hold. "Dr. Frances can see her tomorrow afternoon at two. Would you mind giving me her insurance information now, so she won't have as much to do when she gets here?"

"I'm sorry, but I didn't think about getting that before I called," Terrell replied hesitantly. "All I know is she has Medicare."

There was a long, uncomfortable pause on the other end of the line. "Oh," the receptionist said coldly. "Just ask her to bring all that information with her, Dr. Terrell."

. . .

Dr. Jordan Springer grabbed the chart off the counter at the nurses' station and headed quickly down the hall. Leafing through the front two informational sheets and walking into the cubicle, he said, "Mr. Files, it says here you are being treated for glaucoma?"

The young man looked up. "Yeah, before I'm discharged, I thought you'd refill my medicines so I don't go blind," he answered. "Just give me some prescriptions, Doc, and I'll be on my way."

"It's not that easy. What about your eye doctor?"

"That's the problem," Files replied sheepishly. "He won't fill my medicines until he sees me. I think he just wants my money."

Springer had learned a long time ago that comments like that were better off ignored. "When did you last see your ophthalmologist?"

"Two, maybe three years ago."

"And how often are you supposed to be seen?" Springer paused, looking suspiciously over his glasses.

Mr. Files cleared his throat. Shuffling his feet underneath the stool against the examining chair, he said, "Six months."

It was a familiar story—patients failing to keep scheduled follow-up appointments or take their prescribed medicines. Springer had heard the excuses a thousand times—couldn't afford it, other medical illnesses that took priority—as if their previous problems went away while they were attending to another illness or a sick family member. In many circumstances, there were legitimate reasons. But too often, the truth, always unspoken, was that the patient forgot or just didn't take their illness seriously. If Springer had to bet on this one, it would be the latter.

"Let me get the nurse to call your doctor and see what we can do," he said, jotting a note on the chart.

"I'd rather you not. I still owe him money," Files said weakly.

"That shouldn't make a difference if you've made an attempt to pay. I'm sure he'd be willing to work out something with you that you could afford."

Files looked up, his eyes glaring into Springer's. "I thought so too. Granted, I was a fart off, but when I called up to try to work things out, his whole office had changed."

Puzzled, Springer questioned, "Like what?"

"They told me the doctor was now only doing surgery, and if I wanted any more refills, I would have to pay up in full. It pissed me off bad, not that I really had the right, being that I owed him money for almost two years." Files went on, a note of sadness in his voice. "Weren't you guys supposed to care about your patients, even those of us who stray from time to time? Seems like I recall someone from my Sunday school days who did."

Springer felt embarrassed not for himself but for the growing number of his peers who seemed more concerned about what they earned than the plight of their patients. "Let me see if I can get in touch with him and put in a good word for you."

"You'll probably have to stand in line, Doc," Files said abruptly. "Since he started doing those TV commercials, his telephone stays busy all the time."

. . .

The meeting with Allied American went as expected. The senator patiently listened while their chief lobbyist went through a litany of reasons why the federal government should keep out of the health care delivery system. "Look at Medicare, Medicaid, and now Obamacare," the representative from the insurance company continued. "They have become so expensive and inefficient that there are several of your peers here on Capitol Hill who are talking about privatizing them."

Carlisle could no longer sit idly by. If nothing else came out of this meeting, the senator wanted to see how these people thought. "Mr. Mancuso, since we are both here for the public good, I wonder if I might ask you a few questions."

"Be my guest, Senator. That's what they pay me for." A halfhearted smile oozed across his lips.

"Your company is a publicly owned and traded corporation?"

"Yes, Senator. Allied American went public just four years ago," Mancuso said proudly. "And last November, we were listed on the New York Stock Exchange. Quite an accomplishment for such a young company, if I say so myself."

Carlisle wasn't finished. "And what was your rate of return?"

"Thirty-one cents per share, and we still had enough left over to expand our services into four more states." There was a momentary pause, Mancuso seeming unsure if he had fully answered Carlisle's question. "They tell me we are the fastest-growing company in the business over the last two years."

"Very good, Mr. Mancuso. I know you must be proud," the senator said evenly. "What would you estimate your cost of doing business? No, let me ask the question another way. Out of every dollar your company collects from your policy holders, how much do you spend on administrative costs?"

"I'm not sure I can give you an exact answer on that, Senator," the lobbyist answered hesitantly. "But it's somewhere around 25 percent."

Carlisle slowly pushed back from his desk, looking straight into the eyes of his visitor. "Mr. Mancuso, the cost of running the federal programs last year, even with all their inefficiencies, was 11.5 percent, and there was no profit left over to give out to stockholders."

3

HER GATE WAS unsteady and she held tightly to Allison's outstretched arm. Dorothy Peoples arrived fifteen minutes early for her appointment with Dr. Frances. The last days of nagging discomfort had reduced her to the old woman she was, stripping away not only her strength but also any confidence about her wellbeing. She was scared, vulnerable, and imagining any and every illness that might bring her life to an early end.

"I see that this is your first time here with us at Metropolitan," the young receptionist said through her emotionless smile. "We have a few forms for you to complete before you get started." With that, she handed Dorothy a clipboard with about ten sheets of paper and quickly walked away.

Dorothy's eyes went blurry as she looked down at the stack of papers. Apparently sensing her mother's confusion, Allison gazed around the massive waiting room, spotting a secluded area with two chairs and a lamp in the far corner. "Let's go over there, Mom, and I can help you fill them out."

Almost fifteen minutes passed before Dorothy and Allison had completed all the paperwork. Dorothy made an attempt to get out of her chair but fell back, her hands shaking and sweaty. "Would you mind?" She looked longingly at Allison.

Giving her mother a reassuring pat on the knee, Allison swept up the papers and headed back to the reception area. "My mother might need some physical therapy after filling out all those papers," Allison said, trying to elicit a smile from the young girl. Her gesture was in vain; the receptionist's face froze in an unnerving stare.

Quickly leafing through the pages, the young girl stopped and looked up. "We'll need seventy-five dollars."

Surprised, Allison said, "We gave you her Medicare and supplement policy. What's the extra for?"

"Her deductible," the young girl answered coldly. "She has to meet her deductible for the year before her insurance kicks in. I don't make the rules."

"But what if she's already met it? Can't you just bill us for the difference?" The receptionist's icy stare was answer enough as Allison nervously reached in her purse. "I don't have my checkbook with me."

"A credit card would be fine." It was the first time the young girl smiled since their arrival. "I'm sorry, but we don't take American Express."

. . .

Reassuring Allison she would be okay, Dorothy sat alone in the six-by-eight examining room, waiting for Dr. Frances. Her bare feet dangled off the side of the black, cushioned table. A chill moved through her frail body. The paper gown she had exchanged for her clothes clung loosely to her shoulders, exposing her bare back to the rush of cold air blowing from the ceiling vent in the center of the small room.

She stiffened as the voices in the hall approached. "Good morning, Mrs. ... ah ... Peoples. I'm Dr. Frances," the younger gentleman said as he quickly thumbed through the papers in a red folder bearing Dorothy's name. "This says you've been having trouble with your stomach." Dorothy nodded and started to speak when he continued, "How long has this problem been bothering you?"

"About one—" Dorothy was again interrupted as Frances continued.

"Oh, I see here," he said, turning a page in the chart. "One week. As you probably already know, if it were simple food poisoning or gastroenteritis, you'd have been well by now. I think we need to get some tests on you. Nurse!" he called out loudly, causing Dorothy to almost jump off the table. "Come in here while I examine Mrs. … Peoples."

Dorothy's eyes darted around as the nurse plodded slowly through the door. She must have been fifty pounds overweight, Dorothy thought, as every seam on her brown scrubs was at maximal tautness. The aroma of stale nicotine poured forth as she approached the table. "You need to lie back, dearie," she said, her tone both authoritative and caring. "The doctor needs to check you over."

Lying back on the cold table, Dorothy's vulnerability began to engulf her as she waited for Frances's touch. Oh, how she wished now she had asked Allison to come along. The waiting area was so close but so far away. "Ouch," Dorothy blurted out as Frances's icy fingers dug into her tender abdomen.

Frances's examination concluded as quickly as it started. "Nothing obvious," he said, picking up Dorothy's chart and scanning it once again. "As I said, Mrs. Peoples, to make a diagnosis, we need to do some tests."

Still lying on the cold table, Dorothy silently acknowledged his response, unsure of what her next move. "What should I …"

"The nurse will make all the arrangements," he said curtly. Without waiting for a reply from Dorothy, the young doctor turned to his nurse and handed her the red chart with Dorothy's name at the top. "Do a stool guaiac. I want to see if there's any blood there.

Then order an ultrasound and the GI screen." Dr. Frances opened the door and then hesitated, looking back at Dorothy. "Your son-in-law works here? We're going to be sad to see him go." The door slowly closed behind him.

"You're lucky, Mrs. … Peoples," the nurse said, the stench of nicotine on her yellow stale breath. "Dr. Frances just came to the clinic last month. Trained in one of those fancy hospitals on the East Coast where they have all the latest stuff."

"Except bedside manners," Dorothy muttered under her breath.

The nurse looked up from the chart. "I'm sorry. I didn't hear you, dearie. You can get up now."

. . .

"His insurance isn't going to pay for it," the hospital pharmacist said.

Dr. Springer's hand clung to the receiver while the other nestled the patient's chart. "Why the hell not?"

"The patient's in a Medicare HMO, and the medicine's not on their formulary," the voice on the other end of the line continued. "They claim there're other drugs that work just as well."

"Bullshit!" Springer was beyond frustration dealing with the growing number of encumbrances he faced daily as he tried to carry out his duties as a physician. In some ways, the hospital had turned into a virtual prison—a sea of regulations. On top of that, there were the insurance company restrictions. Additionally, the feds were even dictating the requirements for the size of the doctor's bathroom door and what handle to use on the door, just in case someone in a wheelchair had to take a leak. "You know there's nothing else on the market that works as well."

"Dr. Springer, I just work here," the pharmacist replied sympathetically. "If that's what you want, I'll fill it. But if the patient's not willing to pay, the hospital eats the charges."

Springer threw the chart on the counter. "I'll get back to you," he said. He hung up the telephone and headed down the corridor.

"Mr. Bane, the medicine you've been taking for your heart isn't working any longer. There's a new drug that could possibly make a real difference." Springer looked at the elderly man's sorrowful eyes, his hope flickering away like a dying candle. "The problem is it's expensive, and your insurance won't cover the costs because the drug just came on the market."

Springer thought he saw a tear well up as the old man looked away. "Doctor, I've done a lot of stupid things in my life. Drank too much, even smoked until this damned heart problem set in." He paused, looking down at the floor, his breathing labored. "But the dumbest thing I ever did was invest our money on this land deal. Even our preacher had his money in it. We lost it all. If it wasn't for Social Security, I don't know what my wife and I would do."

"I could get you some samples," Springer said, his concern showing through. "They're pretty good about that with their new drugs."

"Look, I have to cut corners any way I can. We only have $300 a month left over by the time I pay for the essentials—rent, gas, electricity. The drug bill that Congress passed two years ago. There are so many things it doesn't cover, such as over-the-counter products." The old man stopped and coughed into his tightened fist. "What happens when the samples run out, Doc?"

. . .

Lane Foster enjoyed the power afforded to those in Washington who were in the position to make decisions that affected the rest of the country. His anonymity as chief advisor to one of those individuals made it all the better. It wasn't the glory he was seeking. It was control. With a father who had dominated his childhood and Lane's rejection to establish his own identity as a physician, everything was about control. So, when he ducked into the front entrance of Horizon Data Systems, no one took notice.

"I'm sure you can convince your senator to see things our way." Duke Dandridge was a massive man with an even more intimidating personality. Earning the starting tackle position for Michigan his sophomore year, he learned early on that sometimes it was easier to go over people than around them, especially for someone of his size. As president and cofounder of Horizon, he had almost singlehandedly cajoled and bullied his fledging software company to a position of prominence in the industry. Now he was ready to move to the head of the class. The contract to administer the federally funded single-payer health care system would do just that.

"Carlisle's still waffling," Foster said, wringing his hands nervously in his lap. "He's got this King Arthur attitude. He knows the system is broken but doesn't want to bring it down, trying to fix it."

"That's why he's got you," Dandridge answered, a smile creeping across his scarred lips. "You're his go-to guy. And you're our ace in the hole, aren't you, Mr. Foster?"

The senator's chief medical advisor shifted uneasily in the chair. "Look, I said I'd help you," Lane Foster said hesitantly. "I'm not a miracle worker. The senator has everyone in the country that's even remotely associated to the health care industry trying to tell him what to do. Even the president and Congress are waiting to see what comes out of his hearings."

Dandridge held up his massive hand, pointing a finger in Foster's direction. "For the money we have invested in you, Mr. Foster, you had better be a fucking Houdini!"

. . .

Being in the bathroom, Dorothy Peoples was not able to pick up her telephone until the fourth ring. "I was just about to hang up, dearie," came back the voice on the other end of the line. "Mrs. … ah … Peoples, Dr. Frances wanted me to call and tell you about your tests."

Dorothy was filled with emotion. It was the moment she had been both dreading and looking forward to since she had been in Frances's office. She had run over every possible scenario in her mind at least a hundred times. Although she was better with the medicine that Frances had started her on, the nagging fullness in the pit of her stomach still remained. "Yes," Dorothy answered weakly.

"We found no blood in your stool, and the blood tests the doctor ordered all came back normal."

Dorothy let out a sigh of relief at the good news. Her worst fears started to evaporate when Dr. Frances's nurse continued.

"The doctor had some questions about the results of your ultrasound, however," the nurse said, a hint of reservation in her voice. "Something about a mass or swelling in your pancreas."

"A what?" Dorothy shot back anxiously. "Does the doctor think I have … cancer?"

Fear raced to her throat, choking off her words as she tried to find out more.

"He didn't tell me what he was thinking, dearie. Dr. Frances just told me to line you up with a gastroenterologist to check it out."

"Can't I talk to Dr. Frances?" Dorothy pleaded, her voice broken, uneven. "After all, he is my doctor."

"He's very busy, you know, with all his other patients," the nurse replied stiffly, as if her authority were being questioned. "I'll ask him to call you, but it could be a while."

. . .

Jordon Springer was shoving down the last bit of his pita sandwich when the knock came on his door. Looking up, he quickly recognized the face of Art Bywaters through the glass partition. He glanced at his watch—five minutes until he had to face the growing crowd of various pulmonary and cardiac problems that made up the majority of the intensive care unit. "Come in," he said, signaling with his free hand.

"Good to see you, Doc," the always jovial pharmaceutical representative said. "I see you're busy. So, I'll only take a minute."

Springer knew that wasn't true. Bywaters would squeeze in every minute he could to try to get Springer to use his company's line of drugs. He couldn't resent him for that; he was only doing his job. In fact, while still in college, Springer himself had given serious consideration to working for one of the major pharmaceutical firms. What he resented was Bywaters's approach. Instead of just laying out the medical information and letting the drug speak for itself, which is what the good reps did, Bywaters was always trying to buy his way in. No money ever crossed hands; that would have been a direct kickback. Bywaters was too smart for that. Instead, he would cater a lunch at the office. He even brought in a guest speaker, a so-called world expert on diabetes, for a dinner at a fancy restaurant after hours. As it turned out, the expert doctor was in the hip pocket of the drug company and only talked about the merits of the drug Bywaters was peddling at the time. From that time on, Springer always looked on the rep with a calloused eye.

"We've got this great new product coming out for hypertension, Doc," Bywaters said enthusiastically. "It's so slick that after you've tried it, you won't want to use anything else." The drug rep paused, glancing over in Springer's direction. "What would it take to get you to try it on some of your patients?"

Springer glanced at his watch a second time, growing irritated with Bywaters's aggressive approach. "Listen, Art, like I've told you before with other medicine, just get me the printed literature along with enough samples, and if it looks like what you say, I'll give it a try."

"Listen, Doc, you know where I'm coming from," he said, his smile now gone. "I pat your back, and you pat mine. That's how it works, isn't it?"

"Not in my ICU." Springer stood up, facing the startled pharmaceutical rep. "Just bring me the samples. And the money you saved by me not taking you up on your offer, put it into research!"

4

"I'VE PUT OUT feelers to most of the hospitals in the Dallas and Ft. Worth area," Terrell said, picking up a copy of the newspaper. "Except for a few of the smaller ones, they're all facing the same problems. With the insurance companies cutting back on reimbursement and Medicare's recent reductions, all the hospitals are having to look at how they deliver essential services."

Appearing perplexed, Allison said, "Exactly what does that mean?"

"It means two things, my sweet wife. First, I may soon be out of a job. And second, the level of health care in this country has taken another step down the rung on the ladder."

"Why would the smaller hospitals be any better off than the larger ones?" Allison asked, moving closer to John on the sofa.

"That's the irony. They never had those services in the first place—referring their sicker patients over to the larger hospitals for specialized care. Everything is just going to even out, unfortunately at a lower common denominator."

Allison stared blankly at the television mounted in a cabinet at the far end of the den while Terrell slowly turned the pages of the paper. The room was silent as the screams of uncertainty raced through their minds. He was the first to break the silence.

"Maybe I can find something in here," he said, a quirky smile on his lips as he pointed to the top of the section labeled Want Ads. With her continued frown, Terrell could see that his attempt at levity wasn't making the situation any better. "The good news is I have two interviews lined up—one at Baylor Hospital and the other at a slightly smaller hospital out in the Oak Cliff."

A smile broke across Allison's face. "Baylor? Isn't that the largest hospital in the area? They're bound to have room for a bright, young radiologist."

"One would think so," Terrell said hesitantly. "The fact is they're the only large hospital that's even willing to talk to me. I think my chances are better at the other one."

"Which one is that?" Allison asked.

Terrell laid down his paper. "Methodist …" He paused, trying to recall the name. "That's it—Methodist Medical Center."

. . .

"Mr. President, I have never seen anything like it, even when the Clintons tried to reform health care," Senator Rayborn Carlisle said. "We have requests from every organization and special interest group that has anything to do with health care delivery to appear before our committee."

"Ray, I don't see that we can have it any other way." The president slowly pushed back from his massive desk and turned around, gazing across the White House lawn. "I made a promise to the people that if I were elected, this administration would guarantee them access to an affordable health care delivery system."

"It was my promise too. But that's the problem, isn't it, Mr. President?" Carlisle said, his tone somber, strained. "They're just promises—the hopes and dreams of those of us who think we really can make a difference. Then when we get to Washington, reality sets in. We're lawyers; we don't know the first thing about health care."

The president's face turned flush at his old friend's remarks. "I know this. Over twenty million people out there don't have any health care coverage. Another seventy million are paying more than they can afford, sacrificing so they don't have to use up their life savings if they get sick or injured. And no telling how many more are staying in a job going nowhere, for fear of losing their health care coverage." The president paused, taking in a slow, deep breath. "The answer to our promises is out there, Ray. All we have to do is find it."

Carlisle shifted uneasily in his chair. They went back a long way, since their early days in the House of Representatives. The senator was now hardened by the many battles he had waged, cast down over and over again by a system that was almost too democratic. Carlisle marveled how the president, who had fought those same battles, still clung to the same hopes and dreams that brought them both to Washington. Maybe, thought the senator, that's why his old friend was in the Oval Office and he was still over on Capitol Hill.

Although it wasn't the usual protocol, the senator stood up to leave. He knew his old friend would understand. "I've got to go, Mr. President. The committee hearings start back up in twenty minutes."

...

"What have I missed?" Dr. Jordan Springer asked as he edged into a seat at the back of the dimly lit room. The county medical society offices were halfway across town, and with the unexpected arrival of an acute myocardial infarction, just as he was about to go off duty, Springer felt lucky to be there at all.

"Ned's just going over the latest membership stats," the sleepy-eyed physician said, pointing to the slides projected on the screen at the far end of the room. "Pretty discouraging. We're down another 2 percent."

Springer remembered the days when membership in the county medical society was an automatic for any physician in good standing—a show of support for the profession while at the same time ensuring a certain unwritten standard of care. Those days were long gone. Now, maintaining membership had become one of the organization's major concerns, diverting valuable time and energy away from the more important issues involving patient care. Medical organizations were not alone. Even the Boy Scouts were having trouble recruiting troop leaders, and churches seemed the hardest hit of all, frequently running the Sunday services with a skeleton crew of volunteers. The problems appeared to start in the 1960s with the *me now* thinking of the so-called hippy generation. Unfortunately, the attitude had grown into an epidemic of apathy and self-absorption that infiltrated every sector of the American society.

As his eyes accustomed to the darkness, Springer could tell that only about a third of the seats were filled. "I see we're having our usual attendance," he mumbled.

"Hell, Jordan, it's the same old faces. I don't know what's going to happen when we're gone."

Next to Springer, the rumpled physician with a straggly handlebar mustache sat up in his chair, leaned over toward them, and said, "These young farts just want to let somebody else do it for them while they go skiing in Colorado or bang away on their computer."

Springer edged back and whispered, "Dave, I wish it were that simple. Most of them who come out of their training are over a hundred thousand in debt and convinced that nothing we do here at the society meetings is really going to change anything. So the majority have decided to just collect their paycheck and accept the status quo. It's a sad state of affairs, but unfortunately it's reality."

"I don't know who's going to run over us first, the feds or the insurance companies," the disgruntled physician said, no longer attempting to muffle his voice.

The speaker at the far end of the room stopped as all heads turned in Jordan Springer's direction. "Dave, why don't you and Jordan share with us what you were talking about." Ned Townsend's lips distorted in a frown, as his audience seemed to have lost interest in his presentation.

Springer quickly responded, his face flushed in embarrassment. "It's my fault. I started it."

"The hell he did." Never one to hold back when he had something to say, Dave Streeter butted in, his eyes glaring. "I was just telling him like it is. No more bullshit about value or relevance in this organization, whatever that means. The simple truth is that the young doctors aren't here because they don't want to spend the time or pay the money. They would rather be back in the operating room or their offices making money, and a lot of it in some cases, while we work our asses off to allow them to do whatever it is they do for a little while longer. It's the old mind-set of letting someone else do it for them."

Springer had come to know and respect Streeter through their work together at the society. A family doctor in one of the small towns in south Dallas County, he was of the old school, believing that a doctor never stopped being a doctor, even after five o'clock. Usually looking out of sorts, his appearance left a lot to be desired. But he was always there for his patients, and they idolized him for it. He was the last of a dying breed—a true patriarch in his small community.

Ned Townsend appeared speechless as a pall fell over the darkened room. It was Springer who finally broke the silence as he slowly got up from his chair. "Can I come up there?" he questioned the speaker.

Within a minute, Springer was standing before the sparse crowd. An air of calmness surrounded him. He had been in this very spot many times before when he served as president of the society just three years ago. "What Dave said is true. We are just afraid to say it." His voice was measured, calculated. "But ask yourself why."

Heads turned uncomfortably from side to side, but no one attempted to answer Springer's question. Not even Dave Streeter.

"Look at their role models," Springer continued. "Mine was a general practitioner back in Ohio who came by my house after work to check on my tonsillitis. I never saw him ask for any money, only about me. I know he must have gotten paid; my father was that way. But the money was never the issue." Springer paused to look around the room. All eyes were glued to him. Even Ned Townsend had moved over, taking a seat in the front row. "The younger doctors' role models, the so-called heroes of today, retire before they're fifty, appear in the advertising section of the *Dallas Morning News* and spend three months a year at their condos in Colorado. They suck everything out of medicine, giving nothing back, then walk away. What the hell do you expect?"

"I told you it wasn't our fault," Dave Streeter blurted out proudly from the back of the room.

Springer looked up, his eyes full of remorse as he scanned the almost empty room. "Maybe you're right, but I don't see that makes it any better."

. . .

Allison clung to the receiver, stunned as her mother revealed the results of the battery of tests. Her heart ached, knowing what her mother was going through with the uncertainty there might be a malignant tumor deep in her abdomen, stealing her life away. Quickly, Allison's angst bubbled over into anger. "Are you telling me that you have only talked to Dr. Frances's nurse?"

"I asked her to have him call me. She said he was real busy. So far, I haven't heard from him, and that was yesterday."

Allison was on the telephone to Metropolitan Health Care

Associates within minutes after assuring her mother that the swelling in her pancreas was probably nothing and she would ask her husband to check with the doctor just to make sure. Not unexpectedly, she encountered the automated recorder.

"If you are a patient wanting to make an …" Allison's patience already frazzled, she struggled to get through the endless list of options. "If you are a doctor wanting to speak to one of our physicians, dial five at any time. If this is an emer—" It was a reach, but by now, she didn't care. Allison punched five on her telephone.

"Yes, Doctor," the crisp reply came back. "How can we help you?"

Suddenly, Allison felt a sense of guilt, as if she had committed a mortal sin trying to pass herself off as a doctor. "I'm calling for Dr. Terrell." She had already gone this far, she decided. "I would like to speak to Dr. Sidney Frances … if he's not too busy." Her hesitancy was beginning to show through.

"Our doctors are always busy," the operator said indifferently. "Do you want to speak to him now or do you just want to leave a message?"

Allison remembered that her mother had already unsuccessfully tried that option. "No," Allison said, her courage once again bolstered by the operator's arrogance. "He wants to speak to him now, thank you."

The seconds turned into minutes as Allison anxiously waited on the line while infomercials touting the virtues of Metropolitan's clinic blared in the background. Her concern was growing that this might not be the right approach. She was about to hang up when Dr. Frances suddenly cut in. "Yes." His one-word response was hurried. Allison could feel his irritation.

"I'm … John Terrell's wife," she replied, her voice breaking slightly. "Dorothy Peoples is my mother. I had hoped you could give us some information about her test results; she's very concerned."

There was a long, uncomfortable pause. "I thought they told me this was a doc …" He stopped. "They're not all in. I'm not a gastroenterologist, Mrs. Terrell. My nurse was supposed to arrange an appointment for your mother to see one here in the clinic. Has she not done that?"

"Yes. I mean no, not yet. You're her doctor. She wanted to hear from you first before she did anything."

. . .

"Ladies and gentlemen, this meeting is back in session," Senator Rayborn Carlisle said, peering over the horn-rimmed glasses that hung precariously to his nose. A hush fell across the hearing room as an old lady clinging to a battered walker awkwardly edged her way toward the front table. Carlisle picked up the agenda book for the afternoon, leafing through the pages. "I believe the next person to come before our committee today is a Mrs. Hannabel Kornwall."

"That's me, Senator," the old lady said as she flopped down in the chair directly in front of the microphone, still trying to catch her breath from the arduous trip across the hearing room floor. "You can call me Hanna if you'd like."

Carlisle forced a smile, then moved closer to his microphone. "And, Hanna, what's the reason you've asked to come testify before this committee?"

"Senator, my husband and I were married fifty-four years. That was until three weeks ago." A tear edged down her cheek.

"I'm sorry, Mrs. Kornwall," the senator said, shifting uneasily in his chair. "It must be a great loss to you."

The old lady looked up, her eyes fixed squarely on Carlisle. "Oh, he's not dead, sir— just divorced."

Shocked, Carlisle said, "You're telling this committee that you just divorced your husband of fifty-four years?"

"Had to," Hanna shot back, a touch of anger in her voice as her gnarled fingers wrapped around the speaker cord. "Because of you and all your cronies up here on Capitol Hill."

A low rumble echoed across the crowded room as all heads

turned in the old lady's direction. "Do you mind telling the committee what you mean, Hanna?" Carlisle said hesitantly, not knowing what to expect.

"He has Alzheimer's. I'm the only one he knows most of the time." Her voice was sad, unsteady. "I've tried to take care of him, but it was too much for both of us. We even tried bringing in help during the day, but that still left us alone at night. We couldn't afford round-the-clock care. So, I put him in the nursing home." Her tone was somber, dejected.

"I'm sure he's getting better care now," Carlisle said, hoping a little reassurance would be all she needed, and he could move on to the next party on his crowded agenda.

The old lady didn't budge. Instead, she moved closer to the microphone. "Senator, do you know how much it costs to stay in a nursing home?"

Carlisle was prepared for contingencies just like this as he pushed back in his chair to confer with Lane Foster and another aide. Within less than a minute, he was back up to the table. "Twenty-five hundred a month, give or take," he replied cautiously, still unsure where she was taking him.

"More like four thousand, if you count his Social Security," she snapped back. "And don't forget I still have to eat too. Our only choice was Medicaid. It pays for it all, if he's eligible."

The senator felt a sense of relief since he had cosponsored every Medicaid reform package since coming to Washington. "It must be reassuring to know that you and your husband have been provided with some security during this difficult time."

The old lady moved back in her chair and picked up her purse. She reached inside, slowly pulling out a crumbled piece of paper. "Senator, this is my bank statement from last month. Seventy-six thousand dollars. This and our house are all the security my husband and I have. He worked hard all his life, but with six kids and no college education, he didn't have much opportunity."

Carlisle had a full agenda with other witnesses lining the hall, waiting their turn at the podium. "Mrs. Kornwall, Hanna. All of us here are sympathetic to your difficult financial situation. But could you please get to the point that brought you here today," he said, hoping he did not come off as indifferent to her plight.

"Senator Carlisle," Hanna replied, her response measured. "The people at the Medicaid office said we were too rich to be eligible for benefits. I asked them if we could give the money to our kids, and they said no. Guess they thought we might be able to get it back that way if we needed anything."

A hush fell across the room. Carlisle looked back at Lane Foster for an answer. He nodded, his eyes looking at the floor. "She's right, Senator. As cruel as it sounds, according to the rules you helped pass in Congress, they don't qualify for Medicaid benefits," Foster said in muffled tones.

"What should they do then?" Carlisle whispered to his aide.

"Spend it up," Foster said. "By my calculations, with his bills at the nursing home and with hers, they should be broke in about a year. Divorce was the only way she could protect their savings."

Carlisle turned back to the audience, his face flushed with embarrassment. "Mrs. Kornwall, thank you for coming before us today. We are truly sorry for …"

His remarks were cut short as the old lady struggled to her feet. Just as she was about to leave, she turned back to the microphone. "Senator, it would break my husband's heart if he knew the truth."

5

THE MAN HALF-STUMBLED, half-walked into the emergency room at Methodist Hospital. He was holding a bloody oilcloth over his left eye; his car, a late-model Ford, was still idling in the parking lot. Chards of glass from the broken windshield tumbled from his crimson-stained clothes as he pushed his way through the electric doors.

"I need to see a doctor," he said, his breathing labored. "I think I've lost my eye."

Within seconds, one of the nurses arrived at the admitting desk, pushing a wheelchair. "Just sit down here, and we'll take you back so that our doctor can look at you," she said, grabbing a clipboard with blank admitting papers.

The injured man slumped into the chair, his lips ashen as the blood began to drain from his face. He had made it to the hospital on sheer guts and determination, but he was spent and now had to rely on others to get him the rest of the way.

"Dr. Springer," the nurse called out as she passed him jotting down a few notes on a patient in one of the ER cubicles, a young girl with an earache. "Would you take a quick look at the patient in four to see if we need to call an ophthalmologist?"

Springer quickly excused himself, reassuring the patient he

would be right back, and followed closely behind. "What do you have here?" he asked, trying to evaluate the situation.

"Not sure," she said as she pushed the wheelchair into cubicle number four. "He claims he lost his eye. From the looks of him, I would guess he had a run-in with his windshield."

"Mr. …" Springer said, "can you tell us what happened?"

Only partly conscious, the patient's hand dropped to his lap as the bloody cloth that once protected his eye tumbled to the floor. A tickle of bright red blood began to ooze down his left cheek. Springer reached under the man's arms. "We've got to get him on the stretcher before he does any more damage." Trained by years of experience, the doctor and the nurse half-lifted, half-coerced the patient out of the wheelchair and onto the gurney.

"Says his name is Robert Samples," the nurse said, pulling his driver's license from his billfold.

Springer reached over, carefully brushing a few of the glass slivers from his bloody face. "Mr. Samples, looks like you've had a pretty bad injury. It would help me a lot if you could tell me what happened to you."

"Underpass," the patient said, barely above a whisper. "I was driving under this bridge … and that's the last thing I remember. That and the loud crash with all this glass going everywhere."

Springer quickly looked over at the nurse. He had seen it before. Kids, mostly young teenagers, out looking for a cheap thrill, throwing objects off overpasses onto the oncoming traffic below—sometimes with devastating consequences. Without any more to go on, he didn't know for sure, but that would be his bet.

"Mr. Sample, you need to be still so I can examine your eye." Springer reached over once again. This time he was holding a flashlight as he tried to lift up the patient's swollen eyelid. "Can you see my light?"

"Barely," he said weakly. "Everything looks red."

Looking around at the nurse, Springer said, "See who's covering for ophthalmology and let me talk to them." Then he turned back to the patient. "We're going to put a bandage back on your eye while we get an ophthalmologist to come in. It looks like you're going to need surgery."

Springer had just finished placing the last strip of tape over the gauze eye pad when the nurse returned. "We don't have anybody," she answered under her breath, her face tense.

"What about Wharton, Peters, or that new guy who came down here from Hopkins? Teng—that's his name, isn't it?"

The nurse shook her head. "Went to courtesy staff. Peters was the last to leave. Said she wasn't going to take all the call alone."

Springer excused himself, feeling this conversation would be more appropriate away from the patient's inquiring ears, and signaled for the nurse to follow him. Closing the door to the physician's office, he continued his inquiry. "What in the hell are you telling me?"

"Dr. Springer, it's becoming a real problem. It's not just ophthalmology. No one wants to take call. You remember when the board voted that everyone over fifty-five was off?"

"Yeah," Springer said, a sad smile covering his lips. "A real democracy, since all of them are card-carrying members of AARP. But Wharton and Teng aren't that old."

"They went together with about five other doctors, two are ENT, and built a day surgery center. Said they didn't need the hospital."

Springer shook his head in disbelief. "What about emergencies?"

"They claim they take care of their own patients. I'm not so sure since they sent one of their post-op cataracts over here the other night," the nurse said. "The others they refer to us or dump on Parkland, since it's the county hospital."

"What about community responsibility?" he asked, his mind reeling. "What in the hell are they giving back?"

The nurse slowly moved her eyes up. "Dr. Springer, you really are behind the times."

. . .

"I would be giving him the benefit of the doubt if I only called Frances indifferent," Allison said, the sarcasm in her voice obvious. "John, Mom is scared to death, and I really wonder if Dr. Frances cares at all."

Terrell felt caught in the middle. All the reports on Frances were glowing—near the top in his graduating class. Then he completed one of the best residencies on the East Coast, before moving to Dallas. "He's probably just one of those academic types who would rather be working with rabbits than people. Unfortunately, taking care of people pays better; at least it used to."

Allison didn't appear to appreciate John's attempt at humor. "All you doctors are the same," she said. "Always making excuses for each other. If his heart isn't in it, all that fancy training doesn't add up to much. I remember when I was a nursing student on a rotation with old Dr. Strickland. The other nurses on the floor would have to follow along behind him, reassuring the patients that he was such a good doctor, so it made up for his poor bedside manner. The truth was he was an asshole."

Terrell nodded, remembering Strickland from his days at Galveston's John Sealy Hospital—"Black Jack," as his fellow residents referred to him. The very mention he was on the floor brought the house staff to mass hysteria, wondering who the brunt of his insults would be. But he was considered the best. There was nothing he didn't know. John had been told old Strickland even refused to take his medical boards because he felt there was nobody around smart enough to give them to him.

"Frances is another Strickland, just twenty years younger." Allison sighed. "When I was so sick, I remember wanting the best doctor I could get. But what I really was looking for was someone who was both smart and cared at the same time. Now that I'm well, I realized if I couldn't have both, what I really needed was a doctor who cared, because he would find someone who was smart."

. . .

"Parkland's on diversion," the nurse said as she poked her head in the small cubicle where Dr. Jordan Springer was just finishing up writing out prescriptions for a patient who was being discharged from the ICU. "They probably would take him anyway if we just loaded him up in the ambulance and sent him over. But …"

Springer already knew the answer to that scenario. They were called Transfer Rules, passed by the Texas Legislature years ago. Originally, the guidelines, as they were nicely worded, were created to protect hospitals and patients from unfair dumping practices. Unfortunately, more often they shackled hospitals with reams of bureaucratic finagling, while opening them up to a virtual floodgate of fines and potential litigation opportunities. The sad irony was that the benefits of the questionable legislation, if there were any, usually went to line the pockets of the trial attorneys, and patients were forced into long, painful delays in care while the appropriate paperwork was completed. "I've been there before," he said, frustration showing through. "We're not going to take Methodist Hospital down that road again. Who's the backup?"

"Baylor Hospital, but they claim they're full too. Must be the Friday night knife-and-gun club members are working overtime," she said with a smile. "I'll try St. Paul. They're usually pretty good about taking up the overflow when things get rough."

"Let me finish here. Then I'll be up front," Springer answered, turning back to his patient.

The nurse cupped her hand over the receiver as Springer approached. "They'll take him," she muttered. "But they said they wouldn't have any OR time until four tomorrow morning, possibly later. Suggested we try one of the private hospitals to see if they could get him on the schedule sooner."

Within minutes, the nurse had the administrative representative from St. Paul on the telephone. "He wants to talk to you," she said, handing Springer the receiver. "He doesn't understand why we don't ship him to Parkland, since it's the county hospital."

Springer grabbed the telephone, angry at the system. Despite all the political rhetoric, there were two levels of health care in this country—one for those who could afford to pay for anything and one for everyone else. The emergencies fell somewhere in between. Hospitals had to take them in if they presented at their back door, crying for help. This was the law. But to take on someone else's emergencies, that was different. First, most of the time, the hospitals lost money, since many patients refused to pay. Second, that was where most of the lawsuits arose. "We don't have an ophthalmologist on call, and Parkland's on diversion," Springer said, a hint of apology in his tone. "I think he has a laceration of his eye, and it needs to be repaired tonight."

"Does he have insurance?" the unsympathetic reply on the other end of the line came back.

In all the commotion, Springer had not checked on the patient's financial situation. "Insurance?" he questioned, turning to the nurse. She nodded. "Yes, he's got coverage."

"I'll have to check with my doctor to see if he'll accept him."

The administrator was all business. Springer could not fault him for that. Hospitals had always lost money on some of their patients; it was their way of giving back to the community. But with decreasing reimbursement and increasing costs, the days of unlimited charity were over.

It didn't take long, maybe fifteen minutes, until the call came back. Springer was just finishing taking out some sutures on a man he had sewn up six days ago when he heard the page.

"I think he's got a ruptured globe," Springer replied, going on to describe the patient's injury as best he could.

"Let me tell you, Doc. Sounds like you're right," the doctor said, his voice hurried, aloof. "I just do refractive surgery nowadays. Haven't sewn up an eye in maybe five years. My suggestion would be to send him to Parkland. After all, that's why we pay taxes."

Springer set down the telephone, his head shaking in disbelief. "Sometimes, I think we're becoming too damned specialized."

Sensing that Dr. Springer had run out of options, the nurse asked, "What do you want me to do now?"

"Call an ambulance to make the transfer," he said. "Then get me someone from administration. They might want to contact the hospital's attorney."

. . .

"We're glad you could join us for lunch, Senator." The secluded table, tucked in a far corner of the Morrison-Clark Inn's restaurant, had been reserved weeks before, not because the reservations were so hard to come by but because of the importance of the meeting, at least to the small group of people seated around the table.

Rayborn Carlisle felt a wave of uneasiness as he slid into the only empty seat left. Initially, the senator had wanted to limit all communications regarding the proposed health care legislation to the Senate hearing room. But the sheer volume of the special interests' requests made that impossible, delegating much of the committee's work to the individual members when they were not formally in session. Lane Foster had done the background work on this one. Picking up the menu laying across his plate, the senator smiled politely as introductions were made.

"Compared to the American Medical Association, we're a young organization," Jerald Todd, MD, the apparent spokesman for the group, said proudly. "But while the AMA is losing market share, we have doubled our membership over the last three years."

Carlisle nodded his approval, pointing out to the waiter his selection from the menu. "That's commendable, Doctor, but currently how large is the … ah … Unified Medical Association?"

"Senator, I'm our national membership chairman." The reply came from directly to Carlisle's left. The respondent, a young Hispanic female who appeared to be in her late thirties, pulled out a yellow sheet of paper and slid it toward the senator. "As you can see by our latest count, we just passed twenty-six thousand. We fully expect to become the voice of American medicine within four, maybe five years."

Carlisle was impressed, if nothing else than by the sheer growth in their numbers. "Dr. Todd," the senator said, scanning the other members at the table, "what makes your organization different from the AMA or the specialty societies that have represented doctors up to now?"

"Senator, I don't know if you've noticed, but our profession's going down the toilet, despite the efforts of these so-called organizations," Todd said, leaning forward, picking up the knife and tumbling it through his fingers. "First, it was the feds and their false promises with the Medicare and Medicaid programs. Then came the blood-hungry lawyers sucking out their share of the health care dollar. Now, with protections you and your fellow legislators have afforded them, the pencil-pushing insurance company executives are squeezing the last bit of life out of the best health care system the world has ever seen."

Carlisle sat back, the hairs on the back of his neck bristling. "I'm sorry, but I'm afraid I missed your point." If the meeting had not been in such a public place, Carlisle would have taken the doctor's remarks as threatening, rather than just venting his frustration over an increasingly unjust health care system.

"Senator Carlisle, those other organizations will come before your committee and expound on the devastating effects of a single-payer system," Todd said calmly, his steel-blue eyes locked on his guest. "Our organization disagrees. By the time the attorneys and insurance companies take their cut, there's not enough money left over to go around. That leaves us with only one choice—cut out the middle man."

"Your position won't make you very popular with your fellow physicians, Doctor."

"I didn't know that popularity was ever a weapon that was used to win wars." Todd slid his plate to the side, placing the point of the knife into the tablecloth before him. Slowly, carefully, he moved the knife to the right, leaving a deep indention in the material. "That, Senator, is a line. It's a line this organization will not allow our physicians to be dragged across. The doctors of this country have compromised long enough."

The other members around the table shifted uncomfortably in their chairs. Carlisle wondered if they agreed; their continued silence gave him his answer. All eyes turned to Todd.

"Senator, they're only a few real Albert Schweitzers in this world. The rest of us operate somewhere between avarice and altruism. Money does matter. Ask yourself why thousands of Canadian doctors have migrated to this country. Was it because they were being persecuted like the physicians behind the iron curtain? Was it because they were being forced to work beyond their capabilities? Hell no!" His hand thrust the knife into the table, cutting through the nicely starched tablecloth. "Many of them close their offices at the end of October, then take off the rest of the year. Why? Because, Senator, by that time, they're only getting paid fifty cents on the dollar, sometimes, twenty-five. To get quality, this country's going to have to pay for it. We can't afford to continue to give a fourth of the health care dollar away to the leeches who are telling us how to take care of our patients, most of whom have never even been inside a medical school. Many of the best minds in this country are abandoning their childhood dreams of going into medicine and choosing other careers. Can you expect someone to go to school until they are almost thirty, then enter a practice with over a hundred thousand in debt, and not pay them what they are worth? Ask yourself, Senator, would you want that for your own child?"

The table fell silent. Carlisle sat motionless, stunned at what he had just heard. No more beating around the bush or talking about what's good for patients. For the first time, the senator realized the cold, brutal truth.

"If a few people get hurt along the way, regrettably that is the price we'll have to pay. Make no mistake, Senator, this is a war—one we can't afford to lose. That's what makes us different from the other organizations and why you and your fellow legislators will come to the UMA when you arrive at the same conclusion about the inevitable government takeover of this country's health care system."

. . .

Dorothy Peoples patiently held on the telephone as the list of options were reeled off. Suddenly, she punched the number eight. "Would you please hold while we transfer you to our medical records department?" the recorded reply came back.

It was another five minutes before Dorothy heard the sound of a real voice. "Can I help you?"

"I want my medical records transferred to another doctor," she said hesitantly.

"Which of our doctors here at Metropolitan do you want to have them?"

There was a long, uncomfortable pause as Dorothy thought about her response. "He's not in your group," she said. "He's my son-in-law, Dr. John Terrell, a radiologist at Landry."

"That's somewhat irregular," the voice on the other end of the line came back. "Being that he is a radiologist."

"Oh, he's finding me another doctor." Dorothy was groping, hoping she would come up with the right words without telling the truth about why she was looking for a new doctor. "Dr. Frances is just so busy. I need a doctor who can spend a little more time with me."

"That's fine, Mrs. Peoples." The reply came without a hint of emotion. "As soon as we have your seventy-five dollars along with a notarized release form, we will send a copy of your records to Dr. Terrell."

Dorothy was shocked, since she had only seen the doctor one time. How much trouble could it be to duplicate what little records she had accumulated and send them over to John? "Isn't that a little high?" she questioned.

"Company policy, Mrs. Peoples. We have to cover our expenses."

Still confused by what she had to do to get her records, Dorothy asked, "Where do I get this release form you mentioned notarized?"

"That's no problem. For only five dollars, we can have someone in the office do that for you when you bring us your check."

By now, Dorothy just wanted the whole experience behind her. "Can I do that this afternoon?"

"Come on over. We want to make it as convenient as possible for you. We should have your records out by early next week."

"Can't I have a copy today? My son-in-law wants to get me in to another doctor tomorrow."

Dorothy thought she heard a sigh on the other end of the line. "We'll put a rush on it. I hope you understand. That will be another twenty-five dollars. It's company policy."

6

Three Months Later

"COULD YOU GET someone over here from radiology to go over these x-rays with me?" Dr. Springer called out, standing by the row of view boxes just off the nurses' station in the ICU.

Within ten minutes, a young man in a long white lab coat appeared at the front desk. "They said you needed somebody to look at some films," he said, looking around as if he were lost.

"Dr. Springer," the receptionist called out. Springer appeared a little taken back at her lack of formality. "The radiologist is here."

The curtain swung open as Springer headed toward the front. Not recognizing John Terrell, he put out his hand. "You're new here, Dr. Terrell?" Springer said, straining to read John's name from the tag on his pocket.

"Brand-new, just started yesterday," Terrell said, a forced smile covering up his uneasiness. "But I've been at Landry for the last two years. Radiology Enterprises lost the contract, so here I am."

"Methodist is a busy place," Springer said with a half smile. "I don't think you'll get bored over here."

"You won't—"

Terrell's remarks were cut short by a call from the far end of the

ICU. "Dr. Russell, the films of the abdomen are up on the viewer when you're ready."

Springer whipped around, then stopped and turned back toward Terrell. "We've got a sick one over there," he said hurriedly, pointing to one of the small cubicles. "The guy's had abdominal pain for three days, and he's as rigid as a washboard."

"Let me take a look at what you've taken so far," Terrell said as they headed toward the far end of the emergency area.

By the time the two doctors reached the back, the technician had all the patient's x-rays up on the row of viewing boxes. John's eyes darted from film to film as he closely scrutinized every shadow for any aberration. "Air," Terrell said as he moved closer to the x-ray on the end.

At first, Springer couldn't see what John was outlining with his finger. "Where?" he asked.

"Right under the diaphragm." Terrell took out a crayon-type marking pen from his pocket and slowly circled the faint shadow just above the liver. "He's got a perforation somewhere. It's impossible to know where it is from this."

Springer's years of experience had taught him that the air, which Terrell pointed out in the patient's abdomen, was from a hole in his GI tract. Specifically where, Springer had no way of telling. What he did know was that his patient was sick and quickly getting sicker. The patient needed help and fast. "I'll call in a general surgeon," he said, relieved that, with Terrell's help, he now had more to go on. "He'll probably want to put in a laparoscope and look around."

Springer quickly reached for the telephone as John headed toward the front of the ICU where he first entered. "John," Springer called out, "there's a shortcut back this direction."

Terrell stopped, barely avoiding an orderly pushing an empty gurney. "Thanks," he answered, appearing embarrassed by his unfamiliarity with the hospital.

"I've been around here a long time, some may say too long," Springer said, his hand muffling the telephone receiver. "Why don't you stop by during lunch sometime this week, and I'll give you a guided tour?"

A look of relief came across Terrell's face. "That would be great," he said. "They just kind of throw you in around here."

. . .

"How was it?" Allison asked, her tone edgy.

Terrell pulled open the refrigerator door and peered inside. "Scary," he said. "It's almost like starting over. Every face belongs to a stranger, but I met a nice guy—Jordan Springer—and I liked him. We're having lunch together in a day or so, and he's going to show me around."

Allison seemed relieved. "Mom called. She got all her tests back. There's no sign of any problems from the pancreatitis. Her doctor told her to eat anything she wanted but warned her to stay away from alcohol. She got a little miffed since she hasn't had a drink in over ten years. I guess he was just trying to cover all the bases."

In the background, the television was blaring as John poured a glass of orange juice and headed for the den. "What's for dinner?" he asked, slipping into the La-Z-Boy recliner he had brought from Galveston.

"You have your choice—chicken with vegetables or Salisbury steak with vegetables. They both take the same time to heat."

Terrell looked around. "Wasn't that my choice last night?"

"They were on special at Kroger, six for twelve dollars. It's that or another pizza."

Terrell started to reply when his eye caught a familiar face on the television. "Come in here," he called out to Allison.

> Are you tired of those ugly glasses? Does cleaning your contact lenses make you late for work? Well,

> those days are over. Dr. Andrew Bone, leading eye surgeon and world-renowned university teacher, will help … for only twenty easy payments of $199.
>
> Dr. Bone, whose thousands of cases make him one of the most experienced laser surgeons in the Metroplex, has authorized me to make this unprecedented offer. If you don't feel you see better than you ever have before, Dr. Bone will refund all your money.
>
> Folks, this is a money-back guarantee. You throw away your glasses and toss those uncomfortable contacts in the trash. Through Dr. Bone's generosity, for this month only, you can enjoy the freedom of perfect sight though laser surgery. No other doctor is confident enough in his results to make you that offer.
>
> If you mention you heard about this offer on television, Dr. Bone will perform surgery on your second eye at half the price. For more information call 1-800 …

At first, Terrell just stared at Allison, a look of disbelief across her face. "Didn't the dean hold him back?" she asked.

"They caught him cheating on the national boards," Terrell answered. "At first, they weren't going to let him graduate, but his father had pull with their congressman, and they let him repeat the senior year instead."

"I didn't know he went into practice around here," she said, still appearing confused. "I wonder where he got all that experience."

"Probably on laboratory rabbits back in his residency. I heard he only took over the practice of some retiring ophthalmologist last year," Terrell said, still looking at the television. "There were rumors that the first thing he did was buy a van and put his name on it, then sent it out to all the nursing homes. Gathered anyone up who didn't object and brought them to one of the day surgery centers and took out their cataracts."

"I wonder if he's successful," Allison said as she headed back toward the kitchen.

"I guess it depends on how you define successful," Terrell said sarcastically. "It looks like he now owns the day surgery center."

. . .

Carlisle picked up his copy of the committee's report and aimlessly thumbed through the pages. He had gone over the draft at least ten times. It was as if he was searching for an answer, something other than the conclusion he and the other members of his committee had come to after six months of testimony. His basic beliefs had always been conservative—government intervention only when there was no other option. Until the hearings, he had held on to the belief that taking care of the sick was a private matter—one between the patient and the doctor. Intervention from any outside party was a violation of one's most basic right to privacy. But medicine had become big business, an industry in itself, and the senator's point of view had begun to drift to the left.

He reached over his massive desk and pushed the intercom button. "Has Foster arrived yet?" he barked out.

Just then, Lane Foster poked his head in the door. "You called?" The senator's adviser on health care chuckled.

"When this comes out, they're going to call me a flaming liberal." A band of perspiration lined Carlisle's deeply furrowed brow. "I had thought about hanging it up after this term; now I won't have any choice."

"You'll end up a hero, Senator." Lane moved over to Carlisle's desk and pulled up a chair. "At first, it's going to be rough. The doctors will be the most vocal, but their cries are hollow. Some disruption of paperwork, maybe even a temporary work slowdown in scattered areas throughout the country. But their professional ethics will keep from doing anything that could that put real pressure on us to reverse our decision. Their old-fashioned 'do no harm' vow. I don't see the doctors doing anything that might endanger them."

Laying the report on the desk, Carlisle looked over at Foster. "Did you get the numbers on the Unified Medical Association?" he asked, his tone abrupt.

"The folks over there are not sure," Foster answered. "Claim they had to put on two new employees in their membership department and they still can't keep up with the demand. But as of the first of the week, they had just over thirty-one thousand card-carrying members."

Carlisle slid back in his chair and turned toward the window. "Lane, when I met with them at the Morrison-Clark, they were at twenty-six." He paused, looking out at the busy traffic in front of the Senate Office Building. "That's five thousand more in just over three months. What about the American Medical Association?"

"They have so many membership categories it's hard to get comparable numbers," Lane said, appearing confused with what the senator was thinking. "But their numbers stay around three hundred thousand and have been so for about fifteen years, from what I could learn. That may sound good, but with over seventeen thousand new doctors entering practice each year, their market share keeps dropping. Make no mistake, Senator, as far as the public and press are concerned, they are still the spokespeople for American medicine."

"I'm afraid that may not be for long." Carlisle moved back to his desk and picked up the committee's report. "Lane, there is growing discontent among the physicians out there. We both saw that in the hearings. The AMA, the American College of Surgeons, all of them. But the UMA is different. They're not just idle talk. I could see it in their faces. When we put this report out there, recommending federal funding for all health care …" Carlisle let out a slow deep sigh. "The UMA could add fifty employees to sign up new members, and it won't be enough."

. . .

By the time Jordan Springer was able to break away, the reception in suite 315 was almost over. "Come on in," Mandy Jefferson said, her eyes red and teary. "He's the only one I've ever worked for. We started out together, just over twenty years ago. I still can't believe it."

Springer had known Mandy ever since coming to Methodist. In fact, her son was one of his first patients; the youngster had cut his lip when he took a bad tumble off his tricycle. "It took me by surprise too," Springer said sympathetically, also surprised at Gene Broyle's apparent sudden decision to give up his practice. Broyle, the most successful internist at the complex, had taken care of Springer on several occasions. But due to their busy schedules, they had not visited in months.

Springer grabbed a cup of the remaining punch and headed toward the back to find his old friend. Broyle was leaning up against his office door, exchanging pleasantries with the last of the well-wishers when Springer walked up.

"I was wondering if you could break away long enough to come by," Broyle said, appearing pleased to see Springer.

"You really pulled a fast one on us," Springer answered, taking a sip of his punch. "I guess we just didn't see it coming."

"Jordan, I'm just burned out." Broyle looked down the hall as the last guest disappeared from sight, then turned into his office. "Come on in and let's take a load off."

Springer glanced at his watch. There were only two patients in the ICU that needed to be discharged when he left. They could do without him for another fifteen minutes. "Sure."

"I still have two lawsuits pending—one from a child I delivered almost eighteen years ago. In fact, he wouldn't be alive today if it weren't for me. And now the bastard files suit on me," Broyle said, flopping down behind his desk.

Springer pulled up a chair. "What about the other one?" he questioned, feeling Broyle wouldn't have brought it up if he didn't want Springer to ask.

"It's so crazy you wouldn't believe it," Broyle said. "He's the husband of one of my former employees. She came to me saying he had a severe cough and fever and wanted me to give him something for it. I offered to see him, obviously for nothing, but she said he was too sick to come in. So, I agreed and gave her a handful of antibiotic samples instead. Didn't think any more about it until she gave me notice a week later. Her parting comments were that I would be hearing from their attorney."

Springer sat up in the chair, intrigued by Broyle's story. "So what happened?"

"About a month later, I got a letter from their lawyer notifying me they were filing a lawsuit against me for negligence and abandonment." Broyle sighed as a look of sorrow crossed his face. "Never really knew what happened. Evidently, he was hospitalized somewhere else with a raging pneumonia. Fortunately, he recovered. At least enough to take me to court. You get to the point, Jordan, where you don't trust anybody."

Springer shook his head in disbelief. "It's everywhere. Look at that grandmother who spilled hot coffee on herself and walked away with over a million dollars from one of those hamburger chains back in the nineties."

"Not only that. Last week, the largest insurance carrier that I participate with decided not to pay me. No good reason except they were reevaluating their reimbursement codes, and until that was completed, they were holding up all their payments. That added up to over fifty thousand over the last six months they still owe me," Broyle said, his voice angry. "To top it off, since I have a thirty-day notice in my contract, I still have to keep seeing their patients for a month at no pay. I called the state insurance board, and they said I would probably collect eventually. But if I wasn't willing to wait, I could go to arbitration and get fifty cents on the dollar. You tell me how doctors can cover their expenses."

"What are you going to do?" Springer questioned.

"The hospital found someone just out of his residency to come in here," Broyle answered, looking over at the two large cardboard boxes filled with his personal belongings. "Within a couple of months, no one will even notice I'm gone."

Springer was afraid Broyle was going to get emotional if he didn't change the subject. "Now what do you have planned?" he repeated.

"Nothing at first. My wife and I put up a little just in case something unexpected came up. But I can't afford to retire, not at what I've been making the last ten years. There's this start-up medical organization that contacted me about coming to work for them. They evidently got my name when the hospital put out an inquiry for my replacement. Claim they want a representative here in Texas; said before long they'll have one in every state."

Puzzled, Springer questioned, "What's their name?"

"Let me think. I hadn't heard of it before," Broyle said, rolling his eyes up. "I remember. It's the Unified Medical Association."

7

"YOU GOT TIME for a break?" Jordan Springer said as he popped his head into the room where John Terrell was going over the morning's films.

Terrell glanced at the clock above the row of viewing boxes. "Let me take these down first." Terrell started to remove the films when he stopped. "Jordan, look at this," he said, pointing to a small opacity on a chest x-ray up on the screen. "Last year, one of the radiologists read this lesion as suspicious and recommended further evaluation."

Springer moved up to the film, squinting to see the faint shadow John was describing. "That's pretty small. I might have missed it."

Terrell pointed to another film on the same patient just to the right. "This was taken early this morning," Terrell said, frustration in his voice as he pointed to a one-inch lesion on the x-ray.

Springer didn't have to be a radiologist to make the diagnosis. "Carcinoma." He moved back and forth between the two films, comparing the differences. "At this stage, there might have been a 70 percent cure rate, maybe 80 with chemo," Russell said, pointing to the x-ray on the left. "What happened? Did the patient refuse treatment?"

"I wondered the same thing," Terrell answered. "So, I called the physician's office and had them to pull up the chart. According to the staff, this guy sees close to a hundred patients a day. So, he has physician's assistants that do a lot of the screening for him. Our report, along with the recommendation, was on the chart, and it was even initialed by one of the assistants. Evidently, the patient was told everything was okay."

"Does the patient know yet?" Springer asked, still looking at the x-rays.

"Right now, he's too sick to care," Terrell answered. "I think his good doctor should be the one to tell him that if he's fortunate enough to get over this bout with pneumonia, he might have another six months to live."

. . .

Duke Dandridge picked up his glass of Chardonnay. "Mr. Foster, this is to a long and prosperous relationship between Horizon Data Systems and the United States Department of Health and Human Resources."

Shifting uneasily in his chair, Lane Foster raised his glass to meet Dandridge's. "Just because Carlisle and his committee will recommend a single-payer system, that doesn't mean the rest of Congress is going to go along," he said. "I don't think you realize the money and the power of the health care industry, Mr. Dandridge. The drug companies alone have billions at stake, not to mention the hundreds of thousands of doctors and other health care workers who are not all that eager to give up their freedom to Uncle Sam."

"You disappoint me." Dandridge set his glass down without taking a sip. "Do you think I would be dumb enough to put all my eggs in one basket? You give yourself too much credit, Mr. Foster."

Lane Foster gulped down his wine, his pulse starting to rise. "I didn't mean—"

"You are just a part of Horizon's plan to become the intermediary for the government's health care system." Dandridge's tone was more even, less threatening. "We have operatives on both sides of the aisle and in both houses of Congress that will be called upon when it becomes appropriate."

. . .

"Dr. Springer," the nurse said, her tone apprehensive, "while you were gone, they transferred up from the ER this lady in room 6. She's febrile and semi-delirious. Her leg looks terrible."

Grabbing the chart, Springer pulled a pair of gloves out of the box attached to the wall next to the sink. Before he headed down the hall, the nurse stopped him.

"Here," she said, handing him a mask. "You're going to need this."

Springer had not even reached the sick patient's cubicle when the stench first hit him—the unmistakable smell of rotting human flesh. He stopped, holding back a wretch, and put on the gloves and mask. After taking in a deep breath, Springer slowly pulled back the curtain.

"Hello, I'm Doctor …" His voice hung in the putrid air as his eyes locked on the pitiful soul that lay writhing on the stretcher before him.

"Doctor, Doctor … help me," she said, barely above a whisper. The patient, who Springer judged to be in her fifties, held up her arm. A look of desperation plastered across her ashen cheeks. Her long, skinny fingers were reaching out, grabbing blindly for him.

Instinctively, Springer held back, avoiding contact with her at all costs. It was then that he first noticed the sickening gangrenous discoloration that extended up past her knee as greenish, purulent material oozed from several broken-down areas on the skin. "What happened to you?" he questioned, continuing to keep a safe distance until he could better evaluate the situation.

"I cut … my … leg," she said, her breathing labored. "My

brother got me antibiotics from Mexico." She started to cry, rolling her hands back up against her chest as if trying to assume the fetal position. "We got no money for doctors or medicine. That was all I could do."

Springer had seen it before—patients looking for bargains by getting their medicine across the border where the prescriptions were often half the cost. Usually patients were just trying to save money on their prescriptions from doctors back in the United States. Recently, there had been a growing number of cases of self-prescribing, where patients took matters into their own hands. Armed with little to no medical knowledge, the results were sometimes disastrous. This appeared to be one of those times.

Now realizing the gravity of the patient's tragic but precarious situation, Springer moved over to the wall and pushed the intercom button. "Bring me a liter of Ringer's Lactate and a blood culture setup STAT. Call the lab and get someone down here to do a Gram stain."

Within two minutes, the nurse was at his side, awkwardly trying to juggle the bag of IV fluids and the various tubes Springer had requested. "What do you think?" she questioned.

"Sepsis," Springer answered. "Probably Pseudomonas from the color of the puss and the smell. As soon as someone from bacteriology gets here, we should have a pretty good idea." Moving closer to the now subdued patient, Springer took hold of her arm and gently unfolded it from her body. "We need to start an IV on you, so we can find out what's wrong."

The patient offered little resistance as Springer leaned over, searching for a vein along her emaciated arm. Suddenly, his head thrust back, almost knocking him into the nurse. Pain shot out from under his jaw as a blow from the patient's flailing arm struck him squarely on the chin. "What the hell?" Springer called out as the patient's body contorted helplessly on the stretcher before him.

Just as quickly as it started, the patient's body fell limp. Springer watched in horror as bright red froth oozed from her mouth and nose and the color slowly drained from her ashen face. Her eyes, now wide open, stared blankly at the ceiling. "Get me the intubation set!" he called out frantically, knowing that without precious oxygen in her lungs, all the IV fluids and fifth-generation antibiotics wouldn't make any difference.

Springer quickly pulled the stethoscope from his coat pocket and placed it on the patient's now motionless chest, hoping for any signs of life. Silence! He reached up, his fist clenched above his head, ready to make one last, desperate effort to jolt her heart back to life, when he stopped.

Slowly, Springer lowered his hand. His years of experience had given him a sense when all hope was gone. He turned around as the nurse appeared at the doorway; the look in his eyes said it all.

"Irreversible septic shock?" she questioned.

Springer nodded as he stripped away his mask. "System failure," he said, a catch apparent in his voice. "A health care system failure."

. . .

"Mrs. Peoples, I'm not going to be able to see you anymore." Dr. Lori Anderson slowly let the air out of the blood pressure cuff wrapped around Dorothy's arm.

Dorothy stiffened. "What do you mean?"

"Oh, it's not you," Dr. Anderson said. "It's your insurance company. I've been deselected."

A look of bewilderment crossed Dorothy's face as she nervously buttoned up the sleeve on her blouse. "Doctor, I'm afraid I don't understand."

"Insurance companies, trying to save money, have set up their own guidelines. And they want the physicians they use to comply with them." Dr. Anderson's tone was edgy. "If a doctor goes over their limit, then he or she's considered an outlier, and the company does everything it can to get rid of that physician when it comes time to renew their contract." The doctor paused as her eyes slowly moved up to meet Dorothy's. "Mrs. Peoples, I'm one of those outliers, except I'm being forced to give up patients such as you."

"But I have Medicare," Dorothy answered, still confused. "Don't you still take that?"

"Yes." Dr. Anderson laid Dorothy's chart on the examining table and leaned up against the wall. "You have supplemental insurance that is part of an HMO to cover the extra that Medicare doesn't cover," she said. "Well, when you bought that policy, the insurance company bought you. Who you see, even the medications you are allowed to take, are decided by them."

Dorothy's mouth fell open. "I was just trying …"

"Trying to save money. Mrs. Peoples, to them, you're just a number. They don't care about relationships, only transactions." The doctor looked away, and sadness filled her eyes as she gazed blankly at the wall.

"What did you do to get de … se … lected?"

"I just took care of my patients the way I felt was right, and …" Dr. Anderson let out a long, deep breath. "They said I ordered too many tests and wrote more prescriptions than I should."

"My son-in-law said you were a specialist and had lots of complicated patients," Dorothy said, probing for more information. "That's why he had me see you when I had the problem with my pancreas."

Dr. Anderson smiled. "That's a nice compliment, but the insurance company doesn't see it that way." Her smile quickly vanished as she picked up Dorothy's chart. "To them, everything is reduced to the lowest common denominator."

. . .

"Obamacare will seem like a blind date with a prostitute compared to when the press gets hold of this." The blood vessels on Bailey Forman's temples pulsated as he pounded his massive fist on the top-secret copy of Carlisle's report. As majority leader of the Senate, everything went across his desk before it came out of committee. "I thought you ran on a conservative platform. When did you move to the other side of the aisle?"

As a senator, Rayborn Carlisle had grown accustomed to being in control. But in Forman's overbearing presence, he was reduced to a babbling school-kid. "Bailey, I'm as surprised as you," he mumbled nervously. "Once we looked at where this health care system is headed, it seems there's no other choice."

Forman bit the tip off his ever-present cigar and spit the residue in the direction of the tobacco-stained wastebasket behind his desk. "Talk about pissing against the wind."

Carlisle shuddered at the thought of his own excrement blowing back in his face. Once his committee had reached its conclusion, Carlisle knew this meeting with the majority leader would be inevitable. "Don't forget it was you who named me to this position," he said with a slight grin, trying to shift some of the blame back on Forman.

Forman nodded, returning Carlisle's weak smile. "The question, my friend," he said, "is, where do we go from here? Every person and organization that is even remotely related to health care will be waiting to jump on this report."

Carlisle's fingers wrenched awkwardly in his lap. "The only way is to get the people in this country behind it," he responded, clearing the dryness from his parched throat. "The elderly are already seeing a disproportionate amount of their limited income being sucked away just trying to stave off the ravages of their years. Then there are the twenty million Americans who have no health care coverage and probably another fifty million who are stuck in a job they can't stand, just to maintain their coverage."

"That adds up to a sizeable number, Carlisle."

"Since kids can't vote," the senator said, now sounding somewhat more forceful, "that only leaves the rich, who can afford to buy anything they want, those in the health care industry, and the employers. And many of them are all too eager to get the oppressive costs of furnishing coverage for their employees off their backs."

"Impressive." The majority leader slowly sat back in his chair, rolling the giant stogie around his yellowed lips. "I'm afraid you forgot one very important constituency."

Carlisle's eyes grew wide. "What's that?" he questioned, his voice tensing.

"Us!" Forman thundered. "Your fellow legislators on Capitol Hill and the hundreds of thousands of federal employees here and throughout the country."

The senator knew Forman was referring to the generous health insurance programs available to the members of Congress and federal workers. Although by comparison, their numbers were small, it was this group that made the laws and ran the country. Without their support, Carlisle's report wasn't going anywhere.

"For the good of the country, we might all have to make sacrifi—" Carlisle's remarks were interrupted.

"There are two levels of health care in this country," the majority leader blustered, his voice almost pushing Carlisle across the room. "One for the have-nots and one for the rest of us who can pay. No one, not you or anyone else here on Capitol Hill, is going to change that. What you and your precious committee need to do is find a way to offer better health care for those who can't pay—not take away my right to get the care I can afford."

Perspiration ringed Carlisle's collar. "But, Bailey, what about the committee's report?"

"That report, as you put it, will never see its way onto the Senate floor in its present form." Foreman stood up. " Good day, Senator."

Carlisle knew he should go, or he would be thrown out. He decided on the former. "Thank you for the—"

"Let me leave you with just one question," Foreman interrupted. "If we adopt your plan and I don't want to wait six months to get my gall bladder removed, where do I go? South America?"

. . .

Usually the back door light would be on by the time he arrived home, but not tonight. Terrell's concern rose as he fumbled with the key, unlocking the back door and flipping on the kitchen light. "Allison," he called out. The kitchen, spotless as usual, was deserted. A half-full cup of black coffee on the counter was the only reminder that someone had been there that day.

Terrell quickly made his way through the house and turned on the lights as he went, stopping at the closed door to their bedroom. A beam of light from the hall fell across their bed as John slowly opened the door. "Are you all right, honey?" he said, staring at the silhouette that occupied their bed.

"Yes," Allison said weakly, failing to move from her fetal position.

Sensing he was not getting the whole truth, Terrell sat down on the bed, sweeping back the hair that was hiding her face. "Now tell me what's really going on," he said, his voice full of concern. "Are you sick?"

"No," she replied, rolling over toward John. "Not exactly." Her eyes were red and glassy.

Terrell could see she had been crying. "What is it then?"

Allison began to shiver as she reached for her husband's hand. "I think I'm pregnant."

8

HE MUST BE *on vacation*, Springer thought as he scooped up his copy of the *Dallas Morning News*. Except for a few problems when Doc Roberts's sprinklers inadvertently sprayed Springer's yard, the elderly man had been a good neighbor. Jordan would call the two of them acquaintances rather than friends, trading old war stories about Doc's days as a general practitioner in a fork-in-the-road town in deep East Texas before retiring to the big city. Roberts lived alone rather than moving nearer his children after his wife died some five years ago. Other than that, Springer didn't know much about the old man, except that this was not like him. Roberts's lawn was littered with at least a week's worth of yellowing newspapers. The empty trashcan, not retrieved in the last two pickups, still lay on the front curb. Strangely, the old man's car had never left the driveway. Springer tucked the paper under his arm and headed for Roberts's front door.

"Doc, are you in there?" Springer called out after getting no response from the doorbell.

Springer listened carefully, but except for muffled sounds from somewhere deep in the bowels of Roberts's house, there was none. This time, Jordan banged loudly on the door with his fist; again, no reply. Deciding he might have more luck around the back, he made his way toward the patio. As he moved closer, the muted sounds now became more distinct. He let out a sigh of relief, recognizing the familiar sounds of Roberts's television.

Springer tapped on the glass door, interrupting the television's monotonous bellowing. Again there was no answer as Springer strained to see through the sheer curtains that afforded the old man some privacy.

"What the hell ..." Springer's breathing faltered as he recognized Roberts's motionless arm hanging off the large armchair directly in front of the television. This time, Springer's interruption sounded more like crash as his clenched fist banged loudly on the glass partition. Again, no reply.

Still out of breath from his dash next door, Springer had barely made it back to Roberts's front porch from his 911 call when the ambulance pulled up in front. "Hey, Doctor Springer," Lou Bosser said, showing a familiar smile. "Remember me? You're the one who saved my ass. What have we got here?"

In all the commotion, Springer didn't recall their previous meeting. Right now, he was more concerned about his neighbor's wellbeing. "Arlen Roberts—he's probably in his late seventies. He's back in the TV room. I could only see his arm, and he's either sick or ..."

"You sure he's not just hung-over from a little too much football?" Bosser asked, a cocky edge detectable in his voice.

Agitated, Springer fired back at the EMT's apparent indifference. "Just look around at the papers all over the yard, and his car hasn't been moved in over a week."

Bosser looked at the front door—solid oak with a double dead bolt. "Maybe we'd have better luck somewhere else," he said, signaling to his partner. "Get the crowbar out of the truck and meet me around the back. Dr. Springer, you lead the way."

It took Lou Bosser less than a minute to pop the latch on the patio doors. Springer imagined the experience came from his younger days when being street-smart took priority over being at the top of the class.

As the trio rushed the room, the smell of death scalded their throats. Springer held back, the stench causing him to wretch uncontrollably. Bosser and his partner, Sanchez, somewhat immune to these gruesome situations, moved on around the old man's lifeless body. "By the way he looks, I would guess we're about five days late."

Sanchez picked up a tipped-over empty medicine bottle and scanned the label. "I think you have your answer right here," he said, walking over and handing it to Springer, who was looking at the numerous framed snapshots of Roberts and his deceased wife.

"Seconal 100 mg," Springer read, barely above a whisper. "I wonder ..."

"You might want to read this, Doc," Bosser said, unfolding a crumpled piece of paper he had pried loose from the old man's bloated fingers.

Springer took the note and went out on the patio where he could get a breath of fresh air. In the glare of the blaring sun, he strained to read the old man's final message.

> I did the unforgivable sin when I betrayed the Hippocratic Oath. But she was in so much pain I could not let her suffer. Death was her only escape. We are supposed to heal, but when that fails, what else can we do? God knows I did it because I loved her. Now we are both at peace.

...

It had been three days, and Doc's scribbled note still hung in Springer's mind like a neon sign, flashing again and again. The last desperate words of someone who had committed the great mortal sin—the taking of a human life. Even more, it was the life of the person he had loved the most. Now, the old man had paid the ultimate price for his act with the taking of his own life, trying to absolve the guilt that must have been eating him up, thought Springer.

From Springer's earliest days in medical school, he had been taught that preserving life was paramount, and if that was not possible, then to relieve pain and suffering. Anything less was considered an abrogation of the basic tenet upon which the medical profession was founded. Why then was there such controversy within the medical community about physician-assisted suicide? Springer was not sure where he stood—on the side of the American Medical Association and virtually every other medical organization that decried the practice even under the most desperate situations, or on the side of Oregon and several European countries that allowed it when life was terminal and the suffering unbearable. There seemed to be such a fine line between enough medication to relieve pain and that amount necessary to stop breathing, the two frequently becoming one and the same. Why was that any less humane than discontinuing IV feedings and letting the patient die of starvation and dehydration—an accepted practice carried on in virtually every hospital throughout the country?

Looking out his kitchen window across to Roberts's empty house, Springer slammed his hand down on the counter. The advances in medical science were racing in at breakneck speed, conflicting with an archaic bureaucracy unable to deal with their proper allocation or the complex ethical dilemmas they brought along—in many ways so far ahead of past generations, while in others, so far behind. The medical profession had stayed on the sidelines far too long. It was time to move into the twenty-first century. Springer wondered who would lead that charge.

. . .

It was just past six fifteen when Terrell's feet first touched the floor. Although most people would take advantage of their day off and sleep in, that was not the case with him. It was when he could think the clearest, away from all the distractions. Right now, he had a lot on his mind with Allison's unexpected pregnancy. Due to everything she had gone through and her medications, they had become somewhat cavalier, no longer taking precautions to avoid the possibility, a decision they now had to live with.

Until Allison's illness, it was the day they had both longed for—the birth of their first child. Now, all that had changed. Dreams of starting a family were clouded with fears of uncertainty. Would the baby be normal? Would the immunosuppressive drugs that Allison had to take cause the baby to be more susceptible to problems? With all that had happened, could Allison even carry a baby to term? So many questions, so few answers.

Even on Saturdays, Terrell's routine was the same. He watched, as if it would make any difference, as the first drops of dark brown java splashed against the bottom of the Pyrex container of the automatic percolator. He had carefully gone over their limited number of options. *She needs to get this behind her as quickly as possible*, he thought as he poured the steaming brew into his special mug, the sides stained to a darkened brown from repeated usage and improper cleaning. John referred to the buildup as seasoning; Allison had her own less-refined description.

Just as Terrell was about to enjoy his first sip, the kitchen door slowly swung open, and Allison slid into the chair across from him. "Why are you …"

"Couldn't sleep," she answered, the redness in her eyes still lingering from the previous night's crying. "We need to talk."

"I thought this was all settled," Terrell said, his fingers tightening around the hot mug. "We're going to have it aborted. Then we don't have to worry about all those unanswered questions."

"John, this thing inside me is not an it," she answered as tears once again began to fill her eyes. "This is our baby. It all looks different when who we're talking about is me and a baby we created." Suddenly, Allison's tone turned harsh. "You don't just flush *it* down the toilet so you don't have to face the problems."

Flustered, Terrell tried to respond. "But it's not even a baby yet. You're barely seven weeks pregnant."

"Where'd you learn that bullshit? What course in your medical training gave you the right to say what we made together is not a baby yet?" Allison paused, her hands trembling as her eyes slowly moved up to meet her husband's.

Terrell reeled back in the chair as Allison's cold stare dove right to his heart. "What do you want me to do?" he asked, his voice weak, almost apologetic.

"I suggest we find a specialist in high-risk pregnancies and not an abortionist."

. . .

A broad smile crept across his lips as Jerald Todd, MD, reviewed the latest statistics. The growth of the Unified Medical Association had surpassed his most optimistic predictions—just clearing fifty-two thousand three days ago. No one would have predicted that when Todd, a Cleveland cardiologist, threw up his hands just a little less than three years ago and walked out the door on a very lucrative practice, his new endeavor would be this successful. So far, it had all been based on promises. Before long, he would have to back them up with results.

There was nothing democratic about the UMA—a true autocracy with a benevolent dictator. It was Todd's organization, Todd's and his directors'—other disgruntled physicians fed up with watching helplessly as their freedoms were stripped away by the bureaucracies of big government, big hospitals, and big business. Unfortunately, some of the first few to join Todd's cause were hardened radicals, for one reason or another, rejected by the establishment and eager to join any movement that would bring them acceptance. Todd rationalized that as the organization grew, their influence and wayward intentions would be diluted by the whole. In either case, he was in no position to turn down support of any kind at this early stage of development.

"Dr. Broyle is here for his ten thirty appointment," the secretary said over the intercom.

Todd considered Gene Broyle a welcome addition to UMA's staff. Although dissatisfied with the current system, Broyle did not harbor the anger that so often clouded objectivity when difficult decisions had to be made. Todd quickly pulled out the bottom drawer of his desk, removing a manila file labeled Crosstown Medical Center. "Send him in," he said, rising from his chair to welcome his new ally.

"The situation is tearing the medical communities of this country apart," Todd said, his voice grim. "Medical institutions are competing for patients like car dealerships. Children's hospitals are plying on the guilt of parents of sick children to use their facility, or they will be denying their child the best care. Cardiac centers are claiming their survival rates are better than other institutions in the area, implying what—that you have a better chance of dying over there than at our facility? How in the hell do you think patients react to all this? It scares the shit out of them."

Broyle shuffled nervously in his chair. The hot mug of coffee cupped tightly in his hands served as his only source of comfort.

"Since you came, I've been telling you we needed an issue that sets us apart from the other medical organizations." Todd paused, his piercing blue eyes fixed on Broyle. "This is it." He picked up the manila folder and tossed it over on Broyle's lap.

"What's this?" Broyle asked.

"Crosstown Medical Center. It's in your backyard," Todd said. "It seems that the doctors in the community have been forced into two competing camps."

Broyle opened the file, slowly leafing through the pages. "I looked at Longview when I was deciding where to go into practice," Broyle answered. "Sometimes I wish I had made another decision."

"Be glad you didn't," Todd said. "It's like the Civil War down there. The two hospitals control all the beds in the community. So, if you're not aligned with one or the other, you're out—nowhere to put your patients."

"Why not just join both?" Broyle questioned. "That's what doctors have always done before."

"They're mutually exclusive. Somehow the administration of Crosstown got it through their board of trustees. If the doctors want to be on their staff, they can't be associated with any other facility in the area."

"Is that legal?" Broyle was showing more interest.

"Probably not. There are more Federal Trade Commission violations here than we can count, but by the time the case works its way through the courts, the doctors are not only out of business but out of money. So, out of desperation, the ones not already on Crosstown's staff joined up with the other hospital in Longview, which now claims they also must be exclusive to protect their own interests." Todd got up from his chair and walked around his desk. "Former partners are competing against each other, even in one case where the father was passed over by Crosstown and the son got in."

"I'd hate to be at their family reunions," Broyle said. "What about the AMA or the Texas Medical Association? They have a full staff of attorneys."

"They tried. Sent in their lawyers from Austin, even the president's attorney general to arbitrate but without much success." Todd gently lifted the folder out of Broyle's hand. "As you can see here," he said, pointing to an open page, "Crosstown's administration made some vague promises that were never carried out. The attorneys submitted a brief on behalf of one of the disenfranchised physicians who filed suit in district court, but it will be at least six months or more until it comes to trial. By then, all his old patients will be long gone. Even if he wins, it will be like starting over."

Broyle looked inquisitively at his boss. "And what could the UMA do differently?" he asked, his voice hesitant.

"Gene, how long is it going to take until the doctors in this country wake up?" Todd leaned back, pushing against his desk. "Arbitration only works when you're out of options. That's the problem with all the other organizations; they're negotiating out of a position of weakness, because they think they have no other choices."

"Are you going to tell me your other option?"

A smile once again came to Todd's lips. "I thought you'd never ask."

9

CLIPBOARD IN HAND, Allison looked around the crowded waiting room. Taking the only remaining seat in a far corner, she began the arduous process of completing the required paperwork. It wasn't until she tried to make more room by laying down some of the papers that she noticed the large display almost crowding out her small spot. *Rev-New*, she read silently, *your doctor's choice*. Allison looked over the collection of boxes and bottles filled with various colored pills that covered what probably once was a small coffee table.

"What's that over in the corner?" Allison asked, handing her completed forms to the receptionist.

"Oh, those are our special vitamin supplements," she answered, not looking up. "All of Dr. Kinder's patients are on them." The young girl stamped Allison's chart and put it up on the counter in the rack at the end. "You can have a seat, and the nurse will call you back in a few minutes."

Allison turned around and headed toward her chair, only to find it had been taken. She awkwardly scooped up her purse. "I believe that was my …"

"I didn't see no sign on it," the platinum blonde with a nose ring and a tattoo of a dragon on her arm said, her voice coarse and her stare worse.

Deciding she wasn't going to win that argument, Allison moved over against the wall, scooting in between the coat-rack and a sympathetic-looking matronly lady.

Allison looked at her watch. Her appointment had been scheduled for over an hour ago, and she still had not been called back. Fortunately, she had been able to find a seat as the patients moved in and out, so she was reluctant to chance giving it up with another trip to the reception desk.

Another thirty minutes went by before Allison finally stood up, laying her purse on the chair this time. "I'm sorry to bother you," Allison said, "but my appointment was supposed to be over an hour and a half ago. Do you have any idea when the doctor is going to see me?"

The receptionist sighed, Allison's interruption an obvious irritant. "And your name?" she asked, but then she answered her question before Allison could respond. "You're Mrs. Terrell … the doctor's wife."

Allison was taken back by her harsh tone. "Ye … yes."

"Dr. Kinder's very busy," the girl snipped, her eyes rolling up. "With emergencies and everything. No special privileges. Everyone gets treated the same. Being a doctor's wife, I know you understand." She turned and walked away.

That's it! Allison thought. In all of Dallas–Fort Worth, there had to be other doctors who could deal with her complex problems. She would wait no longer. Just as she reached for her purse, a voice called out, "Mrs. Terrell … Mrs. Allison Terrell."

. . .

"Ouch!" Allison grimaced under her breath as Dr. Kinder's long, skinny fingers groped around the far reaches of her pelvis.

"You need to be still," the nurse said sternly, "if the doctor's going to be able to check you."

Allison ignored her comment. If there was one thing that

women universally dreaded, it was the pelvic exam. Allison was no exception. Vulnerable, her bare feet clung to the cold stirrups as her most private parts, somewhere between cold and miserable, lay exposed to a total stranger.

Suddenly, Allison heard a strange ringing as she felt Kinder's hand tighten. Another ring. This time Kinder moved back from the table and quickly ripped off his gloves. "Yes," he said, fumbling with the portable telephone that he had been carrying in his breast pocket.

Allison lifted up her head, only to see the doctor listening intently to whoever was on the other end of the line. Relieved that her ordeal had temporarily come to a halt, she brought her legs together and let out a slow deep breath. For some reason that Allison couldn't explain even to herself, the telephone call seemed like a violation of her privacy. She had been willing to let this unknown doctor in, but she had not consented to the party on the other end of the line. If they didn't have the right to barge into the room during the examination, why was this any different?

Kinder appeared edgy as he looked over in Allison's direction, cupping his hand around the receiver. "Buy three hundred shares," he said, his voice muffled. He quickly folded the phone, turning back toward Allison. "I'm sorry for the interruption, but being a doctor's wife, you know about emergencies."

. . .

Allison sat beside the large oak desk as she anxiously waited for Kinder's report. Not knowing the outcome of her examination, she still felt vulnerable, but at least with her clothes on, she felt less so. Allison glanced at her watch. She had initially arrived now almost four hours ago. She shuddered at the thought of how long she would have to wait when it came time to have her baby.

"Mrs. Terrell," Dr. Kinder said as he breezed into the office. "You're about nine weeks pregnant." He quickly leafed through

Allison's file. "Although there are never any guarantees, I still feel you have a reasonable chance of carrying this baby to term, if you want to." His face was emotionless.

"What do you mean if?" Allison questioned.

"With your myelodysplasia issues and the immunosuppressive drugs, we can't be sure about the baby."

Allison didn't have to ask what he meant; she already knew. "When could we know if my baby is going to be normal?"

Kinder bent over the desk and grabbed a prescription pad, jotting down some instructions. "Here. Take this to the front desk," he said coldly as he handed her the prescription. "We'll do another ultrasound in three weeks that should tell us more." Kinder turned and left as quickly as he had arrived. Allison, alone again, clung to the piece of paper, the outcome of her pregnancy still very much in doubt.

Allison struggled to make her way back to the reception desk, ducking back and forth across the narrow hallway in order to avoid being run over by the mass of people that littered the office. The whole scene reminded her of a grocery store checkout line the day before Christmas—too many people in too small a space, wishing they were somewhere else.

"He wants me back in three weeks," Allison replied, slightly out of breath.

The receptionist grabbed the paper out of Allison's hand and disappeared behind the door. When she returned, she was carrying two large bottles of pills, which she set on the counter directly in front of Allison. "We'll file your visit on insurance—professional courtesy. But we will need sixty dollars for these."

"What are they?" Allison asked.

"Prenatal vitamins," the receptionist said, as if Allison should already know. "The doctor wants you to take them."

"But I already have some. My husband got me a big bottle from one of the drug salesmen."

The receptionist quickly glanced up with a look of disdain.

"Not these. In this area, only Dr. Kinder is allowed to offer Rev-New vitamins to his patients."

Allison was beginning to feel uncomfortable with the young girl's approach. "Aren't all prenatal vitamins about the same?"

The receptionist seemed to ignore Allison's last question as she continued to glare across the counter. "He won't be pleased when I tell him you did not follow his instructions."

Drawing back, Allison fumbled with her purse. "I … I … okay. Do I make the check out to the clinic or Dr. Kinder?"

. . .

"Where did you people put my mother?" The man leaned over the counter, his face only inches away from the triage nurse. "I expect her to get only the best care."

The nurse drew back from his angry stare. "You must be Mr. …"

"Woodlands," he replied, his tone caustic. "Jeffrey Woodlands. My mother is Rose, and they just brought her in here from Cedar Creek Retirement Center. I hope you haven't made her wait long."

The nurse ran her finger down the list of current emergency room patients. "There it is," the nurse said, identifying the man's mother on the page. "She was transferred in here over four hours ago from the nursing home. According to this record, our doctor has been trying to get in touch with you since she arrived."

"Impossible. I would have come right over if I had known she was here." Woodlands cleared the rasp out of his dry throat. "Are you trying to say I don't care about my mother?"

"Of course not. That was not what I was implying at all. I just—"

Woodlands cut her off as he thumped his fingers nervously on the countertop. "Are you going to get me the doctor or not?"

Within minutes, Jordan Springer arrived at the front desk. "Mr. Woodlands, would you mind following me? I would like to speak to you about your mother."

As Springer closed the door to the doctors' consultation room, Woodlands spun around. "I hope this won't take long," he said, a hint of sarcasm in his tone. "My mother needs me, you know."

"Mr. Woodlands, your mother is very sick. I'm afraid there is not much we can do for her but keep her comfortable." To Springer, this was the most difficult part about being a doctor—dealing with the family when all hope was gone. He looked up, fully expecting to be met with an outpouring of grief. To his surprise, Woodlands's response was just the opposite.

"I knew they shouldn't have brought her here to this two-bit hospital where they couldn't do anything for her," he barked, his face flushed.

Springer stiffened. "According to the records, your mother has been in a coma for the last three months. Since she had to be fed through a tube, it was only a matter of time until she developed pneumonia." He paused momentarily to see if there was a response. Seeing none, he continued, "Your mother is not suffering, Mr. Woodlands. It's time to let her go."

"No!" he said, his shaking finger pointed directly in Springer's face. "I want her to have the very best medicine has to offer. I don't care how much it costs Medicare and her stupid insurance company. She's paid for it."

Springer had seen this response many times before—grown children trying to make amends for their own guilt for having to put their parents in a nursing home. "Mr. Woodlands, when did you last see your mother?"

Woodlands stopped, reluctantly withdrawing his finger. "Uh … last month sometime." The anger that had consumed him just moments ago drained away. "I'm just so busy. What with my job and the kids, I don't have the time to …" He buried his head in his hands as tears flowed down his cheeks.

Springer cautiously reached out, putting his hand on

Woodlands's shoulder. "Why don't you go see your mother now, while you still have a chance."

. . .

"They can't have it all," Springer said as he reached across the table for the ketchup. "The problem is they don't know it. Two-thirds of the patients in this country think they are entitled to the best health care available, the other third think they can buy it whether it's indicated or not."

Terrell bit into his sandwich. "Hospital food is a lesson in tolerance. Probably part of a master plan to get patients to leave sooner, so they don't have to eat this stuff."

Springer grinned, pouring the gooey red liquid over his overcooked French fries. "John, I'm worried. We're developing all this technology to prolong life, but we don't have the resources to pay for it. In some ways, many of the other countries in the world are better off. They just say no."

"What's got you going today?" Terrell questioned.

"Some days, I get tired of this facade we put up about only having one level of health care," Springer said as he flicked a French fry in his mouth. "Everyone knows there are two—one for the haves and one for everyone else. And no fancy plan out of Washington, DC, is going to change that."

Terrell dabbed at a drip on his mouth. "You must be talking about the single-payer proposal going through the Senate."

"Bingo," Springer answered, pushing back his plate with the few remaining bits of half-eaten food. "It'll be the end of the medical profession if it passes. Just look at Canada to see the effects."

Terrell moved uneasily in his chair. "I don't see it that way," he said, his tone hesitant.

Springer looked up, not sure he had heard his new friend correctly. "You can't mean you support the idea—what with the long waits for care and all their doctors flocking to this country." He paused, carefully crafting his statements so as to not sound insulting. "You don't want Uncle Sam telling us what to do, do you?"

"They already do." Terrell moved closer, resting his arms on the table. "Think about it, Jordan—Medicare, Medicaid, HCFA, Joint Commission, OSHA, and all the different insurance companies, each with their own set of regulations. When was the last time you really made a decision on your own?"

Now it was Springer's turn to feel uncomfortable. "With that point of view, we're going to give it all away."

"I don't know if you've looked around," Terrell said. "It's already gone. We don't have one Uncle Sam telling us what to do; we've got fifty. At least, with a single-payer system, we'll be back to one. Most days, I feel like a blue-collar worker with a slightly higher pay scale."

Springer was shocked but knew Terrell was telling the truth. As much as he wanted to deny it, Springer and his fellow physicians had watched as most of their freedoms were slowly stripped away. Granted, there had been numerous forays as physicians descended onto Washington or the state capitols to talk to their congressman—even letter-writing campaigns, phonations, and high-priced lobbyists sponsored by the various organizations that claimed to represent the various sectors of the medical profession. Although these attempts had garnered some successes, they had not reversed what would eventually turn out to be a takeover of the health care profession.

"You need to join me at the county medical society," Springer said, hoping he could direct Terrell's frustrations into some meaningful response.

"Too late," Terrell answered as he slid back his chair to leave. "They've had their chance. You can't win a war fighting with gloves on, and that's what physicians have done up to now."

Springer had seen this level of frustration among other young physicians, but until now, not in his friend. "What do you suggest we do?" Springer asked, afraid of what he might hear.

Terrell got up from the chair. "I really don't know." He paused, and a sad look crossed his eyes. "Maybe we're finally going to have to get our hands dirty."

. . .

Rayborn Carlisle tapped his fingers on the massive desk, his frustration apparent. "Forman's got us by the balls," the senator said. "Even with all this work, SB 4215 will never make it to the Senate floor without his approval."

"I was afraid that we were going to have to grandfather the legislation to get it passed," Lane Foster said as he moved awkwardly between the two large stacks of papers on the other side of Carlisle's desk.

The senator appeared puzzled. "Do you mind explaining what you're talking about?"

Foster looked up, a fistful of papers in each hand. "Forman's aide and I have been looking for some middle ground, and I think we hit upon a possible solution."

Carlisle smiled. "So the old fart's finally seeing things our way?"

"I wouldn't exactly call it that," Foster answered with a forced grin. "He's willing to discuss a compromise that would allow your legislation to get to the floor, but at first, it would only cover those who don't already have health insurance."

"That's nothing more than an extension of the Medicare and Medicaid programs," Carlisle mumbled, his frustration again on the rise since his committee had already dismissed the option as only a Band-Aid solution.

Fumbling through the mound of papers, Foster stopped, holding up one. "Here it is," he said. "The bill would include two very important stipulations. First, the Medicare and Medicaid programs would be rolled in within twenty-four months, so we can reduce the bureaucratic costs."

Carlisle was becoming impatient. "You seem to have forgotten. It's only when the rich and powerful can't buy everything they need that they use their influence to raise the level of health care for everyone else."

"That's the beauty of this compromise, Senator." Foster laid the sheet of paper in front of Carlisle. "Point two: once individuals give up their current health insurance, such as with a job change, we've got them. When they move into another group plan with their new employer, we'll levy a 7.5 percent surcharge on the premiums on any new enrollee that is added to an existing program with a private carrier—similar to the tax the feds already have for Medicare. Since the extra money will come out of each of their pockets, the incentive for both parties will be to pick up our less expensive option. At that point in the relationship, the employer's loyalty is still to the almighty dollar."

"Won't most of them just keep their old coverage and pay for it out of their own pocket?" Carlisle asked.

"At first, but the costs will average 40 percent more without the group rate." Foster paused, rifling through his papers. "We ran the numbers. The first year, about one-third will cancel their insurance, with another 15 percent dropping out each year after."

Still not convinced, Carlisle locked on his aide. "The rich and the federal employees won't be discouraged."

"It doesn't matter. Once the carriers lose about 60 percent of their business, they won't be able to charge enough and still show a profit." Foster returned Carlisle's stare with an evil grin. "We estimate that five, maybe six years at the longest, we will be the only game left."

10

THE ELDERLY PATIENT grimaced as John Terrell slowly emptied the syringe full of dye into a vein in the man's right forearm. "You may feel a little flushed," he said. "But it should pass quickly. Please try not to move while we shoot the pictures."

Terrell edged back from the x-ray table, once again checking the position of his patient. Nodding in the direction of the technician tucked safely behind the lead-lined partition at the far end of the room, he suddenly noticed a look of horror in his eyes through the window. Terrell spun around, realizing something was terribly wrong. His patient, who only moments before lay serene and still, was now a mass of contortion—his arms and legs flailing out of control. Terrell rushed back to the table, grasping him around the waist. His attempt was too late as the old man tumbled helplessly off the table, carrying both of them crashing to the floor below. The back of Terrell's head struck the cold tile with the full weight of his patient falling on top of him. That was the last thing he remembered as the darkness closed in.

. . .

By the time Dr. Gene Broyle arrived in Longview, it was after dark. Nothing formal was scheduled until eight the next morning, so he decided to grab a meal on his own. The cafeteria across the street from Crosstown Medical Center seemed the logical choice since it was also just down the street from the Holiday Inn, where he was booked for his visit.

"That would be fine," he said as the waitress offered to pour him a third cup of coffee. "I really need to cut back, but—ouch!"

Broyle jerked back, but it was too late, as the steaming coffee scalded his unprotected hand. "I'm so sorry," the waitress pleaded, fumbling for the towel tucked under her belt. "Here, let me wipe it off."

That was the last thing Broyle wanted—her waving the pot of coffee over his head with one hand, while trying to clean up the mess with the other. "No," he said, grabbing the towel from her outstretched hand. "I'll do it."

It was then he noticed the gnarled joints as her distorted fingers unsuccessfully tried to hold on to the cloth. "Please, I didn't mean to …"

Still recoiling from the pain in his hand, Broyle felt a wave of sympathy cross over him as he dabbed at the spilled coffee. "Rheumatoid?" he asked, now ashamed at his little outburst.

"You a doctor?" She drew back awkwardly in an attempt to cover up her obvious malady.

"Yes," Broyle said. "Well, I was. I just don't practice anymore."

The waitress moved closer. "Do you mind?" she asked as she set down the pot of steaming coffee on Broyle's table. "I hope you're not like my doctor. They ran him out of town." She let out a slow, deep sigh. "That's not exactly the way it was. They kicked him out of this hospital. Now I can't see him no more." She no longer tried to hide her mangled hands.

"Who are they?" Broyle questioned, his curiosity aroused by the pitiful sight of her fingers.

"Those folks across the street at Crosstown," she said. "They kicked him out of their hospital and took all his patients away."

She looked around at her other tables. By this time, they were all empty, except one where the customers were only halfway through their meal. She turned back to Broyle. "I don't understand all that insurance stuff, but it had something to do with his working at the other hospital here in Longview."

She was exactly what Broyle had been hoping for—a perfect example of the carnage that was taking place in this supposedly peaceful East Texas community. "Why didn't you just go with him to the other hospital?"

"They don't take my insurance over there," she said, her voice heavy with sadness. "So far, no one has come in to take his place that's a specialist in my type of arthritis. Fortunately, one of the family doctors who comes to the restaurant refills my medicines for me. At Crosstown, they told me if I wanted to see someone else, I would have to go to Tyler to be covered by my insurance."

Broyle reached over and picked up his cup of coffee with his other hand, his pain starting to subside. "Why don't you just change insurance companies …" He hesitated, not knowing her name.

"Dolly," she said, pointing proudly to her nametag just below her chandkerchief. Suddenly, tears began to well up in her eyes as her crippled fingers tried helplessly to remove a napkin from the container at the far end of the table. "Doc, they just let me stay on here so I can get in on their insurance until I'm eligible for Medicare. I got no other choice. It's this or nothing."

. . .

At first, there was just a faint glow somewhere off in the distance. But as Terrell continued to blink, the picture came more into focus. It was Jordan Springer standing over him, and he was holding a small flashlight. "What the …" Terrell said, his speech jumbled.

Terrell tried to move but was held back by Springer's hand on his chest. "You're not going anywhere until we've had a chance to check you over." Springer's response was compassionate but convincing. "It's your turn to be a patient."

Terrell looked around, realizing he was on a stretcher in the emergency room. A burning pain shot through his temples as he turned his head to the side. Reaching up, he felt a large knot on the back of his skull. "What happened?"

"You probably have a mild concussion," Springer answered. "We've got you scheduled for a CAT scan in a few minutes just to make sure there are no other problems. The old man fell over on top of you just as your head hit the floor."

It was all coming back now—the flailing arms, Terrell's attempt to help, then the darkness. "What about my patient?"

"We moved him into the ICU, but we can talk about that later." Springer appeared edgy as he turned to leave.

"No," Terrell said, his head clearing. "I want to know what happened to him."

Reaching up, Springer slowly pulled the curtain closed. "Right now, it's touch and go," he said with uncertainty. "He apparently had an anaphylactic reaction to the dye you gave him. Fortunately, we got to him right away, but he is still in a coma." Springer paused, seeming to try to get his thoughts together. "John, we had to shock him three times before he went back into sinus rhythm. He's still on a drip, and the cardiologist is talking about a pacemaker if he makes it through the next twenty-four hours."

Terrell was shocked as his mouth fell open. "But he'd had that same dye two days ago, and his doctor just wanted a set of follow-up films." Guilt was beginning to overwhelm him. "I didn't think a test dose was necessary."

"I would have probably done the same thing." Springer's response was cautious. "The problem is they switched dyes on you. No, that's not exactly right. They substituted the dye you had used before for the generic brand. The hospital's been doing that a lot recently—part of their austerity program. The problem is your patient paid the price for it. And in all likelihood, as soon as the old man's family finds out what really happened, so will the hospital."

Springer didn't have to say any more. Terrell knew the rest. Although it was the hospital that had the deep pockets and the one the lawyers would go after the most aggressively, it was John Terrell who was ultimately responsible.

. . .

"I think we've finally got the majority leader on our side," Lane Foster said. "With the compromises I was able to negotiate, he has agreed to let the bill come to the Senate floor."

"Compromises!" Duke Dandridge screamed, slamming his hand on his desk. "For the amount of money I am paying you, I get compromises? You little fart, I ought to—"

Foster interrupted, his voice edgy. "You have to understand how things work in Washington. Everything is a compromise." He pulled out a copy of the revised legislation and passed it across the desk.

Dandridge jerked up the paper, his hand still shaking from anger. "I'm not going through this whole thing. Just tell me what I need to know."

As Foster carefully walked him through revised SB 4215, Dandridge barely opened his eyes except when he got to the parts where it might mean Horizon Data Systems would make more money. "That's where these other people you claim to have working for you in Congress become important." Foster looked up to see if Dandridge was paying attention. "Senator Carlisle has no special loyalty to Horizon. In fact, he could probably get more support from the states for this legislation if he let them pick their own intermediaries to administer this plan. Sort of a *you scratch my back, I'll scratch yours* philosophy."

"I don't think that's going to be a problem," Dandridge said, an evil smile beginning to break through. "The disgruntled doctors with their screaming and doomsday predictions will create such a diversion that an extra rider on the bill supporting Horizon will almost go unnoticed."

Foster shook his head at Dandridge's naivety. "If you think the Blue Crosses and the Aetnas of this country are just going to sit idly by while we run them out of business and give it all to you, you're sadly mistaken. They—"

Dandridge held up his hand. "Mr. Foster, this is corporate America. Health care coverage in the private sector hasn't been profitable, at least not compared to other sectors of our industry, for years. Look at the Blues. They used to be considered the patient's friend, passing on profits by decreasing premium rates. Now through mergers and acquisitions, they are as aggressive as any of them, scratching and clawing for their piece of the pie. And the Aetnas. Name me one sector of society that considers them a friend." He paused, laying down the copy of Foster's proposed legislation on his desk. "No, my uninformed friend, we will become the hero. The only profit left in health care coverage is in the administrative end—distributing the government's money. The private carrier is like the Oldsmobile; they both had their day. Your legislation will see to that. And Horizon, a symbol of corporate America in the new millennium, will only be fulfilling its civic duty as it partners with the federal government to care for this country's sick and needy citizens." A smile slowly crept across Dandridge's pursed lips. "That is for a small profit."

. . .

After hitting the message button with her one free finger, Allison set the sacks down on the counter, still somewhat out of breath from her ordeal to the Safeway just up the street. The first call had been from her mother, wanting a daily update on the pregnancy. Not one to waste time, Allison began unloading the groceries. The second was a recorded solicitation. Allison's head was buried deep in the refrigerator when the word *accident* stopped her cold. She quickly spun around, failing to shut the door, and raced over to the telephone. "… 7747, would you please call as soon as possible." It was all the message she could get.

Her fingers jabbed anxiously, finally hitting the repeat button on the second try. Allison's heart pounded as she went through the first two messages again, afraid that if she hit the erase button she would lose the all-important third call. Visions of untold disasters clouded her mind as the seconds appeared to turn into hours when the third call finally came back up. "Mrs. Terrell, this is the emergency room at Methodist." There was a pause in the conversation as the caller seemed to muffle the telephone. "I'm sorry, but your husband has been in an accident over in radiology, and they just brought him in here. Our doctor is still evaluating his status, but I was told he has a head injury. Our telephone number is 972-620-7 …"

Allison didn't wait for the rest of the message. Almost in a dead run, she slammed the door to the refrigerator and headed back to the garage, her throat tight with fear. The remaining groceries would have to wait; her husband was her only concern. A return call to the hospital would only be a delay. Good or bad, she had to see for herself. Feeling a twinge deep in her abdomen, her face winced at the slight pain as she strapped on her seat belt. She wrote it off to the quick lunch she had gulped down at the deli counter just the hour before as she gunned her car out onto the busy street. When the second, more severe pain hit less than a minute later, she wasn't quite so sure.

. . .

Along with representatives from several other medical organizations, including the AMA, Dr. Gene Broyle had been invited in only as an observer to the first meeting of what had been labeled the Coalition—a loosely knit group of physicians and their attorneys from both Crosstown and its competitor. Not wanting to be tied to one campus, a neutral site at the Masonic Temple was chosen for the occasion. Saturdays, which were usually reserved for quality time away from the problems of the profession, was chosen in hopes of allowing greater attendance. With the deteriorating situation in Longview, that did not appear to be a problem as Broyle took a seat in the back row of the crowded auditorium.

The tapping of the gavel grew louder as the tall, gray-haired man tried repeatedly to gain the group's attention. "Ladies and gentlemen," he called out, his voice echoing through the microphone that had been set up on the podium. "Let's bring this meeting to order."

Squinting to make sure his eyes were not playing tricks on him, Broyle recognized the speaker. Although a year behind, Seldon Rogoff, MD, and Broyle had gone through their residencies together. In fact, as he thought back, it was Rogoff who had accepted the position he rejected in the laid-back East Texas town the year before.

A hush settled across the room as all heads turned toward the lectern. "Let me start by saying that it has been a long time since I have seen many of you, my friends." Rogoff paused, his face drawn, and slowly looked out at the attentive audience. "Entirely too long." His tone was full of sadness. "Many of you are asking, How did we let this happen? Why have we become a town divided amongst ourselves—colleague against colleague, partner against former partner, even father against son?"

Broyle looked over as, two rows in front of him, a young lady, probably in her late thirties, stood up. "I'll tell you how," she said, her voice edgy but resolute. "Because those administrative bastards at Crosstown convinced the non-physician members of their board of trustees that, for financial reasons, it was in the best interest of the hospital."

A round of applause went up around the room at the young physician's comments. She continued, her tone more confident, bolstered by the audience's support. "The irony is that two of the board members are my patients, and they still wouldn't listen to me."

"Thank you," Rogoff interjected, trying to take back control of the meeting. "Dr. Spires is right about how it happened, but the question I put before you today, the question that must be answered before we can even think about a solution, is why we let this happen."

The auditorium fell quiet, reminding Broyle of Sunday church during that part of the service reserved for prayers of confession. A few muted coughs went up, but that was all, as no one was confident enough to give Rogoff an answer. "Everyone in this room knows the answer, don't you? When was the last time you attended a staff meeting at the hospital, except to eat dinner and sneak out the back door? How many have attended a meeting of the county medical society or the Texas Medical Association recently? How many of you are even members anymore of the AMA?" He slowly scanned the audience, looking for a response. "It's because, my friends, we have become so self-absorbed in our own wants and desires that we have abandoned our profession. And when there is a void, all the rats and bloodsucking varmints come in to fill it up. We have turned the practice of medicine into a nine-to-five job—accepting our paychecks, and the rest be damned."

The audience shuffled uneasily in their chairs as Rogoff continued his tongue-lashing. Gene Broyle knew everything his former fellow resident was telling the group was true, but up until now, no one had been willing to say it. Broyle moved closer to the microphone. "So, until the physicians in this community realize that we have a responsibility to our patients twenty-four seven, we are never going to get back the control of what we do."

. . .

Allison clung to the steering wheel; the pains in her abdomen were coming in unrelenting waves. Off in the distance, she could just make out the silhouette of Methodist. Suddenly, not twenty yards ahead, the car in front of her slammed on its brakes, the bright taillights glaring in her eyes almost blinding her. She had been following too closely, but it was too late now. Spinning the steering wheel sharply to the right, she was able to avoid the car in front of her by inches, only to end up crashing headlong into the curb.

It was close to a minute, maybe more, before Allison regained control of her senses. The deflated airbag lay in a crumpled mass over the steering wheel. She checked; the motor was still running. Throwing the car in reverse, Allison stepped on the accelerator, trying to pull away from the curb. There was no movement, only a sickening clanking sound from somewhere underneath the damaged vehicle.

Allison started to panic as the growing pains tore at her insides. She had to get to her husband. Accident or not, he was her only hope. She flung open the door, fumbling to hold onto her purse.

Her second foot had barely hit the pavement when a feeling of lightheadedness began to cloud Allison's thinking. The hospital, less than a hundred yards ahead, took on a strange perspective through her increasing tunnel vision. Her legs, growing heavier with every labored step, were barely able to propel her forward in the direction of the hospital. The small trickle of blood down her thigh went unnoticed. Allison's last thoughts were of her husband and what she would find when the darkness finally closed in around her.

. . .

"You've got to help her!" the passerby called out to the white-clad orderly leaning against the lamppost in the Methodist parking lot. "She's right down the street," he said, pointing to Allison's motionless body, lying on the sidewalk, not a hundred feet away.

Surprised, Stretch Daily looked up, thumbing his half-smoked cigarette into the street. "Let me get a gurney," he answered. He moved quickly across the parking lot and disappeared inside the emergency room entrance.

Stretch was halfway out the door when the nurse stopped him. "Where are you going with that?" Lucille Beating was a veteran of over thirty years in emergency room nursing.

"There's this lady passed out down the street," he said, somewhat out of breath. "I'm gonna go get her."

Beating held up her hand. "Wait!" She walked quickly to the entrance, looking out over the parking lot in the direction of the street. "Is she on the hospital's property?"

The confused orderly gazed in the direction he had seen the fallen patient. "No," he said, his voice hesitant, not sure why the nurse would raise such a question. "Well, almost," he continued. "She's maybe a half a block away, if that."

The crusty nurse spun around, grabbing for the telephone on top of the triage desk. As Beating was dialing, the frustrated orderly said, "What are you doing, ma'am?"

"I'm calling 911," she answered, her hand muffling the receiver. "The hospital could be held liable if you go pick her up and there's a problem. That's what the paramedics are for." She turned away to give the information to the emergency operator on the other end of the line.

Unable to control his frustration, Stretch slammed his hand against the gurney, propelling it against the far wall. Removing a cigarette from his breast pocket, he lit up and took in a deep drag, blowing the smoke in the direction of Beating, who was still tied up with the 911 call.

"What? You can't do that in here," she sputtered as the smoke swirled around her face. "We're supposed to set an example for the rest of the community."

Stretch didn't respond as he walked out the door shaking his head in disgust. He wasn't sure what he could do anymore.

11

"PRETTY NASTY BURN you got there," the stranger said, looking down at Gene Broyle's blistered hand. "Probably ought to get it looked at."

Broyle turned around, still trying to follow the activity at the far end of the room. "It's a long story," he said, drawing back slightly from the man's intruding eyes.

"Why don't we go out in the hall, and you can tell me about it," the man continued. "I need a break."

Shifting uncomfortably, Broyle said, "I think I'll stay. Don't want to miss ..."

The stranger cut him off with a half-hearted wave. "I make my living going to meetings like this all over the country," he answered. "So, my friend, I don't think you're going to get too behind if you step out for a few minutes." He stood up, then turned back to Broyle. "That's the tragedy of it."

It was his last comment that got to Broyle. Wanting to know more, he followed the stranger out of the room.

"Leonard O'Bannon's the name," he said, extending his hand. "I'm the representative from the AMA. And you're?"

Broyle could barely spit out his own name, knowing the UMA was in direct competition to the older, more established AMA.

"It's a pretty big mess they have down here," Broyle said, hoping to divert O'Bannon from finding out why he was there.

"It's a mess everywhere," O'Bannon answered, a note of sadness in his voice. "The boundaries are just more clearly demarcated because Longview is relatively small and there are only the two competing hospital systems." He paused, scratching the back of his neck, then looked back at Broyle. "Let me tell you, living out of a suitcase is hell. These damn overnight laundries always put too much starch in their shirts."

Broyle began to relax when he saw that O'Bannon had a sense of humor. "Just as long as they don't put it in your shorts." Broyle grinned, then decided to change the subject. "Your bosses in Chicago got any ideas on how to solve this?"

"Not any good ones, I'm afraid. We've provided them with legal assistance and submitted several legal briefs, but so far, we've pretty much hit a brick wall. We've offered to send in a team to see about forming some sort of doctors' union, but so far, they have refused. I guess they are just too independent down here. What with our decreasing revenue from membership, we can only afford to put so much into this." O'Bannon's tone was ominous. "The hospitals have the system on their side. By the time this works its way through the courts, a lot of these doctors will be out of money, and their patients will have been forced to go somewhere else."

"I know," Broyle said, looking down at his scorched hand and thinking of Dolly struggling to hold on to her health care coverage.

"We think this Longview situation is a real testing ground for the hospitals," O'Bannon said, his eyes following Broyle's. "If they can get a big win here, it will serve as a model where the hospitals will be able to control the doctors on one side and the insurance companies along with good old Uncle Sam on the other. When that happens, the doctor's uniform will no longer be a white coat but a blue Levi work shirt."

. . .

It was just over seventeen minutes since the nurse had put in the 911 call when the ambulance carrying Allison arrived at Methodist's emergency entrance. "What have you got here?" Beating asked, peering over her half frames.

"Her car ran into a curb just up the street," the EMT answered as he scribbled away on his clipboard. "We found her on the sidewalk, heading your way. Her blood pressure is on the low side, and she's having some vaginal bleeding. Other than that, there's no trauma from what I could tell; probably the airbag saved her." He paused, pulled out the sheet of paper, and handed the nurse the carbon. "We just stabilize 'em and bring 'em in. The rest is up to you guys." His paperwork completed, the EMT was ready to move on. "Where do you want her? She sort of drifts in and out but kept saying something about getting to her husband. Evidently, he's a doctor here. Name's John Terrell."

Beating's eyes grew wide as she adjusted her glasses and looked down at the name on the carbon copy. Nervously, she pointed to one of the cubicles halfway down the hall. "Stretch," she called out, trying to avoid making eye contact. "Would you help the paramedic move Dr. Terrell's wife to number seven, while I get Dr. Springer to come over from the ICU?"

If there was ever a go-to-hell look, it was the one Stretch shot his bitchy boss as he grabbed the other end of the gurney and headed off.

Within less than a minute after she had been transferred to the hospital's stretcher, the curtain to the cubicle swung back. "Allison, I'm Jordan Springer." His voice was calm and reassuring. "Your husband's going to be all right."

Allison sighed, giving the doctor a weak smile. "What happened to him? Where is he?"

"He had a tangle with an unconscious patient and ended up on the bottom of the pile. Looks like he came out of it with only a mild concussion, but we sent him back to radiology for a CAT scan just to be on the safe side." Jordan smiled, moving over to Allison's stretcher, and gently laid his hand on her abdomen. "Now, let's talk about you."

Allison winced in pain as Springer pressed down. "Oh," she said, tightening her stomach muscles.

"You had your appendix out?" Springer questioned as he slowly scanned Allison from head to toe.

"No," she said, trying to hold back a cry. "I'm pregnant." Her voice cracked, realizing what was happening to her. "At least … I was."

Springer looked over his shoulder as Lucille Beating walked by Allison's cubicle. "Let's set her up for a pelvic," he called out, trying to get the nurse's attention.

At first, Beating kept on going; she stopped when Springer moved back out into the hall. He started to repeat himself when she whirled around. "Right away, Doctor," she said hesitantly.

Suddenly, Springer felt a tap on his shoulder. "Doc, I'm sorry," Stretch said, his eyes glassy. "I was just doing what I was told."

"What are you talking about?" he questioned the orderly. Nurse Beating quickly came back.

"Run on up front and help out," she said, glaring at Stretch. "I'll take care of this back here."

Springer was in the dark. "What the hell is going on?" He moved across the hallway so he could look at them at the same time. "Do you mind letting me in on this, Stretch?"

"Nothing!" the nurse screamed. "Now, get on up to the front or I'll—"

Springer cut her off with a wave. "I'm not sure," he said, trying to evaluate the situation, "but the last time I checked, I was in charge here. Now, go on, Stretch."

Springer's eyes grew wide as the orderly began to lay out the sordid story. "I don't know nothin' about that gettin' sued shit; I just know we is supposed to help people around here." Stretch wrung his hands, trying to avoid Beating's penetrating stare. "I know she's going to get me fired for telling you this, but I couldn't live with myself if I didn't. Growing up, we never had no money to give people, so helping out is all we could do. My momma raised seven of us by herself. If it wasn't for my brothers and sisters pitchin' in to help Momma, we'd never made it. " Stretch appeared embarrassed, as his eyes never left the floor.

"Why?" Springer asked, turning to Beating, still reeling from the shock of learning that she had ordered Stretch to leave Allison lying on the street.

"Protocol," she said, moving nervously from one foot to another. "We are not an ambulance service, Dr. Springer. The hospital's malpractice insurance doesn't cover us if we leave the property."

Springer shook his head in disgust. "Damn it, Beating," he said, the hair on the back of his neck bristling. "You're a nurse. Does everything have to be by the book?"

"You might want to take that up with Administration—since we both work for them." She turned around, then paused and looked back over her shoulder. "I'll set up Dr. Terrell's wife for the pelvic—that is, as long as you're through."

. . .

Senator Rayborn Carlisle smiled proudly as the president leafed through his copy of revised SB 4215. "It's the answer to that promise you campaigned on, Mr. President—health care coverage for everyone." Carlisle nervously cleared his throat. "I couldn't get Forman and our colleagues in the House to go along unless we brought the plan in gradually. As much as they bitch about doing away with big government, it seems they're always talking about the other guy. They're for it, until the money starts coming out of their pocketbooks. In one way or another, we all have our hand out. Just look at how many millionaires turn down their Social Security checks: close to none."

The president laid down the proposed legislation, a look of concern still painted across his face. "Ray, you and I came to Washington in order to get Big Brother off our backs," he said, picking up his cup of now lukewarm coffee. "And what's happened since we came?"

Carlisle's smile faded, and he shifted uneasily. "I'm not sure what you mean, Mr. President."

"It's doubled," he said, taking a sip. "You and I have more than doubled the bureaucracy that we promised to control. And now the only answer we can come up with is more of the same. I would have hoped we could have offered the people who put us here something better."

"I'm afraid it's even worse than that." Carlisle lifted his briefcase, setting it in his lap as he extracted a manila folder labeled Confidential. "Since we would be adding about twenty million new names—of people who either could not or would not pay for their own coverage—to the rolls of government-supported programs, the extra costs add up to another $150 billion a year. The Congressional Bureau of Accounting feels we can recoup about $50 billion of that in premium charges, but that still leaves us a hundred in the red."

The president rolled his fingers on the desktop as he looked off across the room. "That doesn't sound so bad," he said. "With the projected budget surplus, we should be able to absorb those outlays without too much difficulty."

Carlisle cleared his throat. "You must remember, Mr. President, the baby boomers are leaving the work force and entering the Social Security and Medicare programs in droves. So with the decreasing tax base, along with Trump's tax cuts, adding another hundred billion will probably put us back in the red again."

Rising from his chair, the president picked up his cup and moved over to the bust of Lincoln nestled in the far corner. "Sometimes, I come down here at night, Ray." He hesitated, then gently rested his hand on the top of the statue. "And I try to imagine what he might have done. His whole world was coming apart—brother fighting brother, father, son. Unquestionably, this country's darkest hour. But through it all, he stood fast—believing above everything else that we should be treated as equals." The president's eyes glistened as he looked back at Carlisle. "You know, Lincoln was right. It may not have all the frills, but everyone deserves basic health care coverage. So if it's one hundred or two hundred billion more, we're just going to have to find a way to make it work."

"We've squeezed the hospitals all we can," Carlisle answered, rustling through the papers he now had laid out across the front of the president's desk. "Almost half of them have closed their doors over the last thirty years. The only extra money is in the administration end and the drug companies. With a federal takeover of the funding aspect, we can control the administrative costs to some extent. With respect to the drug companies, they'll just go somewhere else, and research for new drugs in this country will dry up. You know this is a big world, Mr. President. Unless they're willing to shell out some exorbitant price, all our patients will be able to get after that will be the generics. That is, if they aren't able to take a trip somewhere else." The senator held up his hands in frustration. "We're back to another Canada—having to go to another country for better care. Sort of ironic when you think about why our ancestors landed on these shores four hundred years ago."

"What about the doctors and the nurses?" the president questioned as he plopped down on the overstuffed sofa. "Don't they make a lot of money?"

Carlisle shifted around in his chair so he could face the president.

"One doesn't go into nursing for the money. Next to teachers, they are the most underpaid and overeducated sector in our society." A slight grin came across his lips. "The doctors are another matter."

The president squinted. "Meaning what?"

"Meaning that despite all the sacrifices they make during the many years they spend in training, they could give up 40 percent of their income and still do all right."

"Well, that's it!" the president exclaimed. "We'll take the extra money from them."

"We're not sure that will work either. There're too many variables." Carlisle sighed. "Most of them won't flee to another country, like the Canadian and English physicians. At 60 percent of what they make now, they still couldn't do better anywhere else. We're worried more about the front and the back ends."

The president looked confused as he grabbed for another sip of his coffee. "You've lost me on that one."

"Quitting early," Carlisle said. "It's already happening. If they're close to retirement age and can afford it, they just turn in their stethoscope and walk away. Those who haven't been as fortunate are looking in other areas. Many choose fields where they can still use their medical knowledge, such as working for insurance companies, but those are becoming saturated. I can remember the old doc in our hometown was given a gold watch by the mayor when he finally retired after fifty years. Today, that average is closer to thirty-five years and decreasing quickly."

Carlisle scanned the papers lying before him on the president's desk, then pulled out one. "Here," he said, holding up the page, "is the other end. For the last five years, applications to the medical schools have dropped about 3 percent per year, while the candidates for the law and business schools are up over a third. It looks like many of our smartest are going somewhere else. If we cut their pay by 40 percent, well, you don't have to be a genius to know what that would do."

"So they've got us by the balls," the president said, his voice tense.

"I'm not sure." Carlisle's grin returned. "Oh, they'll holler and kick when SB 4215 first goes through, but if we keep their pay scale up, most of them will quiet down pretty quickly."

"But you said …" The president was becoming impatient.

Carlisle stood up and walked over to the sofa, sitting down across from the president. "At first." The senator's voice was calm and even. "Then we just slowly put on the squeeze. The folks over at HCFA have been playing that game with the doctors through the Medicare program for years—just cut a little bit each year, and before long, we're where we wanted to be in the first place."

"Since you seem to have already figured this out, Ray," the president said halfheartedly, "what if the docs won't go along? Let's say they decide to strike."

"Until recently, I would have said that couldn't happen. The AMA and most of their other organizations might reluctantly support disruption of paperwork, or if they're desperate, maybe even a temporary work slowdown—emergencies only. The whole concept violates the central tenet of the medical profession—patient's interests above all else. Although they consider it their strength, we really think it's their Achilles' heel."

The president glared at Carlisle. "I guess that's of some comfort, but what do you mean by recently?"

"It's this start-up organization—the Unified Medical Association. I met with their leaders at the Morrison-Clark, and to tell you the truth, they scared the hell out of me." Carlisle's look turned sour. "If they make their growth predictions, we could be in trouble. They seem to think of this as war, and with that come casualties."

"Are you telling me they are willing to sacrifice some of their …"

"Patients!" Carlisle said.

An uncomfortable silence fell across the Oval Office. The two occupants were face-to-face with a potential problem even more horrible than Lincoln ever faced—a country without medical care. Rayborn Carlisle was the first to break the silence when he got up, moving deliberately to his briefcase and removing another folder—the large red letters Top Secret stamped across the front. "Just in case, I thought you might want to review this." He tossed it over on the sofa by the president. "I'm sorry, but once SB 4215 passes over on Capitol Hill, the rest is up to you."

The president fingered the folder, squinting to read the smaller letters on the tab. His eyes rose, focusing somewhere in the distance. His whisper was barely audible. "The Reagan administration versus the air traffic controllers."

. . .

Gene Broyle eased his way back through the door of the auditorium. Just as he was about to take his seat in the back, Seldon Rogoff looked up, squinting, then signaled for him to move closer. Broyle waved him off, but it was no use; Rogoff had made up his mind. By now, Broyle had become the focus of the crowd, who were losing interest as a disgruntled physician over on the far side of the large room continued to filibuster. Not wanting any more attention than he already had, he quickly moved down the aisle toward the front. Rogoff's expression changed to a smile as he appeared to recognize his former fellow resident. Broyle gave him a weak wave, diving for the nearest empty chair.

"Doctor," Rogoff interrupted. "Doctor. Thank you very much." The frazzled man tried to continue but to no avail; Rogoff was through with him, and so was the audience. He was just one in a long line of people who had a litany of complaints, but when it came to answers, his list was blank.

"A good friend of mine has joined us today," Rogoff said, pointing to Broyle. "I'm not sure why he's here, but maybe he would like to tell us."

Embarrassed, Broyle raised his hand slightly and shook his head no. "I'm just here to observe." His response was barely audible above the noise of the crowd.

Not satisfied, Rogoff questioned, "Are you here for the AMA, Gene?"

Broyle pointed toward the back in O'Bannon's direction. He had been more fortunate, slipping in unnoticed.

Rogoff looked up, acknowledging O'Bannon, but quickly came back to his old friend. A look of confusion clouded his expression. "Who are you observing for then?" he asked, appearing even more determined.

A flushed feeling swept across Broyle as all eyes in the room once again turned toward him. "The Unified Medical Association."

"The UMA," Rogoff repeated loudly, so the information was now related to all those in attendance. "Welcome, my friend." His tone was reassuring. "Most of us don't know that much about your organization. Would you mind telling the group what the UMA can do for us that the AMA and the others haven't already offered?"

Broyle cleared his dry throat. "Advice, Seldon." His speech was hesitant. "We're small by AMA standards, and we don't have much infrastructure yet. Except for a few secretaries, most of the staff are physicians who for various reasons have given up their practices. I guess you can say that cuts both ways."

"Do you mind being more specific?" Rogoff asked, moving away from the lectern and closer to Broyle.

"Although ancillary staff bring expertise that you and I as physicians lack, they also cost money, which is usually in short supply at the UMA. So what we offer you is the experience of being in the trenches, fighting many of the same battles you have, and perspective by having the time to step back and look at your situation as only another doctor can do." Broyle paused, a little embarrassed he had let himself run on like that. "No ancillary support system can offer you that."

There was an uncomfortable hush that moved across the large room. Finally, a voice called out from near the back, "How about a dollar's worth of your advice then?"

The comment brought out a scattering of chuckles. Broyle drew back, slumping down in his chair.

"I'll add ninety-nine to that," Rogoff said with a grin, appearing to sense Broyle's embarrassment. "We're not going to let you off that easily. Hell, Gene, our old chief was rougher on you than these cream puffs." Then he signaled for Broyle to join him at the podium.

Reluctantly, Broyle stood up and headed for the stage. His heart thumped inside his chest. He now understood why he had been sent to Texas. He was not being paid to sit on the sidelines.

Rogoff stepped aside as Broyle took center stage behind the microphone that hung precariously off the top of the lectern. His mind raced, hoping to find just the right thing to say. "What's wrong with just saying no?" Broyle paused, scanning the room for some kind of response. His knees quivered as he shifted uneasily from foot to foot. He reached up and wrapped his fingers around the microphone, awkwardly freeing it from the lectern, then moved to the front of the makeshift stage. "Ladies and gentlemen, some of you may recall the movie where this middle-aged man who had been pushed to the limit by a bad situation had to make a choice," Broyle continued, his voice now calm and steady. "Either he gave up and walked away, or he made a stand."

All eyes were now fixed in his direction.

"And who remembers what he did?" Broyle paused momentarily. "The man pulled up the window to his tenement apartment and started yelling, 'I'm not going to take it anymore! I'm not going to take it anymore!' At first, his was the only voice that could be heard, but one by one, his neighbors began to join in. And what started out as a single cry rapidly grew into a chorus that shook the whole neighborhood."

Broyle's arm dropped to his side, the microphone hanging limply in his hand. He turned and headed back across the podium toward the lectern, then stopped and faced the audience again. "Longview is your neighborhood. Only you can decide if you are going to keep your windows shut and hope this all goes away. Or are you going to come in from the golf course and move away from your computers to form a chorus that says you are not going to take this anymore? It's up to you. We'll be there to support you, and I would hope so would the AMA." Broyle strained to see if there was a response from O'Bannon. "No organization is going to make that call for you."

12

Three Weeks Later

THE BACK OF John Terrell's head still had a rather large knot, which only hurt when he forgot and rubbed it. So except for an occasional headache from his encounter with the unforgiving floor in radiology, he was pretty much back to normal. Unfortunately, the same could not be said for Allison. The miscarriage had devastated her. She had become so depressed that Terrell had finally arranged for her to see a psychiatrist on the staff. He was relieved that in the last couple of days, she seemed to be doing better, but it was still too early to tell. He knew that wounds of the soul took a longer time to heal.

The reading room was darkened when the receptionist came to the door. "There's a guy from the postal service out front. Says he has a certified letter for you. Can I send him back?"

Terrell squinted in the dim light as he grasped the letter after putting his name beside the X. He held up the envelope and used the reflected glow off the view boxes. The return address was unfamiliar—Donald and Donald, attorneys at law. Tearing open the letter, he let the envelope drift to the table below. Suddenly, his chest tightened as he read its contents:

Attn: John Terrell, MD

Our firm has been retained by the family of C. L. Starnes in their attempt to collect for the damages he sustained while under your care … While it is regrettable …

We suggest you seek legal counsel so that we can bring this matter to the earliest conclusion.

Sincerely,
Raymond S. Donald, JD

Terrell dropped to his chair, his knees weak beneath him. He had witnessed a lawsuit being filed on one his colleagues before, but this was his first. His initial response was anger. How could the patient's family do this to him? He was only trying to help the old man. Didn't these people know all the training he went through just to be a doctor? Medicine was still a fledging science with so many unpredictable elements. There were no guarantees; that point was included in the release form. Didn't they read the small print the old man signed just before he was brought down for the procedure? Terrell had failed to realize the hospital had substituted a generic, but he couldn't check out everything.

Even though there were a few rough days in the ICU, the old man had pulled through apparently unscathed and was scheduled to go back to the nursing home early next week. If the family was so concerned, why wasn't he going home with them? "Those ungrateful bastards," Terrell cursed under his breath, "just trying to wring money out of the system." And the lawyers, the bloodsucking vultures, always willing to help as long as they got their cut. He wondered why they never got sued when they screwed up. It probably had something to do with professional courtesy within the legal profession. Hell, by the time the family and the lawyers were through, the old man wouldn't see a dime.

Terrell slammed his hand on the desk, his frustration bubbling over as he watched the letter slip to the floor. As he reached down to pick it up, unable to see in the darkness, his head struck the edge of the protruding table. "Shit!" he yelled. Stumbling back, still reeling from the pain that shot through his bruised brow, Terrell crashed into the wall in the small room.

"You okay, Dr. Terrell?" the receptionist asked as she rushed back to the door. "I heard the crash all the way from my desk."

"Yeah," Terrell mumbled, reaching up to feel the large goose egg swelling forming over his right eye. "I guess I am going to have to bring a football helmet to work from now on." He grinned as he looked for the fallen piece of paper. "Could you flip on the lights for me? I need to get in touch with my attorney."

. . .

It was now almost five minutes since Allison first nestled the receiver between her chin and shoulder after the receptionist put her on hold. Although he had only recently taken over for Gene Broyle, MD, like so many others, the young doctor was not taking on any new Medicare patients. Allison might not have been so understanding, but as a favor to Terrell, he had agreed to see her mother anyway.

It was frustrating, Allison thought, that this country's senior citizens and underprivileged so often had to go begging for doctors. She knew the public would never understand, since they only saw the image of a doctor riding around in a golf cart and sporting a Polo shirt. The problem had to do with reimbursement from the Medicare and Medicaid patients. There just wasn't enough money in it for the physicians to meet their rising expenses without making up the difference somewhere else. That was unless they ran a mill, seeing one patient right after the other, like cattle moving through the chute, at times going so fast they sometimes missed other, more subtle problems. It was another example of a federal program starting out with the best intentions but ending up with untoward consequences.

"Here we are," the receptionist cut back in without a hint of apology in her voice. "Doctor Benson can see your mother on the twenty-fourth at four o'clock."

Allison blinked. "But that's almost three weeks away. My mother's headaches are bad, and her dizziness seems to be getting worse every day. I don't think she can wait that long."

"That's just the earliest the doctor can get you in," the receptionist answered. "After all, your mother is a new patient for us. And we only have so many of those appointments available. If she gets worse, you might want to take her to the emergency room."

Taken back, Allison hesitated, trying to consider her other options. "Can you at least talk to Dr. Benson and see if there is anything else he can suggest until then?" Allison felt like she was pleading, knowing that all the follow-ups after the emergency room visit would have to be done by whichever internist happened to be on call at the time—and then only for that particular complaint. So, if another problem turned up, it was back to the emergency room and often another doctor. Not a very good way to build a trusting relationship.

Allison could only imagine the go-to-hell look she was getting on the other end of the line as a muffled sigh leaked out of the receiver. "All I can do is tell his nurse," she said, her tone abrupt.

"I'll be waiting for her call," Allison fired back, determined not to be outdone by her indifference.

. . .

"Senator, this software package that Horizon Data Systems has developed will mesh with SB 4215 perfectly," Duke Dandridge said, pointing to the schematics laid out before them. "We are prepared to have full implementation within twelve months from the time the president signs the bill into law."

Lane Foster cut Dandridge a quick smile as Rayborn Carlisle leaned over his massive desk, trying to absorb all the information scattered on the pages of graphs and pie charts. "What do you think, Lane?" the senator asked, turning to his chief medical advisor.

"As I told you, Senator," Foster answered, stepping back from the table while trying to act like the information was new to him, "I will need more time to examine Horizon's proposal, since this is the first time I have had a chance to review it. Mr. Dandridge and his colleagues seem to have addressed most of the problems we have been wrestling with—such as the geographic differences with the cost of delivery and the sensitive issues of prioritization of coverage."

"I don't know," Carlisle answered, fingering his chin as his eyes darted from paper to paper. "The states are going to want more say in how these funds are allocated, and without their help, SB 4215 will never make it off Capitol Hill. Even now, it's a struggle just to get them to go along with the programs we already have in place. Horizon's proposal appears to leave very little room for their involvement."

Dandridge lifted up one of the sheets lying on the table. "But, Senator, that's exactly where the problem is," he said, pointing to one of the tables printed on the page. "There's no uniformity from state to state. Each carrier has its own set requirements when a claim is filed for a particular service. Even in the federal programs, the standards are in a constant state of flux. And what does that lead to? Inefficiency! This country spent almost 24 percent of the money allocated for health care on administrative services last year. We should be able to get that closer to half that number under a single-payer system and Horizon's standardization software. Respectfully, sir, my company can save you folks here in Washington billions."

Lane Foster stayed to the side as the two modern gladiators jockeyed for position. Half of his job was complete—getting Dandridge a meeting with his boss without revealing his personal connection to Horizon. That part turned out to be easy since the senator's office was inundated with requests from parties on both sides of the health care issue. The more difficult half was yet to come—convincing the senator to go along. Being a good businessman, Dandridge had built in contingencies. Besides the other members on Capitol Hill who he had already allegedly recruited, there was Foster's $100,000 payoff. So far, he had seen only the first twenty; the rest would come when Senator Carlisle agreed to go along.

"You're probably correct, Mr. Dandridge," Carlisle said, his tone even and thoughtful. "Developing uniformity is the key to a more efficient health care delivery system. Henry Ford taught us that lesson over a hundred years ago, but as I recall, even though he produced the most cars, they weren't necessarily the best. What the current administration at the White House will not go along with is any program that might compromise quality. I have the president's personal assurance on that."

Foster shifted uneasily, afraid to look in Dandridge's direction as his boss slowly sank back into his chair. "Please, sit down," the senator said to Dandridge. "I am not supporting SB 4215 just to save money. It's about saving lives—taking the money we already spend on health care and removing the waste, so that more of our citizens will not have to lie awake at night worrying that all they have saved for is going to be wiped out just to pay their medical bills."

"I didn't mean …" Dandridge started, but Carlisle held up his hand.

"No, Mr. Dandridge. I understand where you are coming from," the senator said, a look of sadness crossing his face. "That's part of the problem. Don't you see? We've allowed the business community to come in and take over the health care system, and look where it's gotten us."

. . .

Dr. Jordan Springer peered at the dark black lesion through the magnifying loops that wrapped around his forehead. "How long ago did you notice this spot, Mr. Morris?" he asked, having been called to the ER for a consult.

The robust man in his late forties looked at his forearm where the area in question was located, then glanced over at Springer. "It's probably been there for close to a year," he answered. "Asked Doc Bennett about it when he did my physical last fall, but he didn't seem to make much of it then. He called it a freckle or something. Told me not to worry."

Springer picked up the patient's arm and began feeling under his armpit. "So you just ignored it?"

"Well, he's a doctor," Morris said. "I thought he ought to know. That was until it started bleeding about a month ago. I remembered reading about moles that bled, so I went back again."

"Did he suggest you see someone else?" Springer's expression was grim as he continued to mash around under the patient's arm.

Mr. Morris shook his head. "No, he said I must have scratched it. Sort of made me feel like a fool for bothering him with it again. Told me if I wanted to see one of those fancy skin doctors, it would have to be out of my pocket. Since my company is in one of those HMOs, we pretty much have to do what they say. That is, except for emergencies. So, here I am." He grimaced as Springer dug deeper in his armpit. "Hey, Doc, that's hurtin'. Take it easy. I'm just a country boy."

"I'm sorry," Springer answered, removing his hand, letting Morris's arm fall to his side.

"You look worried, Doc," he said. "What'd you find under there?"

Springer began writing on the chart then turned to his patient. "I can't be sure without a biopsy, but it feels like your lymph nodes may be involved."

"Are you telling me this is cancer?" Morris asked, his voice cracking. "And that it's already spread to my armpit?"

"Mr. Morris, you need a specialist—someone who deals with these problems all the time."

The patient's eyes began to moisten as he cowered in the chair. "But, Doc, I can't get no referral." His voice was a faint mockery of his former self. "And we ain't got no money to go out on our own."

Springer swallowed hard, his throat dry as he tried to control his emotions—pity for the poor soul seated before him and disgust for the physician who worked within a system that penalized those doctors who ordered more tests and referred their patients to specialists.

Suddenly, Springer felt a gentle tapping on his shoulder. "One of our old friends is here to pay you a visit," the nurse said. "He's waiting for you in your office when you get through here."

Springer nodded, then turned back to the patient. "Let me give Dr. Bennett a call," he said, forcing a smile. "Unless I miss my guess, you will have a referral waiting for you first thing in the morning."

Springer felt drained as he strode toward his office. His thoughts were still on the patient who some would label a victim of managed care—a method of health care delivery where the incentives are based on doing less. To him, Mr. Morris was more than a victim; he was a tragedy.

. . .

"What brings you back our way?" Springer inquired, pleased to see his old acquaintance but still reeling from the system failure that could ultimately take his last patient's life.

Gene Broyle spun around as Springer entered the small room, splashing a few drips of scalding coffee from the mug he picked up in the nurses' lounge. "Ouch," he said, shaking his already-red hand. "That's the second time recently I've run into problems. Maybe I should stick with iced tea." He shot Springer a weak smile. "The UMA has me working with the doctors in Longview."

"I read about it in AMA's newspaper," Springer answered as he dropped onto the worn sofa that frequently doubled as a bed whenever there was a break in the action. "Seems like the two hospitals over there have those doctors by the balls."

Broyle moved over to the far end of the sofa and sat down, his look deliberate. "That's what the doctors there think," he said. "In fact, that's what they all think, including the representatives from the AMA and the Texas Medical Association. But we don't necessarily agree."

"*We* being your bosses at the UMA?" Springer questioned, shifting to the other hip in order to get a better look at Broyle.

"Them but me too," Broyle answered. "I guess I've changed since getting on board with them. I always thought that doctors had to play by the Marksbery's rules, and if you did, everything would work out for the best, since we were doing things for the right reasons. Well, the last thirty years have taught us that line of thinking is a crock of shit." He paused, taking a sip from his steaming mug, his eyes dancing around the room. "The problem is, until the UMA came along, everyone still followed those same rules, even the organizations that claim to represent the doctors in this country."

Springer's jaw tightened. "What do you mean followed?" On one hand, what his former colleague said made sense, but the whole line of thinking made him uncomfortable. And coming from someone who had been considered part of the establishment, he just wasn't sure.

"Reminds me of the Redcoats during the days of the

Revolutionary War," Broyle continued, appearing to ignore Springer's last question. "Even though they knew the casualties on the front lines were going to be astronomical, they just kept throwing more and more waves of soldiers into the battle, the idea being the last man standing—which often turned out to be some raw recruit from the reinforcement brigade—won the battle." He sighed, then turned to Springer. "Jordan, what amazes me is the dumb bastards on the front lines went along just because that's the way it had been done before. Almost 250 years later, and we're still doing the same thing."

"Gene, I didn't know we were at war."

Broyle shook his head. "That's exactly the problem. The physicians have been so caught up in taking care of their patients and stamping out the little grass fires that pop up that they've missed the fact they have been at war for a long time. That's why we're losing. If you don't put up a fight, you can't expect to win."

Springer looked away, unsure how to respond. Suddenly, a tapping on the door broke the uncomfortable silence. "Yes," he said, happy for the intrusion.

John Terrell poked his head through the door, glancing over at Broyle. "The nurses told me that one of our alumni had decided to pay us a house call." Terrell smiled, then moved into the room, tucking the envelope under his arm. "If you've come back for some fatherly advice, you're in the right place. I was just about to ask for some myself," Terrell said affectionately, extending his right hand.

"I'm afraid it's Gene who has the advice," Springer answered, barely breaking a grin. "He's here on behalf of the Unified Medical Association to help those doctors in Longview who are getting screwed."

"Got your brochure in the mail. Otherwise, I don't know much about the UMA," Terrell said. "What are you guys planning to do that hasn't already been tried?"

Broyle leaned forward, clenching his hands. "Show the doctors of Longview how to take their patients back," he said. "Everyone seems to have forgotten that all the people in the hospitals out there are our patients, and we are *their* doctors."

"I wish you'd tell that to the lawyers." Terrell clutched the envelope once again, then held it out for the other two occupants of the room to see. "My first lawsuit," he said, his voice taut. "It's from the family of the old man I nearly knocked off with the generic dye."

Springer shot him a look of disgust. "You're in good company. By now, most of us have had at least one," he said, looking back over at Gene Broyle, remembering his unfortunate situation with several lawsuits. "My guess is they're not just after you. What they want is the deep pockets—the hospital and the pharmaceutical company who made the drug. They're worth a lot more to them than you are."

"Those damn lawyers," Terrell said. "They're always trying to get us."

"Not always, John," Gene Broyle said. "Who do you think your malpractice company calls first when you notified them you were being sued?"

Terrell paused, shuffling from foot to foot. "A lawyer?"

"You got it!" Broyle exclaimed. "They're just the facilitators for both sides. It's the system that stinks."

13

LANE FOSTER TAPPED in the number on the phone after retreating to the small alcove just down the hall from the Senate hearing room. The call was to Duke Dandridge's back line. Trying to not look suspicious, he shot brief acknowledgments to the familiar faces as they scurried to and fro.

"We worked a deal with Senator Forman's aide to bring SB 4215 to the floor next Tuesday," Foster said, slightly above a whisper. He felt a sense of elation from his skillful maneuvering. "I pushed for that because it's probably the most difficult day of the week for the doctors to be there, especially on such short notice. Many just won't come because it wipes out their whole schedule."

"What about the amendment to get Horizon's name on the bill?" Dandridge queried, apparently focused on his company's best interests.

A wave of disappointment dulled Foster's enthusiasm. That was just Dandridge, thought Foster—asshole to the core or just a good businessman, loyal to whoever paid the highest salary. If it didn't benefit Horizon, Dandridge couldn't care less. "That'll come at the joint conference committee at the last minute, just before the final bill gets pushed up to the president. Hopefully, it won't leave enough time for the other intermediaries to put up much resistance."

"Very good, Mr. Foster." The news seemed to please Dandridge. "Maybe you're worth the money we pay you after all."

Foster smiled at Dandridge's rare compliment. "For this to work, your contacts in the House can't drag their feet, or the medical community could kill the whole thing."

"You've made your point," Dandridge shot back.

"Maybe it would be better if I dealt with whoever that is directly?" Foster asked. "Since everything has to be closely coordinated at the conference committee."

There was an uncomfortable pause as Lane Foster waited for Dandridge's response. "That might be necessary in time. But for now, the less you know about Horizon's involvement, the better."

A chill made the hairs on the back of Foster's neck bristle as he hung up.

. . .

Allison was feeling a growing sense of panic by the time her third knock went unanswered. She fumbled through her purse, looking for the extra set of keys to her mother's apartment, almost dropping the cluttered bag several times. *They were in here the last time I looked*, she thought. But that had been several weeks before. "Mother," she called out, her voice breaking.

Dorothy had called less than an hour before, telling Allison her headache had become so severe she could no longer take the pain. Adding to her growing concern, her mother had also noticed a weakness in her right arm and leg. Allison suggested calling an ambulance, but her mother had rejected the idea, wanting Allison to take her to the emergency room instead.

Desperation setting in, Allison dumped the contents of her purse on the doormat, spreading out the collection of items for closer inspection. She let out a sigh of relief when the key tumbled free of the clutter. Ignoring the mess that lay before her, Allison grabbed the key and jammed it into the lock, then rushed into the darkened apartment.

"Mom … Mom!" Allison's calls went unanswered as she quickly made her way toward the bedroom. She squinted in the dim light that streamed through the partially opened door. "Are you all right?" Allison blurted out, her throat clutching in fear.

Slowly pushing open the door, Allison was taken back by the eerie silence that seemed to envelop her mother's semi-darkened bedroom. Other than the faint silhouette of Dorothy's still body lying facedown on her bed in the far corner, everything seemed in its proper place. "Mother, are you …" Making her way across the room, Allison's question fell short as her foot struck an unseen object, toppling her forward. She thrust out her hands into the partial darkness, attempting to cushion her fall to the floor. Pain shot through her left ankle as she came to rest atop the unknown object.

Allison reached back, half-pushing and half-kicking to free her leg as she recognized her mother's suitcase. Judging from the weight, it was already packed for the trip to the hospital. In the low light, Allison could not fully evaluate the extent of her injury, but for the moment, that was not her major concern. She whirled around in the direction of her mother, still lying unresponsive on her bed. "Mother," she called out, her voice pleading as her heart pounded wildly inside her aching chest.

Her throbbing leg dragging along behind, Allison crawled quickly the rest of the way across the room to her mother's bed. Trembling, she reached out, touching her mother on the back. "Speak to me," Allison said, waiting for a response that she feared would never come. Tears began to cloud Allison's eyes as she pulled herself up onto the side of the bed and quickly rolled her mother up on her side. There were no spontaneous respirations, and Allison was unable to find a pulse, only her open eyes staring blankly at the darkened wall. Allison knew from her two years in nursing school that it was only a matter of time until the first signs of rigor mortis would set in. The pain in Allison's leg was clouded out by the realization that her mother was gone. Suddenly, Allison felt an overwhelming need to help as she jumped up from the bed, lunging toward the closet and the blanket that her mother always kept tucked away on the top shelf for those infrequent cold nights.

Allison slowly limped back to the bed, the blanket gripped in one hand trailing behind. She bent down and gently kissed the back of her mother's head, then neatly arranged the blanket over Dorothy's exposed body—a gesture founded by a lifetime of kindness and love that only a mother could give.

It was only then that Allison reached over and turned on the light on her mother's bedside table. Picking up the receiver, she dialed 911 and waited for the response.

. . .

"Are you going to be all right?" the sympathetic EMT asked, turning to Allison as his partner continued to tighten the straps that held Dorothy's covered body to the gurney. "You can ride with us if you want to."

Allison shook her head, then looked away. "No," she said, her voice broken and weak. "I'll meet you at the hospital. I need to do a few things around here first."

As the door closed, the apartment once again fell into silence—that deadly silence Allison first encountered when she arrived. She slowly made her way back toward the bedroom; the acute pain in her leg had dulled into pulsating throbs. Her mind reeled as thoughts seemed to come at her from all directions.

Tears turned into sobs as Allison plopped down on her mother's bed, her strength evaporated. A chill surged throughout her body, while the deafening silence pulsated inside her head. She reached for the blanket that had protected her mother's still body and brought it up around her shoulders. Why did her mother have to die? Why had a system that had brought her back from the edge of death failed so miserably with her mother? So many unanswered questions! One thing Allison knew for sure—her mother did not have to die alone.

Allison's tears slowly subsided as her sorrow turned into anger. She sat up on the side of the bed, her strength returning, fueled by her growing frustrations. Maybe if the doctor had been willing to see her mother sooner, none of this would have happened. Allison vowed to find answers to these questions—no matter what it took.

. . .

"Dr. Terrell," the receptionist said, "they need to see you over in emergency."

Terrell laid down the x-ray he was holding over the viewing light and turned toward the door. "Did they say what they wanted?"

Terrell's question went unanswered as the receptionist disappeared down the hall. Frustrated that he never seemed to have enough time to finish one job before being pulled to another, he grabbed his lab coat and headed out the door.

Emergency rooms, even the one at Methodist, which was considered more like a walk-in clinic, were either in mass confusion with everyone running in two directions at the same time or dead as a doornail. By the time John arrived, it was the former. "I'm Dr. Terrell," he said to one of the nurses who was hunched over a mound of papers on the large counter. "Do you know where they want me?"

She looked up, appearing to recognize Terrell immediately. "Ah … yes, Doctor," she answered, her voice edgy. "Let me see." She stood up, scanning the large open area to one of the other nurses on the other side who returned her glance with a nod. "Dr. Springer asked if you'd wait for him in the doctor's lounge. We'll send him right back as soon as he finishes with a patient."

Terrell paced back and forth, his level of anxiety growing. Even though Springer was a good friend, the work was piling up. He would wait another two minutes; then Springer would just have to reach him by phone. Suddenly, the door to the doctor's lounge swung open.

The look on Springer's face was not one Terrell had seen before. "It's your mother-in-law," Springer said, his tone sullen. "They brought her in here about twenty minutes ago. According to the EMT, your wife found her at her apartment. I'm no pathologist, but it looks like she's only been gone a couple of hours."

"Gone! Do you mean she's dead?"

Springer nodded as Terrell staggered backward, practically falling into the overstuffed sofa that filled a large part of the tiny room. "I'm sorry, but by the time she got here, there was nothing anyone could have done for her."

Terrell's lip quivered as he tried to speak. "Except see her sooner," he mumbled, barely above a whisper. Terrell stared at the floor, his hands clasped tightly in his lap. "We tried to get her into that Dr. Benson who took Broyle's place, but he put her off for three weeks. Something about only seeing a certain number of new patients. Allison asked them if the doctor could make an exception since her mother's headaches were so bad, but the nurse never even returned her call." Terrell cut Springer a shallow grin. "Maybe we should just consider ourselves lucky since most of the other internists on the staff weren't even taking any new Medicare patients."

A knock interrupted the conversation. "Dr. Terrell's wife is out front," the nurse said, poking her head through a crack in the door. "I think you need to take a look at her, Dr. Springer."

"Me?" Springer questioned, puzzled by the nurse's request.

"She's sitting over in the corner of the waiting room," the nurse answered. "Looks like she banged her left leg up pretty good, but she won't let any of us touch her. Said she just wants to be left alone."

Terrell shot past the nurse on a dead run, barely missing a patient coming out of the bathroom. By the time he reached the waiting area, his heart was beating out of control. In the far corner, he could see Allison, a bloodstained kitchen towel draped around her leg. "What happened?" he questioned, his eyes filled with tears.

"We let her down, John," Allison said in between sobs. "When I was sick, she was there. No questions. She just closed up her home and moved to be with us. But when she came to us, all we could do was ask her to wait."

Oblivious to others in the waiting area, Terrell knelt down, lifting off Allison's homemade bandage that covered a large scrape in her shin. "You need to let Jordan look at this," he said softly.

Allison nodded and then, with John's help, slowly rose to her feet. She grabbed his arm, her sobs temporarily abated as they made their way back toward the treatment area. Suddenly, Allison stopped, her eyes fixed. "John, we are going to help her, aren't we?"

Terrell understood what Allison meant. She wasn't just referring to her mother. Allison was talking about all the Dorothys who had been betrayed by a health care system that discriminated against the elderly and the disadvantaged. He wasn't sure he knew the answer or even where to look, but he knew he had to try.

. . .

Springer was too busy to open the letter when the receptionist from the front desk first brought it back to him. Since the return address from the medical director's office of the Health Care Financing Agency's intermediary for the Medicare program in Texas didn't arouse much interest, he stuffed the correspondence in his lab coat for a quick review later before depositing it in file thirteen. Now with a break in the action, he removed the envelope from his pocket and tore open the flap.

"What the hell?" Springer blurted as he began to read the

correspondence again. This time he was much more deliberate, not wanting to miss a single word.

His face was flushed, and the vessels on his temples pulsated as he grabbed for the receiver on the wall phone, dialing zero. "Get me administration," he said, his voice taut.

It took close to five minutes until Springer was able to make the connection he wanted, since the chief executive officer of Methodist was already on another line when Springer's call first came through. "Jordan, what can I do for you?" Britt Barkley asked.

"Those sons of bitches at HCFA say I owe them over $22,000."

"Looks like they're back to their old tricks," Barkley answered. "I just got off the line with the administrator at Medical City, and three of his ER doctors got their recoupment notices today too. My guess is that some pencil pusher in Washington ran out of something useful to do and decided to go back after the docs again. It crops up every five years or so where the feds get a hard-on about paying out so much money for health care services and decide to yank our chain. It's their way of letting us know who's the real boss in this reimbursement game."

Still befuddled, Springer continued, "But they've already paid me the money, and now they want some of it back. It's their damn fault if they made a mistake."

"You'd think that, but they operate like the Internal Revenue Service," Barkley went on. "The rules are what they make them."

"But they're laws?" Springer's frustration was growing by the minute. "I'll just take them to court."

"Dr. Springer, it sounds like you've never been to tax court," Barkley said. "Speaking as someone who's been there on behalf of this hospital, the feds win 75 percent of the time, and the lawyers walk away with at least $50,000 of your money whether you win or lose."

Springer crumbled the paper in his fist. The extra money he had put away to add on to his den—well, that would just have to wait. "Are you telling me I have no other choice?"

"Let me see if the hospital's attorney can negotiate a settlement for you. Usually the feds are willing to settle for less if they can get something up front," Barkley said, his tone reassuring.

"Thanks." Still seething, Springer slammed down the receiver and turned to one of the nurses standing beside him. "Would you look up the telephone number of Dr. Bennett? You know, the one who missed that melanoma on our patient earlier. I think I'm going to kick some butt before I call it a day."

. . .

Dr. Jerald Todd sat stoically behind his cluttered desk. "It looks like they have enough votes to get SB 4215 through," he said to the group of UMA leadership crammed into his tiny office. Due to the many demands put on them by Todd, this was the first time in months the group of disgruntled but dedicated physicians had been able to get together. He was a hard taskmaster in every sense of the word, driving them constantly with a common cause—to save the medical profession from the sharks of the world that would confiscate medicine's profits for their own best interests. And they would follow him, whatever it took to accomplish their goal.

"My email is loaded with messages from the different medical organizations asking me to lobby my congressman to veto this bill," a slightly balding physician said. "I hope we're doing the right thing by staying out of this battle; otherwise you can kiss our membership goodbye."

"We're going to take a hit at first," Todd answered calmly. "The AMA and the state medical organizations, even many of the specialty societies who don't normally get involved in the political fracas, are up in arms about this. Claiming it's Armageddon—the end of an era." Todd slowly stood up and walked around his desk. "Bullshit! That era ended the day the white collars at Medicare and the executives in boardrooms of the insurance companies in Hartford started telling us how to practice medicine."

A collective gasp permeated the small room as Todd continued his tirade. They had heard it before, at least in bits and pieces. What set Todd apart from the other physicians who were fed up with the system was his ability to see the big picture. He was a strategist—understanding when to give and when to take. That's why they had joined on. Maybe they weren't as passionate as their self-appointed leader, but they believed in his message just as deeply. The methods used by the traditional organizations that represented the medical profession just weren't working. No one would deny there had been small victories along the way. But in the long haul, the battle was in a slow downward spiral, with the doctors and their patients cowering in the trenches, reacting in self-defense. No war had ever been won from the bottom of a bunker.

"You can't lose something you don't have," Todd thundered. "What we're trying to do, ladies and gentlemen, is position the doctors in this country so that we can take back something we lost a long time ago—freedom for our patients and ourselves. As I recall, that was the same reason our forefathers authored what has become the most important document in the history of our country—the Declaration of Independence."

Wedged in tightly between two of his overweight cohorts in the far corner, Gene Broyle, MD, said, "Just exactly, how do you see us in a better position to deal with all the intrusions under a single-payer system?"

"You can't beat your enemy if you can't get to him. Today, we have the feds, the private insurance companies, and those groups that are self-insured," he said, counting them out on his fingers. "Then we have OSHA looking over our shoulder to see if our workplace is safe, JCHA to monitor the hospital, and then a good part of the legal profession waiting to take a piece of our hide if we screw up. The list goes on and on."

"I hope you're not telling us that doctors should be set loose without some way to monitor what they do," Broyle said uneasily. "Our patients deserve better than that."

"No!" Todd thundered back, irritated that his authority was being questioned. "I'm talking about consolidation—bringing the enemy together—so we can get our arms around them. It's just like putting out lots of little grass fires. To get all of them under control, you have to divide up your resources, thus weakening the overall effort. Whereas one big fire, even with its greater destructive power, can be taken on by surrounding it and directing whatever efforts one is able to mount in the same direction. The great military leaders down through the ages taught us that very important lesion."

A light seemed to go on in Broyle's head. "So, you want to let our friends in Washington, DC, do that for us?"

"Sort of ironic, don't you think?" A big smile broke across Todd's face. "The enemy puts its own head in a noose." Suddenly, his smile faded. "That's if our cohorts in the other medical organizations don't screw it up for us by blocking the proposed legislation."

A rumble rippled throughout the crowded room as the participants questioned Todd's last remark. "I don't think you're going to get the other organizations to back off their protests," said one of the younger female physicians. "This has become their top priority."

"They may scream and cry, but their heart isn't in it." Todd's eyes glimmered as he waited for the small crowd to turn their attention back to him. "Physicians aren't just fed up. They've also given up---at least a large portion have. Just look at how many participate in the running of their organizations. I saw in my own state medical association times when they had to go find volunteers in another meeting just so they could have a quorum. That's why many of the specialty organizations operate more like an autocracy, so they don't need input from many of their members. The state medical organizations and the AMA haven't caught on yet, but recently they have turned over much of their important business to an executive-type board. Most hospital medical staffs have done the same thing. Unfortunately, the docs on the street couldn't care less how the decisions are made as long as they can take care of their patients and get paid for it."

"The doctors are only going to get paid less if the feds take over," Broyle said as he loosened his collar. "And as far as taking care of their patients, all you have to do is look at Canada where they wait for months for elective procedures. Our physicians can get the same thing done the next day."

Todd turned around and lifted a small folder off his desk. "When the Medicare program first began in the 1960s, physicians actually made more money, since many of their existing elderly patients were either low pay or no pay. It ultimately turned out to be a way to sucker the doctors in. It was only after the feds had enough of us signed up that they started increasing their regulations and decreasing what they paid. It's an old government ploy, and history usually repeats itself. So my guess is Congress will do the same with SB 4215 in order to try to quell the protests and get most of the doctors to buy in."

"But what about the delays in being able to get the care we've all come to expect?" a voice sounded out from the back. "The doctors aren't going to put up with that."

"You might be right," Todd said calmly. "Hopefully, we can use that to our advantage when phase two of our plan starts. Besides, where are the physicians going to set up practice if they get fed up here? Mexico?"

The group rumbled again when another hand shot up. "You haven't said anything about the patients. They're not going to be too happy with Uncle Sam sticking his finger into their business."

"Is that a question or a statement?" Todd asked, not waiting for a response. "First, except for those who are financially well off or already on government-sponsored programs, most will support the changes with open arms. They will no longer be locked into jobs they can't stand worrying about losing coverage if they leave. Over twenty million more people will be able to get coverage they don't have now. And for at least that many more, with the decreased premium costs, it will free up essential cash reserves they need for other things." Todd paused and looked around the room to make sure he had everyone's attention. "And maybe most important of all, they can once again choose their own doctor—not some unknown face off a list they got through the mail." Todd stopped and held up a piece of paper from the folder in his hand. On it were several columns of numbers. The onlookers squinted to see, but except for several seated close to Todd, the letters were too small to make out. "Just look at virtually any survey taken where the citizens of this country and Canada are asked about overall satisfaction with their present health care delivery system. Even with all their delays and limitations of resources, our neighbors to the north win hands down."

A hush fell across the crowded room as Todd's remarks slowly sunk in. "Don't think it's not going to cost more," a disgruntled voice shot out. "You don't just add more than twenty million people to the system and expect it to be a wash."

"You're right," Todd said, searching the audience. "First, some of the money is going to come from the retired population who can afford to pay. Just because you're eligible for Medicare and Social Security doesn't mean you get it—a political pariah but the only reasonable way to put real dollars back into the system. Second, we must accept the reality of rationing. England and Canada already do it, but in this country, we operate behind a veil of denial that everyone is eligible for all the latest technology our profession has to offer. No more. There are simply not enough resources to go around no matter how much money is out there."

Gene Broyle again cut in. "I wouldn't call the Centers for

Medicare and Medicaid Services' performance stellar with their handling of the Medicare and Medicaid programs. So, I hope you're not going to propose turning this much more complex system over to them too."

"Initially, they have to be involved." Todd frowned. "That's the reality of politics. But Congress will quickly come to realize CMS is in over its inefficient, bureaucratic head. And that's where we here at the UMA come in. The wheels have already been set in motion—the second part of our plan. It will be the first of its kind—an organization of physicians joining with a respected intermediary in the insurance industry to run the world's most advanced health care delivery system. And, my friend," Todd said, looking at the balding physician over to the side of the room who had brought up the question of losing membership. "The rest of the medical profession will be beating down our door to get in."

14

THE SITUATION HAD been gnawing at him since it happened. So, with the few minutes left he had in his lunch break, Springer decided to drop by suite 315. "Is anyone in there?" he questioned, tapping on the frosted glass window that separated the waiting room from the treatment area. Springer quickly looked around and noticed that, except for the lack of patients, things looked pretty much unchanged even though Dr. Gene Broyle had now been gone several months.

Suddenly, the partition slid back. "Can't you see we're still on our lunch …" The obese, graying lady seated at the reception desk cut off her remarks. "Oh, I'm sorry, Doctor." She laid down her half-eaten sandwich. "What can I do for you?"

Springer recognized Mandy Jefferson, Broyle's former assistant, bent over a file cabinet across the room. "I was hoping to talk to Dr. Benson before he started seeing patients," he said to the receptionist, trying to catch Mandy's attention.

"I'm afraid that won't be possible," the receptionist answered curtly, her mouth still half-full. "He's very bus—"

"Come on back," Mandy interrupted, shooting her fellow employee a go-to-hell look if Springer had ever seen one. "Just have a seat in his office," she said as she pointed toward the rear. "He was just going to run over to the cafeteria to get a quick bite."

Springer stopped as he passed Mandy and turned around, everything familiar since he had been in Broyle's office on numerous occasions. "Looks pretty much the same except for the princess at the front desk," he said under his breath.

Mandy returned his remark with a quick glance. "That and the prince in the back," she whispered. "But you'll see for yourself soon enough."

Springer barely had a chance to pick up a journal before the door swung open. In rushed a man he guessed could not have been much past his thirtieth birthday. He glanced over at Springer, his black knit shirt unbuttoned at the top, revealing a full chest of curly black hair outlined by several gold chains. "Dr. Springer," Benson said, his tone hurried as he reached for his white jacket slung over the back of the chair. "Ms. Jefferson said you wanted to see me?"

"Yes, I thought you might want a follow-up on Dorothy Peoples," Springer said, his eyes burning from the thick layer of cologne mixed with the musty smell of stale cigarette smoke that surrounded the young physician.

Benson looked over at Springer, sliding his other arm through the sleeve of his coat. "I don't believe I recognize the name," he said indifferently.

"She was Dr. Terrell's mother-in-law," Springer answered, his impatience growing. "He's on the radiology staff here."

"I remember now," Benson answered, straightening his coat. "Something about headaches as I recall. We set her up for an appointment next week, I think. You know with the way Medicare pays, we don't make any money off those old people. I just can't afford to fill up my practice with them. We did schedule her for a CAT scan just in case."

"That's good of you. But it won't be necessary any longer."

"Great," Benson said, not picking up on the tension in Springer's voice. "I guess her headaches went away. You know they say over

90 percent of illnesses get well on their own if you just give them enough time."

"Unfortunately, the other 10 percent don't." The blood roared through Springer's temples. It was all he could do restrain himself from wrapping his fingers around the arrogant doctor's neck and squeezing the life out of him. But he had made a vow to preserve life, not take it. "Dorothy Peoples died the other day." Springer's voice trailed off, his anger dissipating into disgust for the charade of a physician standing before him. He turned and headed up to the reception area, Benson close on his heels.

"She … she really never was my patient, you know," Benson said defensively. "I never got a chance to see her."

"Yeah. You're too damned busy." Springer slammed the door and left through the empty waiting room.

. . .

Sliding into a seat in the second row, Springer balanced the paper plate full of barbequed brisket and baked beans in one hand while juggling an oversized piece of pecan pie with the other. The meal violated everything he preached to his patients about eating healthily. He rationalized if the food was being served at the county medical society meeting, there must be some redeeming value. At least it was enough to relieve his guilty conscience.

Dr. Ned Townsend banged his gavel on the podium. The meeting, in one of the mammoth ballrooms at the Anatole Hotel just down the road from the county society offices, had been hastily put together to discuss organized medicine's read on SB 4215 and, if passed into legislation, what impact it would have on the practice of medicine. Since he was already in Texas because of the problems with the doctors in Longview, Dr. Leonard O'Bannon was invited to give the AMA's position. "Ladies and gentlemen," Townsend barked, trying to quell the noise of the sparse crowd, "it's been a long day, so let's call this meeting to order."

More than five thousand invitations had been extended to the active membership. But as Springer looked around the giant room, he counted only a hundred, maybe 120 heads—most gray or balding, except for the few female participants.

"With AARP and the labor unions strongly supporting the single-payer legislation, there is a tremendous pressure being put on Congress," Townsend began. "Now with the National Business Coalition joining in, we could be in real trouble. It seems that everyone is fed up with the managed care companies, and Uncle Sam seems like the easy way out."

"I don't understand AARP's support since their constituents are already covered," came a voice from the back of the room.

Townsend looked up, squinting. "You might want to move up closer," he said. "It's the 20 percent co-pay and all those Medicare HMOs going under. They feel trapped just like the working class. If their doctor dies or retires, they can't get anyone to take care of them except for emergencies. And the labor unions, that's a no-brainer. Anytime they can get the government to pay for something, it's less money out of their pocket."

"What's organized medicine doing about the bill?" Springer called out from his position just in front of the lectern, deciding to get the conversation away from what couldn't be done to stop the legislation and on to a more positive note.

"The Texas Medical Association and several of the state specialty organizations have essentially moved their lobbyists to the capital for the duration," Townsend answered. "From what I'm told, the response has been polite but not one you'd take to the bank." He paused and turned to O'Bannon, who was seated beside him next to the podium. "Maybe our distinguished guest from the AMA can give us a better idea from the national perspective."

O'Bannon stood up, promptly moving over to the microphone as

Townsend stepped back. "When the opposition got the support of the National Business Coalition, that hurt us," he said, not breaking a smile. "Except for our position with the managed care companies, business has been on our side from the start. The less the feds were involved, the better. But it looks like they've given in. Too expensive! The businesses can't keep passing on the expanding costs of health care coverage for their employees to their customers and continue to compete. Not with the global economy the way it is today."

"So, what's the AMA's position?" Townsend questioned.

"They're going to fight it all the way," he answered. "The single payer is the issue they plan to go to the mat for." O'Bannon paused, his face taut, and walked out from behind the podium, approaching the physicians on the first row. "If we lose this one, it's all over. At least with managed care, you could elect to participate or not. If SB 4215 comes into law, the only choice you'll have left is where to mail your salary check."

The room fell silent as O'Bannon's prediction sunk in. Springer slowly raised his hand. "What if it passes?"

O'Bannon shook his head. "We don't know. At first, you'll probably see a rise in your income since all the uninsured will then be covered. Our best guess is the real impact of the legislation will start to show up somewhere between the fourth and sixth year when all the private insurers start to go under. From that point on, Uncle Sam will just start putting on the screws. If they can't get the physicians to go along with their prices and regulations, then there are plenty of pseudo-doctors waiting in the wings to take over. And we all know who they are." O'Bannon's face started to flush with anger. "The ones who decided the four years we spent in medical school building a foundation based on peer-reviewed scientific evidence before we went off into our specialty training wasn't necessary."

"The public and many of our own congressional leaders think we're just trying to protect our own golden asses when we bring that subject up—the so-called midlevel practitioner shit," Dr. Dave Streeter bellowed, no longer able to control his frustration. "I say screw 'em. Let those bellyaching sons of bitches have their single-payer system. As soon as one of those senators' wives has to wait three months to get her gall bladder out, they'll come running back sniveling like an old hound dog that's been out sticking his pecker where he shouldn't."

O'Bannon blushed, apparently not accustomed to the salty talk of the seasoned Texas family practitioner. "Doctor, you do have a way with words, but I'm afraid it's not that simple. Once John Q. Public gets used to having something paid for by the government, getting them to take it back is next to impossible. Take Social Security for example; it's almost unheard of for someone to turn down their check." The AMA representative stopped and looked around the room. "Let me see a show of hands of those of you who would voluntarily send Washington money to cover the defense and education budget." He again paused, waiting for a show of hands that never came. "I rest my case."

Townsend stepped back to the microphone, his eyes scanning the shaken crowd. "Each one of you knows who your elected leadership in Washington is. Some you voted for and probably a few you didn't. But they are all keenly aware that it's your vote that will keep them there or send them home," he said. "Our lobbyists can only do so much. The rest is up to us."

Each of the participants in the sparsely filled meeting hall knew what they had to do.

. . .

Terrell cracked the back door, calling out to Allison. Except for the light over the stove, the kitchen was dark. He was later than his usual arrival time but not by much. So, when his first attempt went unanswered, he became concerned, calling out once again.

"Allison," he said, making his way up the dimly lit stairs to the master bedroom on the second floor. He tried to push back the door but was met with resistance, as Allison's blouse was caught underneath. Forcing his entry, Terrell found the bedroom in mass disarray—totally out of character for Allison. Squinting in the uneven darkness, all he could see was a crumpled pile of blankets strewn across their bed. Panic began to set in as he rushed across the room and reached out to the lifeless form that now appeared before him on the unmade bed. Suddenly, he stopped cold as Allison slowly rolled over, her eyes puffed closed to bare slits.

"You're all I have," she sobbed quietly. "Our baby, now my mother and the lawsuit. I thought that when I was given a second chance, it would all be different." She reached out in John's direction but drew back, tucking her arm underneath her chest. "I'm so tired," she whimpered, barely above a whisper as she rolled back over, almost disappearing into the protection of the overstuffed coverlet that surrounded her.

He sat on the side of the bed, unable to respond. All Terrell wanted to do was climb into the bed beside Allison and pull the blankets up over his head—shutting out the cruel world that had brought them so much pain.

Terrell bent over, tucking the blanket snugly around his wife, then slowly left the bedroom, making an attempt to pick up some of Allison's clothes along the way. By the time he reached the kitchen, he had already removed his billfold from his hip pocket. Flipping on the light, he took out the business card he had placed behind his driver's license and laid it on the counter.

Grabbing the portable telephone off the wall, John strained to read the small numbers to a telephone line in Washington, DC, printed in the bottom corner and punched them into the buttons on the receiver.

"I'm sorry," was the reply of the prerecorded message. "Dr.

Gene Broyle is out of the office, but if you will leave your number at the sound of the tone, he will return your call as soon as he returns."

. . .

Senator Rayborn Carlisle pulled out his handkerchief and blotted the band of sweat that dotted his brow. He knew from the start that when the time finally came to bring SB 4215 to the floor of the Senate, there would be pressure. But that didn't make the process any easier. On one hand, he felt like a savior to the downtrodden in this country who lived in fear that what little security they had been able to stow away in these uncertain economic times would be wiped out by some unforeseen medical malady. On the other, there were times when he felt like a pariah—a satanical father figure hell-bent on destroying the best health care delivery system the world had ever seen. In reality, he considered himself neither—just someone in a position to address the inequities in the process.

Presidents Clinton and Obama had failed. Why did Carlisle think his attempt would fare any better? Mainly because, unlike the Clintons, he was already part of the system—not some hotshot outsider with a questionable social history from a small Midwestern state house, Carlisle thought as he watched his fellow colleagues file past him into the hallowed Senate chamber.

Lyndon Johnson, a master when it came to working the system, had been his hero growing up. Even in his role as Senate majority leader, Johnson wielded more power than the sitting president. It all had to do with who one knew—or maybe even more important, what he knew about the individuals who were entrusted with making decisions that would guide this country's future. J. Edgar Hoover, Carlisle's other hero, dominated Washington's elite in this manner during his tenure atop the FBI. Carlisle, unfortunately, possessed one trait his two role models did not, a trait he often considered a curse—scruples. Not that Johnson and Hoover were amoral. Far from it! They were just willing to persuade others to the make sacrifices on their behalf if the cause was great enough—an essential trait of all good military leaders. One of the reasons, Carlisle rationalized, for his decision to join the army's Signal Corps during Vietnam instead of a combat division. Not that Carlisle didn't believe passionately in the causes he championed, but he wasn't willing to take others down with him.

The hand on his shoulder brought Carlisle back to reality. "I'm glad we could work out our differences," the Senate majority leader said, his eyes fixed. "My aides tell me the gallery looks like a medical convention in there. I'm going to hold off bringing out 4215 until after the morning recess. Usually works to thin out the crowd a little. Today, I'm not so sure." Carlisle thought he saw a faint grin cross Forman's yellowed lips.

"Thanks," Carlisle answered, nervously stuffing the handkerchief back in his pocket. "I'm going to need all the help I can get. Last night, we had 'em by two votes. But those AMA lobbyists were still in Dunn's office when I left, and he only came over to our side yesterday." Shifting to the other foot, he continued, "So, right now I don't know. What about the House?"

"The Speaker tells me if we get this through the Senate, that with AARP and the labor union's influence in the House, it should be a slam dunk." Forman looked away at the growing crowd appearing ready to get started, then turned back to Carlisle. "Hope you got your ducks in order, Ray. Otherwise, you're gonna have a lot of buckshot up your ass if you dip into the pockets of any of those guys in there—especially mine."

. . .

"Missed you at the meeting the other night," Springer said, already knowing that Terrell was only one of over several thousand other physician members who for a myriad of reasons decided not to come.

Terrell barely looked up from the morning paper laid out on the cafeteria table. "What meeting was that?" he asked, distracted.

"The meeting the Dallas County Medical Society sponsored to see what we can do to stop the single-payer bill in Congress." Springer was frustrated that so many physicians like Terrell seemed to be uninformed or did not care about what was going on around them. In larger numbers, he watched as many doctors seemed to just want to collect their paychecks. What happened after five o'clock did not appear to matter, unless they were on call. Springer felt like he and a handful of his mostly older cronies were carrying the fight for the medical profession—not just on this issue but also in malpractice reform and insurance injustices. The list went on and on. He fought to suppress his growing cynicism. "If the physicians don't get off their asses and come together to block this legislation, we're all going to be working for Uncle Sam."

Terrell gathered up the paper and laid it on the chair beside him. "Want to sit down?" he asked. "I've been in touch with Dr. Gene Broyle. He said the Unified Medical Association is telling their members to back off. Something about being easier to deal with one payer than a bunch of them and that they had a plan if it went through."

Shocked, Springer set his breakfast tray down, sliding into the chair across from Terrell. "Why in the hell are they taking that position? Haven't they been paying attention to what happens when the government takes over the health care delivery system? It turns to shit!"

"I guess you might say that's a matter of perspective," Terrell said evenly, taking a sip of his lukewarm coffee. "By in large, most doctors would appear to go along with your conclusion; maybe that's because they don't make as much as we do here. But not necessarily their patients. Broyle said that generally more patients are satisfied with their system than ours—that's if you're talking about Canada and England. It's not fair to compare third world countries because they don't have enough of anything."

Springer picked up a piece of dry toast and shoved it in his mouth, then swallowed hard. "I guess that's why all those patients from Canada come down here to get their gall bladders out and their bypasses done rather than wait six months."

"I didn't say there weren't problems," Terrell said, apparently not persuaded by Springer's example. "At least their care is paid for, and they get to see the doctor of their choice—number one and two on patients' top-ten list of concerns about their health care coverage, respectively."

Springer sat back in his chair, his eyes now staring right through Terrell. "I just don't understand," he said, shaking his head. "You and your generation have such different ideas on where you think the medical profession should be headed."

"I'm not so sure I agree with you, Jordan." Terrell's look was pensive as he folded his arms on the table. "With all that's happened to Allison, both good and bad, the crap you and I put up with at work every day, the lawsuit, and now the screw-up that resulted in Dorothy's death, I've spent a lot of time thinking." He looked over at the chair beside him and picked up the copy of the morning paper. He pointed to the article he had been reading, hidden on the back page of the first section. "I knew what meeting you were talking about," he said with a grin. "I chose not to go because I feel it's a waste of time."

Springer squinted to read where Terrell had pointed. "Senate debates single-payer issue …" His voice trailed off. "So, you're just going to let the feds take over because Broyle and his radical organization told you to." His voice turned harsh.

"Don't you think radical is a little judgmental?" Terrell questioned. "I imagine there were plenty of our ancestors back in England who said the same thing when Washington and his ragtag volunteers decided to break away from the crown and start their own country." Terrell paused and looked around the employee cafeteria. "What do you see?" he asked, extending his arm in the direction where most of the people were congregated.

Springer felt uncomfortable, unsure where his friend was taking him, but decided to go along. "Hospital employees, nurses, technicians, and … doctors."

"Exactly!" Terrell drew his arm back in. "What I want for this profession is the same as you. We're all in this together. For what reason? Because we want the people lying in their beds on the floors of this hospital and those waiting to see you in the ICU to get well. And each of us has a unique role to play in trying to get that done. So, if you want to try to accomplish that goal through the AMA and the other more established organizations, it's fine by me."

Springer felt relieved. Finally, Terrell was making some sense. "Then why don't you want to get on board?"

"Because it's time doctors went back to working for their patients and quit working for the health care payers," Terrell answered as he picked up the paper and started to read out loud. "Said the official from the AMA, 'If SB 4215 passes, we will take the fight all the way to the Supreme Court if it's necessary.'"

Springer smiled and eased back up to the table. "Sounds like they're right on target."

"Bullshit!" A reddish hue broke out across Terrell's face. "The Supreme Court wouldn't dare buck Congress and the president on this one. And throw twenty-plus million people back out on the street without health care coverage? Never."

Springer said, "I respectfully disagree."

"They're throwing our dues dollars down the drain." Terrell stood up, knocking part of the paper on the floor. "Instead of where they should be spending them."

"And where might that be?" Springer asked as Terrell turned to leave.

Terrell paused, looking back across the crowded room. "Where it could really make a difference."

15

"I HAD A FEELING this was coming," Britt Barkley, Methodist's CEO, said. "It's happening all over the country. The docs just aren't willing to take call anymore."

Springer stiffened in the chair at the news that his ICU might be shut down. "They've given us ninety days to work something out," Springer stated, but in his mind, it was more of a question. Without better specialty coverage, the intensive care department would be turned into storage, and he would be out of a job. He could find another position picking up shifts no one else wanted on nights and holidays at some other busier hospital until something more permanent came up. With closings of many of the smaller ICUs in the suburbs for the same reasons and the growing attractiveness of the specialty of emergency medicine, even that was becoming more difficult. But finding a place to work was not Springer's major concern. Having moved into the position as head of the department almost two years ago, Methodist had become his home. Closing it down would be like losing a member of the family.

"The last two orthopedic surgeons gave us notice only a week ago that they're moving to the day surgery center over on McArthur at the end of the month," Barkley continued. "That means we'll have no neurosurgery, ophthalmology, or orthopedics. To top it off, the one ENT doc who still works here regularly said we could no longer expect him to take all the call by himself and is threatening to move to the same surgery center if we don't come up with a solution."

Springer shook his head. "I just don't understand why we let them get away with it," he said. "When they need a place to put their really sick, paying patients, they come here. Those who don't have coverage are punted to Parkland, letting the city pick up the bill. And the cream, the easy bread-and-butter stuff is sucked off to the day surgery centers."

"The fact that many of the physicians have vested interests in those operations—putting a little extra money in the other pocket—has nothing to do with it either, I suppose," Barkley said, his tone harsh. "Besides, Dr. Springer, it was you and your fellow physicians who voted that courtesy and consulting staff don't have to take call as long as their own admissions are under ten patients a year."

Springer remembered well. It had been a controversial decision; the hospital staff was almost evenly divided on the issue. But fearing a loss of all the internal medicine subspecialty consultants, the family practitioners had won. Emergency call was only for those physicians with active staff privileges. "Damn, I get discouraged," he said, slapping his hand on the arm of the chair. "We've turned into a society of takers. And I'm not just talking about doctors; we're talking about everyone. As long as there's something in it for me, count me in. Otherwise, piss off."

Barkley rustled in his chair, apparently uncomfortable at Springer's outburst. "That may be," the CEO answered hesitantly, "but that doesn't get us any closer to a solution as to what we do about the ICU. I need to have something to tell the board of directors by next month's meeting on the ..."

Barkley's remarks were cut short as his secretary popped her head through the door. "I'm sorry to interrupt," she said, "but they're paging Dr. Springer to a code blue in 224."

Springer quickly looked down, punching the readout button on his pager to see why he hadn't gotten the message about the cardiac arrest. His eyes widened at the blank screen—not the first thing that had failed him today. He bolted toward the door but stopped momentarily and turned around in Barkley's direction. "You ask the board who's going to respond to these when I'm gone."

...

Fortunately, the resuscitation effort had gone well. Springer followed the unconscious patient another ten minutes before heading back to the nurses' station. With the visit to the CEO's office and the unexpected code blue, he was late for his appointment. So, he decided to take a shortcut through the professional building to make up some time.

"Hey, watch out!" the man in blue coveralls barked, trying to balance a box stuffed with medical records under each arm.

Springer looked up just in time to miss the unexpected collision—his thoughts focused on the ICU and what would be waiting for him after his prolonged absence. "Excuse me," he said, snapping back to reality. "What's going on?" Springer asked, peering into Marvin Breedlove's office. The door had been propped open with a half-full wastebasket.

"Can't say since this is an ongoing investigation." With that, the man headed down the hall, leaving Springer without an answer. He noted the name stenciled on the back of the man's blue coveralls—Allied Security.

It was then Springer saw the notice taped to Breedlove's door.

> Until further notice, Dr. Breedlove will not be accepting patients. Copies of medical records as well as emergencies will be handled through Dr. Will Strother, suite 115.

Looking past the door, Springer thought he saw movement in the back of the office. "Marvin," he called out.

Suddenly, a face popped up from behind the receptionist's desk. "Hey, Jordan." Marvin Breedlove slowly moved toward him, his face drawn and sullen. He plopped down in one of the chairs that lined the far wall in his waiting room. "Got a minute?"

"Yeah, uh … sure," Springer said, glancing at his watch, knowing he was already late for his meeting. "I didn't know you were ready to retire."

"I wasn't," Breedlove said. "But it seems Big Brother in Washington has other ideas. They made me an offer I wasn't able to refuse." He looked away to the far corner of the waiting room as tears began to glisten in his eyes.

Springer walked over and slid down into the chair next to his distraught colleague. "I couldn't get much information out of your security friend," he said, his tone sympathetic. "Want to tell me about it?"

"I was hoping you would ask. Unfortunately, that's part of the arrangement—that I don't tell anybody, or the deal's off." Breedlove let out a long sigh. "But I'm not sure I give a shit at this point. My career is already in the toilet. Other than throw me in jail and take away my life savings, what more can they do?" he said, a half-hearted smile breaking across his lips.

Springer tried to force a smile in return. But after all the preceding events of the day, he was fresh out. He could only wonder what dastardly deeds this now helpless physician had performed to bring on such a disastrous response.

"Coding errors," Breedlove said, his voice barely above a whisper. "My secretary billed under a full exam code when, according to the guidelines, they say I should have used the intermediate one."

"What?" Springer stated in a near laugh. "Your telling me they're putting you through all this just for some silly-ass billing?"

The man in blue coveralls came through the door. "Just two

more boxes, and I'll be out of your hair, Doc," he said, brushing by toward the back of the office.

"I guess some of it's my fault," Breedlove continued. "The people down at the county medical society kept sending out brochures offering courses on how to file Medicare claims—even offered to come visit the office—but I just threw them in the trash. Gretchen works so hard around here; I was afraid to ask her to spend her free time taking a course on something she's been doing for me for over twenty years. And I sure as hell wasn't going to go do it myself." He paused as the security employee came back through with the final two boxes.

"I'll get the door after I unload these," the man said, sweat dripping off his brow.

Breedlove waved him off. "Don't worry; I'll get it," he said in a sarcastic tone. "It's the least I can do." Turning back to Springer, he continued, "So, this is what it got me. Gretchen and I are both out of a job."

Springer was shocked. "Aren't you going to fight it? The feds can't just come in and take over your practice."

"The legal people call it intent to defraud," Breedlove said, a hint of anger in his voice. "The HCFA representative claims that I willfully—I believe that was the term she used—deceived the Medicare program. That's bullshit, but I'd have to go to court to prove it."

"Well then, that's your answer," Springer said, sure he had given his fallen colleague a way out of his dilemma.

"I talked with a law firm that handles these kind of cases, and they would give me fifty-fifty at best," Breedlove said. "Even if I win, they estimate my legal fees at over $75,000. And if I lose, it could cost me as much as $5,000 per patient in fines, plus court costs and legal fees."

Springer tried to calculate the costs, but the numbers were way over his head. "So, what did they offer you?"

"A five-year suspension from the Medicare program and a little over $60,000 in fines," he said as an eerie smile crept across his lips. "You know the irony is that I still lost money on most of those patients."

"Why are you quitting?" Springer looked at his watch and then stood up to leave. "You can make a good living without Medicare, and I'm sure the bank would loan you the money if you can't come up with that much right now."

"I'm just fed up," Breedlove answered. "Fightin' those bastards over every dollar. It's just not worth it anymore. Besides, I got another offer."

"What's that?" Springer questioned, his curiosity aroused.

"Starting Monday, I'm going to work for Aetna." Breedlove broke out in a laugh. "Would you believe as a medical consultant in their insurance department?"

. . .

"He's in am pretty bad way, Doc," the elderly lady said, dabbing at her tear-stained cheek with a wadded-up handkerchief she had retrieved from under the sleeve of her blouse. "The doctor told us he was doing everything possible. But every day my husband just seems to be getting worse. So, that's why I brought him here to you."

Springer leafed through the patient's chart. "It says here your husband has cancer of the prostate." Then he looked over at the grieving lady huddled in a chair next the old man's bed. "Why is he on all these herbs?"

"Because Dr. Sotono prescribed them for him," she replied, her voice weak. "He told us to stay away from radiation and the hormones. Said they were the devil's poison and we should use only natural things to fight the cancer."

"What's Dr. Sotono's specialty?" Springer asked, not recognizing the initials A.P. printed after his name on the copy of one of the old man's prescriptions.

"He's a doctor of alternative medicine," she answered, seeming almost apologetic by this point.

Then Springer remembered that despite organized medicine's strong warning, last year the Texas Legislature had established a State Board of Alternative Medicine. There had been a major battle at the capitol, but with the influence of the legislators from many of the state's under-populated areas, they had been able to pull enough votes together to get it through. The claims that alternative medicine was better than no medicine at all seemed to hold sway—that and a great deal of campaign funding in just the right places.

Reaching over, Springer placed his hand gently on the old man's abdomen and pressed down. "Ouch!" the man screamed out, and Springer quickly drew back.

Springer spun around. "Call radiology down here and get me a flat plate of the abdomen STAT," he barked out to the nurse who was standing nearby. "Then draw a CBC and a SMAC 18." He turned back to the elderly lady, her face now buried in the tear-soaked handkerchief, and laid his hand on her shoulder.

Suddenly, she stopped crying and looked up. "Thank you, Doctor," she said, her eyes glistening, this time from hope.

Within thirty minutes, John Terrell had joined Springer in front of the view box at the far end of the ICU. "The spine and pelvis are riddled with mets," Terrell said solemnly, pointing to the numerous dark spots created by spreading tumor cells that gave the old man's bones a honeycombed appearance.

Springer doubled up his fist and struck it against the wall below. "Those sons of bitches pretending to be doctors when they're not," he said. "We all know conventional medicine can't cure everything, but the old man probably could have had a couple more years, and who know what they would have come up with by then."

"It's not your fault," Terrell said. "They made the choice not to go to a real oncologist."

"You're right," Springer answered. "It's not my fault. It's the fault of a political system that allows anyone with enough money to buy their way in, no matter what the public good. We see it in the industry all the time." He looked down at the red splotches that were beginning to break out on his bruised hand. "Maybe it's because I'm a doctor, but when it comes to innocent patients, I take it more personally. Every time the legislature meets, they seem to give away more medical care to those pseudo-doctors who want to be physicians. They all claim we are just trying to protect our own asses. But you know who really loses when the smoke clears? The patients." Springer stopped and looked down the hall. "That old man over there."

Terrell slowly took down the two x-rays of the old man's abdomen and started to put them back in the folder. "I wish I could have given you better news."

Shaking his head, Springer looked up at Terrell. "You've got a lot more time left to practice than I have," he said, his voice troubled. "I hope you can do more with what remains of this profession than my contemporaries and I have."

. . .

His frustration growing, Rayborn Carlisle tapped his fingers softly on the desk as he ruffled through his briefing papers on SB 4215. At the speaker's podium, his fellow senator from the great state of Arizona had gone on for now close to forty-five minutes about the pitfalls of a single-payer system. Loss of freedom to Big Brother. Patients becoming numbers instead of people with problems. Doctors turning into blue-collar workers whose only concern was their next paycheck. Carlisle had heard it all at least a hundred times. Enough of the rhetoric. It was now time for a vote.

Suddenly, Carlisle heard a gasp. To his horror, he looked up to see Bailey Forman, his eyes rolled back in his head, slip out of his chair, disappearing behind his massive desk above the podium. "Someone get help!" came the call off to the side. "The majority leader has had a ..." The cries were drowned out as people from all directions rushed frantically to the front of the Senate chamber.

Carlisle, glued to his chair in a state of shock, could only watch as the events unfolded before him. The paramedics, arriving within minutes, huddled around Foreman's motionless body. Carlisle strained to see, but only the majority leader's legs were visible, extruding out from behind the desk at the top of the stage.

No longer able to stay back, Carlisle eased out of his chair and headed toward the stage. "Out of the way!" a voice barked behind him. Spinning around, Carlisle came face-to-face with a paramedic—a look of desperation across his face—pushing a gurney toward the fallen senator. Carlisle quickly moved aside only to collide with the good senator from Arizona, now appearing all too eager to give up his position on the podium.

"Excuse me," Carlisle mumbled, still confused by the turn of events.

Grabbing his coat sleeve, the senator from Arizona glared at Carlisle as he said above the noise of the crowd, "In your new system, Senator, if our esteemed colleague makes it to the emergency room, do you think he would have to draw a number and wait in line?"

. . .

"I had hoped you have a few spare moments to show him around," Britt Barkley said as he nudged the reluctant figure in the white jacket into the partially darkened room. "Dr. Zamora's duties don't officially begin until tomorrow, but I thought he might want to get a head start." Methodist's CEO did not wait for Terrell's reply before heading back down the hall.

Dr. Ramon Zamora, a board-certified radiologist from Harlingen, had been hired by Terrell's group to fill the one remaining vacancy at the medical center. Terrell knew very little about him other than his impressive curriculum vitae on the American College of Radiology's website.

Terrell laid the film on the counter, extending his hand. "Looks like it's just the two of us. It was time for a break anyway," he answered, his eyes squinting in the bright light that filtered through the door.

After a brief look around the department, John and his new colleague headed to the cafeteria. "Barkley's not a bad guy for a hospital administrator," Terrell said, looking around to make sure Zamora was keeping up. "Just a little assuming, but that must go with the territory."

Zamora cut John a quick smile but didn't comment.

After picking up two Styrofoam containers of straight black java, John plopped into his favorite seat in the far corner, and Zamora slid in across from him.

"I assume your first question is, why am I here?" Zamora said, reaching for two small packets of Equal in the bowl at the edge of the table.

Terrell nodded as the steam from the fresh coffee swirled around his face. "That might be a good place to start," he answered, noticing the gray flecks scattered through Zamora's otherwise jet-black hair.

"It's the lawsuits," Zamora said. "They're killing the practice of medicine in the Valley."

Terrell had heard rumblings of the growing problems in South Texas where, in some areas, much of the economy revolved around three things—the hope of winning the state lottery, the Medicaid program, and money derived from lawsuits.

"At least half of the doctors are looking for positions elsewhere," Zamora continued. "With four generations of my family from around there, it broke my heart to leave, but I had no other choice. My malpractice carrier notified all of us that as of the first of the year, they were pulling out of South Texas."

Terrell sat down his coffee, pulling up to the table. "What about other insurance companies?" he asked, noticing the slight tremble in Zamora's hand. "Doesn't the state have to offer you coverage through some sort of insurance pool?"

"For three times the price," Zamora said. "At that rate, the first four months of the year, I would be working just to pay off the premium. Giving up my practice of over twenty-three years was probably the hardest decision I've ever had to make." He paused and looked down at the table, picking nervously at the empty packets of artificial sweetener. "It was that or …"

"Or what?" Terrell said.

"I'd better not say." Zamora shuffled uneasily in his chair.

Terrell was not going to let him off that easily. If they were going to be working together, he felt he had the right to know more. Something about Zamora's story did not add up. "What part of this are you not telling me, Ramon?"

"I went into medicine to take care of patients. Compared to most of the people in the Valley, the doctors have so much more. But if you look at what doctors in other areas of the state make, we are far behind because so much of what we do is either Medicaid or from across the border. I felt I had an obligation to these people because they were part of my ancestry. But many of the doctors are not like …" Zamora's arm flung out to make his point, knocking his half-full cup of coffee over. "Excuse me," he said, reaching quickly for the pile of paper napkins as the end of the table, his face turning crimson.

Terrell scooted out of the way as the first drips made it to the table's edge. "No problem," he answered in a half grin. "Maybe that's why we didn't go into surgery. What about the other doctors?"

"Don't get me wrong," Zamora said, continuing to dab at the

mess he created. "These are good people. But they have big debts, mostly left over from their training, and they have obligations to their families. Many of them came from this area, just as I did, and they don't plan to leave. At least not without a fight."

Reassured that the problem with the spilled coffee had passed, Terrell moved his chair back up to the table. "So, how are they planning to deal with the situation?"

"They've tried the courts without any real relief," Zamora answered, his look discouraged. "We've gone to the legislature with the help of the Texas Medical Association and the AMA, and although there's a lot of sympathy, there's not much help. Seems that education and law enforcement have a higher priority."

Terrell was becoming frustrated as he slid the pile of soiled napkins to the side. "You haven't answered my question." His eyes were fixed on Zamora.

"Strike." Zamora's reply was barely above a whisper.

Arching back, Terrell's gaze never broke from his new colleague. "You mean a work slowdown—emergencies only, screwing up the insurance company's paperwork?"

Zamora slowly shook his head from side to side. "I was not prepared to go that far, not to my people, but there are others who are, and their numbers are growing daily." He stopped and drew in a deep breath. "John, do you remember what happened in California in the seventies when their malpractice problems were out of control?"

Terrell rolled his eyes. "Something about the anesthesiologists bringing about reform," he said, his response unsure.

"More specifically, they brought the state to its knees," Zamora said. "They stopped doing anesthesia for all elective surgery, and in just three weeks, the governor called their legislature back into special session."

Trying to recall the outcome, Terrell asked, "So, what came out of it?"

"Even today, almost thirty years later, their malpractice premiums are half of those of the doctors in Texas."

They sat in silence as Terrell contemplated the meaning of Zamora's revelation. "So, you're telling me ..." His remarks trailed off as he took another sip of coffee.

Zamora nodded. "John, many of the doctors in the Valley are prepared to go a lot further than that."

16

"THE DOCTORS HAVE decided to go forward." Dr. Seldon Rogoff's face was grim as he closed the door to his office in the back of the clinic. "Until our plan is more formalized, we don't want anyone else in on it, even our own staff. That's where you come in."

Feeling the fatigue of the predawn flight out of Washington, followed by a three-hour drive to Longview, Gene Broyle laid his briefcase on Rogoff's desk and sat down in an overstuffed chair in the corner. "What made you change your mind?" he asked, still confused by Rogoff's urgent call the day before.

"EMTALA," Rogoff answered. "The bastards pulled the Emergency Medical Treatment and Active Labor Act on us."

Caught off guard at first, Broyle tried to recall the particulars of the legislation. "That's the bill that restricts hospitals from transferring sick patients to another institution unless they are first stabilized and the other hospital agrees to accept the patient, isn't it?"

"There has to be medical coverage during the transfer, but that's pretty much it," Rogoff said. "In fact, the legislation came out of a complicated pregnancy case here in Texas maybe twenty-five years ago. The problem is with another part of the bill. It was in the fine print that somehow slipped through."

"I'm not sure I'm following you," Broyle said.

Rogoff moved over to his desk and picked up a sheet of paper. "The legislation also states that the physician who is in charge of treating a patient in the emergency room can call on any specialist who happens to be providing coverage for help if deemed necessary."

"Somewhere along the line, I must have missed something, Seldon," Broyle said. "You and I have been doing that since the first day of our residency."

Walking over, Rogoff pointed to the third paragraph on the page he was holding and handed it to Broyle. "As the consulting specialist, you have thirty minutes to respond or face a fine of $50,000."

Shocked at the revelation, Broyle scanned the Xerox copy of the legislation. "This law has been on the books for a long time, and I've never heard of anyone getting fined."

"Until now." Rogoff's brow furrowed from disgust. "Do you remember Larry Murdock?"

Broyle shook his head no.

"He was at Parkland with us in the Cardiac Surgery program. One of the ER docs wanted him to see a patient with chest pain. I don't know why he didn't call the cardiologist first, but that's the other problem: the ER docs decide who to call. So, no matter what the consultant thinks, if they call, you go!"

"So, how does this Murdock fit in?" Broyle questioned.

Rogoff backed up to his desk and flopped down. "Well, the guy's in surgery. I mean, he's got someone's chest open, doing a bypass when he got the call. So, he sends out the message to get someone else. Murdock claims he never heard anything else from the ER doc until yesterday, when a certified letter from the Attorney General's office arrived."

Broyle's eyes widened. "He couldn't break scrub and endanger his own patient's life," Broyle said, thinking the decision was obvious.

"Evidently, that's not the AG's position," Rogoff answered, his jaw fixed. “Murdock’s lawyer told him he might be better off just paying the fine. With the legal fees, he might spend even more money and still lose his appeal in court. Everyone around here is really pissed. Claims that was the final straw.”

“Something doesn’t add up,” Broyle mumbled. “I know plenty of emergency room physicians, and they wouldn’t have made this into a problem.”

Rogoff’s eyes widened. “You evidently haven’t met these guys. They work for a company out of Houston. They come up here for a month then move on somewhere else. Lately, we never see the same one more than once. That’s part of the problem. Some of them are pretty cooperative, but a few have been real assholes. And since they’re employed by the hospital, they don’t really care what we think. To them, it’s just a job—get ’em in and move ’em out. That’s what they’re paid to do.”

“Have you complained to the hospital?”

“Wouldn’t do any good,” Rogoff said. “They fired the group who was here and brought these guys in.” He stopped and moved closer to Broyle, lowering his voice. “I’ll get to it in a minute, but I have indirect proof the hospital administrator has a master plan to run us all out of town, and then the hospital would bring their own doctors in as employees.”

“Couldn’t most of you just move over to the other hospital?” Broyle’s concern was growing.

“That’s the real surprise,” Rogoff said, looking up nervously at the closed door. “Mercy, the other hospital, has hired the same group to run their emergency room, and from what I can tell, they’re doing the same thing over there. The two hospitals have never agreed to anything before, but it’s like they’re working together. A pretty neat scheme, if it’s true, to take over all the medical care in Longview. But they forgot one thing.”

Broyle moved forward. “What?”

“The bylaws,” Rogoff said as a smile crossed his lips. “It’s the only thing the hospital has not been able to take away from us. The bylaws allow each specialty section to set the rules on who takes emergency room call."

"So, you're saying—" Broyle stopped when Rogoff put his finger to his lips.

"Exactly," he whispered. "We just vote ourselves off the call schedule. Then the damn EMTALA doesn't apply. If we want to respond to the emergency, we can, but if we don't, the attorney general can't do anything about it."

Broyle drew back at the apparent genius of the plan, but he still had doubts. "What about the hospitals bringing in doctors to take your place and locking you out? Your patients are going to have to go somewhere if they're sick. You know their loyalty only goes so far. We learned that lesson with managed care."

"That's why this can't get out," Rogoff said. "For the plan to work, the medical community has to get off their asses and participate—all the doctors on both hospital staffs coming together at the same time. If not, the hospitals will play us off each other until they can bring in their paid reinforcements. Then we're out of here, and the hospitals will have complete control."

"I'm still worried about the patients during all of this," Broyle said. "Some of them are bound to get hurt if one of your doctors decides to play another round of golf rather than come in for a ruptured appendix."

"That's a potential problem," Rogoff answered, his voice sober. "We're still working on how that situation will be handled. Back in the days before the payers and the hospitals took over the practice of medicine, doctors did a pretty damn good job of disciplining themselves through the county medical society review boards. If a doctor screwed up or got out of line, a group of his peers got involved. He or she was either rehabilitated or they were out of there. The system worked a hell of a lot better than what we have today."

"Aren't the emergency rooms going to be flooded with patients with no place to go for follow-up care?"

Rogoff turned back toward his desk, ruffling through a stack of papers. "They already are." He stopped and pulled out a sheet. "The volume of patients seen in Crosstown's emergency department has increased 30 percent a year for the last ten years. The patients who don't have insurance have turned the emergency rooms of this country into giant outpatient medical clinics, making it even more difficult for those patients who really are acutely ill to get seen." He let out a slow sigh. "Hopefully, this would push the not-so-sick ones back into their doctor's office where they belong."

"The hospitals aren't just going to lie down and let the doctors of Longview take over," Broyle said.

"They will if they think the Federal Trade Commission will get them for collusion." Rogoff reached in his pocket and pulled out a set of keys. Unlocking the bottom drawer of his desk, he pulled out a manila envelope and handed it to Broyle. "The only other copy is in my safety deposit box."

"What's this?" Broyle whispered.

"A letter from the president of Allied American Insurance Company," Rogoff said, "offering Crosstown's administrator a six-figure bonus along with stock options if he could deliver 80 percent of Longview's doctors into Allied's capitated health care plan. The only way he could do that is to cut a deal with his counterpart at Mercy to get rid of all of us and bring in a whole new set of doctors."

"How'd you get this?"

"Let's just say one of my patients works in very high places," Rogoff answered with a grin.

"Why me?" Broyle said. "Why not the AG's office or even the AMA?"

"I figure if Allied is making the offer here, there must be other places where the same thing is going on," he answered. "And not just with Allied but the rest of the carriers who think of their policy holders only in terms of how much of their premium dollar they can hold on to."

Broyle held back his impatience. "You're avoiding my question, Seldon."

"I'm scared," Rogoff said. "Gene, you and I go back a long way. If our plan to boycott the ERs turns sour, a lot of innocent people could get hurt—me included. I need someone I can trust."

Broyle stood up, slipping the envelope into his jacket pocket. "Let me run this by Todd and the guys back in Washington. With the single-payer legislation steamrolling through Congress, we've got a lot going on. The UMA has some connections that might come in handy if things get ugly." He headed for the door, then stopped and turned around, smiling. "You know, it's time we took back the profession. Longview, Texas, just might be the right place to start."

. . .

"They *what*?" Terrell spun around in his chair as the bright light streamed through the hallway door. "How can they just lose our insurance claims?"

Sylvia Veller, billing secretary for Methodist Hospital, shifted uneasily from one foot to the other. "Dr. Terrell, Allied American is one of the few insurance companies that still requires paper claims," she said, her voice hesitant. "They tell us they never got them. Said if we wanted our money that we would have to resubmit them."

"Should be no problem then." Terrell turned away from the light, relieved but unsure why she would interrupt him with something that was already being handled. "Except that they've been able to hold on to our money a little while longer. Medicare has been doing that forever."

Sylvia moved toward Terrell, her steps cautious in the dimly lit room. "It's not quite that simple," she said. "They're not going to pay any claim that's over sixty days old—said it's in the contract you signed with them when you agreed to be a participant with their company."

As she came closer, Terrell could see she was carrying a stack of forms. "So, what does that mean in numbers?" he asked.

"Close to 75 percent we can't collect on." She laid the pile of unpaid claims on the counter next to his stack of unread x-rays. "They've really worked out a slick system," Sylvia continued. "Allied can wait to pay our claim for up to forty-five days after receiving it. Remember when our previous governor vetoed the Prompt Pay legislation that would have made that time shorter. Some political jargon about raising the costs of health care premiums. By the time our people in billing pick up that the claim hasn't been paid, make the inquiry, and file a new form, the time has almost expired."

Terrell had a puzzled look on his face. "Can't we call earlier to see if they have received the claim?"

"You would think so." A half-hearted smile broke across Sylvia's lips. "That's where these managed care companies have one up on you doctors. The law that says they have to pay you within forty-five days isn't specific. So when we call, Allied and a few others just give us the runaround with terms like it's probably 'somewhere in the system,' which adds up to a big fat zero until their time runs out. Then they either pay or lose the file. I know because I worked in the insurance industry before coming over here two years ago."

"They can't do that," Terrell said, his anger mounting. He reached over and picked up the stack of forms. "What are these?"

"Unpaid claims on your patients with Allied American coverage over the last six months that have passed the sixty-day limit," she answered quickly. "One hundred and twelve to be exact. At fifty dollars average per claim, that adds up to about $6,500 Allied has stiffed you for."

Terrell's jaw clenched. "Why not bill the patients and let them work it out with the insurance company? After all, in the end, it is their responsibility."

"Again, read the fine print in your contract," Sylvia said, moving aside to give Terrell room as he stood up. "The doctors who participate in their programs aren't allowed to bill the patients for covered services, even if Allied reneges on its obligations."

The stack of unpaid claims rustled in Terrell's shaking hand as his anger mounted. "Are you telling me that with all this work I did on these patients, because some insurance conveniently loses the original bills, I get nothing?"

"Not exactly," Sylvia answered, a hint of sarcasm in her reply. "You're not alone. Along with the other doctors on the staff and the monies owed the hospital for its bills, Allied is into Methodist for slightly over $300,000. Our attorney has threatened to put all the claims together in a class action lawsuit. So, Allied has agreed to work out a deal. That's why I'm here—to see if you want to join with the hospital."

Terrell's eyes brightened as he plopped back into his chair. "Well, just as I was about to lose faith in the system. Why didn't you just tell me the hospital had worked out a solution?"

Sylvia's hands clenched as she edged back toward the door to the hall. "Allied has agreed to settle for fifteen cents on the dollar."

. . .

"Fusdgert drinheg gat dhefs kogghei," the rotund man coughed out, his shaking finger stabbing at a spot just above his navel.

Springer shot a glance of uncertainty toward the nurse, then quickly turned back to the patient lying on the stretcher. "I'm sorry, Mr. ... Magannaih," he said, looking over at the name the patient had written down on the top of his emergency room chart. "But I can't understand what you're trying to tell me. Is there somebody with you who speaks English?"

An outline of perspiration outlined the armpits of the middle-aged man's soiled white shirt. His face was clouded in frustration as he tried to substitute gestures for the language barrier that kept them miles apart. "No English! Wirfedst non gedvfirt."

Springer reached out, his hand now pressing down firmly on the patient's abdomen. "I'm just going to check you over," he said, his tone reassuring. Springer knew that what he said was not as important as how he said it, since the patient wouldn't understand him anyway. His hand moved slowly around the abdomen, probing each quadrant carefully for any sign of pathology. He saved the spot in the center where the patient had pointed for last.

"Oh …" Suddenly, the patient recoiled as Springer finally reached the area in question, his flailing arm with a giant fist catching Springer's unprotected ribcage with its full force.

Springer lurched backward, his head striking the solid partition that separated the small cubicles. His mouth flung open, but Springer's cry was silent, as the unexpected blow had extracted all the air from his lungs. Springer, still gasping for air, waved off the nurse who had come around to offer her assistance. "I'm … okay," he puffed out, feeling embarrassed as oxygen slowly returned to his lungs. "He just … caught me … by … surprise."

A rapid movement caught Springer's eye as he looked back toward the stretcher. The patient grabbed at his shirt pocket, his fat fingers probing deep inside. Springer winced backward when the man removed something from the pocket and thrust what appeared to be a folded piece of scrap paper in his direction. "What!" the man barked, gesturing for Springer to take the note from his outstretched hand.

"What's this?" Springer questioned as he cautiously reached out. He grasped the note, then quickly drew back to the safety against the partition. Slowly he unfolded the paper, straining to read the contents before him. Temporarily blurred by the tears from the blow to his chest just moments before, Springer dabbed at his eyes with the sleeve of his jacket.

The note contained a ten-digit telephone number, followed by a four-digit extension. He did not recognize the area code but was sure it was not local. He motioned to the nurse. "I'll be right back," he said, knowing he had no choice but to make the call.

"World Wide Interpretation Services," was the prerecorded message on the other end of the line. "If you already know the extension for the language that you need the services of one of our translators, please enter the four-digit number at this time. If you need further assistance, please stay on the line, and one of our service representatives will be with you shortly."

Springer squinted again at the crumpled piece of paper laid out before him on the counter at the nurses' station. Then he punched in the four-digit extension.

"You have selected ... Barshwar," the computer-generated voice said. "The rate for our services is eleven dollars a minute. At the completion of the tone, please punch in your credit card number, followed by the expiration date. If you need further assistance, one of our service representatives will be with you shortly."

Springer started to reach for his billfold with his credit card but held up, deciding it wasn't his responsibility to pay for the call. He looked up, signaling one of the nurses. "What's the hospital's credit card number?" he asked.

She shot him a go-to-hell look, picking up a chart off the desk. "It's time you took a long weekend, Dr. Springer. You must be working too hard, if you think the hospital is going to turn its employees loose with their credit card number." She quickly turned away, leaving Russell to solve his own dilemma.

"Can I help you?" the operator on the other end of the line interrupted.

"I hope so," Springer answered. "I'm a doctor, and I have a patient whom I can't communicate with. He gave me this number. My guess is he speaks this Barshwar. So, we need a translator."

"That's what we do, Doc. Just give me your credit card number.

Then put your patient on the line, and I'll patch him through to a translator," the indifferent operator said.

Springer was growing frustrated, feeling he was fighting an uphill battle. "Can't you just bill me?" Springer knew he had a better chance of getting the hospital to accept the responsibility of the charges with a bill to show them.

"Doc, I don't run no charity here. I've got phone calls going to all parts of the world, and that don't come for free. You've got to pay if you want to play."

"Listen." Springer's anger was seething. "I've got a sick patient who needs help and—"

Springer's remarks were cut short. "I guess you ain't heard about the Clinton law? Says the doctor has to pay for a translator anytime the patient asks for one. He signed it into law through some sort of presidential order just before he left office. So, the way I figure it, you give me your credit card number, or that patient of yours reports you to the proper authorities, and if he don't get well because you wouldn't pay for an interpreter, well, that would be between you and your attorney."

17

"SENATOR MAYNARD DUNN, Wyoming!" The call came from the podium as all heads in the Senate chamber turned in his direction.

The vote on SB 4215 had gone pretty much as expected to this point. The final outcome, however, was still very much in doubt. The opposition currently had a one-vote lead. If Dunn cast a nay, then it was back to the drawing board. With his support, the vice president could be counted on to break the tie in the president's favor. The diminutive senator from Wyoming, never a focus of much attention before, had become the swing vote in the most important health care legislation to come to Capitol Hill since the 1960s. Over the last several weeks, he had unwillingly been propelled into the number one target of every lobbyist and special interest group even remotely associated with the proposed bill. Unaccustomed to all the exposure, he had finally taken refuge in his office, communicating only through his advisors. The commentators who filled the late night and Sunday-morning airways were almost evenly divided as to what side of the fence Dunn would be on when the roll was finally called. Today, they would get their answer.

A ghostlike hush fell across the massive room. Those not able to crowd into the chamber sat glued to their television sets. From the president, sequestered in his study just off the Oval Office, to most of the congressmen on the other side of the Capitol, Washington held its collective breath.

"Senator?" The call for the long-awaited response went out again.

"Yes," the senator answered, his voice barely audible from the back of the overflowing room.

A brief conversation took place at the front of the room as the sergeant at arms stepped away from the microphone to confer with the Senate majority leader, still adjusting to the effects of his newly implanted pacemaker, and the vice president, who were seated directly behind him. He quickly returned to the lectern. "We are not quite sure we heard your reply. In a matter of this importance, we must be certain of your decision. I hope you understand," the gentleman atop the podium said, squinting in Dunn's direction. "If you responded in the affirmative, please raise your right hand."

Dunn shuffled uneasily in his chair as all eyes in the room locked on the small but pivotal figure from Wyoming. At first, he appeared to freeze—his arms limp at his side.

"No!" an unidentified voice from the balcony screamed out. "Don't do it!" Immediately, the attention of the audience shifted to the balcony where two security guards quickly made their way toward a partially shaven man dressed in a surgical scrub suit. Within a minute, he had been escorted from the proceedings, still yelling that the end of the great American health care system that was assured with the passage of SB 4215.

At first it was just a murmur as the audience began to settle back down. But quickly the noise began to escalate into bursts of applause, his shouts almost drowned out by an equal number of boos. For amidst the mayhem that was unfolding in the Senate chamber stood the senator from Wyoming—his outstretched right arm, like the Statue of Liberty, thrust high above his head.

. . .

It was just after midnight, and the lights in the boardroom at 515 North State Street in Chicago were still burning bright. With the passage of SB 4215, an emergency meeting of a select group of leaders from the various prominent medical organizations had been convened. Notably absent was the representative from the Unified Medical Association. The headquarters of the American Medical Association had been selected because of the Windy City's central location and the AMA's continued prominence as the largest organization of physicians in the country.

"The most we can hope for is a compromise bill in the House," Dr. Leonard O'Bannon said as he scanned the participants seated around the rectangular conference table. O'Bannon had been selected to chair the meeting because of his expertise on the subject of the downfalls of a single-payer system. Experiencing firsthand the problems in his native Canada before migrating to the United States almost fifteen years ago, he did not want to see the same thing happen here.

Suddenly, the light went on just in front of the participant from the American College of Surgeons, a signal she had something to say. "Dr. O'Bannon," she said, her voice taut. "It seems that's all we have done for the last thirty years is compromise. And where do we find ourselves? Sitting around this table, sniveling about how we are going to compromise some more."

"Dr. Tragus," O'Bannon said, "all of us in this room share your pain, but this is reality. Our organizations have not been able to solve the problems of those unfortunate souls who live from month to month trying to decide whether to put what little money they have been able to stash away toward food to stave off the pit of hunger they carry in their stomach or toward medications that will keep their aching bodies going until it's time they have to make the same decision again. So, when the next election is held back in their home districts, the poor, the elderly, and the labor unions carry a lot more weight than a bunch of doctors and hospital administrators."

Dr. Tragus was apparently not swayed by O'Bannon's argument.

"I did my residency at Walter Reed, so I know what it's like to have Uncle Sam foot the bill for everything. If I'd wanted to work for the government for the rest of my life, I'd have stayed." She dropped back in her chair, a look of disgust across her face.

Chagrined that he had not brought the group to a consensus, O'Bannon fingered the microphone attached to his desk as he waited for further responses. He glanced over as a hand shot up at the far side of the room. It wasn't the hand of one of the participants gathered around the conference table but that of RJ Talkington, who had been called in for staff support.

"Dr. O'Bannon," she said, "may I make a few comments?"

"Would you mind coming up here to the microphone, so the group can hear you better?" O'Bannon asked hesitantly, afraid that with the competition between the organizations, if there was too much AMA input, the rest of the group might not go along with whatever approach was worked out. For now, though, hers was the only input being offered.

Rebecca Jane Talkington, affectionately called RJ, was an institution at the AMA, having been around since before records were kept on such matters. Although she was somewhere in her eighties—no one ever had the nerve to ask—except for the cane that she carried like a scepter, she showed no signs of slowing down. She was unquestionably the go-to-person on matters of historical perspective. Whether they knew it or not, as she sat down in the chair just to the right of O'Bannon, she was about to give the group of befuddled physicians a lesson on the profession they had vowed to preserve.

"One doesn't have to be a soothsayer to know that someday we would be forced to deal with the problems that are facing this country today," she said, her raspy voice an unfortunate reminder that she had not been able to free herself from the cigarette addiction that in one way or another contributed to more deaths in this country than any other entity.

An odd hush fell across the conference table when RJ reached in her pocket and removed a handful of Hershey's chocolate Kisses, scattering them on the table before her. O'Bannon, who had known RJ only in passing since first becoming involved with the AMA, edged back in his chair, unsure of what was to follow.

"In the end, it all comes down to two things—money and control of that money," she continued, picking up one of the candies. "It seems that every country in the world, including ours, is headed in the wrong direction." She paused, removing the foil covering and popping the chocolate morsel in her mouth. She slowly looked up, her eyes searching the room. "Would you eat more of these if they were already paid for and given to you?"

The reply was a deafening silence as the transfixed participants waited for RJ's answer. Even the physician from the American College of Surgeons was now on the edge of her seat.

"Sure you would. We all would," she answered, clearing the last bit of chocolate from her mouth. "So, why shouldn't our patients try to get every dollar they can out of the health care system if it's already paid for? It doesn't matter whether it's a single-payer or managed care. That's why these systems fail; it's not their money. The patients have no incentive to conserve our limited health care resources because we've taken that decision away from them."

RJ pushed back her chair, struggling to her feet as all heads in the room followed her every move. "Now that it looks like SB 4215 is about to become law and everyone is going to have coverage, I would suggest your organizations work with Congress to allow all the patients in this country to own their own policies, even in those cases where the government is funding most of it." She scooped up the remaining chocolates and deposited them back in her pocket, save one. "Or, one day when you go to the store, the shelves will be empty."

RJ turned to leave but hesitated, reaching out to the one

remaining piece of candy and sliding it over in front of O'Bannon. "Why don't you give this one to your kid before it's all gone."

. . .

"What in the hell is this?" Martin Bohannon, administrator at Crosstown Medical Center, said as he picked up the large manila mailer off his desk.

The secretary, accustomed to Bohannon's foul language, headed back to her desk. "Don't know," she said. "A courier service just dropped it off five minutes ago. I noticed there's no return address."

Always close to the edge, Bohannon tore into the oversized envelope, agitated by the unexpected interruption. He quickly extracted the document, letting the folder fall to his desk. Slumping back in his chair, his oversized hands clung to the pages. Bohannon's lips barely moved as he took in the contents of the first page:

> Attention: Martin Bohannon, Chief Executive Officer
>
> We the undersigned formally submit this document to inform you of the decisions reached by the medical staff of Crosstown Medical Center. These decisions were made only after serious consideration was given to all sides of the issue at a duly congregated meeting of the majority of the medical staff (see enclosure for those in attendance) and with appropriate legal counsel.

In accordance with Medical Staff Bylaws Article 6, Section 2B,

> the majority of the physician members will determine the emergency room call for their particular section.

As of forty-eight hours from the date of receipt of this document, in compliance with the results of an election held at the above-mentioned meeting, and in accordance with the bylaws of this institution, the attending medical staff of Crosstown Medical Center will no longer be bound by the hospital's compulsory emergency room call schedule.

> Any arrangements for coverage consultation and assistance at Crosstown's emergency room will be on a private contractual basis between that individual physician or group of physicians and the Crosstown Medical Center administration.

Only those physicians who are duly licensed and credentialed by the medical staff of Crosstown Medical Center will be allowed to participate in such contracts with the hospital.

> Physician reimbursement for services rendered through the emergency room will be guaranteed by the hospital with Crosstown Medical Center assuming the responsibility for collection for these services.
>
> Respectfully ...

Bohannon's eyes darted back and forth as he plowed through the three pages of familiar signatures that followed the cover sheet. "Those sorry sons of bitches. I'm going to ..." He stopped abruptly when his secretary stuck her head in.

"It's Darnell, the administrator over at Mercy on line one," she said. "I didn't know the two of you were chums."

"Shut the door!" Bohannon said as he reached for the receiver, trying to decide if he should let his old adversary and new business partner in on the latest revelation. "Darnell, didn't I tell you never to contact me here?"

He paused, waiting for Darnell's reply, when his mouth fell open from the shock of Darnell's news. A similar ultimatum had been delivered to him from the Mercy medical staff just moments before. "I just was handed the same thing by my doctors," Bohannon said. "Looks like we've got a conspiracy going. Those bastards only want to cover our emergency rooms on their terms. Can you imagine how bad it would be if we let physicians run our hospitals? I think we ought to take their asses to court and rub their almighty noses in this crap. We should be able to get them for abandonment and dereliction of duty. Maybe even triple damages for restraint of trade. At the very least, we'll now be able to convince the good folks of Longview that we are the real heroes, so that when we bring in our salaried physicians, there won't be ..."

Bohannon stopped in midsentence at Darnell's interruption. "Did I see what?" he said.

"Collusion!" Bohannon wedged the receiver between his sweaty chin and shoulder. "I must have missed it." He bent down, his trembling hand picking up the fallen mailer. Reaching inside, he quickly extracted a letter-size sealed envelope he had overlooked and tore it open. He gasped when he recognized the copy of the supposedly secret communication from Allied American Insurance Company, the one that had promised him a hefty bonus and stock options if he could deliver most of Crosstown's medical staff into Allied's fold.

Bohannon rocked nervously back and forth in his chair as Darnell explained that he had gotten a copy of Bohannon's letter too. Darnell seemed convinced that it was only a matter of time until whoever was behind this insurgency would also discover his private arrangement with Allied.

"If they go to the attorney general with this," Bohannon said, drawing in a deep breath, his oversized belly heaving at the buttons of his perspiration-soaked shirt, "not only would you and I be out of a job, but if the authorities find out, we could have our asses in prison."

. . .

"Can you come over and look at a chest x-ray for me?" Jordan Springer's voice was agitated.

Almost twenty minutes passed by the time Terrell was able to break free and make it over to the ICU. "Where is he?" Terrell asked, looking around as the maze of people crisscrossed around him.

The nurse pointed toward one of the back cubicles, then disappeared into the nurses' station as Terrell eased his way to the far end of the emergency room area.

"Over here," Springer said, standing by the row of view boxes. "What do you see?" he asked pointing to a chest x-ray.

Terrell squinted at the film, carefully going over every shadow and light spot. "Not much," he said, wondering why—with all the x-rays Springer had signed off on in the past without calling over a radiologist first—he was so concerned about this one. "Maybe a little thickening in the major bronchioles here." Terrell pointed to several vague shadows in the middle of the film. "Want to give me a little history?"

"According to the patient's family doctor, who sent her over here, she's growing methicillin-resistant staph out of her sputum," Springer answered, looking closer at the area pointed out on the film. "I've gone over her from head to toe, and the only thing I can come up with is a persistent bronchitis."

"What are her symptoms?" Terrell asked.

Springer wheeled around and slowly headed back toward the front, with Terrell trailing behind. "A nagging cough with a low-grade fever, and that's about all," he said, a tinge of frustration leaking out.

"So, what's the big deal?" Terrell asked. "Unfortunately, we're all seeing more and more of these new super-germs that are resistant to the usual antibiotics. But if she's in good health otherwise, she should do well on one of the new big guns."

"It's a hundred dollars a day," Springer said, his face in a scowl. "And Medicare won't pay for it unless she's in the hospital. Since she can't afford the medicine on her own, we're going to have to admit her for the ten-day course of therapy."

Terrell shot Springer an offhanded smile. "Not very cost-effective, if you ask me."

"One thousand dollars versus the $10,000 that Medicare is going to end up spending because some bureaucrat makes an uninformed decision." Springer's disgust was obvious. "Why don't you tell your Unified Medical Association about that one when they encourage their members to not get involved in the single-payer debate?"

. . .

Lane Foster's fingers trembled in anticipation as he punched in the nine-digit code that would access the secret account that Horizon Data Systems had opened for him. The bank, one of hundreds that set up storefront operations on the Cayman Islands, was nothing more than a façade to hide questionably earned revenues from the world's taxing authorities. How the monies were earned and what happened to the funds after the deposits were made was of no concern to the bank's executives as long as they got their cut—analogous to the rebellious stepson. As long as he showed up for Sunday brunch with his hair combed and his teeth brushed, it didn't matter how he got there.

A slow sigh of relief escaped Foster's lips as the computer-generated voice read out the five-figure total in the account. Duke Dandridge, for all that he wasn't, was at least true to his word. If

Foster wanted to see his account move into six figures, he had more work to do at the joint conference committee that was sure to follow whatever variation of SB 4215 came out of the House.

Foster pushed the end button on his cell phone, dabbing at the ring of sweat that rimmed his brow. He just wasn't cut out for this sort of thing. If only he had been born rich like many of his boarding school classmates, he wouldn't have to work for a living. The millions his father had been able to put away as CEO of a giant hospital corporation were just that, his father's. The old man, as Foster secretly called him, was adamant that, after the best education money could buy, it was Foster's responsibility to make his own way. Still jogging six miles a day, the elder Foster was the youngest sixty-two-year-old around and a long way from turning over any inheritance to his son.

The LED readout lit up again as Foster placed his next call. "Are you in a position to talk?" Frustrated that he was not privy to the other contacts on Capitol Hill that had signed on with Dandridge to make Horizon the national intermediary for the new national health care system, Foster decided to purchase some insurance on his own.

Foster's eyes darted from side to side as he waited for the response on the other end of the line.

"It's got to look like the amendment is coming from your congressman when we put out the final draft for review," Foster continued. "Since you and I will be doing the editing before submitting the proposed legislation to the joint committee, that should be no problem, as long as he goes along."

A smile eased out across Foster's face as the reply came through. Then he frowned when the party on the other end of the line continued.

"You'll get your ten thousand when the bill is on the president's desk—just like we discussed," Foster said before pocketing his phone in disgust.

18

Six Months Later

RAYBORN CARLISLE FINGERED the fountain pen the president had given him. It would be treasured then handed down to Carlisle's grandchildren and then to their grandchildren. For the pen had been used to sign into law the most comprehensive health care legislation to ever come out of Washington, DC. With passage of the Universal Health Care Protection Act, no American citizen would have to live in fear that all they had ever worked for would be wiped out to pay for unexpected medical bills. Although his was not the original attempt to address the growing problems of the uninsured and the underinsured, Foster was considered the father of the legislation, since it was through his influence that the dreams of many previous administrations had finally been brought to fruition.

"Senator," Foster's secretary blared over the intercom, bringing him back to reality. "Senator Dunn is here for his meeting."

Foster quickly rose to his feet, his hand extended to greet and thank the individual whose deciding vote had made the sweeping health care legislation possible. "Maynard, how are things back in Wyoming?" he asked, still wondering why his colleague had asked for the private meeting.

"I wouldn't know," Dunn answered, his gaze stiff and awkward. "With all the talk shows and interviews, I haven't been able to get back there." Dunn cleared the catch out of his throat. "Ray, that's not why I wanted to talk to you."

Carlisle could sense something was bothering the senator. "Can I get you some coffee?" he asked, signaling for him to sit down.

"Cream, no sugar." Dunn nodded, easing into the chair across from Carlisle's desk. "I voted for your bill not because it had all the answers but because the alternative, which was no legislation, was wreaking havoc on millions of this country's disadvantaged." He paused, his eyes following Carlisle as he moved into position on the other side of the desk. "They literally couldn't afford to be sick."

Carlisle flicked on the intercom, barking out the coffee orders to his secretary. Then he turned back to Dunn. "It seems everything we do here in Washington is a compromise, but I would like to think that this legislation will make a difference," he answered cautiously, still unsure where Dunn was headed.

"Ray, I spent a great deal of time with physicians and their advisors from the organizations that support their interests, such as the American Medical Association," he said as he straightened up in his chair. "And they're convinced that any payment system for health care services where the monies come from a single source will eventually erode the quality of that system."

Carlisle sat back, rocking in his chair. "That's the beauty of this legislation, Maynard. We leave the insurance companies intact," he said, reassured he had addressed the senator's concerns. "For those who choose, except for the surcharge on the premiums for any new employees who elect to join an existing plan from a private insurance company, everyone can still purchase coverage through their job or on their own if they're not working."

"Cut the crap!" Dunn said, his nostrils flaring. "That's a bunch of bullshit, and you know it."

The hairs on the back of his neck bristling, Carlisle stiffened at the sudden change in Dunn's demeanor. "I'm … I'm not sure what you mean, Senator," Carlisle said, trying to control his surprise.

"I agree with the compromise we reached with the House about not waiting the full twenty-four months to roll the Medicare and Medicaid programs in with our new participants," Dunn said. "Since saving money was one of the goals, the sooner we can decrease bureaucratic duplication, the better. But the part about tax deductibility—forcing individuals to pay for their health care premiums with after-tax dollars if it's not through their employers or this new federal program—is a sham."

Carlisle wiggled uncomfortably at Dunn's evaluation of the new legislation they helped to initiate. "Coupled with the existing Medicare and Medicaid programs, it was the one way we could keep enough money coming into Uncle Sam without significantly affecting the funding for Social Security and disability, while still making it affordable to the disadvantaged we are trying to serve." Carlisle picked up the cup of freshly made coffee his secretary had just set down beside him and blew off the steam. "If the rest of the country wants to continue to get their health care coverage elsewhere, they'll just have to pay a little extra for it."

"Little!" Dunn said. "How about 40 percent more. Those of us in Washington made sure we protected our own asses since we are still under the federal option program. But what about when we are no longer in office? You tell me how many of us are going to shell the money out of our own pockets when we can stick it to the IRS."

Carlisle knew he was losing the argument. From the start, there had been compromises. But if that was what it took, both he and the president had decided to make them. That's just the way it was in the nation's capitol.

Apparently not willing to wait for an answer, Dunn continued, "There are probably a few who will keep their private insurance coverage, along with those who stay employed with the same company." Dunn stopped and pulled some lose papers out of his briefcase. "But as an increasing number of individuals switch to the federal program so they can pay with pretax dollars, it will be the insurance companies who can no longer afford to offer competitive rates." His sad eyes looked up at Carlisle. "Then it's only a matter of time until the feds are the only game in town."

His hands wrapped around the hot mug, Carlisle drew in a deep sip of the java, then set it to the side. "Ingenious, don't you think?"

. . .

"How many stitches did ya take, Doc?" the young man asked, his eyes scanning the oversized gauze bandage wrapped around most of his daughter's right forearm and hand.

Dr. Jimmie Fouts looked back over his shoulder at the young girl lying on the stretcher. The bloodstained towels clumped on top of the tray of scattered instruments waiting for removal almost blocked the view of the patient whose right hand he had put back together over the last hour and a half. "I lost track after seventy-five," Fouts answered as he continued scribbling notes on the young girl's chart. "Carlos, I did all I could for her now. There's a hand specialist who comes down here from San Antonio once a week. I'll see if we can get her an appointment with him," he continued, after looking at the father's name on the young girl's chart. "She may have cut some tendons, which might have to be repaired later. In either case, with rehab here at the hospital and time, she'll probably get back most of the use of her hand. We'll just have to wait for the final answer."

Carlos brightened at the news of his daughter's probable recovery. Even though there were lingering concerns, at least she was in good hands. "I should've never let her help me in the shop," he said, his tone regretful. "With the way things are here in the Valley, I couldn't afford to hire outside help."

Fouts slipped the chart under his arm and spun around. "I've lived here all my life, except for my medical training, and each year it seems to be getting worse," he said. "My father had been with Sears for twenty-seven years, and in May, they gave him a choice—take early retirement or a pink slip."

Fouts had been lucky—the only child in the family who had been able to break free of the Valley's growing poverty. Three hard freezes in the last five years had almost wiped out the grapefruit producers and all those who relied on its revenues for sustenance. Only those few with deep pockets or undying optimism continued to hold on. As with so many other types of produce, the industry was moving to more tropical climates where, except for the threat of hurricanes, a continual supply was more of a certainty.

"At least we got that new insurance to protect us, so I won't have to sell my business if one of my family gets sick," Carlos said, his eyes quickly moving back to his daughter's bandaged arm.

Fouts shuffled uneasily on the stool. "My partner and I aren't going to be part of that program."

"What?" The concerned man's jaw dropped in disbelief. "Why didn't you tell me before you started working on my daughter, so that the hospital could've gotten us a doctor who would? I can't afford to pay you—not without borrowing the money."

"Neither of us had any choice in the matter," Fouts said firmly. "Your daughter had to be treated now rather than waiting to be transferred to San Antonio or Galveston." He got up from the stool. "And I'm the one on call for the emergency room, which means I'm obligated to take care of everybody who comes in, whether they can pay or not."

"But what about the new law that gives everybody without other insurance protection?" he asked, has face a mass of confusion. "I already sent 'em my fifty-five dollars a month ago."

Fouts shifted to his other foot. "It's called the Universal Health Care Protection Act, or UHCPA for short," he answered. "And, Carlos, it's a good thing—something this country has needed for over fifty years. The problem is the guys in Washington put the responsibility in the wrong hands."

Carlos blinked. "I don't understand."

"Unfortunately, it gets down to money," Fouts answered, almost embarrassed. "If we sign up as participants in the program, then we have to abide by prices the feds say we can charge. Since the rates they have set are the same as Medicaid, most of us lose money on many of the patients we see, if you take into account the overhead we have to pay. Even here in the Valley, with all the patients who I don't collect anything on, I'm still able to charge those who can afford to pay enough to make up for the difference. It's called cost shifting and the only way a lot of us and the hospitals get by. With UHCPA, cost shifting will become a thing of the past if most of the private insurers pull out of the area."

"Doc, I dropped out of school after the fourth grade to help my mother and father in the field," he said, wringing his hands. "I don't understand about no cost shifting, just that I'm going to owe you a big bill for fixing my daughter. I ain't got much, but what I do have is my pride. I always pay my debts."

Fouts sighed, knowing he had taken the exasperated father too far in his convoluted explanation. This was not the time or place to vent his frustration over UHCPA. "Listen, Carlos, my secretary is going to send you a copy of my bill," Fouts continued as he moved out into the hall. "Do us both a favor and mail it to the UHCPA offices in Washington. Put a note on it to send the money to you they would have paid me if I were part of their program. Whatever you get back from them, we'll call it even."

Fouts had now put the responsibility for his bill in the right hands. He knew Carlos would never understand the true meaning of his gesture. He only hoped that someday those with the ability to make a difference would.

. . .

At first Jordan Springer thought he was dreaming when he walked through the automatic doors just off the loading dock at Parkland Memorial Hospital's emergency room. He was still feeling the pains of an especially busy shift at Methodist. But he had made a commitment to give something back for his years of training, and volunteering at the large city-county hospital was his way of keeping that promise. Springer had missed last month because of the growing demands at the hospital; he wasn't about to make it two in a row.

"Where is everybody?" he quipped to the triage nurse as he scanned the almost deserted waiting area.

She slowly looked up from an open copy of *Cosmopolitan* spread out before her. "Are you talking about the doctors or the patients?" she asked, her tone subdued.

"I guess both," Springer answered.

The nurse pointed in the direction of the doctor's dictating room just off the main hall. "You might want to ask Dr. Atkins," she said. "He's in there with the interns and residents. The last time I checked, they were involved in a hot game of stud poker."

Springer headed back, his footsteps echoing, no longer muted by the moans of patients' cries or barking orders of various medical personnel who normally populated the emergency area. "The word must have gotten out on you guys," he said as he popped through the door of the small dictating room.

"I wish it were that simple, Jordan," Atkins answered, his gaze still fixed on his handful of playing cards. "Since the UHCPA went into effect, we've seen an almost 70 percent drop in our patient flow."

Springer edged behind one of the younger doctors seated at the rectangular table that filled most of the cramped space and slipped into a chair in the far corner. "I guess I must have missed something," he said, reflecting on his own workload, which had almost doubled over the last three months.

"Now that they've got coverage, nobody wants to wait long to be treated," the chairman of the emergency department continued. "Can't say that I blame them." Atkins laid down his cards, turning to Russell. "No, it's much more serious than that. They know this is a training program for these interns and residents, and I think they're tired of feeling like guinea pigs."

The other young doctors shuffled uneasily but appeared reluctant to add to the dialogue.

Springer slid his chair up to the table. "You and I know that's not true. In fact, if I had a life-threatening injury, this is the first place I'd want to be."

"We understand that, Jordan," Atkins answered, his face long. "Unfortunately, most of the public doesn't. To top it off, the other hospitals are working against us. Now that everybody is eligible for some type of coverage, the other health care facilities in the community are more than eager to keep the emergencies that come to them. Lately, we've just been ending up with their overflow—that and the illegal aliens. The boys in Washington still haven't come up with an answer to that problem. They're coming across the border by the thousands, and you and I, the taxpayers of Dallas County, are picking up the bill for all their health care. To top it off, if they deliver in this country, their babies become certified US citizens and are eligible for all the subsidy programs available to the underprivileged. Sort of ironic that we have to end up taking care of people who are not supposed to be here in the first place. But that group of patients alone is not enough."

"So, what do you think is going to happen?" Springer gestured at the residents and interns crowded around the table.

"We're going to have to get our training somewhere," the young, curly-haired doctor with a soiled white laboratory coat answered. Russell judged him to be in his mid-twenties.

Atkins said, "That's the real problem that has come out of this sweeping health care legislation. Besides taking care of the sick, our primary responsibility is to prepare the next generation of doctors to take over for us. If we don't have the patients to train them, health care education as you and I knew it will be a thing of the past. That may not be all bad, moving those responsibilities into the private sector, but I question whether we can adequately do all that's required to accomplish our goals."

Springer looked around, the unfinished poker game a thing of the past as the young doctors in training waited for their chairman to continue.

"You see, Jordan, we also need to be able to continue to advance this fledging science of medicine through research too." Atkins stopped momentarily, appearing to realize that the tone in the small alcove had taken a much more serious turn. "Until recently, most meaningful research has come out of the underfunded, behind-the-scenes laboratories of this country's teaching institutions. With the growing corporatization of this industry, research has also begun to move into the private sector, as drug company money and the need for profit has slowly replaced the philanthropic and federal-funding programs. The net result is if there's no way to make money out of it, the project doesn't get funded."

An oppressive pall engulfed the room, as each physician seemed to be contemplating their own uncertain future in the profession they had chosen to follow. Suddenly, the silence was broken by an announcement over the paging system. "Doctors, we have a patient in treatment room 1."

Within seconds, the room stood empty, as all the occupants sprang for the door, each eager to gain any experience they could from the dwindling load of patients—except for Jordan Springer, his eyes fixed on the individual piles of cards laid facedown around the table, waiting for the game to continue. Springer drew in a deep breath and wondered, when the participants returned, how each would play the hand that had been dealt them.

. . .

"What does this mean?" Allison's voice cracked. "Are we going to lose everything?"

John Terrell shuddered not so much from the cool breeze blowing across their back porch but from the realization that the lawsuit was actually going to take place. "My lawyer seems confident that the patient's family will settle before it goes to court," he said, trying to cover up his lingering doubts. "He feels they're really after the hospital's deep pockets. What they can squeeze out of me is just an added bonus."

"Doesn't it matter that it was an honest mistake?" Her voice was filled with growing anger. "You didn't know the hospital was using a different brand of dye, and besides the several days extra in the hospital, the patient is back in the nursing home without any permanent problems." Allison kicked her foot against the railing, pushing her chair back on its hind legs. "I just don't understand," she said, her eyes glassy.

Terrell shook his head. "My attorney said it's a game to them. The plaintiff's lawyer just throws out a net and sees what he can bring in. Then he takes out a minimum of 30 percent as his contingency fee, plus expenses. What little is left over goes to the client after expenses." Terrell picked up the envelope off the table and fingered the return address in the upper corner. "I wonder if they ever stop to realize how much pain they cause in the name of justice—all so we guarantee everyone the right to proper counsel."

"Justice!" Allison said, her face flushed. "There's no justice in a system that threatens to wipe out our security just because you accidentally gave a patient the wrong medicine."

"Allison, doctors aren't supposed to make mistakes. Don't you know that?" Terrell slung the envelope against the sliding glass door that led back into their living room. "One of the first things we were told when I entered medical school was to be honest with my patients," Terrell said. "That's a joke. If I tell them, 'Look, I screwed up. You really didn't have the disease I thought you had,' or 'I didn't do the right surgery,' at the very least, they're going to look for another doctor."

Allison reached over and rested her hand on Terrell's arm. The anger in her eyes melted into disgust for a judicial system that, like a cancer, had eaten into the very core of what once was the most, noble profession.

"My own attorney even advised me to keep quiet," Terrell mumbled, his voice barely above a whisper. "Not lie … just not tell them everything unless I was specifically asked. He said even though it was the truth, I was just setting myself up for more risk."

"Why can't they do like baseball players do when they want to renegotiate their contract?" she asked, her foot dropping back to the floor.

"You're talking about arbitration," he answered. "We've been working in that direction for a long time. No one questions that patients should be compensated if they have been wronged. It's the level of compensation that's the problem. That and the sick mind-set in this country that if something doesn't go one's way, it's sue their ass off. Poor outcome now is equated to negligence. And feeding the frenzy of more must be better, the juries of their peers are going along, awarding unreal judgments that make no sense at all. It's the lotto mentality, and they're just helping one of their own grab the brass ring. True justice, which is an unbiased evaluation of the interests of both parties, unfortunately is all too often the furthest thing from their minds."

Terrell moved out of his chair, bending over to pick up the fallen envelope. Tucking it in his hip pocket, he slid back down, moving his chair closer to Allison.

"Why is arbitration better than a jury trial?" she asked, nuzzling against her husband's warm shoulder.

Terrell cut his eyes down at Allison, then wrapped his arm around her. "It's not always, such as with criminal proceeding, although lawyers plea-bargain for their clients all the time.

Arbitration levels the playing field, so that both parties' concerns are addressed in a non-prejudicial manner by a disinterested third party."

"You sound like a lawyer," she said, her demeanor now more of acceptance. "If arbitration is better than a jury trial, why haven't the doctors been able to get legislation to change the system?"

"Look at what most of our elected representatives did for a living before they went into politics." He gazed off in the distance as the silence surrounded them.

19

IT HAD BEEN months since Lane Foster had heard from Duke Dandridge when Foster got the call for an emergency meeting at Dandridge's office. Although Dandridge had made good on his commitment once the law went into effect and Horizon had been appointed as the intermediary, the farther Foster could distance himself from his former associate, the better. He just didn't like the arrogant son of a bitch. Still out of breath from his dash across town, he approached Dandridge's secretary. "I'm sorry I—"

"He's not going to be happy," she said, looking at her watch. "He started the meeting fifteen minutes ago and told me to send you in when you got here."

Foster decided any explanation for his delay would just fall on deaf ears, since his experience had already taught him that the only concern of Horizon was Horizon. "I'll just slip in the back," he offered as the secretary turned away to the file cabinet, obviously no longer interested in continuing their conversation.

Dandridge looked up as Foster eased the door shut, trying to remain as inconspicuous as possible. "Foster, didn't I tell you …" Dandridge shook his head in disgust as he towered over the three other participants huddled around his desk.

"Listen, I don't work for …" Foster cut off his remarks, realizing he would only make the situation worse. It was then that he recognized the three occupants seated at Dandridge's desk—all faithful members, as was he, to the fraternity of advisors who worked for the elected representatives populating Capitol Hill. The only thing that changed with each election cycle was their employer, and with that, their loyalty to whatever party or special interest that was paying their salaries.

"Come on over and sit down," Dandridge demanded, motioning with exaggerated gestures. "I don't believe introductions are necessary, except to say that it was through your combined efforts Horizon was able to assume its role as the national intermediary for the UHCPA."

Foster moved over to the one remaining chair in front of Dandridge's desk, shaking hands with all in attendance before taking a seat—except for Dandridge, whose chronically flushed face was becoming even more distorted with the ongoing delay.

"Gentlemen," Dandridge said, "it seems that some of the damned doctors don't want their money. And I don't know what in the hell to do about it."

Foster turned to the others beside him, noticing that they too seemed to be in the dark.

"Can you believe that?" Dandridge barely broke a smile. "Doctors not wanting money. Hell, that's some sort of oxymoron." He picked up a stack of papers, shaking them in the direction of the small group. "These are statements for unpaid medical bills on patients in our UHCPA program. The problem is the doctors who delivered these services are not participants in our program."

"That's nothing new," Foster said, still puzzled over Dandridge's apparent concern. "Just like managed care, if the physicians haven't signed up with the plan, they don't get paid. The patient has to go somewhere else."

Dandridge's look of disgust was obvious. "It's not quite that simple, Mr. Foster," he said, his tone sharp. "Except for a few isolated docs, who are already seeing more patients than they should, there's nobody else to take care of them."

Foster was still unsure why he was once again the focus of Dandridge's interest. He had delivered on his pledge to make Horizon the intermediary. The problem of how to disperse the government's allocated funds was now theirs.

"There are notes on some of these statements from the patients asking that we send the money to them so they can pay their doctor directly." Dandridge smirked as he pulled an example from the pile. "Can you imagine trusting the patients with the money? Hell, someone down there must think we're one brick shy. Those patients will just go out and buy a refrigerator or something else with it."

"Can't we just send the money to the doctors directly even though they haven't signed up with the program?" the aide seated next to Foster asked.

Dandridge dropped the paper and flopped back in his chair. "It's against the law, except when the service was for an emergency medical problem," he answered, scanning the four faces across from him. "That's where you come in. The Texas Valley is a somewhat unique area—high unemployment rate, vast areas of sparse population, and too few doctors. Some of the people qualify for Medicaid and the other subsidy programs, but for many, it's the UHCPA program or nothing."

"You can't just make the doctors join up," Foster said as he reached forward and picked up one of the statements.

"Can't you, Mr. Foster? That's an interesting dilemma." Dandridge's eyes glistened as he continued. "I haven't been able to prove it yet, but I'm convinced there's some sort of conspiracy going on down there. Most of the docs have participated in the other programs. Why not this one?"

Foster looked up, the paper dropping to his lap. "Are you saying that the docs are in collusion?"

"Anything is possible." A smile broke across Dandridge's ruddy face. "All we have to do, gentlemen, is create the perception that the doctors down there have conspired to deny patients proper health care, and your bosses over on the Hill or even the president will be forced to legislate that they come into the program."

. . .

"The first round is going to be the hardest on the doctors who don't participate with the UHCPA financially, since they are turning down the potential funding," Dr. Jerald Todd said as he gazed out the window of the conference room adjacent to his office that overlooked the Washington landscape. "It has to look like they're acting independently—each doctor making his or her own decision not to become part of the program. If there's even the hint we're involved or that there's collusion among the doctors down there, the feds will be all over them. And, I might add, us too."

Dr. Gene Broyle and the seven other dedicated members of the Unified Medical Association's full-time staff huddled around the conference table were waiting to see what Todd would propose next. Not that they agreed with everything he said, but he was a visionary—a chess master of modern medicine, steps ahead of everyone else when it came to charting unknown territory. And bucking the federal government with a large-scale boycott of the UHCPA program was definitely in that category.

"Since there is essentially nowhere else for the patients to go in the Valley," Todd continued, massaging his brow as he tried to pull out thoughts from the deepest reaches of his mind, "my hope is the feds will buckle under and send the doctors' monies to the patients. As long as they can't prove a conspiracy, then we've opened that long-awaited crack in their system." He turned around to the group. "You see," he said, his eyes glowing, "that's the point those who have been speaking out for doctors have been missing all along. It's not as important who pays the moneys; it's to whom they make the payments. It really doesn't matter if the money comes from the managed care conglomerates or the federal government.

As long as they send the reimbursements directly to the doctor, the patient becomes a disinterested third party. If they aren't made to assume some responsibility—getting the money to the doctor and working out any differences they might still owe—then the patients have no incentive to use their limited health care resources wisely."

"Your arguments fall apart when the patient pockets the money instead," Broyle chimed in.

Todd nodded as he moved back over to the table. "You're right, but when that happens to you, if you're smart, you won't see that patient again. Before long, that patient runs out of doctors, especially when the next physician asks for a copy of the previous records and there is a big Past Due Balance stamped on the first page. We were duped into thinking it's a common practice by the feds at the start of the Medicaid program, and the same premise has been fostered by the managed care companies even today. In reality, paying the doctors directly was a way for the payers to cut the patients out of the decision-making process. It was an easy next step to start ratcheting down the controls since the relationship was then only made up of two parties—the payer and the payee."

"In your system, Dr. Todd," the young female physician of Hispanic descent said, "what if the patients can't afford to pay any more than they get in reimbursement from the UHCPA?"

Todd pulled out the vacant chair at the head of the table and eased down. "Dr. Martinez, that's the second key part of a successful health care reimbursement system. The patients have to be made to pay for the remainder of what they owe—but only to the point they can afford."

"A means test," Martinez said. "That's a dead issue as far as Congress is concerned, if they want to go back to Washington at the next election. The rich and powerful of this country would shoot that issue so full of holes it would drown in six inches of water."

A smirk went around the small conference room at the young

physician's retort. Todd edged closer to the table, temporally joining in on the moment of levity.

"The way things stand now, you are correct," Todd answered softly, bringing the dialogue back to the head of the table. "But someday this country is going to have to wake up to the fact that the rich and well off, whether they earned it or not, will have to forgo the benefits of the federal subsidy programs in order for the programs to remain viable for those who were not so fortunate, even if that was also by their own doing."

Dr. Martinez shook her head. "Although I send them what money I can, my parents are still very poor people. Their only chance is through Social Security and Medicare. So, as you can see, I am more than eager to let the wealthy fend for themselves if it means my parents live out the remainder of their lives with a little dignity," she said.

"We all bring our biases to the table, Dr. Martinez." Todd's compassion for his fellow physician was obvious by his tone. "But each of us seated here today has to use those feelings in a constructive way to search for the right answer to the very difficult problem of ensuring that everyone in this country has access to an affordable array of basic health care services."

Todd slowly rose out of his chair, returning to the window that looked out over Washington. "In the months ahead, we're going to be asking physicians from all areas of this country to make some very hard sacrifices," he said, his voice ominous. "Maybe even violate the very tenets on which medicine was founded. But if we're to reach our goal, then we may have to let our noble profession sink before it can soar."

. . .

Jordan Springer shoved the stack of unopened mail to the side of his desk as he fingered the internal memo from the membership department at the American Medical Association. Intended for the chief executive officers of the component state medical societies, he had circuitously obtained a copy of the document through a contact at the state's headquarters in Austin. A look of concern covered Springer's face as he scanned the five paragraphs for the second time. According to the latest statistics, renewal rates for membership in the national organization were down almost 30 percent compared to the previous year—a frightening revelation if the trend continued, he thought. The lost revenue from dues dollars could have disastrous effects on the AMA's ability to influence public opinion and Capitol Hill on the critical issues that faced the medical profession.

From what the experts at the headquarters in Chicago could tell, the downturn started within two weeks after the AMA weakened its position on the UHCPA issue. Not that the organization supported the proposed legislation, only that their opposition had softened. The internal document went on to point out that although the AMA was not alone in its acceptance of the inevitability of the proposed bill's passage, the organization appeared to be taking the brunt of the criticism of physicians who felt they had been abandoned on this very contentious subject. From Springer's perspective, it appeared the AMA was always held to a higher standard than most of the other organizations that spoke out on health care problems—that or, because of their size, they were just an easier target.

The content of the final paragraph was a plea for the state executives to use the influence of their respective organizations to try to turn the trend around, citing a weakness at one level of the so-called federation of medicine ultimately would lead to problems elsewhere. Springer tossed the paper back on his desk then reached for the pile of correspondence resting just to the side. Within seconds, he had extracted a large envelope with the AMA's logo in the upper left-hand corner.

"Here," he whispered as he pulled out a sheet of paper with Membership Outreach Program stenciled across the top. Below were listed twenty names with their accompanying addresses and telephone numbers. Six weeks before, he had volunteered his services to recruit former members of the giant organization who for various reasons had decided to spend their dues dollars elsewhere. Until now, he had not gotten around to honoring that commitment.

"I'm Dr. Jordan Springer from Irving, Texas," he said, after placing a call to the first name at the top of the list. "I wonder if might speak to Dr. Fredrick Dolittle."

Springer tapped his fingers anxiously as he waited for the doctor to come on the line. Although some of his peers seemed to revel in the process, Springer had always found solicitation of his fellow physicians difficult. He just wasn't a salesman. Even in grade school, he hated the fundraisers where he was asked to hit up his relatives, selling second-rate candy to underwrite some school function. Even though it was for a good cause, he hated the process just the same. That was one of the reasons he chose medicine instead of business; they came to him, instead of the other way around.

"Yes." The voice of the doctor brought him back to reality.

"I hope I'm not bothering you," Springer said. "I just wanted to know if there's anything I could do that might convince you to renew your AMA membership." Hearing no response, he continued, "Because of its diversity, representing virtually every aspect of our profession, there are going to be isolated issues that each of us might individually disagree on, but—"

Springer was cut off as the irate doctor poured forth a deluge of alleged transgressions against the giant organization. Every time Springer tried to interrupt, Dolittle batted him down. He was finally forced to hang up as his only means of reprisal.

After nineteen more tries, ten of which he was unable to make the connection, Springer laid down the receiver—one maybe the only consolation for his effort. Although none were as openly hostile as Dolittle, the others clearly had decided the AMA was no longer the organization they wanted representing them on a national level. To Springer's surprise, three had already joined the Unified Medical Association, and four were contemplating doing the same.

Springer pulled out the AMA directory he kept stored in the bottom drawer of his desk, leafing through until he came to the Os listed under the staff section. He dialed the eight hundred number to the organization's Chicago headquarters, then punched in the four-digit extension at the tone. "Could you connect me with Dr. O'Bannon?" he asked.

Apparently, O'Bannon was lost somewhere between meetings, so Springer was put on hold while his secretary tried to track him down. He again picked up the memo, reviewing the numbers until the line clicked back on. "Dr. Springer, this is Leonard O'Bannon. May I help you?"

"Doctor, I think you're in trouble."

. . .

"Dr. Rogoff, are you and your fellow physicians trying to put me out of business?" Martin Bohannon glared at the hospital's current chief of staff as if he were the devil himself.

Since the physicians had begun their campaign, now just over a week ago, Dr. Seldon Rogoff had known this meeting with Crosstown's executive director was coming, but that did not make it any easier. Bohannon had requested the encounter take place in his office, but Rogoff, now accustomed to confrontational situations since taking over as the hospital's top doctor, opted for a neutral site. The cafeteria across from the hospital complex was the logical compromise.

"No, I don't believe that is our intention," Rogoff answered, rolling the spoon handle through his fingers as he slowly stirred his steaming cup of coffee. "It has more to do with going back to what doctors are supposed to be doing—taking care of patients instead of needless paperwork. They did teach you that back in hospital administration school, didn't they, Martin?"

Bohannon's cheeks flushed. "You and I both know the hospital is not going to get paid unless your doctors complete the required forms. That's the damn law, or don't you care about the law?" The administrator grabbed at his Danish, ramming half of it past his puffy lips.

"Whose law is that, Martin? The joint commission's, the fed's, the state's, or maybe even yours?" Rogoff's tone was threatening. "There are so many laws and regulations doctors have to follow today. I just want to make sure we're talking about the same ones."

"Refill?" the waitress interrupted, her gnarled fingers struggling to hold on to the half-full pot of hot coffee. "Mr. Bohannon, you don't look so good today," she continued, staring at his sweaty collar. "They must be working you too hard over there at the hospital."

Bohannon waved her off. "I'm fine, Dolly," he said brusquely. "We're full up. Just give us a little peace and quiet over here." The administrator turned back to Rogoff, his nostrils flaring. "Don't play your silly-ass word games with me. You don't do the proper chart documentation, and we don't get paid. I can't make it any simpler."

"Chart documentation!" Rogoff fired back. "I believe, if you check, every chart has a history and physical admission note, daily progress notes, signed orders, discharge summary, and op report where indicated. So, don't tell me about proper chart documentation."

Bohannon reached for a sip of his coffee. "The discharge sheet, the length of stay documentation, the utilization and review—"

Rogoff held up his hand, stopping the executive director in midsentence. "Do any of those forms add any benefit to the patient's care? Do they help us take care of the patients better the next time they have a problem? No!" The doctor slammed his open palm down on the table.

Bohannon jerked back in disbelief, spilling his cup of coffee across the table as all eyes in the establishment turned in their direction. Dolly quickly set out the drink order for a table of police officers in the far corner, then headed back toward the commotion.

"So, I would suggest, Mr. Bohannon, that you let all the administrative assistants you hired to make sure the doctors are in compliance do the paperwork themselves and climb down off our butts so that we can get back to taking care of our patients."

His mouth dropped open. Bohannon was still speechless when Dolly, finally making her way across the crowded room, intervened again. "Listen, you guys," Dolly said, her voice stronger than her arthritis-riddled body as she flopped down a towel and started dabbing at the spilled coffee, "maybe if the two of you spent less time arguing and more time worrying about patients like me, this community would be a lot better off."

20

"THE PROBLEMS SEEM to be isolated so far, Mr. President," Rayborn Carlisle said, crossing his legs as he attempted to get comfortable. As many times as he had been there, the senator was always a little on edge when he was in the Oval Office, and the straight-backed chairs the First Lady's decorator had positioned directly across from the president's massive desk didn't make it any easier. "Overall, the UHCPA has been able to achieve about 80 percent of its goals. But these incidents, if left unchecked, could undermine the whole program."

The president leafed through the briefing papers Carlisle had brought along. "Ray, I can't see where a small group of doctors in the Texas Rio Grande Valley who won't go along with the program are a real threat," he said, his eyes quickly moving across the pages.

"It's more than that, sir," Lane Foster interjected. "There's also the doctors in Longview, Texas, who won't complete the required paperwork—in effect, virtually shutting off the only two hospitals in town from all the federal-funding programs."

"Seems like those Texans are trying to live up to their reputation." The president chuckled. "Operating just outside the corral."

Foster's frown remained. "Maybe so, sir. But the problem still exists. We also have received scattered reports that similar job-related work actions have been initiated in an area of Minnesota and in Las Vegas."

"So, what are you trying to tell me, Mr. Foster?" the president asked, laying down the briefing papers. "That this is some type of orchestrated conspiracy to undermine our legislative efforts?"

A lump hung in Carlisle's throat as he looked across the president's desk. He had been doubtful when Foster first came to him with the theory. But after his aide's explanation, the senator couldn't rule out the possibility. Foster wanted to push for an immediate presidential order to force the physicians to comply—even emergency legislation off the Hill if necessary. Carlisle was reluctant to ask for such drastic action without more proof of collusion. For some reason, which the senator wasn't able to explain, the almost devout resolute expressed at the meeting with the leadership of the Unified Medical Association at the Morrison-Clark kept coming back to haunt him.

"I'm not in a position to answer that so far," Foster continued. "There are similarities to all the incidents that make them troublesome, however. First, the vast majority of the physician population in each location appears to be involved. So, if they're not working together, they must have ESP. Second, the site of each of these incidents is remote enough that the majority of the patient population is being forced into going along with the doctors' demands rather than seek care elsewhere."

"What do you think, Ray?" the president asked, shifting uneasily in his chair.

The senator shook his head. "There's a lot of dissatisfaction among the physicians out there. Some of it's downright anger," Carlisle said, resting his hand on the corner of the desk. "And it's not just because of the UHCPA—managed care breathing down their necks at every turn, the threat of lawsuits at the slightest transgression, loss of autonomy with the predatory practices of the business community that used to be their friends, just to name a few. Ten years ago, I would have told you any action on the part of the physicians of this country that might remotely endanger even one patient was out of the question. Today ..." The senator paused, looking deep into the president's eyes. "I'm not sure how far they would be willing to go in order to take back the control of their profession."

...

"Do you remember when Broyle told me it was the system that stunk?" John Terrell questioned, his white coat silhouetted against the glow off the view boxes in the darkened reading room.

Springer's tightened fist clenched a wadded piece of paper. "But this!" He tried to control his anger. "The doctors have a system that deals with these problems that has been in place for more than 150 years. If more of you would get involved instead of just sitting on your asses casting stones, maybe we wouldn't be where we are today."

"That's what I'm doing," Terrell fired back. "In case you haven't checked lately, Jordan, your system isn't working. So, while you and your cronies at the medical society are rubbing your graying heads, the profession you have vowed to defend is being stolen right in front of your eyes."

"John, the UMA is made up of a bunch of malcontents who either couldn't or wouldn't succeed in the system." Springer's tone grew harsh. "Criticism is easy when you're not willing to take the blame. Being a doctor often takes a twenty-four-seven effort—something many of your generation seem to have missed."

Terrell glared at his friend. "Now, you're getting personal. I guess that's what the British royalty said about our ancestors when they decided to break away from the Crown."

Springer tossed the crumpled wad of paper at the younger physician's feet. "You can take your damned meeting and put it where the sun don't shine," he said, spinning on his heels and exiting the Radiology Department without another word.

Bending over, Terrell scooped up the paper as disappointment coursed through his veins. He slowly unfolded the wrinkled flyer that he had posted in the doctors' lounge earlier that morning.

> Worried about your future in medicine?
> The Unified Medical Association might be the answer.
> Tuesday, 8:00 p.m.
> Ramada Inn, 5543 MacArthur Blvd.
> Guest speaker: Gene Broyle, MD
> Sponsored by John Terrell, MD, Department of Radiology

It was sad, Terrell thought. They both wanted the same thing—a health care system where the patients really did come before the dollar, one that didn't bend to the pressures of the nation's capitol or the legislative mandates out of the state houses every time the governors and their cronies wanted a few extra dollars to put toward one of their pet projects. With increasing restraints being heaped on the profession from so many directions, the apparent ineffectiveness of the organizations that had carried the medical profession through the twentieth century was rapidly diminishing. Terrell had reluctantly come to agree that what was needed was a totally new organization—one that didn't fall back on tradition but was willing to take risks, if necessary, to free a health care system that was slowly strangling to death in a sea of red tape. Unfortunately, he and Springer were generations apart from a solution.

. . .

Solomon Page stroked back his unwashed, sticky blonde hair, so that it would fit under his size 7.5 baseball cap as he slowly moved up the teller line in the Austin National Bank. If it had been during the sixties, he would have been called a hippie or a beatnik, but in the university town where the computer industry ruled, the young man, barely in his twenties, was considered just one of the hundreds of so-called geeks that populated the hill country landscape.

On weekends, the hearts and minds of the American public might still belong to the gridirons and baseball diamonds that made reality for the rest of the week tolerable. But come Monday morning, the hard drives and keyboards took control once again. The twenty-first century was a new dawning where power was no longer measured in truckloads or touchdowns but nanoseconds and gigabits. Information was king, and the geeks, whose ethereal minds operated at levels unknown to previous generations, were firmly in control of how that information was collected, stored, and distributed to the less enlightened who naively still thought they ran the country.

A feeling of exhilaration coursed through Solomon as he moved one more space up in line. He was ready for the payback of a childhood where his only real friend was a parakeet named Joie and the seventeen-inch monitor that linked him to the outside world. When his father never came back from Vietnam, Solomon's mother was forced to hold down two jobs, leaving the young boy to fend for himself most nights. Hoping to find some solace in his lonely existence, Solomon stayed tucked away behind the locked door of his bedroom, roaming the Internet. Feeling the same frustrations of denial that he was experiencing in his own life, he began deciphering codes that allowed him to peer into corporate America's most private secrets. Through years of parental neglect and self-training, he had developed hacker skills that put him with the best. Unfortunately, except for a few select individuals who also operated on the dark of the Internet, his abilities were unknown. His initial opportunity to use his talent for profit came when he was the first to break an anonymous encrypted call for assistance. The request was simple—substitute a three for a seven in Horizon Insurance Company's database.

In order to preserve anonymity on both sides, the deal was worked out through a secure chat room with the payment promised in the form of a bank draft on a dummy account from somewhere in the Caribbean. Not surprising, Solomon was able to break down the code of his unknown sponsor that turned out to be linked to a terminal inside the headquarters of Allied American Insurance Company. He did not really care who was footing the bill, but the extra insurance of knowing made him feel a little more secure.

In the quiet of the early morning, Solomon sat down to accomplish his task. To his surprise, Horizon's firewalls crumbled like a papier-mâché fortress as his lithe fingers were able to break down their code in less than an hour. Then, it was only a matter of seconds until he had made the agreed-upon changes. He started to close down when his genius took over. This would bring him the respect he had not found in the other world outside his bedroom, he thought, even if it was only by the ghostwriters of the Internet that struck terror in the hearts of those who tried to maintain world order.

Just over twenty minutes had passed when he finally pushed back from his desk. A look of satisfaction oozed from his pursed lips. In front of him on the screen were the fruits of his labor—not one virus but two. The first was a decoy to cause an immediate disruption in Horizon's ongoing operations. Solomon knew that it would only be a matter of hours until the problem he had created was remedied, and the giant company would be back to business as usual. It was the second virus that would show his true genius. For the second virus would silently attach itself to Horizon's outdated scanning program, taking it to every sector of Horizon's massive system. Then with the firewalls safely back up, this dormant virus would slowly leak its disruptive venom into the system. He would coin the term exponential sequencing, equating his second virus to forms of cancer that spread silently throughout the body before being discovered. The principle was simple; the substitution of three for a seven would only show up in Horizon's system periodically. But with the passage of time and slowly increasing frequency, the effects would be devastating. It was only then that Solomon was contented to log off, knowing that his deadly creations were neatly tucked away in a file at Horizon's regional hub in Austin. What happened from that point on was no longer his concern.

The cashier's check for $10,000 held tightly in his clenched hand was far and away the largest amount of money he had ever deposited. Just thinking about it made him nervous as he finally made it to the teller's counter. "Put nine thousand in my account," he said just above a whisper. "And give me the rest back in hundreds." His skinny fingers trembled as he tapped the marble counter, waiting for the teller's response.

Her squinty look of scorn sent a chill down his pale, thin body, but he stood his ground. She scanned the draft from a bank on the Grand Cayman Island, which was listed under the account Chicago Development Corporation, then typed in the seven-digit number before slipping the wrinkled piece of paper into the scanner attached to her register. "Looks like your ship came in," she said, waiting for the clearance code to come up.

Solomon chose not to respond as his heart pounded inside his chest, hoping that the dummy account set up by Allied American Insurance Company for its illicit operations would check out. A gentle sigh of relief passed from his lips when the code popped up on the screen. As far as Solomon was concerned, he had earned the money; at least, he had performed a service at Allied's request that entitled him to the proceeds of the bank draft.

"Don't be like those lotto winners and blow it all on a used pickup truck," the teller said, thumbing out ten crisp hundred-dollar bills.

"Never been in one. It's for my mother," the diminutive man with an oversized head mumbled as he quickly slipped the bills off the counter and straight into the pocket of his tattered khakis. "The folks in Washington have owed her this money for a long time, and now they're getting ready to pay it back—and then some."

...

"You look like your mother-in-law just moved into your guest bedroom," Mandy said to Springer.

His thoughts miles away, Springer's head jerked up at the interruption. "You remember, I don't have one," he said, still out of sorts. "At least not anymore—just a misguided friend who seems hell-bent on taking the wrong bus."

The graying ICU nurse blinked, seemingly confused by Dr. Springer's comments. "Want a shoulder to cry on?"

Springer scanned the ICU. "What do we have?"

"The guy in three with the fever and the old lady in the next cubicle with the pulmonary embolus that's waiting for the consult," Mandy answered, glancing at the flowchart on the wall beside the triage desk. "Someone is checking in now, but he doesn't look like he's in much pain."

"How about a cup of coffee?" he said, heading down the hall toward his office.

Maggie closed the door as Springer handed her a Styrofoam cup full of the steamy brown liquid from the pot on the small counter. "Two sugars, no cream as I recall," he said, trying to break a smile.

"Good memory." She reached for the cup. "Want to tell me about it?"

"Maggie, I think I was born thirty years too late," Springer said, settling down on the sofa. "This new generation of doctors and I just don't think alike. To many of them, the practice of medicine is just a business—not carrying their problems past the back door of their office."

The nurse took a sip and slowly looked up. "My husband was a general practitioner in Waxahachie, a small town just down the road from here. It was his dream for our daughter to go into medicine, but he never even got the chance to see her graduate from medical school," Maggie said sadly, a tear glistening in her eye. "He carried his patients' problems with him everywhere he went—until he died one week short of his fiftieth birthday. I've had a lot of time to think about it since he's been gone, and I'm convinced that as long as doctors show they care what happens, the patients understand that they have a life outside of medicine."

Springer gulped to clear the lump stuck in his throat. "I'm sorry," he said. "I didn't know."

"Don't be," she answered, reaching up to dab the tear from her eye. "He probably would have had problems with a lot of what's going on today too."

"Maggie, we're being turned into businessmen." Springer leaned forward on the sofa, awkwardly moving his cup to the other hand. "Many of the so-called successful doctors today seem to measure their accomplishments by how many warm bodies they can get through the door—their payoff counted in terms of net receivables instead of satisfied patients. No longer willing to rely just on referrals from their patients or other doctors, they now depend on newspaper deadlines and infomercials."

Maggie stuffed the moistened Kleenex under her sleeve. "Went for an eye exam the other day. The ophthalmologist I go to has turned into one of those radio docs and only wants to do surgery now. So, I think they stuck me in hoping they could talk me into one of those new refractive procedures—even offered to do one of my eyes for free and two tickets to a Cowboys football game if I referred a friend who might need the surgery. When they found out I wasn't interested, it was like adios, trying to get me out as soon as possible. Except for the technicians, the only time I saw the doctor was for maybe two minutes to review the results. Once he saw that I was a nurse, all he could do was bitch about how the optometrists were trying to steal his business." She smiled, taking a sip of her coffee. "In case he hasn't noticed, they don't have to steal his practice. He's giving it to them, since all he wants to do is surgery."

"Although many of them make a lot of money, acting as nothing more than high-priced technicians casts a pall over the whole profession. But the problem goes much deeper, Maggie," Springer said, a note of sorrow detectable in his voice. "When doctors begin to act like businessmen, then patients think like customers. The expectations of both parties change. The doctor's primary concern becomes the monetary reward from the services rendered. The patients, on the other hand, think they are paying for results. In that scenario, if their expectations are not met, they either consult their lawyer or want their money back. The relationship has been changed from professional to transactional." Springer paused, looking down at the floor. "And doctors wonder why their patients don't flock to their rescue when Uncle Sam slaps another restraint on them."

"What does your friend on the wrong bus have to do with this?" Maggie asked.

He glanced over to the door as if he expected Terrell to walk in at that very moment. "He's one of them, but he's not."

"You've lost me on that one," she answered.

"My friend is getting involved with an organization that's willing to take risks that could put some of our patients in trouble or, at the very least, land a bunch of doctors in jail."

Maggie's eyes lit up as her confusion appeared to lift. "You must be talking about the UMA? My daughter says they are the profession's only hope." She moved uneasily on the sofa. "I think you'd be surprised to find that my daughter and your errant friend on the bus have very similar goals to yours for the profession that you chose to follow."

Springer felt uneasy now that Maggie had made the issue personal by bringing her daughter into the discussion. "I didn't mean to …"

"Yes, you did, Dr. Springer," Maggie said, cutting him off before he could continue. "You and my husband were from the old school—do everything possible to protect your patient. That's singular. Managed care under capitated systems have taught us to think more broadly." Maggie let out a sigh. "In a system with a group of patients and only a certain amount of money that can be spent for all their health care needs, the doctors have to think about all the patients they are responsible for—giving those limited resources in such a way so as to do the most good. Unfortunately, some patients must do without certain benefits or look elsewhere outside of the system."

Springer's jaw fell. "How do you know so much about this stuff?" he asked.

"When my husband died, I needed something to occupy my nights and weekends," she answered. "So, I went back to school. With six more hours of credit, I'll have my master's."

"Congratulations. Your daughter must be proud," Springer said. "But I still don't understand the connection between managed care and the UMA's position."

"Dr. Springer, my daughter and your friend care about their patients just as much as you do yours," Maggie answered, her gaze serious. "But they don't just look at the one patient sitting on the examining table across from them. They're also thinking about the patients who are still left to come in." She paused, her hand fumbling nervously for the Kleenex under her sleeve. "If a line is not drawn somewhere to say no more, then all those patients still waiting to be seen won't have a chance."

"And the patient on the examining table?" Springer asked hesitantly.

Maggie stood up and moved toward the door. "They may have to make their contribution to help the others who come after them."

. . .

The security guard's feet hit the floor with a thud as his boss, Duke Dandridge, flew past him on the way to the bank of elevators that led to Horizon's operations complex. Surprised by the unexpected middle-of-the-night interruption, the crimson-faced security officer grappled with the half-eaten salami sandwich that tottered precariously on his lap. According to the rules, no employee was to eat or sleep when they were on point in front of the six ten-inch television screens that constantly monitored Horizon's giant complex. He had been caught doing both. The guard's only hope was that in Dandridge's haste to get to wherever he was headed, he had not noticed.

Rubbing his eyes to clear the haze, the guard bent over, scanning the monitors on the console before him. His heart froze when he locked on to the third screen to the left. To his horror, the monitor, the one that went to the giant computer complex on the third floor, the heart of Horizon's operations hub, was black.

. . .

"What in the hell!" Dandridge bellowed out as his giant hands flung open the steel-plated doors that blocked Horizon's operational systems from the outside world. His nose wrinkled as the faint smell of smoke permeated his senses. He gazed wildly around the darkened computer-clogged maze for any signs of human habitation. "I said …"

"Over here," came the faint reply from an area tucked into the far corner of the massive room, filled with row after row of the oddly silent technological wonders.

Dandridge squinted in the dim glow as he awkwardly made his way in the direction of the light. Shuffling cautiously, he tried to sidestep the overfilled wastebaskets still waiting for the night crew pickup. Dandridge finally made his way over to the three pale-faced employees, flashlights wedged under their arms, huddled around the blackened central control panel. A lit cigarette straddled an empty Coke can that now doubled as an ashtray.

The plume of smoke caught Dandridge as he leaned over the board. "I thought I told you about smoking in here," he said, trying to swallow a cough.

"I'd say that's the least of your worries, sir," Barton said, his wrinkled white shirt's collar rimmed with perspiration. He picked up the half-burned cigarette, flicking the ashes in the small hole in the top of the can, then took in a deep drag, exhaling in the opposite direction from where Dandridge was standing. "We first got wind there was a problem when two of the mainframes over on aisle three started spewing out crazy data," he said calmly. "I was in the middle of backing up when the rest started to do the same thing, like a bunch of dominos."

Dandridge's cheeks twitched as he swung around the panel, quickly displacing the other two employees who had been looking over Barton's shoulder. "So, what in the hell did you do then?"

"The only thing I could if we were going to try to save anything," Barton said, not giving up anything to his aggressive boss. "I shut the whole son of a bitch down." The computer genius without even a high school diploma took another drag off his cigarette, then looked up at Dandridge. "I don't need to remind you it was your decision to have the regional centers link all their data directly into our servers here."

Dandridge shrugged, trying to ignore Barton's last comment. Letting his greed override his common sense, Dandridge had gone against the recommendations of his child prodigy and the other computer geeks who worked under Barton. They had suggested that the regional hubs around the country collect and process the massive amount of data that was going through Horizon's system since the UHCPA program started. That way, if a problem developed in one center, it could be isolated, allowing the other hubs to take over temporarily. Dandridge did not even want to consider the other reason. Always thinking of ways to improve the company's bottom line and the very generous stock options that awaited him on retirement, Dandridge had opted for the less expensive option of putting everything under one roof. Now, he would have to face the consequences of that decision.

"Do you realize the embarrassing situation you've put my ass in?" Dandridge said as his eyes, growing accustomed to the darkness, scanned the giant room of silent machines. "Come eight o'clock in the morning, my phone is going to be ringing off the wall."

"I had to make the decision. That's what you pay me for," Barton said, a hint of uneasiness showing through for the first time. "It's your company. You have to tell us how you want to bring them back up."

Dandridge's nose flared. "Just turned the bastards back on," he said, his tone condescending. "It's probably one of those computer glitches like on cable TV. You just turn it off, wait sixty seconds. Then when you turn it back on, everything is working again." He paused and looked at the other two employees behind him. "Something about the computer reprogramming itself."

Barton choked as the smoke off his cigarette got caught up in the back of his throat. "I'm afraid it doesn't quite work that way, sir," he mumbled, still trying to catch his breath after Dandridge's naïve statement. "We think it could be a Trojan horse."

"A Trojan what?" he said, spinning back in Barton's direction.

"It's a virus that sneaks into the computer system undetected," the young computer geek answered as he reached for another cigarette out of his breast pocket.

Dandridge grabbed the young man's hand to stop him. "You know the rules about smoking in here. Besides, that shit is going to kill you—if I don't do the same to all of you first. Now, I thought we had virus shields and firewalls to protect us from those problems."

Barton jerked back his hand in defiance of Dandridge's threat. "We do," he sneered. "But again, I might remind you, Horizon hasn't had an update in fourteen months. That was your decision too."

"How did this virus get in?" Dandridge's tone was more settled.

"Probably one of the regional centers was contaminated because their firewalls are easier to breech. Some hacker with knowledge of the system attached it to a file. So, when we opened it up here at headquarters, the virus started infecting all the other files," Barton said, his look pensive. "That's why I shut them down until we could see how to contain it."

Dandridge broke a smile. "Good work, son," he said, his relief obvious. "At least we have it backed up."

Barton shot a look at his two coworkers, then turned back to his boss. "We're not sure of that either," he said. "If the virus is dormant, it could have been in the system for weeks before it was triggered."

"Meaning what?" Sweat again broke out on Dandridge's forehead.

Barton reached for another cigarette. This time, Dandridge did not try to restrain him. "Meaning that everything in Horizon's system could be infected."

. . .

It was just past noon when Barton brought the last server back online. He typed in the code to activate the Norton virus scan as the screen went to dark gray. The group of red-eyed employees along with Dandridge held their collective breaths as the dark blue strip at the bottom of the screen grew longer as the program burrowed its way through every file in the server's database.

"Yes!" Barton called out, when CLEAR flashed on the screen. "I would say we lucked out, Mr. Dandridge. The hacker who did this was strictly an amateur—trying to slip in a Love Bug knockoff." He shook his head in disgust. "I just don't understand why these jacklegs can't get a normal job." He then turned to his fellow employees. "Ladies and gentlemen, the interruption is over. We can get back to work."

Within minutes, the familiar whir returned to the massive room as the computers began to once again spit out their payments to the health care providers across the country. For now, no one would notice, but for a brief thirty-second period, the 360 checks spewed out of the printer were incorrect. For some, the error was only off by four cents, an amount that would probably go unnoticed. But for others, such as a hospital or a large group of doctors, the discrepancy on a few of the payments was as high as $40,000, enough to raise serious concerns with the entire system.

In twenty-three and a half hours, the Trojan virus would raise its ugly head once again. This time it would be for forty-five seconds. The next day, it would be thirty minutes sooner and for fifteen seconds longer as Solomon Page's exponential sequencing began to take its toll. It was anyone's guess how long it would be until Horizon's system was in total disarray.

21

One Month Later

BRITT BARKLEY, METHODIST'S CEO, moved from foot to foot as he waited in front of the makeshift podium hurriedly set up in the hospital's dining room. "Could we get started?" he called out, his edgy voice barely audible above the noisy crowd. "Thank you for coming tonight on such short notice."

After filling his Styrofoam cup with fresh coffee, Jordan Springer plopped down in a chair in the back row as Barkley tried to call the meeting to order. Springer's eyes flicked around the room until they fell on John Terrell, who had taken a place near the front. He had gone to great pains trying to avoid Terrell since their confrontation over the UMA meeting, now over a month ago. Russell missed their close relationship but felt his young colleague was alienating himself with a constituency that would take their profession down a path of destruction. He wasn't the enemy, but Springer felt he was no longer a friend either.

The group of physicians on Methodist's staff turned in Barkley's direction as the hubbub of voices quieted down. Springer had first heard about the surprise meeting earlier in the day. Although rumors had circulated through the corridors about the hospital's financial situation, no one seemed to know the real reason the

CEO had called them together. Based on past experience with hospital administrations, there was an undercurrent of distrust as Barkley signaled for the group's attention.

"In the last several weeks, the hospital's billing department has experienced an increasing number of errors in the payments we have received from Horizon Data Systems, the UHCPA's intermediary in Washington," he said, reaching for a stack of papers to his left. "To date, our department has picked up twenty-two of our accounts."

A low rumble started to well up from the audience as the group of fatigued physicians began to voice their dissatisfaction at Barkley's surprise late-evening meeting for such a trivial matter. Springer cut a look in John Terrell's direction, hoping to get his take. "Hell, Barkley," came the response from Ted Tyler, a crusty internist with bright red suspenders and horn-rimmed glasses, who was standing over by the water fountain at the side of the room. "I suppose you're wanting our billing staff to straighten your problems out for you."

"Not exactly," Barkley answered, appearing to ignore the scattered chuckles that percolated through the audience. "Three weeks ago, there was one incorrect payment. Last week six. This week fifteen—to the tune of $93,945.32."

"Excuse me," Tyler said without a blink. "I was mistaken. You want us to float you a note with all the extra cash we make off that stupid program?"

Barkley's look was strained as he tried to lead the staff of his hospital to the point he was making. "Not that either, Dr. Tyler. Let me break it down to you in another way," he said, picking out several of the papers he had been holding. "Here is an explanation of benefits that's off by $40,000. Another for $404. Here's one that has an error of forty-four cents." He stopped and looked out at the crowd. "Does anyone here see a pattern?"

"The pattern, as I see it," Tyler answered, after he took a gulp of water, "is, like Medicare and Medicaid, the boys in DC have found another way to screw us."

This time, the crowd of disgruntled physicians could not hold back their emotions, as bursts of laughter erupted throughout the room. Even Barkley saw the humor in Tyler's retort, a smile breaking across his face.

"They're all off by a factor of four," the CEO said, shaking the papers in his outstretched hand. "We did a comparison to the original bills the hospital sent to Horizon, and in each of these cases, every time the number seven was anywhere in the total, the number three was substituted."

An odd hush fell across the crowd. John Terrell's hand shot up as Springer leaned forward to hear what he had to say. "Mrs. Veller in your billing department told me the other day that she had resubmitted several claims of mine. Something about they were incorrectly paid on two of the patients I had read x-rays on that were in the UHCPA program, but she didn't say how much they were off."

"We ran those too," Barkley answered as he turned around to a stack of papers resting on a chair behind him. After less than a minute, he turned back to the audience, holding two pieces of paper. "Four dollars and forty-four dollars to be exact on your two patients, Dr. Terrell." The CEO laid the papers down and walked around the desk toward the audience. "We're now checking into all of Methodist's hospital-based physician practices. So far, we've come up with thirty-five payment errors, all with the same discrepancy over just the last three weeks. Before that, they all seem clean."

"Maybe the feds just have something against Methodist," Jordan Springer called out from the back of the room, no longer able to hold back since his bills were now possibly involved.

A frown clouded Barkley's face. "I called the administrator at Presbyterian yesterday," he answered. "They had been aware of some recent discrepancies but hadn't picked up a pattern until I asked them to check."

The audience waited for Barkley to continue. Springer's hand gripped his Styrofoam container, his breathing shallow in anticipation.

"Got the answer back this morning when I arrived," Barkley said, scanning the group of bewildered faces. "Ladies and gentlemen, *we* have a problem."

. . .

After a few pleasantries, Jordan Springer headed for the door. He was stopped by a tug on the back of his jacket. Spinning around, he came face-to-face with the person he had been trying to avoid for the last month.

"What'd you think?" John Terrell asked, his face showing concern.

Startled by his former friend's appearance, Springer was at a loss for an appropriate response. "I don't know," he mumbled. "Looks like the government is messing with our money."

"I don't think so," Terrell said, acting as if the two had never had a falling-out. "At least not intentionally. Can I walk you back over to the ICU?"

Springer nodded, then headed off. If his young colleague could put their differences behind, so could he, Springer thought.

"I'm no computer expert," Terrell said, sidestepping a toddler who had strayed from her mother as they passed the waiting room of the intensive care area. "But I think the problem is in their system, either a programming error or a virus."

Springer stopped and shook his head, a slight smile on his lips. "You've been working too hard."

"No, really." Terrell's hands waved in frustration. "I talked to Barkley after the meeting. The errors that are showing up on the bills of those of us who work in the hospital are increasing in the same progression. Evidently, something similar is happening at Presbyterian Hospital."

Springer slipped through the back entrance to the emergency area, holding the door so Terrell could follow. "Look, I've had a hell of a day," he said as the fatigue of his ten-hour shift, plus the meeting, finally began to set in. "Barkley asked the private docs to look back at their payments from the UHCPA's intermediary. He also said he was going to do some more checking with his administrator friends around the country. So, why don't we just put this whole thing to bed for the night? Allison is not used to her radiology husband being out this late. She might just throw your dinner away."

"More likely just put it back in the freezer with the rest of the TV dinners," Terrell answered, his voice suddenly somber. "Jordan, the AMA and the UMA need to get together on this, if it's what I think it is."

"John, you're letting your imagination run away with you," Springer said sympathetically. "It's probably just some rookie programmer who got as far as computer 101 in one of those instruction courses that you take by mail."

Terrell sighed, the look of concern still showing. "Let's hope you're right," he said. "My worry is it's the one who's teaching 101."

. . .

"Dr. Rogoff, I believe you could be in a great deal of trouble." Martin Bohannon cut an evil smile as Crosstown's attorney laid out the grim facts to his chief of staff. "We have in our possession numerous instances where you and your peers have used the hospital's protected medical information in violation of the Health Insurance Portability and Accountability Act, better known as HIPAA to you."

Rogoff's mouth fell agape in response to the hospital's charges against him and most of Crosstown's medical staff. "This is all a bunch of bullshit, and you know it, Martin." He knew that Bohannon and his cronies would try to retaliate for the way the physicians had gotten to him on the emergency room call and the required UHCPA paperwork, but this was preposterous.

Bohannon held up his hands. "We're just trying to uphold the law, Doctor—protect the patients. I know you have appointed a privacy officer for your office, who has 'implemented written privacy policies, trained your staff, obtained new consent forms, developed a method for tracking and recording disclosures, assured that your patients' records are handled and stored in a secure fashion.' And they've also secured written privacy contracts with all business associates who might have access to individually identifiable health information," he said, partly reading from a memorandum lying on the desk.

"I believe if you closely examine the fine print in the act," the legal counsel said, "you'll find the definition of Protected Health Information is 'oral information or information recorded, maintained, or transmitted in any form … that's created or received by a covered entity.'" After quoting from the paper he was holding, Crosstown's attorney laid down a copy of the act he had brought along for the meeting. "That covered entity is us."

Rogoff looked at Crosstown's administrator and legal counsel in disgust. "You know the physicians can't get paid for surgery or most major procedures without the hospital's operative report, and frequently the payers want a copy of the admitting history and physical too."

Crosstown's attorney sat back in his chair, his intertwined fingers resting under his outstretched jaw. "It's unfortunate, Dr. Rogoff, but it seems that on occasion, when your staffs have sent out claims, and let's call it the substantiating data electronically or over the fax machine, somehow that information has ended up in the wrong hands."

"Are you implying that my fellow physicians and I are intentionally releasing that information to a party other than the one intended?" Rogoff's tone was defensive and angry.

"We're not implying anything, Doctor," Bohannon cut in. "The facts speak for themselves. We have put together a file on each of you filled with examples where either you or someone in your office made available protected information to someone who was not authorized by the patient."

"But those were mistakes," Rogoff answered. "An incorrect fax number or email address. Besides, there's also a Notice of Confidentiality stating that if the information ends up at the incorrect location, the sending party should be notified."

Bohannon said, "Sort of like, if the doctor cuts off the wrong leg, that's okay because the op permit made a reference to unforeseen complications." He turned to Crosstown's legal counsel as they shared a laugh. "Doctors are so naive." Then he whipped his head back around, his smile gone. "You violated the law, whether it was intentional or not, and you're going to have to pay the price. According to the HIPAA, that could be up to one year in jail and a $50,000 fine."

Rogoff pushed back his chair and started to stand. "I've had enough of your Gestapo-like tactics. This meeting is over. Now get out of my office!"

"Doctor, now settle down," Crosstown's attorney said, motioning for Rogoff to sit back down. "I'm sure we can come to an arrangement that will satisfy both our needs."

. . .

"What in the hell?" Duke Dandridge screamed as the door to his twelfth-story office atop Horizon's headquarters burst open.

Barton, the giant health care intermediary's chief of operations, charged in unannounced, almost stumbling over his own feet. "The virus has now infected our Medicare and Medicaid programs!" His shrill voice shattered the serenity of Dandridge's sanctuary. "We're not able to contain the problem, sir. My guess is it's only a matter of time until the virus gets into every health care reimbursement program in the country."

Dandridge jumped up, his rumpled jacket that hung on the side of his chair falling helplessly to the floor. "How did it get into our other operations?"

"This is the most virulent interruption I have ever encountered," Barton continued, dropping down into the chair in front of his employer's massive desk. "The virus seems to contaminate everything it touches. Since we act as the intermediary for other programs too and, as you know, virtually all health care companies overlap, either as the primary or the secondary payer, it doesn't take a computer geek like me to figure out what happens from here."

"Can't you stop it?" Dandridge gripped the edge of his desk as the veins on his temples pulsated in frustration.

"We've tried," Barton answered, removing an envelope marked Confidential from his hip pocket. "I even brought in Microsoft's top troubleshooter to see what she could do."

Dandridge's eyes bugged. "You what? I thought I told you no one else was to know about our family problem."

"It's all on the QT." Hoping to avoid eye contact with his infuriated boss, Barton never looked up as he pulled a folded sheet of paper out of the envelope and passed it over. "Right now, Mr. Dandridge, I would think Horizon would be glad to accept any help it could get."

Horizon's president scooped up the confidential memo with Microsoft's logo at the top. "What the hell is this?" His lips moved silently as he read the final paragraph at the bottom of the page before throwing the paper back in Barton's direction. "She must be crazy!"

Barton quickly drew back. "She recommends the sooner the

better, sir," he said, his confidence slipping away with the growing tension that choked the air from his lungs.

"You're telling me the only thing we can do is close down all our systems and start over?" Dandridge started to hyperventilate. "Look, you have to buy me some time. I've got friends in high places that will help us. All we have to do is convince the powers in Washington that we are the victim of some sort of corporate guerilla plot, and we'll be back in favor again."

Barton shot Dandridge a look of doubt. "That might be the case, but proving it would be next to impossible. It's much more likely just a hacker whose social life is in the toilet, and he wants to take the rest of us down with him."

Dandridge fell back into his chair, his strength drained from the ominous recommendation. "How long would it take for Horizon to recover?"

Barton shook his head while tugging nervously at his shirt pocket. Within moments, he had extracted another piece of paper, and with a trembling hand, he passed it over to Dandridge.

"What's this?" Dandridge said. "Another one of your damned memos?"

"No, sir," Barton answered. "It's my letter of resignation."

. . .

"I know you have impeccable credentials, but why didn't Mr. Dandridge come to me directly with this information?" The secretary of Health and Human Services thumbed through the small stack of papers Barton had brought with him for their highly irregular meeting.

Barton shuffled uneasily, knowing that bypassing his former boss as well as Horizon's board of directors could have devastating effects on his future. A snitch was a snitch, even when it was for the right reason. "I would guess he still thinks the problem can be fixed internally. Just continue to pay out the claims, even though more and more are coming out incorrectly. Then go back to those who complain and make up the difference. Horizon has done this for years and gotten away with it, just on a smaller scale."

The secretary looked up, his hand caught in midair at Barton's last statement. "I'm not sure what you mean," he said.

"If you'll look at the EOBs you have there," Barton said, pointing to the stack of papers laid out before the secretary, "the mistakes in many of them are for less than five dollars. Most doctors, especially in large groups, never question anything if it's only off by that amount or less. It's not economical from the point of employee time spent trying to collect, especially through big companies like Horizon. The telephone time they spend on hold alone wipes out any profits they hope to regain—and don't think that's by accident either. Four to five dollars spread over millions of claims means hundreds of millions of dollars to the payer's bottom line each year."

The secretary frowned. "That doesn't say much for your industry, does it?"

"This is much bigger, Mr. Secretary," Barton continued. "That kind of practice is penny-ante compared to what's about to happen to the health care reimbursement system if we don't shut it down long enough to fix the problem."

"Shut the whole health care payment system down, even for a couple of days—that's impossible!" the secretary said. "With no money going to the hospitals and doctors, the results would be cataclysmic."

"I think that term could also be apropos if you don't do something, sir." Barton sat back in his chair as a look of calm spread across his face. "I know it was before our time, but there was a day when patients were responsible for their own medical bills, and somehow they survived."

22

IT LOOKED LIKE a medical convention as they were all huddled around one table in the far corner when John Terrell walked into the hospital's dining room. "What's going on?" he asked, tapping one of his white-coated peers on the back.

"It just came out over the hospital's hotline," the young physician answered. "The feds have shut Horizon down."

Hearing the familiar voice, Jordan Springer got up from the table, motioning for Terrell to follow him to a quieter area. "They claim it's only temporary, but considering the government and how long it takes to get anything accomplished in Washington, you never know. A real shocker, but after the meeting the other night, I guess I'm not surprised."

"Do we know what this means?" Terrell asked.

"What it means, my friend, is that we aren't going to get paid on any claims we submit on patients in the UHCPA program until further notice." Springer pulled out a chair and sat down. "There's something in the memo about submitting paper claims until the problems in DC are worked out. Hell, we haven't submitted anything on paper in years. You can bet we won't see any of that money for a long time to come."

Terrell joined him at the table, the concern showing in his face. "We can't just abandon those patients in the program." He picked up a small packet of sugar, nervously flicking the edges with his finger. "On the other hand, we can't afford to see them for free either."

"It's going to be a real problem," Springer said, watching Terrell's aimless fidgeting. "Before they had coverage, we could just take care of their emergencies, then shunt them off to Parkland or some other city-county hospital where our taxes would cover their needs. In those situations, when that was not possible, such as out in areas where those services were not available, we could at least bill them for what they could afford. Once the program was instituted, that kept us from billing the patients except for services that weren't covered by the UHCPA. Now that it looks like we aren't going to get paid, at least for a while ..." His voice trailed off as he contemplated the uncertainties that lay ahead.

Terrell looked up as the packet fell from his hand. "At least we've got the other insurance programs to keep us afloat."

"Maybe," Springer answered, clearing the dryness from his throat. "The memo also mentioned that they would be evaluating the other funding systems over the next several days."

"Meaning what?"

Springer's gaze locked onto Terrell's inquiring eyes. "The memo left out Horizon's name when they referred to other sources of health care funding." Terrell paused, reaching nervously for his friend's fallen packet of sugar. "The omission might have been intentional, or it could mean that virus of yours has infected the whole health care funding system."

. . .

"How long does it take for him to come to the telephone?" Senator Rayborn Carlisle asked, his patience pushed to the limit.

Lane Foster shifted the receiver to the other hand as perspiration began to rim his collar. "They're looking for him," he answered. "His secretary has me on hold."

"You've got my ass in a lot of trouble," Carlisle said as he paced back and forth across his cluttered office. "It was on your recommendation that I put this Dandridge and his Horizon company in control of the UHCPA. If I didn't know better, I'd say you had something going with them."

Foster's grip tightened on the telephone. He had no intention of following up on that line of thinking.

"I used up a whole term's worth of favors to get that one through Congress," Carlisle continued, "and now we have to shut down the program because the son of a bitch can't keep his computers in line."

"I'm sure Mr. Dandridge can give us a good explanation when—" Foster stopped in midsentence as the voice returned to the other end of the line.

Carlisle came to a sudden halt, waiting for his aide to continue. The stress of Horizon's problems had fallen on his shoulders, for he had shepherded the groundbreaking legislation through Congress. And at the very end, just as the bill was about to come out of the joint conference committee, it was Carlisle who gave his final stamp of approval—appointing Horizon as the only intermediary for the entire UHCPA program. It was a move that put him at odds with many of the states' hierarchies as well as most of the major insurance conglomerates that had run the other federal subsidy programs. His political ammunition, the fodder that fueled the Capitol's engine, was down to the bottom of the barrel. If Horizon went down, so would he.

"He *what*?" The blood drained from Foster's face as he dropped the receiver into its cradle. He tried to stand, but his weakened knees buckled under him as he fell back in the chair at Carlisle's desk.

Carlisle rushed toward him, his chest heaving in anticipation of what he was about to hear. "What the hell is going on?"

"He's gone!" Foster stared straight ahead in disbelief. "Left on a flight late last night on a one-way ticket to Zurich." He slowly turned toward his boss. "He also transferred close to $100 million of Horizon's assets to a Swiss bank account just before he left."

. . .

Britt Barkley spun around when Dr. Jordan Springer jerked open the door to the small office Springer called home during those brief moments when he was not up front in the ICU seeing patients. "Maggie told me you were back here," Springer said, somewhat surprised since the administrator almost never ventured out into the treatment areas of Methodist unless it was a matter of utmost importance.

"I don't want to start a panic," Barkley stammered, his face drained of its color. "But I think we're in big trouble." He handed Springer a small stack of invoices, then fell back onto the couch. "They started showing up three days ago, just like the ones from Horizon."

Springer looked quickly over the papers. "This one's from Aetna," he answered. "And here's two from Blue Cross and ..." Springer stopped, his mouth ajar as he pondered the consequences of this latest development.

Barkley nodded, gripping the arm of the sofa. "The same substitution was made on all the EOBs, and each day we are turning up more." He sighed. "Whatever caused Horizon's problem appears to have metastasized to the rest of the system."

"Why are you coming to me with this?" Springer asked.

Barkley's eyes clouded with a look of despair. "We've got to be together—the doctors and the hospitals—or we'll all go down on this one." He reached up and loosened his tie. "With our reserves depleted by Medicare's fee cuts over the last several years, the hospital can't afford to run in the red for long. Just like you, we've got mouths to feed. And if the other payers tell us to go to paper claims like Horizon until they solve the problem, we won't be able to hold on."

"What are you suggesting?" Springer cautiously moved over, joining Barkley on the couch.

"Think about it," Barkley said, appearing to relax a little. "It's simple economics. The feds just want the problem to go away. Their only concern is that their Medicare, Medicaid, and UHCPA programs don't go over budget. Then there're the private carriers who have those same worries. However, since most of those in the positions of leadership are also stockholders, they have the added personal financial incentives. In more simple terms, although both advocate for a fairness, they all want to hold on to their money as long as possible—leaving us, the hospitals and doctors, to carry the system until they work out their problems."

Springer was cautious, since he never fully trusted that Barkley had ever put the doctors' interests on par with the hospital's. "You still haven't explained why you're coming to me."

"If the authorities shut down the other payment programs even temporarily, we'll go under in three weeks, maybe four tops, without other income to fall back on," Barkley said, rubbing his sweaty brow. "Revving back up to do paper claims, it will be at least forty-five days until we see the first payment come in, probably closer to sixty. So, what I'm proposing is turning the problem over to the patients."

Springer was confused. "You're going to have the patients go to the feds and the insurance companies to get them to give us our money sooner?"

Barkley nodded. "It's all about responsibility. The patients must assume some of the responsibility for the payments of the health care services they use. In the last part of the twentieth century, we took that away from them," Barkley continued, his eyes flickering as he appeared to search for just the right thing to say. "At the same time, the payers must be responsible to their policy holders, because they are the ones who support these companies with their premium dollars. The legislators are also responsible to the patients of this country, because it is only by their continued support through campaign contributions and in the voting booth that these elected officials continue to remain in office."

Springer shifted uncomfortably. "We can't let the patients get hurt in this battle, no matter what the cost."

"That line of thinking is the Achilles' heel the feds and the payers have been able to exploit—the physicians' unwillingness to jeopardize the health of even one patient," Barkley said. "In some ways, it may be your greatest asset, but it has also become your greatest weakness. Those who are in control of doling out the payments for health care services know the doctors and the hospitals will just keep on going. So they push and squeeze until we have nothing left to give. It's a business to them. Those of us who provide these services have to begin to think differently—not just about the patients we treat today but also about the patients we will be asked to see tomorrow and the day after. We have just as much responsibility to them—to fix the problems of our current health care system—so that when their day comes, they won't have to suffer the way many in this country are today."

Springer got up from the sofa and headed for the door. "I've got to get back to work." His uneasiness about the administrator's proposal was obvious.

"Listen, Jordan, this is a problem we can't walk away from." Barkley's face was wrought with emotion. "We have to get our patients involved."

Springer spun around. "And exactly how do you propose doing that?"

"Bill them directly," Barkley answered. "Give our patients a paper claim that they can submit to their insurance company—the one they or their employer picked. If it can't be worked out to the patients' satisfaction, you can bet they will take their premium dollars elsewhere when it comes time for policy renewal. It's worked before, and there's no reason it can't work again."

"Why me?" Springer was growing more frustrated as he reached for the door.

"This won't work if we can't get most of the doctors and the hospitals in Dallas to go along. I can try to pull the hospitals together, but I need help with the doctors. Since you're president of the county medical society, I thought you …" Barkley stopped when Springer held up his hand.

"Was," he answered. "That was several years ago. I'm no longer involved."

Barkley's sorrowful eyes told a story all their own. "Dr. Springer, if you take care of patients, you're involved."

. . .

"Are you sure?" Senator Bailey Forman said, cigar smoke hanging like a cloud above his head.

The secretary of Health and Human Services nodded. "This virus has somehow infiltrated virtually every program in the system," he said, his nasal passages, not accustomed to the blanket of tobacco stench that coated everything in the Senate majority leader's office, crying out for a breath of fresh air. "We've brought in experts from Microsoft and IBM, and they feel shutting down the entire electronic billing system for health care services until new programs can be written that are not susceptible to this virus is the only solution. If we don't, they think the substitution problems will keep compounding until we'll never be able to rectify the discrepancies."

Forman bit off the tip of his ever-present stogie. Mixing it with of a wad of his yellowed saliva, he spit the residue in the direction of a government-issue wastebasket that substituted for a spittoon nestled beside his right foot. "I was never much for this computer shit anyway," he said, pointing to a legal pad of lined paper and a ballpoint pen laid out before him on the desk. "Anytime you've got to rely on a metal box hooked to a little mouse to tell you how to take your next piss, you're in trouble."

"You should really cut back on that stuff," the secretary said, waving the smoke away, recalling the senator's recent medical problems. "It's going to kill you."

"It what?" the senator said, taking in another deep drag off his chewed-up cigar.

"Nothing, sir. It's not important." The secretary cleared his parched throat, hoping Forman would agree to his request and not throw Capitol Hill into turmoil over this tumultuous issue. "The president really needs your support on this. The pressure from the medical community is going to be relentless, claiming we're going to bankrupt them. They might just have to dig into their fat little savings accounts, but they'll survive. I'm committed to getting the system back online in forty-five days. We'll try to buy some time to let them blow off steam by having them send in paper claims, but the truth is we don't have the trained personnel to handle it. The carriers and the folks over at CMS phased out most of those positions years ago. It was just too expensive to keep both once all the health care providers were required to go to electronic billing."

"What happens if the physicians and hospitals won't go along?" Forman's gaze cut through the cloud of smoke like a laser.

"You don't have to worry about that, Senator," the secretary answered quickly, a smile coming to his lips. "They may bitch and moan, maybe even slow down on some of their nonemergency care in protest, but they're doctors."

Forman leaned forward in his chair, resting his smoldering stogie on the edge of his desk. "And exactly what does that mean?"

"The docs took an oath when they graduated from medical school to never abandon their patients." The secretary rolled his hands together, a look of confidence beginning to show through. "We've got them by their white-smocked balls, and the dedicated fools don't even know it."

. . .

The cell phone in Gene Broyle's coat pocket played out the intro to *2001: A Space Odyssey*, signaling he had an incoming call. "Yes," he answered, his breathing shallowed, knowing the impact of what was to follow could change the course of health care delivery in this country for well into the twenty-first century.

Within moments, Broyle was properly identified and patched into the prearranged conference call with Dr. Jerald Todd and the other members of the UMA's leadership who were scattered in strategic locations throughout the country. "Dr. Broyle is now on line," the operator said, then cut away.

"Gene, I hope they're treating you right down in San Antonio," Todd piped in. "It's cold as hell up here in Seattle."

Broyle glanced at the briefing papers spread out on the bed before him as he pulled up a chair from the desk. "I haven't made contact yet," he said, scanning the twelve-by-fourteen-foot room on the second floor of the Ramada Inn that he would call home during days or weeks ahead. No one could be quite sure.

"I think we're all on," Todd continued, his voice taking on a more somber tone after concluding with the pleasantries. "We have been able to confirm that the Horizon *virus* has now been identified in most of the other software programs throughout the country. It is only a matter of time until every carrier will be shut down while the problems are being rectified." Broyle could hear shuffling of papers on the other end of the line through a brief lull in Todd's presentation. "Each of you should have a list of UMA members in your area, along with a point person who will help you coordinate our efforts."

Broyle nodded, his hand moving to the six-page list of names of physicians who, by joining the start-up organization, had made their own commitment to move the war raging against their profession to a different battlefield—one where casualties were a given. But with the gravity of the current situation, it was a price worth paying.

"Our market share in your locations varies anywhere from 15 percent in Memphis where Dr. Martinez is stationed to Broyle's 40 percent in San Antonio. Even in Memphis with the lower numbers, with full compliance from our membership, our efforts will shake the very foundation of the health care delivery system," Todd said, the sadness apparent in his voice. "Hopefully, when our fellow physicians realize what we are trying to achieve, they will quickly join us in this endeavor of bringing the payers to their knees. We can only pray that any suffering our patients are forced to endure will be kept to a minimum."

The stark reality of Todd's statement sent an icy chill to the far reaches of Broyle's body. Never in his wildest imagination did Broyle think he would ask his fellow physicians to turn away sick patients. Todd's plan had been carefully thought out, so that to every extent possible, the patients could not bring chargers of abandonment against any physician who refused to treat them. Life-threatening emergencies would be handled without delay. It was with the non-urgent and elective treatments that the plan would have its greatest impact. The physician's request would be simple: pay at the time of service, or if that was not possible, sign an agreement that the patient or those who were acting as the representative would agree to assume responsibility for settling the patient's medical bills. Those without the ability to pay would be referred to institutions that had been established for that specific purpose. In locations where those services were not available, as had been done in the past, the patients would be asked to pay what they could afford—charity care continuing to play a major role in the way the doctors and health care institutions gave back to those who were not so fortunate in their community.

Glaringly absent in Todd's plan was any reference to a third-party payer—federal or private. That was, according to the UMA's approach, once again between the patients and whatever entity they chose to establish a relationship with. The plan did allow for one concession, however. The doctor would furnish an itemized statement that the patients could submit to their carrier for reimbursement.

"Apparently our friends in Washington are going to make it easier on us," Todd continued, a trace of sarcasm in his voice. "From our contact inside HHS, the secretary has been all over Capitol Hill, lining up support for a presidential order to shut down all electronic billing for health care services until the problems can be rectified, even in the private sector."

"When do you think that might occur?" Broyle cut in.

"Anyone's guess, Gene. But at the rate the payment mistakes are showing up, every day they delay just compounds their problems." Todd answered. "Our job is to get them prepared, but we can't let the physicians move forward until the order comes down, or our loyal members could face stiff fines. And as for us, since we will be seen as the instigators, a little prison time to boot."

Everyone involved in the UMA plan knew timing was critical in order to avoid charges of abandonment as well as criminal prosecution for contract violations. The abandonment question was reasonably straightforward. In addition to posting a notice in their waiting rooms, the physicians, who chose to participate, would have to attempt to notify every patient they had cared for in the last two years of their intentions. The patients would be given thirty days to find an alternate source for their care before the plan went into effect.

The contact violation questions would be more difficult—the small print varying all over the board, from thirty days with no cause to the life of the agreement, which came up for renewal on a yearly basis. Although UMA's legal counsel was somewhat divided on the issue, the thirty-day notice to the payer would probably stand up in court since the contact had been unilaterally altered by abandoning electronic billing. Especially since the physicians would be able to demonstrate significant financial hardship with the projected reimbursement delays. In addition, the sheer number of physicians involved would make it unlikely that a given carrier would try to challenge them in court. Since most of the participants were independent providers, a class action lawsuit would probably be unsuccessful.

"The major worry will be the criminal charges of collusion," Todd said. "But then again, this is war, and in war, nothing is certain."

23

Three Days Later

"I DON'T SEE HOW we can go along," Dr. Leonard O'Bannon, the American Medical Association's spokesman on the UHCPA issue, said as his eyes darted across the secret memo he had just received from a fellow member. "What the Unified Medical Association is recommending, if Washington shuts down electronic billing, will put patients at risk. The board of trustees would never agree to that."

Rebecca Jane Talkington slowly reached over to the side of her desk and picked up her cane. "That may be the reason the UMA is rapidly becoming the spokesman for the doctors of this country," she said, tapping the end of the walking stick on her desktop like a school mom of a hundred years ago. "Until the UMA came along, virtually every medical organization thought of the patient-doctor relationship in the context of one doctor taking care of one patient—an admirable but archaic point of view."

"That's the very tenet that holds this profession together," O'Bannon answered, somewhat put off by her remark.

"It still is but in a more global sense," Talkington said. "In the latter part of the twentieth century, the technological advances in health care delivery outpaced our ability to make them available and affordable for each and every patient. It was at that very crucial point that doctors were, for the first time, forced to make allocation decisions—having to decide which patients were eligible for a particular test or therapy and which ones weren't."

O'Bannon felt like a school-kid as Talkington's cane tapped out its message of sage advice on the desk before him. He was getting a lesson not by some pale-skinned liberal holed up in an academic think tank but by someone who had devoted more than sixty years of her life to the profession she had made not only her job but her best friend and family too.

"You can sugarcoat it all you want, but the reality is health care services are being rationed. Put more simply, every day there are patients who are being denied tests and treatments that would make their recovery more likely and their suffering less, because they are either too old, too sick, too poor, or the service is not covered in their policy." Her tone turned more somber. "Besides temporarily stemming the growth of health care expenditures, that's the only good that came out of managed care. By getting their employees to participate in health care coverage that limited their access to certain health care services, the employers of this country made many of those allocation decisions for you."

O'Bannon sat up in the chair. "I'm not sure how that changes what we have thought of as the traditional patient-doctor relationship."

"By agreeing to participate in managed care plans, especially those that are capitated, with limited access to the hospital, the doctors de facto agreed to think more broadly when making medical decisions." Talkington eased back, her cane resting across her lap. "Those doctors assumed the responsibility of allocating what resources were available such that all the patients covered under a given plan received the most benefit. If selected patients used up a disproportionate share of the limited resources, there would be none left over for the others."

"So, where does the UMA's plan for the doctors to bill the patients directly fit into this expanded patient-doctor relationship?"

Talkington looked over at O'Bannon. "You see, Dr. O'Bannon, the UMA is not just thinking about your one patient but the patients you will see for the tomorrows to come." She paused, pushing her chair away from her desk. "Since the 1960s, we have been giving this profession away a piece at a time because the organizations that spoke for the doctors in this country were afraid that if they made the sacrifices necessary to save this profession from those who would turn it into a trade, their patients might be harmed. As you can see, that approach has not worked."

"But ..." O'Bannon stammered, his mind full of contradictions.

She leaned forward on her cane, slowly raising herself to an upright position. "Doctor, I would suggest you go to the board and ask them to reconsider their position."

. . .

John Terrell tossed the hospital's emergency memorandum on the counter. "We might not see another check for a while."

Allison tapped the long spoon she was using to stir a batch of her homemade spaghetti sauce against the side of the large pan, then picked up the paper. "Is this about the lawsuit?"

"No. At least we've got insurance to protect us from that," he answered. "Evidently, the president signed an executive order late last night that suspended all electronic billing for health care services across the country."

"I haven't seen anything about it on the news," Allison said.

Terrell reached in the refrigerator and pulled out a Diet Coke. "Doesn't surprise me. The press isn't interested unless the story involves sex or violence, preferably both. Besides, the administration is all too happy keeping a lid on the whole thing in order to avoid a panic."

"Panic?" Allison said. "Just because doctors can't use the Internet to collect their bills? I don't see the big deal."

Terrell took a gulp from the can, then plopped it down on the counter. "According to the billing department at Methodist, once this round of checks clear, which should take another week or so, there won't be any payments coming in from the payers for forty-five days at the minimum."

Allison's eyes began to glass over as her trembling hand laid the spoon on the counter. "Without borrowing from your retirement fund or going to the bank, we won't be able to get by that long."

"We're not alone," Terrell said, moving closer to his wife. "The hospitals and their employees are in the same situation. There's going to be layoffs and closings. And without the hospitals, we have no place to take our sickest patients. When that happens, you know who also gets left out in the cold."

An eerie silence enveloped the young couple as they pondered what lay ahead. With Allison's near brush with death from myelodysplasia, they were no strangers to adversity, but this was different. The health care profession was standing at the brink of total collapse. Drained of many of their assets by the health care funding problems of the last thirty years and the rise of for-profit institutions where much of the extra profit was being siphoned off to line the pockets of stockholders. The hospitals were in no position to withstand a cutoff of their funding resources. In the past, these edifices had been the cornerstone of stability, where those from all walks of life could come in their darkest hour for refuge and solace. Now their very existence was being threatened by the insatiable appetite of a population who had grown accustomed to having all medicine had to offer. The hospitals were literally drowning in the debts of their own accomplishments. Now the country would have to face the stark reality already accepted by the rest of the globe; from this point forward, there would be two levels of health care, one for the haves and one for the have-nots. Those with the resources could avail themselves of medicine's best and latest discoveries. Those without would get the leftovers. It was a cruel world but one where reality had finally trumped beneficence.

"We don't have to let that happen," Terrell said, his voice barely above a whisper.

Allison looked over at her husband. "What do you mean?" she asked, reaching for the stool as her weakened knees began to give out beneath her.

"It's the third-party payers that are squeezing the life out of this system. Not only do they funnel off billions of dollars from the health care system, but worse, they have caused the providers of care to lose their direction. Clocked in a veil of protection and improved efficiency, they have literally torn the heart out of our noble profession and the patients we serve." Terrell reached over and put his hand on Allison's shoulder. "Patients no longer have reasonable expectations as to their outcome. By paying their premium to the carrier, in their mind, they have ensured that each and every need will be fulfilled. If the outcome is not what they wanted, they sue. Many physicians, caught up in the avarice of their own unreal expectations, have turned patients into numbers, measuring success by how many surgical procedures they can crowd into a day or the zeros added to their bottom line."

"You don't paint a pretty picture," Allison said, resting her cheek against his hand. "How do you think you're going to change things?"

Terrell smiled, then squeezed her shoulder. "Not just me but us." His voice was soft, even. "The doctors of this country have cowered from the payer's bureaucratic bullying long enough. It is time to take back the control of our profession, by whatever means necessary."

Allison jerked her head up. "With you and whose army?"

His hand dropped to his side as Terrell gazed off into the distance. "Our patients."

. . .

"The AMA's board of trustees has agreed to take no position," Britt Barkley said, resting his elbows on his desk. "I just got off the telephone with the EVP's right-hand man. Evidently, the majority of the trustees voted to go along with the Unified Medical Association's plan to boycott paper claims. According to him, they thought it was time to draw the line. But since they could not reach a consensus that was the best they could offer. Typical of that organization," Barkley said with a shrug. "They're just too damn democratic."

Jordan Springer's jaw tightened, never realizing until then that being more democratic was considered a liability. "What about the national specialty societies and the American Hospital Association?" he asked, choosing to not get into a debate over the virtues of a democracy versus an autocracy at this time.

"This is all behind the scenes, since everyone is afraid the feds will slap a huge fine on them for collusion." Barkley flipped over the page on his notepad. "By my calculations, it's about eighty-twenty in the UMA's favor with the specialties. The exec at the AHA is telling the hospitals when they call for advice to go along with their medical staff. If the docs don't boycott, and the hospital does, then that particular institution could be setting itself up for some big fat lawsuits for abandonment."

"Where does that leave Methodist?" Springer was growing uneasy, since he knew Barkley wouldn't have requested the meeting unless he wanted something from him in return.

"That's the pisser," Barkley said, his eyes lighting up. "The UMA's plan is almost identical to the one we talked about several days ago. But our hospital can't do it alone. To pull this off, the majority of hospitals in the Dallas area and their medical staffs need to go along. That's where you come in—getting the physician leadership of all the hospitals together through the county society."

Springer looked up, knowing Barkley had finally gotten to the heart of the matter. "I told you I wasn't involved anymore."

"You can't walk away from this."

"Why the hell don't you call John Terrell and get him to do it?" Springer fired back, angered that Barkley was putting the pressure on him. "He's a card-carrying member of that damn organization and would probably jump at the chance."

Barkley slowly pushed back from his desk, picking up his notepad. "Why don't you call him, Dr. Springer. If we're going to be successful, it's time your two points of view worked together."

. . .

John Terrell nervously thumbed the stack of unread x-rays on the stand beside him. It had taken close to forty-five minutes, but he was finally able to track down Gene Broyle.

"You'll have to … speak up … John." Broyle's voice was broken by gaps of interference. "I'm about fifty miles out of Longview, heading back to San Antonio. Tomorrow, they've got me going down to the Valley to coordinate the effort there. So far, the response has been very encouraging. What did you say about the doctors in Dallas?"

"Dr. Springer is getting the physician leadership together through the county society, and they want me to be the guest of honor," Terrell said, not sure he was up to the challenge. "Evidently, we've had the tacit approval of the AMA. Their board of trustees voted not to take a position on the UMA's plan. I'm not sure whether they just want us to take the fall if it backfires or they really are behind the effort but for political expediency are afraid to take a stand."

"With their membership numbers continuing to struggle, it may be a little of both," Broyle answered, his voice distant but now clearly understandable. "But hell, who cares if they want to stay at the negotiating table with the payers? The important thing is we're not divided on the issue. From my experience over the last two days, it's the hospitals that are pushing their doctors to get behind our position. They don't give a rat's ass about what the other medical organizations think. Most of the hospitals have been operating from month to month. So, don't kid yourself into thinking they have decided to become our big brother all of a sudden in the name of altruism. It's about their survival. A forty-five-day payment delay could put a lot of them out of business. In the past, if there were a funding problem, we would be fighting each other to see who would control the health care dollar. For the first time in as long as I can remember, we seem to be on the same side of this issue. I'm just glad they woke up and realized they needed our support, because the hospitals and the doctors make a formidable force. We need to capitalize on it, because when the next issue comes along, they may be back on the other side again."

Terrell spun around in his chair as the light from the hall spilled into the darkened reading room. "I'm just not sure I can pull this off, I …"

"Sure you can," Broyle said, his tone reassuring. "You're just the messenger. The UMA's plan is only a template—something for the physicians in Dallas to work off. Each community is unique, depending on the situation. One with a city-county referral hospital will have to be set up differently from somewhere there is only one hospital for a hundred miles. Dr. Terrell, it's essential that the majority of the physicians and the local hospitals agree on which approach to take. Otherwise, the whole effort turns into a bloodbath, with the patients caught in the middle. The way I see it, either all the medical community in any location goes along, or they stay out. There's no straddling the fence on this one."

Terrell gulped. Sweat coated his palms as the reality that he had been chosen to present the UMA's plan enveloped him. Just becoming a physician had been a challenge. There were thousands of careers and thousands of lives that would be affected by decisions that would be made in the days ahead. He believed in the position that medicine finally had to draw a line in the sand and say, "No more." He had watched from the sidelines as his chosen profession had been beaten into submission over and over again. Physicians' choices slowly stripped away by bureaucrats and politicians who, although they claimed to mean well, were often doing it to feather their own pockets and political careers. And the patients, the very ones he had vowed to protect, were drowning in a sea of paperwork, overcome with despair and disillusion. From his vantage point, he could sense their growing frustration as they were told which doctor they could see, which of the treatments they were eligible for, and depending which drug company had submitted the lowest bid that month, the medicine they could take.

"I'll do it," Terrell said, his response forced as he punched off the receiver. He knew he couldn't stay in a profession where a growing number of its participants, stripped of their independence, had switched their ultimate priorities from what was best for their patients to how much they could put toward the bottom line. Frustrated by their own ineffectiveness to stem the tide of increasing restraints coming at them from all directions, Terrell watched as many of his colleagues counted the time until retirement, so they could move on to a second career. Something had to change that would instill once again what it meant to be a doctor. He would move on to the playing field and take up his position. Slowly, Terrell turned back, his face silhouetted by the glow from the viewing boxes that allowed him to look at the very heart of his patient's problems through their x-rays. In the silence, he could only hope that his fellow physicians would join him and commit to doing the same.

. . .

"I'm hearing rumors from both sides, Ray," the Senate majority leader said. "That's why I'm relying on you."

The senator didn't want to admit it, even to himself. But with the computer virus essentially gutting the country's medical payment system and then the president of the government's largest health care intermediary taking an unexpected sabbatical along with millions of Uncle Sam's dollars, Carlisle was feeling the heat. He hadn't sought the job as the Senate's resident expert on health care issues. It was Forman who had made that decision when he assigned the committee appointments. Being a good soldier, Carlisle had reluctantly taken on the role. "Until recently, I would have agreed with the secretary's opinion that the doctors wouldn't do anything that could hurt their patients," Carlisle answered as he scooted the chair around so he could face Foreman. "They have been angry for a long time. But after meeting with at least one group, I'm convinced some of them are not just talk. Now that we've effectively cut off their revenue stream, nothing would surprise me."

Foreman chomped down on his cigar. "You don't think they'd strike?" he asked, leaning forward in Carlisle's direction.

The senator held up his hands in frustration. "We're living in a new era," he said. "With the destruction of the Twin Towers, the American public has come to accept that with any conflict, there are potential casualties. Nothing is sacred anymore."

"Hell, we'll just slap a big old fine on their asses if they try something crazy like that." Forman's eyes glared through the haze of stale cigar smoke. "Get them for collusion or abandonment or whatever. Maybe even let their leaders do a little jail time for inciting them to act. That's what we pay the attorney general to figure out."

"It won't be that simple," Carlisle said. "If you look back at the bill that was passed when the Medicare program was first introduced in the sixties, the original stipulations specifically excluded any federal interference in the way doctors took care of their patients. Since then, you, our esteemed collogues, and I have done nothing but pass more and more legislation that has allowed the bureaucrats over at CMS to gut almost every piece of that landmark legislation."

The Senate majority frowned. "Sounds to me like you're going soft on them."

"I've learned a lot since we started the hearings on the UHCPA legislation," Carlisle said with a sigh. "First, we have taken our health care system for granted. Lawmakers in the state houses across the country and here in Washington have made the assumption that no matter how much the reimbursements for medical services are cut and regardless of the compounding rules and regulations health care workers are asked to comply with, the health care system would be there for them when they needed it. Well, they're wrong!"

"So, what are you trying to tell me?" Foreman's face showed his confusion.

"That we haven't been listening, Senator," Carlisle said, pulling at his shirt collar, trying to get a little air in the smoke-filled room. "The doctors and the hospitals have been trying to tell us for a long time. If this country wants to continue to have the best health care system in the world, then we're going to have to pay for it."

Foreman sucked in a draw from his mangled cigar and slowly exhaled. "It's all about money, isn't it? Those selfish bastards just want to stuff more in their velvet-lined pockets."

"I think you've misjudged them if you feel that way," Carlisle answered, somewhat surprised considering the senior senator's recent near brush with death. "It's more about their freedom to practice the way they feel is appropriate—to deal with the patients as to how their services will be paid for, rather than some faceless pencil pusher on the other end of a telephone line. It's about taking their profession back from the bureaucrats." Carlisle pushed his chair back and stood up. "The doctors of this country have been playing by our rules, and you can see where it's gotten them. I'm afraid we're about to start playing by theirs."

24

THE TELEPHONE LINES to the American Medical Association's headquarters at 515 N. State Street in Chicago were jammed with all the incoming calls. Patients, their moods ranging from irritated to desperate, from all parts of the country were turning to the only voice they knew as thousands of doctors began notifying them that after thirty days, they would be responsible for their own medical expenses. Almost to the person, there was a feeling of abandonment, especially intense in the elderly who relied so heavily on a continuous stream of health care services, and mothers of newborns, many who had cash flow problems of their own.

The news was quickly picked up by the media as, in growing numbers, other physicians and hospitals joined the boycott. What made the situation even more critical was that except for life-threatening emergencies and existing relationships during the previous two years, it appeared the changes would begin immediately.

"There's a camera crew down in the lobby from CBS," Rebecca Jane Talkington said through Leonard O'Bannon's intercom. "Claims they've been trying to get through for an interview all morning. We contacted the chairman of the board, and he said you should be the AMA's point person on this issue."

"Be sure to tell him thank you the next time you get him on

the phone." O'Bannon squinted at the email from the Washington office. "All we have so far are the calls, nothing official from the Unified Medical Association or any of the doctors who are participating in the boycott," he answered.

"My guess is that's all the answer you're going to get," Talkington said. "The thing they're all afraid of is collusion. The feds can suspect it all they want, but to make any charges stick, they've got to have proof—a paper trail that can be traced back to the UMA. Todd and his cronies are too smart for that."

O'Bannon squirmed in his chair as the realization set in that he had been thrust into the position as spokesman for an issue that he neither created nor necessarily supported. "That son of a bitch," he said, chuckling. "I'll bet he planned it all along that the AMA would be forced to take the limelight. Since our official policy is no position, he knows we can't be held accountable."

"Maybe not by the legal system," Talkington said.

O'Bannon gulped. She was right. In the end, it wasn't the courts he would have to worry about. It was the doctors who were putting their careers on the line trying to prevent the extinction of the world's best health care system—doctors who were also members or potential members of the world's largest and most respected medical organization. Not only was the weight of the medical profession being thrust on his shoulders but also the future of the AMA and possibly the other medical organizations that portended to represent their physician members. Sweat broke out across his furrowed brow. "Tell them I'll be down in a minute," O'Bannon said, desperately trying to hold it together while he collected his thoughts.

"Doctor," Talkington said, a hint of sympathy breaking through in her tone, "I'll tell our media relations people to set it up in the boardroom, since this probably won't be the only interview you'll be doing over the next several days."

. . .

"Although our organization has taken no position on these particular actions to this point, the AMA has always objected to any outside interference in the patient-doctor relationship," O'Bannon said, forcing a smile in the camera's direction.

"You are skirting the issue, Doctor," came back the impatient voice from the tiny speaker hidden in O'Bannon's left ear. "Aren't these doctors and hospitals, in effect, abandoning their patients if they can't pay up?"

O'Bannon shot an edgy look in Talkington's direction, hoping for an answer. "It's not about money," he answered, squinting from the lights that surrounded him. "The issue is about freedom—the ability of the physicians to practice medicine without Big Brother questioning their every action and, in the end, being able to charge what they feel is appropriate."

"It's always about money, Doctor," the belligerent anchorman said.

There was a long, uncomfortable pause as O'Bannon stared into the faceless camera. "Maybe in your profession but not in ours."

. . .

John Terrell winced as he pulled open the door to the back entrance of the ICU at Methodist and peered through. It was a sight he had not witnessed, except on one occasion during his residency at John Sealy Hospital when there was a major pileup on Galveston's causeway that temporarily inundated the emergency room. "What's going on?" he asked, catching an orderly, loaded down with various medical supplies, by the jacket sleeve just as he was about to step over the outstretched legs of a young mother, cradling her baby, propped up against the wall.

"This is the overflow from the emergency room. I think you'd better talk to one of the nurses or Dr. Springer if you can catch them, Doctor," the orderly said hurriedly, pulling his arm free just before he disappeared into the throng that almost obliterated Terrell's view down the ICU's long hall.

Deciding he needed a better answer, Terrell headed off in the direction of the front entrance area where the nurses' station was located. An uneasy feeling of claustrophobia tightened his chest as unfamiliar hands pawed at his laboratory coat from various directions, accompanied by pleas for help. Trying to avoid eye contact as much as possible, he continued to gently push forward through the mass of people that surrounded him. Terrell's pulse quickened, catching glimpses of the anguished faces of those reaching out to him. *Strange*, he thought. These patients didn't look particularly ill, just …

At first, he couldn't make the connection. Then it struck him. Terrell stopped and kneeled down, lifting up the chin of a young man seated on the floor; crystals of dried tears coated his smudged cheeks. It was at that moment Terrell recognized the familiar smell of ketosis and the mournful look in his eyes. The young patient wasn't just sick; he was desperate!

"What's wrong with you?" Terrell asked, afraid of what he was about to hear.

The young man slowly looked up. A glimmer of hope seemed to light up his face when he recognized Terrell's white jacket. "I just want a prescription so I can get my insulin refilled." His speech was weak but still understandable. "I know it's partially my fault since I don't keep my appointments as often as I should … but I check my blood regularly and take my medicine the way my doctor told me," he said proudly.

Terrell was puzzled by the young patient's response. "Then why won't your doctor fill your prescription?"

"His nurse told me it's because I hadn't been in for a while," he continued, "and that I would either have to pay for the visit out of my own pocket or sign some sort of paper saying I'd work out the bill with my insurance company."

Suddenly, Terrell realized that the young patient was one of the first victims of UMA's plan. "All the nurse was trying to get you to do was agree to work with your own carrier, then pay the doctor after you'd been paid." At least that was the way it was supposed to work, Terrell thought.

"Hell, Doctor." The young man lunged forward, his voice full of anger, forcing Terrell to recoil. "I work for a living. I don't understand nothing about filling out all those forms. Besides, my company pays for my insurance, and the doctor's been filing on it before. With a wife and two kids to support, we ain't got no extra money for medical expenses. In fact, that's why I stay in this job. With my diabetes, that's the only way we can afford the coverage in case one of us got really sick. And now my doctor has abandoned me if I don't ..." His voice trailed off to a whisper as he fell back against the wall.

"It's not meant to be like that," Terrell tried to explain, his mind jumbled with contradictions. "Your doctor is only trying to—"

The young man, tears once again spilling down his cheeks, cut the flustered doctor off in midsentence. "Doctor, are you going to write me a prescription for my insulin or not?"

...

The 95-watt light globe that hung precariously from a cord suspended over the worktable in the back of Carlos's shop cast an eerie glow across the littered room. With the day's work moved off to the side, laid out neatly in front of him were his daughter's unpaid medical bills. Carlos had repeated the process almost nightly for the last several days. He was a man of great pride, but the heaping debt from his daughter's injury had reduced him to a shadow of his former self.

"Yes, ma'am, but ..."

Carlos's grip tightened around the telephone receiver as the party on the other end of the line put him on hold for the fourth time. The reassurances by Dr. Jimmie Fouts that he would accept whatever payment Carlos could get from the UHPCA program had temporarily buoyed his hopes of avoiding financial ruin from his daughter's tragic accident. But those hopes were dashed by the two subsequent surgeries to repair the torn tendons by the specialist from San Antonio that were missed by Fouts when he treated his daughter's initial injury. Carlos wasn't angry, because that was just the way it was when major medical problems occurred far away from specialty care in remote rural areas—you do the best you can. With his daughter's hand finally on the mend, it was now time for Carlos's health insurance to pay up, or he would be held accountable. Without cashing in what little money he had been able to set aside and taking out a second lien on his ramshackle shop, he had no other means of settling his debts. Carlos sighed as he waited nervously for the representative from the UHPCA insurance program to come back on the line.

Suddenly, she clicked back in. "Mr. Rodriguez, I'm afraid you have a problem. You see, the physician who treated your daughter initially is not affiliated with our program, and the other has temporally stopped accepting payments from us."

"So, what are you trying to tell me?" he asked. "That you're not going to pay my daughter's bills because you and my doctors are having problems? I thought you worked for me."

"I don't make the rules," the representative said. "If we're going to pay your bills, we have to have somebody to mail the checks to."

Carlos's voice was now almost pleading. "Why me? Aren't I the one who sends you the premium each month for this coverage in the first place?"

"That's beside the point. Our company is authorized to pay the providers of health care services directly," she answered. "We can't be sure that the money ends up in the right hands if we send the payments to the patients."

"Are you saying you don't trust me?" Carlos felt pushed to the breaking point. "Somehow I don't understand. I'm supposed to trust you to protect my family and me if we get sick, but you can't trust me to pay off my bills."

"You have to understand, Mr. Rodriguez. It's nothing personal against you." Her voice grew edgy. "But we run a business. Patients have been known to keep the money. We have an obligation to our doctors and hospitals to make sure they get paid for their services."

Carlos now realized who the voice on the other end of the line was working for, and it wasn't him or the countless other patients the company claimed to represent. In frustration, he suddenly lashed out as the neatly laid out medical bills were sent scattering across the floor. "I want to speak to your supervisor," he said, hoping that somewhere he could find someone with compassion for his seemingly irresolvable problems.

"That would be operator sixteen," she said. "Would you mind holding while I connect you?"

"Wait!" Carlos said before she cut him off. "What's your name?"

"I'm … operator twenty-six."

. . .

"You conniving son of a bitch," Dr. Seldon Rogoff roared as he bolted through the door of Martin Bohannon's office.

Bohannon lunged for the telephone at the far edge of his desk. "How dare you come in here threatening me. I'll have security all over your …"

Rogoff blocked Bohannon's hand as the startled hospital administrator recoiled in defiance. "Listen, I thought we had a deal," Rogoff said, laying the receiver to the side, out of Bohannon's reach. "You agreed that Crosstown and Mercy would go along with the physicians and let the patients deal with their insurers instead of filing for them."

"I … I told you the board would have to give its support and that I'd try to convince them that …" Bohannon's upper lip began to quiver as Rogoff's stony glare bore through him. "Listen, Doctor, despite your laudatory ideals about turning this profession around, I've got mouths to feed and bills to pay. This hospital has been running on the margin for a long time. With direct billing on hold and now your crazy-ass plan to get the patients involved, I don't think we can hold out."

Sinking back into the chair, Rogoff's eyes never left the squirming hospital administrator. "Martin, it's one thing to not want to go up against the feds, but to bring in a bunch of scabs to try to take our place? That's even hard to believe for someone of your caliber."

"These are respected doctors," Bohannon answered, his tone defiant. "I have reviewed each of their credentials personally. Besides, they are willing to work with the hospital as we try to make the best out of a very difficult situation."

"You mean work *for*, don't you? I wonder if the state board of medical examiners would agree with you about how desirable they are," Rogoff said. "From what I hear, most of them don't even speak English."

Bohannon ignored Rogoff's last statement. "I can assure it's all on the up-and-up. The state board will be issuing hospital permits on any of our new physicians who don't already have their Texas license."

Rogoff's eyes grew wide. "You can't do that!" He stood up. "Crosstown isn't a teaching hospital."

"It is now," Bohannon answered smugly, shooting a quick glance in the direction of his disabled telephone. "We have been able to recruit a well-known physician in the field as our medical director. You might have seen him on television from time to time. Until recently, he's been making his living traveling around the country, providing expert testimony. Seems he was ready for a change, and Longview was as good a place as any for him to hang up his spurs."

Steam could have easily come out of Rogoff's ears. It was all he could do to keep from grabbing the self-serving administrator around the neck and strangling every ounce of life out of him. "You sorry bastard."

"Under the conditions, I'll let that slanderous remark go," Bohannon said, seeming to gain confidence. "Since the majority of your physicians in Longview appear to have severed their ties with the payers, the board felt it was essential we step in to protect the good patients in this community and reestablish that relationship with, let's say, doctors with whom we are more compatible. So, Dr. Rogoff, it appears we are at a stalemate, or maybe a more appropriate term would be checkmate. If you don't mind, I think we both have things we would rather be doing."

. . .

The oppressive pain boring through his chest and the darkness closing in around him were the last things Dr. Jordan Springer remembered.

"Jordan, you're in the holding room outside the Cardiac Cath Lab," Dr. Jeffrey Schooner said, his voice even but authoritative. "For a moment, you really gave the folks in the emergency room a scare—being you were the doctor in charge and going out on them like that."

Springer rearranged himself on the stretcher and looked around. "Must have been those double shifts I've been pulling since the boycott went into effect. All of us over there have our tongues hanging out, trying to pick up the slack until the patients realize the doctors are still there for them. The only thing different is the way the payments are handled." For the first time, he noticed a distinct soreness in his chest and the wires hanging from sticky pads snaking down his stretcher and into a wall outlet.

"It's too bad you guys have to catch the brunt of all that unrest, but I'm afraid there's more going on here, Jordan." Schooner's tone turned serious. "You may have had a myocardial infarction or, at the least, a severe ischemic episode. Then you developed an arrhythmia, most likely V-tac, and went into fibrillation. As you can probably tell by now, we had to shock you." The doctor reached in the oversized pocket of his lab coat, pulled out his stethoscope, and fixed it to his ears. "When you get over this, you might want to thank your buddies over at the ER, because without them, you probably would have been another statistic in the obits section." He bent down, placing the diaphragm end on Springer's chest. "Now, take in a deep breath and hold it."

Springer did as he was told, holding the air inside his lungs while Schooner listened to his heart. The cardiologist's revelation and cold stethoscope sent a shiver throughout Springer's aching body, lying half-naked and vulnerable under the sheet. "What now?" he asked after Schooner stood back up, his question only touching the surface of all the unknowns clouding his mind.

"We've already given you the enzyme to dissolve any clots you might have," Schooner said, pointing to a small bag hooked up to the IV tubing that ran directly into the back of Springer's right hand. "But your T waves are flipped across the anterior chest leads, and you have some early ST changes." He picked up a copy of Russell's electrocardiogram, running his finger across the page. "We aren't going to know exactly what's going on until we get in there."

His fingers gripping the rails of the stretcher, Springer quickly put two and two together. To make a definitive diagnosis, he was going to have to undergo an arteriogram—the dye injected through a small plastic tube inserted into a large blood vessel in his groin and threaded up to his heart was the only way to adequately evaluate the full extent of his damage. "When do we go?" he asked hesitantly, torn between wanting to know everything because he was a physician and just closing his eyes, only to wake up and have the whole ordeal behind him.

"As soon as you sign the papers," Schooner answered, picking up a clipboard from the stand beside Springer's stretcher. "We tried to locate your sister, but evidently she had turned off her cell phone. We were about to go ahead as an emergency anyway, but now that you decided to wake up and join us, we'll let you make it legal. Once the formalities are over, I'll get the nurse to give you something to take the edge off."

Springer forced a smile, reaching out to the clipboard holding the medical release. "It's in your hands," he said, scribbling his name at the bottom of the page without so much as a glance at the fine print above. Although most patients would have gone over the document giving Schooner the right to invade their bodies with a fine toothcomb, not Springer. He knew the medical release form backward and forward. As far as he was concerned, the only purpose the piece of paper served was as a veil of legal protection for the doctor. Even then, most courts did not give much weight to the document, since the patients often claimed they were confused by their stressful situation and didn't know what they were signing. In today's environment, what counted were results, not some paper crammed full of medical and legal terminology. And results were all Springer cared about anyway.

"Jordan, depending on what we find, we'll try to open any blockage up with a balloon angioplasty, or, if we need to, we'll put in a stint," Schooner said, leaning his arms on the side rails of Springer's stretcher. "If neither is possible, we've notified Mack's team to be on standby."

Springer swallowed hard. Dr. Preston Mack was head of Methodist's heart surgery team. Mack and his colleagues were called in when the cardiologist's efforts at relieving the blockage of vessels to the heart failed. He could only hope he was not facing bypass surgery and the weeks of soreness and rehabilitation that would follow. A weak nod was all he could muster, his precarious medical situation draining him of any confidence that might still remain.

The door closed silently, leaving Springer alone to ponder his uncertain future. His only connection to the outside world were the three cardiogram leads glued to his chest that were connected to a monitor somewhere else in the Cath Lab. Springer rolled over and gazed up at the ceiling. Although this was not the area where he often worked, he had stood in this same room many times before. This time it was different. He was not there in his role as a physician but as a patient—frightened and shivering like a baby under the thin sheet. His only defense was an undying confidence in a profession that Springer had made his life's calling—that and his God. He closed his eyes and did the only thing left he could—pray.

25

RAYBORN CARLISLE'S EAR screamed for relief. It had been close to ten minutes since the senator's secretary first patched Peidmont Glick's call through, but Cleveland's largest car dealer and Carlisle's major contributor wasn't finished.

"My employees are all over me," Glick railed on. "They're telling me that because of a screw-up in Washington, their health insurance isn't any good. And that their doctors aren't going to treat them unless they sign some sort of document guaranteeing their bill. That's a bunch of bullshit. I didn't contribute no telling how many thousands to your campaigns to have you piss away your time up there, while the rest of us ..."

The senator fought to get a word in. "Peidmont, it's not Washington's fault. A virus got into the government's UHPCA program. Then it spread into all the other health care payment systems. So, we had to temporarily shut them all down until the problem was corrected. The doctors are just overreacting."

"My advice to you," Glick said, his tone loaded with resolve, "is that you and the rest of your cronies on Capitol Hill stop wasting time worrying about whose fault this whole thing is and worry about how you're going to fix the problem. Do I make myself clear, Senator?"

"We always appreciate your input," Carlisle said, choking

back the urge to tell him what he really thought. But this was Washington, and the Peidmont Glicks were the reason he and all his fellow legislators were there. Without their campaign dollars to put his face in front of the voting public, he would still be an alderman in Toledo's first district, sorting out salary problems between the local police and bus drivers' unions. "Give my best to your wife."

Carlisle hung up the receiver with one hand and punched the intercom through to his secretary with the other. "Tell Lane Foster to get in here as soon as possible. And, Maggie, send in two cups of coffee—black. I think we're going to be here for a while."

. . .

John Terrell's eyes strained against the subdued lighting. "Schooner tells me you're going to make a full recovery," he said, trying to put his best face forward for his friend.

"If you call giving up double shifts and hamburgers to get there," Jordan Springer answered, rolling over in his bed to face Terrell. "I guess I'm lucky. They only found one vessel that was severely affected, and Schooner was able to get a stint into it. So, they tell me if I watch my diet and get back on the treadmill, I should be able to see my grandkids grow up."

Terrell blinked at Springer's last comment, knowing that up until now, his friend had claimed to be a confirmed bachelor. "I didn't know that you and Cindy were making plans." He reached out, pulling a chair up beside Springer's hospital bed.

"We aren't. I mean, we weren't. She's waited a long time for me to come around." Springer's eyes grew glassy. "The last several days have given me a lot of time to think, John. If I hadn't already been in the ICU, Schooner tells me I probably wouldn't have made it. This has given me time to think about what I've done. Up to now, it has been about me. What I've wanted. What benefit

I could get out of what I did. Sure, if I had died the other day, people would have said he was a doctor who dedicated his life to easing the suffering of others. But did I make a difference—a real difference to patients? Not just to my patients but those who went to other doctors. Up to now, the answer is no. Initially, I think most people who choose medicine as a career probably do so for the right reasons. But after years of sacrifice, essentially living from month to month, watching their college classmates drive up to new homes in fancy sports cars while they still face thousands of dollars in debt just to get to where they actually can take care of patients, a lot of young physicians change. Many feel they are owed a debt for what they have gone through. I think I have thought that way but never realized it before."

Springer's candid evaluation of the medical profession caught Terrell off guard. If he didn't know better, he would have thought Springer was giving his deathbed confession. "Jordan, I'm not sure where you're going with all this," Terrell said.

"I'm talking about footprints—visible signs that when we're gone, something we accomplished made our brief stay on this planet worthwhile. I know it sounds sappy, but, John, we've turned into a me-first society. If I help you, how does that benefit me? Maybe it's more money or a job promotion. It all turns out to be the same. We tend to only undertake activities that benefit us—even those of us who claim to represent the medical profession." Springer rubbed his brow, his expression troubled. "Despite what many of our colleagues think, it's not what we get that's important; it's what we give. And the reward for that effort, which appears to elude the growing number of physicians who seem to act and think more like businessmen, is a sense of satisfaction. In some ways, that may be why these so-called physicians keep crowding more patients into their already loaded schedules and pouring thousands of dollars into attracting more patients. They're searching for something they'll never find—because they never slow down long enough to realize the answer is in the next examining room, waiting to be seen."

Terrell went numb, rocked to his core. He eased up from his chair as his own sense of guilt, coupled with the stuffiness of the cramped room, choked at his lungs. "I need to get some air," he said, his head starting to swim.

"John, I think you're right." Springer's response was barely above a whisper. "About the boycott and what we have to do to save this profession."

Terrell spun around, grabbing the top of his chair for support. The cobwebs that were sweeping over him just moments ago evaporated.

Springer's wide-open eyes, glistening even in the subdued lighting of the hospital room, stared right through Terrell as if he was looking into the future. "If I'm lucky enough to get a second chance, I'd better start thinking about my grandkids and the problems they are going to have to face someday—and not just myself."

. . .

"President Truman probably gave old John L. Sullivan a heart attack when he sent down that federal order breaking the coal miners' strike of the late forties," Lane Foster said, leafing through the stack of briefing papers he had brought with him to Senator Carlisle's office. "Then they said it wouldn't last when Reagan fired the air traffic controllers and hired his own. As long as we can convince the president this boycott by the doctors and the hospitals is a threat to our national security, he has almost unlimited powers to intervene, if he chooses. That's where you come in, Senator."

Rayborn Carlisle shook his head in frustration as his aide continued to lay out his plan to use a presidential order to force the physicians back into the federal subsidy programs. "There must be another way," he grumbled as he pushed back from his oversized desk. "There seems to be a contradiction here. On one hand, we portend to trust these physicians with our lives, while at the same time we're essentially reinstituting a doctor draft, because we feel they aren't going along with what we want them to do. Lane, you're either naïve or stupid if you think that under those conditions, they're going to put out their very best. They're doctors, not POWs. And if you look into the future, what about the young people who are thinking about a career in medicine? I suppose the best and brightest of them are going to continue to line up for a life of indentured servitude."

"It'll only be temporary, until Congress and the president can work out a universal health care payment system that the country can afford," Foster answered, continuing to rifle through the pile of papers scattered across Carlisle's desk in front of him. "Then, when everybody is covered under a single payer, they'll be no need to keep them federalized since we'll be the only game in town."

Carlisle shot his aide a scowl. "Let's hope this plan of yours works out better than appointing Horizon and its illustrious president head of our UHPCA program. I agree we need to find a way to cover the uninsured, but a single payer for everyone? The affluent and the upper class aren't going to tolerate it. Besides, you know what happens to the dollars for research and updating our health care facilities under that system." He picked up the article on *Truman v. The Coal Miners' Union*. "It might have worked for the coal miners, but the doctors … I just don't know."

Foster's gaze moved up as Carlisle's indecisiveness and accusatory, offhanded remarks appeared to take their toll on his patience. "Look, Senator, the doctors and the hospitals really haven't given us much choice. They've dumped the problems into their patients' laps, trying to make us look like the bad guys. And we all know when the next election cycle comes around to keep you here in Washington, where most of your votes come from. If we don't nip this in the bud, no telling what might happen."

The senator stood up, throwing the article back on his desk. "Yeah, the senior citizens of the good state of Ohio could vote me out of office, and the physicians might just take their own profession back."

. . .

"The doctors in Longview want us to tell them what to do," Dr. Gene Broyle said, his voice raised. "Seldon Rogoff feels the Unified Medical Association got them into this, and they're expecting us to get them out."

Dr. Jerald Todd switched his phone to his other hand as he looked out his window to the Washington landscape unrolled before him. "Up to now, one of the problems of our organization, or any other that represents physicians, is that we have no inherent power, only influence through our constituent membership. Unlike labor unions, because we are voluntary, we are prohibited by law from bringing physicians together to collectively negotiate—whether that's about fee structure, work slowdowns, or even a strike if it became necessary."

"So, that means we fill our members' heads with all these lofty ideas about how the UMA is different and how we're going to change the system," Broyle said, his anger showing through. "Then when some sorry-ass hospital administrator in the middle of deep East Texas calls our bluff. We throw up our hands and walk away, leaving our members high and dry. That's bullshit, and you know it!"

"Calm down, Gene," Todd said with an authoritative ring. He moved over, picking up a file from his desk. "Like I told you before, we have entered a war—a fight to take back our profession. Strategically, you don't want to bring in all your artillery for the first battle. When the time comes, we may have to draw that line in the sand. For now, I would suggest we let the current system work for us."

"What system?" Broyle questioned, distrust of his new boss still showing through. "For the last forty-plus years, every time the medical profession has asked for help, they have been screwed by the so-called system—tort reform, managed care with third-party payers dictating how we treat of our patients, federal mandates telling us when they're going to pay and what they're going to pay us. Need I go on?"

Todd fingered the file before him. "Get Rogoff and the other physicians to ask the legal teams from the Texas Medical Association and the AMA to help them petition the district court for a restraining order, claiming the two hospitals' attempt to bring in replacements denies them of their right to earn a living. If they lose, then they can appeal the decision to the federal court and maybe even the Supreme Court if it goes that far. Additionally, I would recommend the physicians file a lawsuit for any lost revenues that might incur during the time it takes for the case to be decided. If the hospital loses the first part, the settlement on the lawsuit could end up costing the hospitals millions, with the courts possibly awarding treble damages for restraint of trade. With the narrow margins the hospitals have been running the last several years, my guess is their pockets are fairly shallow, and they could not afford to take that hit."

"Couldn't the Longview hospitals do the same thing and countersue the doctors?" Broyle asked.

"That's always a concern," Todd answered. "But if the court at least grants a stay while the case is being heard, the costs the hospitals would owe in salaries to these so-called doctors they've hired and the ongoing expenses they are already incurring should be enough to take them down. With respect to recouping their losses out of the doctors' pockets, it is very unlikely the courts would look favorably on that, since it was the hospitals who initiated the action by trying to replace their current staff."

Broyle's tone turned from anger to guilt for questioning Todd's judgment. "Look, I didn't mean to ..." he said sheepishly.

"No apologies," Todd said. "Let's just hope my suggestions work. Or this war could be over before it really gets started."

. . .

"If I didn't know better, I would have thought you'd come over to our side." Dr. Jerald Todd's comments were laced with a hint of insincerity as he tapped nervously on the windowsill of his office overlooking Washington, DC. "Well," he continued awkwardly, nuzzling the telephone to his ear, "I just wanted to thank you for not criticizing us in front of the media."

The call to Dr. Leonard O'Bannon, the AMA's spokesman on the physician boycott, had been one of the most difficult he had made in a long time. Todd, a onetime AMA supporter, felt a wave of shallowness move over him as he recalled his decision to drop his membership in the prestigious organization over a position the AMA had taken on what turned out to be an inconsequential reimbursement issue. The real reason, which even Todd tried to deny to himself, was money; since the AMA was so big, they would not miss his several hundred in dues dollars, or so Todd rationalized. Now with thousands of his peers breaking ranks and joining other organizations that targeted their own special interests, the onetime voice for the profession was in real danger of being put in mothballs. In a small way, Todd felt responsible and guilty at the same time, especially when the larger organization had not seized upon the opportunity to criticize its upstart rival. Fortunately, the press had not appeared to catch on to the AMA's declining influence in the medical community—still lining up to get its point of view each time a story broke on the health care front. Afraid that his own board of directors would see the move as an act of weakness, Todd decided to make contact secretly in hopes of using the organization's lack of rebuke in the media to his advantage. By not coming out publicly, in a sense, the AMA was giving its implied consent. Hopefully, thought Todd, the call to O'Bannon would keep it that way.

"I wasn't defending you or what your organization is doing. I was speaking for the profession. If we come down against you, it only hurts the doctors. They've already got enough on their plates with no money coming in. I know you probably wouldn't understand how we approach problems around here, since you dropped out several years ago," O'Bannon said, not using the conciliatory tone Todd had hoped for.

Todd started to jump on O'Bannon for his condescending remark but held back, realizing it would only add fuel to their widening differences. He would have to take the bad with the good, if he had any hopes of getting the AMA's continued silence. "A regrettable move on my part," Todd said, trying to dampen O'Bannon's obvious hostility. "There should be plenty of room for both of our organizations. In fact, I've put in a request for another AMA application. I don't see why the physicians in this country can be members of both."

"Because, Dr. Todd," O'Bannon said, "our organization does not believe in putting patients at risk as you and the UMA appearing to be doing."

"You do it every day," Todd said without hesitation. O'Bannon had given him the opening he had been waiting for, and Todd was prepared to pounce on the critical difference that divided the competing organizations.

"How dare you accuse us of—"

Todd cut back in before O'Bannon could continue. One thing he had carried with him from his early days on the boxing team at Syracuse University was once you have your opponent on the ropes, don't let him off. "The AMA isn't alone. Most of the organizations that claim they support the doctors and their patients are doing the same thing each time they let the government put in another useless regulation that takes more time away from patient care.

Or when some bureaucrat, lounging around in a plush office atop a high-rise built with funds that should have gone to health care services, cuts their company's reimbursement so the stockholders will get a higher return on their dollar." Todd paused and took in a deep breath. "Don't you see?" he asked.

"I … I'm not sure it's quite the same," O'Bannon replied, his air of confidence apparently shaken by his meek response.

Todd looked out the large picture window, his eyes straining to put sense into the dotted Washington skyline. "It's exactly the same." This time his answer was slow and deliberate. "Our organization may be putting a few patients at risk now. But by your reluctance to take a stand and continued compromises over the last fifty years, you've been putting those same patients at risk too. The only difference between our respective organizations is when we decide to end our patients' suffering by drawing the line and saying no more—now, as the UMA is trying to do, or in the future. Good day, Dr. O'Bannon. I trust we can count on the AMA's continued support."

26

THE PRESIDENT HUNCHED over his desk, his face almost buried in the stack of papers scattered before him. "Bailey, do you agree with all this?" he asked, looking up to the Senate majority leader seated across from him.

"Unfortunately, Mr. President," Forman answered, his hands projected forward in frustration, "Carlisle's man appears to be correct in his analysis of the situation. I'm just not sure his proposal is the best solution. If we're wrong, our asses could fry."

"You mean my ass, don't you?" the president fired off before turning in the direction of Lane Foster. "Tell me, Lane, why you think such a dramatic step is necessary."

Foster shifted in his chair as all the participants in the Oval Office focused on what Senator Carlisle's aide and chief medical advisor had to say. "The doctors are a greedy bunch, Mr. President. All they care about is padding their pocketbooks, and they don't care where the money comes from—as long as they get it. So, the only way to resolve this situation before our health care system goes to hell in a handbag is to take over—"

"Excuse me, sir," Carlisle interrupted, hoping to cut off his aide before he got in too deep. "Lane is a bit opinionated on the subject. What he meant to say was that a growing number of physicians seem to be putting their own self-interests above that of their patients. But I think the majority of physicians are still dedicated to what is best for their patients."

"I agree with Senator Carlisle," the secretary of Health and Human Services said. "By in large, they probably are committed to their principles, but that's their problem; they don't see the big picture. The reality is there isn't enough money to go around. They feel that because of their years of sacrifice to get to where they are, we owe them. When they don't get the level of income they expect, they rebel—the reason for Foster's point. Many of them get greedy and forget the reasons they went into medicine to begin with. Up to now, they have mostly just bitched and moaned. But this boycott, well, I can tell you it's thrown my department into a panic."

Pushing back from his desk, the president slowly stood up. "Although we seem to have some difference in opinion as to why the problem exists, my concern is what do we do. Just because doctors are some of the most respected members of our community, we can't just kneel down and give them everything they want. Next, it'll be the schoolteachers and the policemen." He looked back over at the secretary of HHS. "How serious is this threat?"

"It's hard to get exact numbers," the secretary answered as he fumbled through his papers. "Somewhere between 35 and 38 percent of the doctors are currently participating, from what we can tell. What's even more alarming, the numbers keep going up about 10 percent per week. At around 50 percent, they will have paralyzed our system, unless we acquiesce or whatever is decided here today."

The president's expression turned sour. "Can't we negotiate with them? See if we can find some common ground."

"There's no one to really talk to," Carlisle said, concluding that after chairing the hearings, he was as qualified as anyone in the room to answer the president's question. "We're the ones who slapped the Federal Trade Commission guidelines about collective bargaining on them. If we can't prove there is a collective action on their part, they've got the law on their side."

"What about their American Medical Organization?" the president asked.

"You mean Association," Carlisle answered, deciding it was time the president learned more about the profession that might well define his administration when the historians decided to write the final chapter. "The AMA is a volunteer organization, which means it has very little control over the actions of its members. They can lay out standards, but as far as putting any teeth behind what they say, forget it. There are also the national specialty societies. In some ways, they have more influence since they control the board certification process, but that predominantly affects new doctors or recertification." The senator paused and scanned the occupants in the room. "Let me tell you, if any of these organizations tried to restrict a physician's credentials for political reasons, they would have a lawsuit slapped on them so fast you couldn't begin to count the money they would be paying out."

"So, you're telling me there are over a half a million doctors out there," the president said, flopping down on the sofa. "And there's no one we can talk to. Hell, the lawyers wouldn't get away with anything like this. The Bar would be all over them if they tried to pull off any sort of shenanigans like this."

"That's a whole different problem, Mr. President. Let's just say we take care of our own since the majority of legislators are attorneys and leave it at that." Carlisle turned around in his chair, his head in an awkward position. Thoughts of the Unified Medical Association and the key role they might be playing behind the scene in the boycott crossed his mind. But the senator decided to remain silent, since the UMA was in a similar situation as the other medical organizations; by their own doing, Congress had made it illegal for any organization to collectively speak for the doctors of this country. "To be exact, Mr. President, the number is around nine hundred thousand, and that's not counting the chiropractors, podiatrists, and midlevel practitioners, most of which participate in our programs. If the physicians are successful, it's only a matter of time until the rest come over to their side."

A hush fell across the room as all the participants pondered their next move. First, it was the president. Then all heads turned in the direction of Lane Foster, waiting for him to further explain his proposal.

"In 1946, when he felt there was a threat to our national security, Truman authorized a federal takeover of the nation's coal mines and then ordered the workers who were on strike back to work," Foster said, scanning the papers on the Truman presidency he had brought with him to the meeting. "Later, during that same year, he petitioned Congress for permission to draft the railroad workers who were then on strike into the military so that he could force them to get the trains moving once again." Foster laid the file down and picked up another labeled Reagan and the PATCO. "We were all around when President Reagan had a falling-out with the air traffic controllers. He didn't mess around trying to draft them or use a federal order to get them back to work. He just fired the whole lot."

The president blinked at Foster's historical insights relating to prior events where one sector or another was at odds with the leadership in Washington. "You're not suggesting …" the president said, encouraging Carlisle's aide to continue.

"Oh no, sir. We can't fire them. There's no one else to take their place," Foster said, a broad smile breaking out across his lips. "But if you feel their growing refusal to participate in programs that serve to protect the good voters in this country, who are less fortunate, poses a threat to our national security, then you sure as hell can conscript them."

. . .

Jordan Springer winced, letting the English muffin he had just retrieved drop to the countertop as the sharp pain bubbled up through his chest. His cardiologist had given him the green light, but his recent brush with catastrophe was never far from his mind. Every passing ache and pain was analyzed for its significance—a constant reminder of what might have been and could, without warning, reach out and slap him down again. Besides being frightened, the whole ordeal was humbling for Springer, because for the first time, he faced the precarious balance everyone walks throughout whatever lives they are allowed to enjoy. A small belch eased out through his lips, and just as suddenly as it began, the pain in Springer's chest was gone. He cracked a smile, remembering the plate of spicy enchiladas he had put down the night before, then retrieved the muffin and headed for the cashier. The sweat that had moments before begun to rim his collar evaporated without a trace.

Springer slipped the change into his pocket, then lifted up his tray and looked around the hospital cafeteria. As usual, the landscape had taken on a subdued look with the only remnants being the nightshift personnel trying to cram in one last bit of solitude before heading back to their assigned positions somewhere throughout the now darkened medical complex. It was a far cry from the usual hustle and bustle of just hours before.

Springer tightened as his eye caught the sight of a familiar figured huddled over a tray in the far corner. Springer's immediate response was to ignore the chance sighting, but unfortunately, it was too late. Dr. Larry Benson, Gene Broyle's replacement, signaled for Springer to join him—the last thing Springer wanted to do after their previous encounter concerning Allison Terrell's deceased mother. Begrudgingly, Springer moved over to Benson's table, sliding into the chair across from the overconfident young doctor.

"Working late?" Benson questioned, apparently searching for the right words to open the conversation.

Miffed he had not been able to muster the fortitude to reject Benson's offer, Springer put down a gulp of his Diet Coke. "Do this four nights a week," he answered, his tone indifferent. "The other week, I've got the day shift."

"Look, I'm sorry about Dorothy Peoples," Benson went on. "I've gone over her case a thousand times about what I should have done differently. We all get calls by patients who think they need to be seen immediately that we can't fit into our schedule."

"Don't you mean *won't*?" Springer picked up the English muffin and bit out a chunk. "In some ways, you're playing God, deciding which patients you're going to see and when you're going to see them." His gaze never broke from the young physician.

Benson nodded sheepishly. The nauseating air of superiority that had almost choked Springer on their previous encounter evaporated along with the overpowering odor of men's cologne. Only the rancid smell of stale cigarette smoke remained. "In that respect, you're luckier than I am. Being in intensive care, you don't have to make that choice—just who you're going to see first, depending which one is the sickest. At the end of your shift, you turn your patients over to somebody else. In what I do or, maybe I should say *used to do*, we can't just walk away, because those same problems are still there waiting when we return."

Springer recoiled, not sure if he had just been insulted or given a lesson in the wide disparity of responsibilities by those who cared for the sick. Deciding he was in no mood to open their encounter into a more confrontational situation, he opted for the latter. "I guess it all goes back to why we initially chose our particular specialty," Springer answered in an uneasy tone, noticing for the first time the various array of stains on Benson's wrinkled shirt. "What did you mean by you used to do?"

"The irony is I'm not even participating in the boycott, and my practice is still off 80 percent," Benson said, picking up the crumbs scattered across his empty plate and popping them nervously into his mouth. "Had to lay off my receptionist last week and move Mandy up front. If things don't turn around, she'll have to go too."

What started out as a feeling of aversion for the brash young doctor now turned into an awkward type of pity. "Look, I wish I could ..." Springer mumbled, taken back by Benson's unfortunate turn of events. "They tell me we should begin to see the money from our paper claims in about forty-five days, if we can hold out. In the meantime, can't your patients just pay?"

Benson shook his head. "Broyle's practice was almost 70 percent Medicare, and most of them live month to month. Rather than pay me up front, they appear to be turning to you for their urgent needs through the ER. The routine stuff they're just putting off until the feds work this mess out."

Springer thought back about his own busy workload, some of who could have been Benson's former patients. "What about a loan to tide you over?" Springer asked, his mind drifting to Mandy Jefferson, his favorite nurse who had worked for Broyle before Benson took over the practice.

"I'm maxed out. What with the loans I still owe from my training and buying your friend's practice, the banks say I've reached my limit."

Springer sat back in his chair. The hunger that had seemed so important just moments before faded as the reality of the ominous situation facing the medical profession fell on him like a sack of unformed concrete. Without uttering a word, he slid the uneaten portion of his English muffin over in front of Benson. He got up, leaving the cafeteria behind but not the concern for the tragic situation that was unfolding all around him. If he wasn't already, it would not be long until Springer and every other physician in the country was swept up in the turmoil. He could only pray that when the fog of uncertainty lifted, the price extracted in terms of the lives of patients and their doctors would be worth the sacrifice. A wave of nausea forced a portion of the undigested muffin back up in his throat. He swallowed hard and swung open the door into the cool night air.

...

"You can't just let him go," John Terrell said. "He has a wife and his daughter with the spina bifida. Where are they going to find insurance until he gets on somewhere else?" He held back with what he really wanted to say about the hospital's decision to lay off his associate, Raymon Zamora, at the end of the month.

Britt Barkley straightened his jacket, his eyes darting around the darkened reading room nestled in the back of the Radiology Department. "Look, John, it's a difficult decision all around, but with the downturn in our census, we just can't afford to keep the staff at the level it was before the boycott," Barkley said, sounding as if he was talking about dropping a product line instead of a decision that uprooted someone's life. "He had the least seniority on the staff. I guess I don't need to remind you who is just above him."

Terrell's jaw clenched at the realization that if Barkley was forced to let anybody else go in his department, it would be him. Suddenly, Terrell realized Barkley's argument for letting Zamora go didn't add up. "He collects from the payers and the patients for what he does. The hospital only sends out the bills for him and charges a healthy commission for what they do, I might add," Terrell continued, recalling his own arrangement with Methodist. "So, unless his contract reads differently from the rest of us, I'm not sure I understand the problem." Terrell's face twisted in a look of confusion.

Barkley shuffled uneasily, scraping his foot across the floor. "Let's just say we couldn't reach an agreement that was satisfactory to both of us." The administrator took an awkward step in Terrell's direction. "Zamora just didn't understand what it took to get along around here, with the decreased hospital census and everything," Barkley said, just above a whisper. "Look, Dr. Terrell, the hospital has made a pact to go along with the doctors because, in the long run, what helps you helps me."

"I'm sure you're trying to tell me something, or you wouldn't have come all the way over here just to let me know you're letting

Zamora go," Terrell said, swinging around in the chair so he could face the administrator directly. "But so far, I'm not getting it."

Barkley's hands became animated, flinging back and forth in the subdued lighting. "Our occupancy rate is off almost 50 percent," he said. "We can cut back on some services, such as food costs, spread the nursing staff out further, and temporarily shut down one of the floors, but it looks like that's not going to be enough. We're going to need more money coming in from somewhere. Otherwise, the board of directors has advised me we may have to shut the whole place down."

Terrell's eyes grew wide. "Can't you just dip into the hospital's reserves until the paper claims start coming through?"

"We used up most of them over the last several years with the increasing reimbursement cuts. In case you haven't noticed, the business of running hospitals hasn't been very profitable as of late. That's the reason the hospitals in the Dallas area have gone along with the boycott. We just can't keep giving the level of care that is expected for the amount we're being paid. It's Economics 101; when there's more going out than coming in, it's impossible to keep our doors open for long." Barkley stopped gesturing, his hands hanging limply at his side. "John, we're not asking for much. Just an extra test here and there would make a big difference."

Terrell felt the blood drain from his face as he fought to remain composed. "You're asking me to do what?"

"It's no skin off your nose, as they say. It's the payers who are going to get stuck with the extra costs." Barkley's level of assurance appeared to climb once the subject had been broached. "Everyone in pathology and the rest of your cronies in radiology agreed to go along, even the ER docs I've talked to so far. For some reason, Zamora just didn't get it—something about loyalty to his principles. We'll see how far that loyalty gets him when it comes time to pay the bills."

Everything inside John Terrell wanted to scream, "No!" But he couldn't find it in himself to tell Barkley to go take a flying leap into hell. *What a contradiction*, he thought. Here Terrell was willing to lay it all on the line so that he could make his own decisions—to once again become part of a profession whose participants only did what was in the best interest of those they served. Now he was being asked to betray one of the basic tenets of that profession—honesty. He felt like he was borrowing from the devil to try to buy his way into heaven. By Terrell's continuing silence, it could be interpreted he would go along.

And that was exactly the way Barkley took it. "All you have to do is when you see an x-ray and there's any doubt, just order another series of films. A few of those on everyone's part, and we shouldn't have trouble staying in the black." The confident administrator turned to go but then stopped, looking back at Terrell. "Except for Jordan Springer, you were the last one on my list. I hope he turns out to be as understanding as you."

Terrell hung his head as Barkley disappeared down the hall. The acrid taste of his own cowardice swirled around his mouth like the stench of his early-morning breath after a night on the town. It wasn't as bad as he imagined, getting in bed with the devil—as long as he didn't have to look at himself in the mirror.

. . .

"You must be sick," Allison said, watching John Terrell pick at the pork roast and potatoes she had fixed him for dinner. "Normally, you'd have been going back for seconds by now. I know I'm not as good a cook as your mother, but ..."

Terrell cut her a weak smile as he twirled the fork on his plate. "It's not you," he said, hoping to spare his wife from the frustration he was facing after his encounter with the hospital administrator. "I've just lost my appetite."

"When did we start keeping secrets from each other?" Allison bent her head down, then looked up to catch his gaze.

"Brit Barkley paid me a visit this afternoon." Terrell looked away as he spoke, ashamed at what he was about to confide in his wife. "Wants me to order unnecessary tests on some of the patients I see in order for the hospital to stay out of the red. He claims it would only be until the electronic transfer and boycott problems are resolved."

Allison grimaced as she pushed away from the table. "You told him to shove it, didn't you?"

Terrell remained silent, just as he had done with Barkley. His head dropped to his chest—a pitiful profile of his former self.

"I take that to mean you didn't tell him no."

"I didn't tell him yes either," Terrell said, his response weak. "I didn't say anything. He just assumed. Look, Allison, I'm not in a position to buck the system. With the downturn in patient load, no one in the area is hiring, from what I can determine. And besides, my income is off too. So, the extra money coming in won't hurt us either."

"Are you saying that to convince me that what you're doing is justified under the conditions, or are you just trying to appease your own conscience?" Allison's question was laced with disgust. "What about the other doctors? Are they going to go along like you?"

Her husband shook his head. "I'm not sure. Barkley said he still had to talk to Jordan Springer, but according to him, everyone had agreed except that new radiologist from the Valley. He kept saying the guy wouldn't violate his principles. Made it sound like a dirty word."

"John, in the end, what we stand for is all we've got." Allison got up, picking up her husband's half-eaten plate of food. "What happened when he told Barkley no?"

"He was told to find another job by the end of the month."

"Couldn't he take Barkley to court and create a real stink for the hospital?"

Terrell grabbed the other dishes and headed to the sink

to help Allison. "I guess so, but he's got that sick child. He's probably just worried about getting on somewhere else, so he has benefits in case anything happens to her. Besides, with all that's happening, his case wouldn't get on a court docket for at least six months." Terrell gently nudged Allison to the side and began rinsing the dishes in the sink before popping them in the dishwasher, thinking it was the least he could do to try to get back in Allison's good graces. "I really feel sorry for the guy," he said, feeling more confident now that he had diverted the conversation away from his own response to the administrator. "He's given up everything for his principles."

Allison shut off the water and turned to Terrell. The look of disappointment on her face said it all. "John, he hasn't given up everything. He still has his self-respect."

. . .

"What did you tell him?" John Terrell pushed his friend for a response, closing the door to Jordan Springer's small office in the back of the ICU so their conversation wouldn't be overheard.

Springer's usual confidence was missing as he appeared to be searching for the right response. "I told him I'd think about it." Springer's voice was almost apologetic. "The bastard is asking us to sell our souls for a few measly bucks."

"According to Barkley, those few measly bucks, as you say, are the difference between you and I having a place to work or sitting at home waiting for some high-priced headhunter to give us a call about an offer to work the night shift in Hico, Texas."

"I'd lay odds Barkley is exaggerating just to cover his own ass," Springer continued. "But in the end, it really doesn't matter. If we don't play along, we'll be joining Zamora in the unemployment line. Those of us who are hospital-based physicians may direct bill for our services, but the reality is we work for the hospital. What the board of directors says is what you and I do, or come time to renew our contracts, we won't be around."

Terrell glanced at his watch, knowing the longer he was away from the Radiology Department, the higher the stack of unread films when he got back. "Although some of the extra costs will filter down to the patients, the irony is that Barkley is primarily asking us to put the screws to the third-party payers—the ones who started the problems in the first place, and for whatever reasons, we feel guilty," he said with a half smile.

"It all goes back to price, John," Springer said as he reached for the door and his return to the hectic pace of the ICU. "When we didn't stand up to him, he determined—right then and there—we had a price."

Terrell raised his hands in confusion. "I'm not sure …"

"A whore is a whore," Springer answered, his tone upbeat. "The only real difference between them is what they charge."

27

SAVE ONE, THE straw poll vote had been unanimous. Even though the sweeping proposal had come from one of his own staff, Senator Rayborn Carlisle could not bring himself to throw his full support behind a federal takeover of the health care delivery system. In his travels as the resident health care expert in the Senate, he had witnessed firsthand what happened when the doctors and other providers of health care services became employees of the government rather than independent practitioners. Carlisle did not want the same for this country, but with the growing crisis, he was in the minority. By last count, the number of physicians who were no longer willing to work directly with the government's payment programs and the other third-party payers had crossed the critical 50 percent barrier. From an operational perspective, the health care delivery system as it had functioned for the last forty-plus years had come to a screeching halt. Either the government buckled under—authorizing those who were responsible for payments of health care services to reimburse the patients directly—or initiated federal action until a long-term solution could be worked out. From the results of the vote, it was obvious the elite group of individuals gathered around the conference table in the West Wing of the White House had chosen the latter option.

"We're not going to be able to keep this quiet for long," the secretary of HHS said, the fatigue from the long hours of debate showing in the furrowed lines of his face. "The doctors are going to put the fear of God into their patients—claiming we have thrown the health care system back into the Dark Ages. It's a good thing the next election cycle isn't for a year and a half. With the money that will be poured into a media campaign by the medical organizations, the drug companies, and the insurance carriers, none of us seated around this table would see the inside of the Washington Corridor again. Even then that might be too soon."

Carlisle scanned the small room of leaders from the House of Representatives, the Senate, the Department of Health and Human Services and the executive branch. His eyes fell on the president, who had acted more as an observer than a participant in the debate that had gone on for just under five hours. Lane Foster had done a beautiful job of laying out the grim facts surrounding the rapidly escalating crisis that could well be the defining issue confronting the current administration. In his own way, without distorting the facts, Carlisle's aide had been able to paint the president into a corner. Anything less than intervention on the part of the commander in chief to defend the public's well-being would be seen as capitulation—in time, probably leading to similar confrontational situations by other sectors of society if and when they became disgruntled. According to Foster, who today sounded more eloquent than any plaintiff's attorney Carlisle had witnessed in a long time, this could be the president's shining hour—or darkest, thought Carlisle, watching the president as he appeared to struggle with the agonizing decision that he alone had to make.

"If you sign the executive order, Mr. President," Bailey Forman said, looking across the conference table to his counterpart from the other side of the aisle in the Senate, "you can count on us to ratify your position. We're going to miss those contributions to our campaign funds from the medical organizations and the pharmaceutical conglomerates come the next election, but it appears they have put us in an untenable position."

The president looked over at the Speaker of the House, who nodded his approval. Then he moved to the minority leader of the House, receiving a similar sign of reassurance.

"It's decided then." The president nervously straightened his tie. He then turned to his secretary of HHS. "Can your people handle the load?"

"Our systems have all been debugged and should be back online by the end of the week," the secretary answered. "We can handle our programs but not everyone else's."

Lane Foster motioned for the president's attention. "Sir, wouldn't it also be possible to federalize the private insurance carriers so that they can do the work for you."

"Shit!" the president blurted out as his closed fist struck the conference table, causing all the participants in the room to jerk back in surprise. "Before long, we're going to put the whole damn country under our wing. My conservative supporters back home are going to piss all over themselves."

It was obvious the stress of the situation was getting to the president, so Senator Carlisle decided it was time for him to join the debate. "Let me offer a compromise to Foster's suggestion," he interrupted, hoping to introduce some of his own thoughts. "If you move forward, Mr. President, there are two prerequisites as I see it. First, whatever action you take must be done quickly. As the situation stands now, the health care delivery system is on the verge of total collapse. With the increasing number of doctors and the hospitals not accepting payments from third-party payers and the funding agencies not willing to send the reimbursements to their subscribers, the patients are caught in the middle. They are afraid to seek help for their medical problems out of fear they will be responsible for their medical expenses, while at the same time still continuing to pay for coverage they can't use and often afford. Second, in order to minimize disruption and hopefully avoid panic, we need to incorporate as much of the present system into the plan as possible."

A look of relief spread across the president's face as he leaned forward on the conference table. "And just how do you propose we do that, Ray?"

"I wouldn't federalize the insurers," Carlisle answered, pleased that he now had the group's attention. "Instead, turn all of them into our intermediaries, subcontractors so to speak, for the part of their operation that deals with health care coverage. They would still offer insurance and collect the premiums on the lives they cover. But when it comes time to make the payments, we'll be the ones to cut the checks out of the revenues they have collected, minus an appropriate administrative fee to cover their normal operational expenses. That way, we can still set the reimbursement levels and make the decisions about which services will be covered. The government will be the repository, managing these intermediaries throughout the country. It's just like we do with the Medicare, Medicaid, and the UHPCA programs now. The difference is all the physicians and hospitals will have to be involved if they want to get paid. Because we will be the only game in town."

The vice Speaker of the House leaned toward Carlisle. "What if the insurance companies don't want to put that part of their operation under Uncle Sam's control?"

"I think our friends in the state houses can be of help there," Carlisle answered. "Even though the majority of insurers have operations throughout most of the country, they must obtain a license in each state where they do business. In turn, for the state bureaucracies to continue to operate, they must draw down on federal funds for many of their essential programs. We would just put a stipulation on those monies, tying the two together. You license only those insurance companies that agree to do business with us, and Big Brother in Washington will continue to take care of you. We've done it plenty of times before, such as setting the speed limit on the interstates if the state wanted to continue to get funding for their federal highway system. And the private insurers, they also need that license to conduct any business in the state. That means life, auto, and all the others. So, I think it's unlikely they wouldn't agree to go along."

The president's expression grew long once again as he fumbled with the briefing papers spread out before him. "What about the doctors and the hospitals under your proposal?"

"The hospitals are strapped for cash with their high operating expenses and lowered profit margins in recent years. But as long as they can hold on, they will tend to go along with their doctors," he answered without delay. "Because that's where their patients come from …" Carlisle's voice trailed off as the room full of Washington's leadership waited for him to continue.

"And the *doctors*, Ray," the president said. "What if the doctors won't go along?"

. . .

Jordan Springer's jaw dropped when his car rounded the corner, just down the street from Methodist. Not twenty yards ahead was the familiar face of one of his former colleagues at the hospital, jogging down the pavement. Initially, Springer started to honk, but then he held back after remembering the circumstances under which Dr. Ronny Leopold retired from practice. Without a word of warning, the busy sixty-year-old rheumatologist abruptly sold his practice, claiming he was unable to continue because of persistent neurological problems. No one but his private physician, an orthopedic surgeon of marginal reputation named Luther Curtis, knew his real diagnosis. It was rumored Leopold was suffering from an increasingly debilitating case of spinal- stenosis—a frustrating and painful condition caused by a progressive deterioration of the lower spinal column. As Springer recalled, Leopold was awarded 100 percent disability by his insurance carrier, which, according to one distant source in the department, he accepted begrudgingly.

Springer marveled at Leopold's agility as his apparently effortless strides showed no signs of the debilitating disease that just months before had caused him to give up his lucrative practice. Just as he was about to pull up even with his former colleague, Springer turned off, deciding he should find out more in case their paths crossed again. Besides, he had promised to have lunch with John Terrell before he was scheduled to go on at two o'clock.

"I'm telling you it was him," Springer said, reaching for the ketchup to put over his warmed-over French fries. "Running down the road like he didn't have a care in the world."

Terrell just shook his head. "I knew it didn't add up when I reviewed his films."

Now, Springer's interest was piqued even further. "Are you telling me you were the one who made the diagnosis on him?"

"Not exactly," Terrell answered, eyeing Springer's potatoes. "One of the technicians brought me Leopold's films to see if the quality was good enough or whether she should shoot some more before letting him go. They looked fine to me. So, I asked the technician to put the films on my pile and said I would look at them more carefully later. That was the last I saw of them."

Springer picked up on his friend's hungry eyes. "Here—take one," he said, shoving the plate across the table. "You mean the films are gone?"

"According to the ledger, Curtis came in almost immediately and checked the x-rays out before I had a chance to get back to them," Terrell said, popping one of the smaller fries in his mouth. "It's against department policy to take films out of the area until there is a final read by one of the radiologists, but according to the technician, he was persistent to the point of almost being rude. So, she gave in when he promised to bring them back the next day. That was two months ago, and we haven't seen them yet."

By now, Springer had forgotten all about his French fries as he pushed the young radiologist for more information. "Didn't you tell somebody about Curtis not returning the films?"

"My chief. He told me that since Curtis brings in so many patients to the hospital, I should just let it go."

"And that's what you did?" Springer's question was tinted with suspicion.

"I know it was only a quick look, but the films I saw on Curtis were normal." Terrell pushed the plate of partially eaten food back over to the other side the table. "Jordan, I tried to increase the limits on my disability insurance a couple of months ago, and they turned me down. Told me that since more and more doctors are using it as a way to retire early, they couldn't afford to go any higher. According to the representative, the company is thinking about not writing any more new business on doctors—said we have gone from being the best risk group in the industry to the worst."

"Are you saying ..."

Terrell looked up at Springer as a sad look spread across his face. "I went back and pulled up Curtis's last two hundred patients that came through our department. The x-rays were missing on six of them—all checked out under the heading admitting physician. What's even more troubling, the patients were all physicians, and they were all x-rays of their spines."

"Couldn't Curtis just have just been doing them a favor by looking at the films himself?" Springer questioned. "The personal touch, so to speak."

"You might say that and more." Terrell seemed uncomfortable. "I followed up on each of Curtis's doctor patients, and five have recently retired from practice on disability."

"And the sixth?"

"He's scheduled to turn over his practice to a younger associate next week because of chronic back problems," Terrell continued.

"That is, after he returns from the British Virgin Islands where he is participating in a sailing regatta."

. . .

Just then, the door to the conference room swung open as a tall man of Asian descent in a three-piece suit slipped in silently. He quickly moved over, grabbing an unoccupied seat in the far corner. The president looked up and, from what Carlisle could tell, gave a weak signal to the new attendee.

"I don't believe it's necessary to introduce Attorney General Stokley," the president said, looking around the crowded room. "I have asked that he be here today because Stokley and his team over at the Department of Justice will be responsible for enforcement of any plan we decide to enact."

The group collectively turned in the attorney general's direction. The discomfort of being the center of attention was obvious in his expression as he moved uneasily in his chair.

"Stokley," the president continued, "would you mind going over with the group what our options are with respect to dealing with the doctors?"

The attorney general cleared his throat. "Currently, they are considered independent contractors, even the ones who are employed by hospitals or HMOs, because they work for companies who, by law, must also operate independently. So, any collective action on the part of the government will take an act of Congress or a presidential order to federalize them."

Lane Foster said, "Isn't what they're doing a threat to national security?"

Stokley looked over at Carlisle's aide. "The doctors would probably contest those charges in the federal courts since they have not refused to give care, only file for reimbursement from the third-party carriers—claiming their old contacts null and void, and any new agreement only between themselves and their patients. In the end, they would probably win, but by the time the argument is decided after the case works its way up to the Supreme Court, most of them will have been forced to comply with whatever the administration proposes. After all, doctors have to eat too."

The president still looked confused by the direction of his attorney general's presentation. "Stokley, do we federalize them or not?"

"That's your call, Mr. President," Stokley answered, appearing to not want to shoulder all the responsibility. "If you don't conscript them under a federalized system, it is much more likely that if the Supreme Court finds in their favor, Uncle Sam could be paying out damages to the doctors and their families long after you and I are gone. On the other hand, if you do draft them and put them under the department of HHS in the name of national security, then for those physicians who fail to comply, we can use a system akin to the military tribunal rather than the normal courts. It's not exactly the same circumstances, but this country has drafted doctors into military service until after we were run out of Vietnam. How that option would play out with the Supreme Court is anyone's guess. Except in the past, the justices tend to be more sympathetic when Congress and the administration are on the same side of an issue."

"And I suppose that if you treat them like POWs," Carlisle interjected, no longer able to hold back his frustrations, "they're going to continue to bust their butts taking care of you day or night, whether they're sick or tired, 365 days a year. Well, think on." Disgust oozed from his voice.

Stokley shuddered at the senator's caustic comments. "I didn't mean to infer they were …"

"I know what you meant, Mr. Stokley," Carlisle answered, his voice sounding slightly more sympathetic than a few moments ago. "We are all under a great deal of stress right now. A much less disruptive alternative would be to link the doctors' state licensure to their participation in our program. Once again, we would use our influence through the allocation of federal funds to let the states do our dirty work for us. The states could give the doctors sixty days to sign up; after that, those who failed to comply would have their medical licenses invalidated. That way, we wouldn't have to assume the responsibilities that come with making them federal employees or draftees, such as retirement programs and health care benefits. They could still remain as independent contractors and charge for non-covered services—something we here in Washington could not afford to take on—as well as those patients who had not obtained coverage through our program."

"Damn, I think these doctors have got you buffaloed, Senator," the secretary of HHS said, his egotistical pessimism apparent. "What do you think they're going to do—go on strike and let their patients die if we push them too far? Not in a million years."

Carlisle strained in the direction of the secretary. The breakfast meeting at the Morrison-Clark Inn with the leadership of the Unified Medical Association flashed before his eyes. The senator blinked at the image of Dr. Jerald Todd wielding one of the restaurant's knives as he drew a deep line in the tablecloth—the line, the impassioned doctor vowed, he would never let his doctors be dragged across. "Let me give you one piece of advice, Mr. Secretary." Carlisle's message was barely above a whisper. "If you persist in your hard-line approach to their concerns, just don't get sick."

28

Two Weeks Later

THE REGISTERED LETTER from the Texas State Board of Medical Examiners had arrived earlier that morning, along with the rest of John Terrell's correspondence. The receptionist at the front desk of the Radiology Department had signed for it, along with similar letters to the other doctors in the department, before dumping the envelopes onto each physician's pile. Terrell had been so backed up reviewing the films left over from the busy weekend that going through the stack of usual drug company brochures and various other solicitations was not high on his priority list—until Jordan Springer's urgent call was patched through to him in the reading room.

"I can't believe the feds think they can make this stick," Springer said, his voice laced with anger. "Those son-of-bitch liberals have wanted to socialize medicine since before the Medicare program was pushed down our throats in the 1960s. If this doesn't nail the lid on the coffin, I don't know what else would."

Terrell fumbled through the pile, finally identifying the official correspondence to which his friend was referring. He felt his chest tighten as he tore open the envelope. "What the hell?" He tried to make sense of the curtly worded text on the page before him:

> … failure to comply within sixty days of the above date will result in the revocation of your license to practice medicine in the state of Texas.

"The people at the county medical society finally got through to the AMA, and according to them, the same thing is happening all over the country," Springer said. "You'd think with all the money we pay to these organizations, someone somewhere would have given us a heads-up on this so we could have gotten an injunction to stop it, at least until we had our day in court."

The only thing John Terrell could think about was getting in touch with Gene Broyle or even Jerald Todd at the Unified Medical Association to get their read on the situation. "So, what this means …" Terrell fumbled for his words as his mind reeled out of control. "If we don't sign on to be part of the UHPCA program and start accepting their payments directly, we'll be out of Medicare and Medicaid too."

"Read the small print, John. The feds have taken over all the health insurance programs. In an ingenious way, they have instituted a single-payer system with this move. The way it stands, any patient who has health insurance, either through a government plan or with a private carrier, is covered by this federal statute. To ensure we comply, my guess is they put a stranglehold on federal funding to the states. We either sign up or lose our license."

Terrell threw the letter against one of the viewing boxes and watched it fall to the counter below. "They even washed their hands of the discipline problems too, since practicing medicine with an expired license is a violation of state law."

"And they say those guys in Washington don't know what they're doing," Terrell said. "That's what happens when you give a bunch of lawyers too much power and too little money. They're going to take from the haves and give to the have-nots—after they've taken out a percentage for themselves."

Hearing a clatter behind him, John Terrell spun around in his chair to see a familiar face heading his way. "Jordan, I've got to go. It looks like another of our compatriots got his letter too. I'll try to call Broyle and get back to you at lunch. See if you can find out any more from our legal staffs in Austin and Chicago," he said, then rested the receiver back in its cradle.

Apparently unaware John Terrell had been in the midst of a telephone conversation, Ramon Zamora, whose time was almost up at Methodist, burst into the darkened reading room. "First, I get fired for not going along, and now this," he interrupted, his personal communication from the state board of medical examiners tightly clenched in his outstretched fist. "You know, John, if my daughter or son asked me if they should go into medicine, I think you know what I would tell them."

. . .

"I'm afraid he'll have to call you back," the receptionist at the Unified Medical Association headquarters said. "We've been snowed under with all the … wait … Dr. Broyle just got off the line. Let me put you through."

"John, I'm sorry, but we were blindsided," Gene Broyle said, sounding fatigued. "We didn't get a hint that this thing was being considered, even by our fellow physicians in Congress. I guess the old adage about forgetting where you came from once you get to Washington is true. According to our source, the edict came down as a presidential executive order, based on what the leadership in Washington sees as the boycott's growing threat to national security. Then night before last, in a top secret conference call, both sides of Congress ratified the president's proposal, making any question as to whether it was valid to equate national security with health and well-being null and void."

John Terrell felt a wave of hopelessness sweep over him. "Can't you guys get a restraining order to delay implementation until we can try to work through a compromise?"

"Don't forget, John, the UMA doesn't have an in-house legal staff. Besides, all the medical societies are volunteer. There are legal questions as to how far they can go when negotiating on behalf of the whole medical profession, many who are not even members of these organizations," Broyle explained. "The AMA, many of the state organizations, and most of the national specialty societies do have attorneys who work for their organizations or are kept on retainer. Todd has been on the telephone all morning trying to put some of them together to seek an injunction, but they've been resistant so far."

"Why in the hell wouldn't they want to do something?" Terrell questioned, moving the telephone to the other ear as he picked up his communication from the state board.

Terrell heard the rustling of papers through the receiver as he waited for Broyle's response. "Two reasons. First, the other organizations don't see this as their fight, although, like the AMA, their silence in the boycott has been taken by the media as implied support. As you know, that's not necessarily the case. Now that we're in trouble, they're not eager to get dragged down with us. It's the *I told you so* attitude."

Terrell was growing more resentful by the minute. "What's the other reason?"

"We really don't have an organization that can speak for the whole profession. In theory, the AMA is supposed to be the spokesman for all the doctors in the country. But with only a 20 percent penetration of the eligible physician market, they can no longer function in that role," Broyle said, his tone turning contemplative. "The problem is that organization has been run the same way for now close to one hundred years—its governance structure created when most doctors were white males in general practice. Today, that's all changed, but not the old guard of the

AMA, only applying patchwork remedies instead of undergoing a major restructuring to bring it in line with the way the physician population is currently aligned. Consequently, their membership percentages have plummeted, and instead of coming together under a properly constituted umbrella organization, the different medical organizations, including the AMA, that speak for physician interests are in competition with one another for members and dues dollars."

Terrell detected a note of cynicism in Broyle he had not heard before. "Don't you think you're being a little hard on them? After all, the people who run these organizations are just docs like you and me, giving of their time for what they believe in," he said, feeling a little guilty that he and Broyle were criticizing the very organizations that had allowed them the freedom to practice in the best health care delivery system in the history of humankind.

"You're right, John," Broyle answered, the stress of his responsibilities showing through. "I just get pissed when it's time to stand up and be counted while the organizations that are supposed to be representing us are fighting among themselves as the profession is about to go down the toilet. Then on top of that, I look around and see the same guys giving their time, over and over again, to fight the problems that face the profession, while the majority just sit back doing their own thing. I know it's not just with doctors. Hell, there's public apathy about getting involved that has affected all sectors of our society from the churches to the Boy Scouts. They're all in trouble when it comes to volunteerism. By in large, we're still willing to support these causes with our paychecks, but if it takes time away from what we want to do, forget it."

"Sounds like you need a vacation," Terrell said, trying to lend a little unsolicited support.

"Write me a prescription, John, and I'll hop on the first plane heading south. When I get there, I'll bury my face in a good book and let the waves lap at my toes while I sip on a double piña colada."

Broyle let out a slow sigh. "Maybe, when I get back, this nightmare will be over."

The frustration swimming around in Terrell's chest showed no signs of abating with Broyle's continuing pessimism. "You know, there're a lot of doctors who have put their careers on the line because of the UMA. We came on board because Todd made us believe that if we made sacrifices now, this profession did not have to be enslaved by the bureaucrats on Capitol Hill and the corporate pencil pushers of the giant insurance companies." Terrell crumpled the letter from the state board in his tightened fist. "It's like the story of the Pied Piper when it comes to trust and commitment," Terrell said, a tinge of sadness in his voice. "Maybe we just lined up to follow the wrong person."

"That vacation you were going to prescribe for me?" Broyle said, clearing a catch in his throat. "Looks like I'm going to have to take it later."

. . .

The nondescript meeting room just off the long corridor of the O'Hare Hilton was selected because of its central location as well as its relative anonymity. Chicago's International Airport was a stopover for virtually every flight that crisscrossed the northern half of the country. It was also a business mecca. And the hotel—not luxurious by any stretch of the imagination—was the pride of the Hilton chain because the row of small conference rooms on the second floor that stretched from one end of the structure to the other was where much of that business was conducted. One could literally fly halfway across the country, attend a meeting that changed the course of the future, and be home in time for cocktails—all without taking one breath of fresh air while being gone.

Dr. Jerald Todd eased to the side of the crowded hall, then

stopped, reading the three-by-five-inch card affixed to the front of the door. He moved on until he reached the one where the card read Task Force on Health Care Facilities. Taking in a deep breath, he tossed his coat over his shoulder and pushed open the door.

"Well, we finally get a chance to meet face-to-face," Dr. Leonard O'Bannon said, getting up from his chair and extending his hand in greeting. "We were just getting an update on the situation from RJ Talkington."

Todd scanned the room, quickly realizing he was the last one to make an entrance. "I'm sorry I'm late, but you know how airport security is, especially in and out of Washington." He then moved around the table to meet everyone in attendance, sitting down at the opposite end from the representative from the AMA, where a place had been reserved for him.

Rebecca Jane Talkington, briefing papers spread out before her, once again started to describe to the small group in attendance the latest on the boycott and the government's alarming response. "Let me back up for Dr. Todd's benefit," she said, picking up a file. "As of last Friday, over 55 percent of the physicians are no longer filing claims with the third-party payers. The hospitals are slightly behind that number, probably because they have inpatients where they already have established a commitment. Additionally, due to the low profit margins the institutions have experienced in recent years, they're more reluctant to cut off their funding resources even though no one is getting paid right now."

"Best-guess estimate," Dr. Arlene Tragus, the spokesperson for the American College of Surgeons, said. "When is funding going to resume?"

"The people over at HHS tell us they have begun to process the electronic claims that were already in the pipeline when everything was shut down," Talkington said. "They're evasive about the paper claims, however. I'm afraid it's going to be a long time until the doctors or the hospitals see any of that money, since, from what our people in Washington can tell, the government has made no attempt so far to put on anyone extra to work them."

O'Bannon motioned for attention. "RJ, what do you hear about the president's ultimatum?" He leaned back in his chair as all eyes in the room were riveted on the AMA's longtime legal expert.

"They see the boycott as a threat to national security," she answered, putting down the file and turning her attention to Todd. "They view the doctors as the enemy and plan to make any lack of compliance stick to a tune of $5,000 per day in penalties for those who don't go along by the time of the deadline."

Todd shifted uncomfortably in his chair as the group followed Talkington's lead. "Mrs. Talkington, I have been try—"

"It's *Miss*!" she said.

"Excuse me, Miss Talkington," Todd answered, sweat beginning to rim his collar. "As I was saying, I have been trying to get your legal staffs to file for an injunction until our organizations can come together on this." Even though Todd's attention was directed toward Talkington, he was speaking to all those in attendance, since that was his purpose in asking the AMA to convene the fly-in meeting of representatives from the three largest medical organizations.

Leaning forward in his chair, Dr. Lawrence Raven, the representative from the American College of Physicians, said, "Why in the hell didn't you think of that earlier? Maybe if you had taken the time to check with those of us in this room before you asked your members, many of whom belong to our organizations too, to walk the plank, we wouldn't be facing a virtual takeover of the health care system."

Suddenly, the air was thick with tension—Raven's remark landing a bull's-eye in the middle of Todd's chest. Talkington looked to O'Bannon for direction. "Maybe we should ..." she started.

Todd interjected, "Dr. Raven, I would concede that in some

respects you're correct." He made sure he selected his words carefully. This was the moment of truth he knew he would have to face to have any hope of reaching his goal of emancipating his profession from its increasing bondage. "If I had come to you and the other people in this room earlier, your response would most likely be more of the same—trying to set up meetings with our elected representatives or some green-behind-the-ears aide who suddenly became an expert on health care delivery because he or she put together a few briefing papers, mostly referenced by ivory tower idealists who never saw a patient one-on-one. Then trying to coerce them to your way of thinking by contributing to their campaign war chests so they will not support legislation that takes more of our freedoms away." Todd stopped, straightening in his seat. "We never go forward with that approach; we only slow down our unending descent into the abyss of socialized medicine."

"I believe our organizations have done a pretty good job of protecting your butt, Dr. Todd," Raven said, cutting him a smug look. "The doctors in this country still make more money than anywhere else in the world."

"Is that all there is to what we do?" Todd questioned. "Making money—our freedoms being bartered away for a price. What about the freedom to select who we treat and how we take care of them? What about spending more time justifying what we do on paper than treating the patient? What about living our lives in fear that if we make a mistake, we'll either be sued for everything we have worked for or fined by some government agency because we didn't post the right signs in our office or mention a patient's name in the correct context? Need I go on, Dr. Raven?" Todd's growing hostility was obvious as the veins stood out on his sweaty forehead.

Leonard O'Bannon intervened. "Dr. Todd, I don't think any of us in this room would disagree with the concerns you have raised. The problem our organizations have is the approach you have taken has put all of us in jeopardy. We have spent years establishing relationships and working in election campaigns to get where we are today."

"And just where are we, Dr. O'Bannon?" Todd moved back in his chair as his question hung over the small group of participants.

"He's right!" Dr. Arlene Tragus said, breaking the deafening pause. "The College of Surgeons might not agree with me, but Todd and his organization have brought us to a crossroad the rest of us were afraid to face. Everyone in this room knows where the medical profession is headed. All our efforts have only slowed down our eventual demise. What Dr. Todd has done is give us a chance to be something other than highly paid blue-collar workers."

"I'm not sure I understand why you have ..." O'Bannon appeared confused.

Todd moved back up to the table, assured that he had at least one ally present. "Because the UMA can't do it alone. It's just like the military needing the assistance of its four branches to win a war. We don't have the funds or the infrastructure to pull this off without your help."

"Don't you think you're a little too late?" Dr. Lawrence Raven said.

Todd's eyes turned glassy as frustration clawed at him. "You tell me, Dr. Raven. Are we too late?"

29

DR. LEONARD O'BANNON shifted nervously from foot to foot waiting for the audience noise to die down. Behind him, lined up in a tidy row, were Drs. Raven, Tragus, and Todd standing in as representatives of each of their respective organizations totaling over 550,000 physicians. "Ladies and gentlemen," O'Bannon called out, moving closer to the battery of microphones attached to the podium set up in the boardroom at the headquarters of the AMA. "We will take questions later, but first I would like to make a statement on behalf on the organizations represented here today."

Todd had won the day. Although the AMA and the other two organizations still had not committed to a full-fledged support of the UMA's boycott, they would not oppose it either. What all those in attendance could agree on was an unwavering opposition to the federal mandate taking over the health care payment system. For Todd, this was victory enough. His rapidly growing army of physicians, along with the technological and legal support that he was now getting from the more established organizations, would carry the battle to its conclusion.

"I have filed for an injunction in federal court to delay implementation of the order by the president that would for all practical purposes turn doctors into indentured servants." O'Bannon looked up from the podium, having completed his prepared remarks. "Yes," he said, pointing to the young reporter in the front row from the *Chicago Tribune* with her arm raised. "What is your question?"

"Doctor, you have laid out the reasons for your collective opposition to the federal mandate," she said, looking down nervously at some scribbles on the notepad in her hand. "And maybe I missed it, but I don't believe you discussed the recent move by now over half of the physicians in this country to only treat patients who pay up front, which, we are told, was the reason the president issued the response he did."

Todd, who was directly behind O'Bannon, noticed the muscles on the back of the AMA's spokesman's neck tighten at the reporter's question. He knew it was only a matter of time until the controversial subject would be brought up. But on the first question? Now, he could only hope O'Bannon would be true to his word.

"Ah … yes." O'Bannon seemed to be caught a little off guard. "First, let me clarify one thing you just said. Although the AMA has not supported their actions, we have been told the doctors you are referring to have not refused to treat any patient unless they pay, only that the patients agree to be responsible for their own bills at an appropriate time."

"Haven't these doctors in effect cut out the patient's insurance company?" the reporter followed up.

The AMA spokesman cut a smile for the first time since the briefing began. "I believe you got it correctly when you said the patient's insurance company. That seems to be something we have all forgotten—that the relationship should be between the patient and whatever entity they obtain their insurance from. I believe many of the problems that have brought us to where we are today is because we have incorrectly assumed the relationship is between the doctor and the third-party payer—leaving the patients out altogether."

Todd let out a slow silent sigh of relief as O'Bannon spun himself out of the question, answering only the part that made his point. Something the folks in Washington had turned into a science, he thought.

"Next question," O'Bannon said, leaving the befuddled reporter to scramble through her notes.

"What happens if the federal district court won't grant a delay?" called a reporter in the back row.

The AMA's spokesman hesitated, looking down at his briefing papers, then slowly raised his eyes. "Ladies and gentlemen, all of you in this room have had the privilege of being able to access the best health care delivery system in the world. When you or your loved one gets sick, you have known that a doctor will be by your side, day or night, 365 days a year. If the federal mandate is allowed to stand, those days may well be over." He paused, scanning the audience. "To answer your question, we'll appeal to the Supreme Court, and I would hope that with so much at stake, we will have your support."

A low rumble moved through the audience of reporters and assorted media. "And if the Supreme Court won't grant a delay?" the young reporter from the *Tribune* asked, having regained her composure.

O'Bannon stiffened. "I'm not quite …" His hands gripped the podium as he appeared to be searching for a response, his uncertainty obvious. Suddenly, he looked around, as Todd, moving up, signaled that he wanted to take over the AMA spokesman's position. O'Bannon stepped back, his face contorted in a mix of confused relief.

His heart beating in his throat, Todd adjusted several of the microphones and then leaned forward. "If the Supreme Court won't grant the physicians of this country a delay that could allow an opportunity to save our health care delivery system, well …" He paused as every ear in the room waited for him to continue. "I don't believe this country is prepared to deal with that option."

. . .

"What do you think he meant by that statement?" Lucille Beating asked, handing over a chart to Jordan Springer. The nurse bent over and adjusted the volume on the small television set affixed to the counter that wrapped around the nurses' station. She was too late; Todd's final comment of the briefing earlier that day was all that had been picked up by ABC for its national coverage. The program was now on to its next story.

Springer tucked the ICU patient's chart under his arm. "Check another channel," he said, moving back toward the counter. The patient would just have to wait, he decided.

"… deal with that option." Todd's face faded from the screen as the reporter cut back in. "It seems the American Medical Association and the nation's three other largest medical organizations have put down an ultimatum—negotiate or else. We can only wonder how far the doctors in this country are willing to go in their standoff with the administration. This is Clarise Bennet for CBS News."

Springer shrugged. "You've got me," he answered then headed down the hall to see the patient with a fever and chills. As soon as he got caught up, he would check with John Terrell and see if he had any inside information on Todd's comments.

Almost an hour had passed before Springer had a chance to put in a call to his friend. "When did the AMA and Todd crawl into bed together?" he asked, taking a sip off coffee he had just poured out of the pitcher in the small kitchen area near the back of the ICU.

"Surprised me too," John Terrell answered. "Broyle said Todd was able to work out some sort of an arrangement with the Big Three, as he calls them. Evidently, they aren't willing to go along with everything he wants, but …"

Russell cut off Springer, agitated that the other organizations appeared to be selling out to Todd's upstart UMA. "You wouldn't know it from that press conference."

"Seems he caught them all off guard with his remark," Terrell said. "Caused quite a ruckus after the briefing was over, but by then, it was too late for the other organizations to take it back."

"Todd has already gotten our asses in so much hot water—and now this." Springer bit nervously at the edge of his Styrofoam cup, the steam tickling his nose. "If I'd ever heard a dare. It sounds like he's just looking for a fight."

"We didn't get to hear the whole news conference. Broyle told me the media kept pushing and pushing with what-ifs, and the AMA spokesman just ran out of answers. So, Todd gave them one." John Terrell's tone changed. "Jordan, the reason I bought into the UMA was because Todd told us that if we kept on conceding, one day there would be nothing left. I think the message he was trying to get across was that instead of looking for a fight, he wasn't going to let that day come without putting up a fight."

. . .

"The president is mad as hell!" Bailey Foreman barked, spitting a bit off his cigar butt in the direction of his tobacco-spattered wastebasket that served as a spittoon behind his desk. "Feels that this son of a bitch Todd has thrown down some sort of gauntlet against him personally. And you know the president; he's not real good at backing down."

Senator Rayborn Carlisle, still slightly out of breath from his quick trip over to the Senate majority leader's office, shuddered, then pulled up a chair in front of Foreman's massive desk. "When you called, you said the network was sending over an unedited copy of the whole press conference. Has it arrived?"

Foreman picked up the remote and clicked on the monitor resting on a cabinet against the far wall. Carlisle adjusted his chair as a picture of Dr. Leonard O'Bannon filled the screen.

"Ladies and gentlemen, I don't believe this country is prepared to deal with that option."

Carlisle blinked as Dr. Jerald Todd's hardened stare faded into the darkened television screen. "What in the hell do you think?" Foreman's impatience was apparent as he pushed his colleague before giving Carlisle time to collect his thoughts. "This Todd has just flat-out told us to rescind the presidential order or he's going to shove it down our throats."

"The doctors in this country are angry about a lot of things," Carlisle said. "Up to now, except for a work slowdown in California over malpractice premiums about fifty years ago, they have avoided involving their patients in their battles. Sort of an unwritten code of honor that comes with their profession—protect the patient at all costs. Unfortunately, those of us who make the rules have exploited that weakness. You know, it's ironic."

Forman leaned forward, resting his chewed-up cigar on the side of his desk. "In what way?" he asked.

"Just like their patients, you and I have trusted the doctors to make things right, no matter how much money those of us here in Washington or in the headquarters of the third-party payers wring out of the system or how many hoops we give them to jump through. Well, Bailey, from what I saw at my breakfast meeting at the Morrison-Clark Inn with Todd and the leadership of his organization, those days may be over."

The Senate majority leader reared back, his nostrils flaring. "If they think they can intimidate the United States government, we'll just fine their asses off," he said, his tone indignant.

"All five hundred thousand of them and growing?" Carlisle said. "In case you're a student of history, when the doctors in California pulled the work slowdown, treating only emergencies, the governor was forced to call the state legislature back into session within about three weeks to deal with the problem."

"What happened?"

Carlisle eked out a faint smile, since he was about to prove a point. "The doctors won. Malpractice rates ended up being cut almost in half."

Foreman gulped. "They wouldn't?"

His question hung in the air as both leaders looked at each other. Carlisle broke the silence with a nod. "To Todd and his followers, this is war. There may be no proof that Todd is behind the boycott, but his unwavering dedication to stopping the continual erosion of his profession's influence into its own destiny tells me, in one way or another, he's involved."

"Can't we get the attorney general's people to charge him with something like inciting or collusion, just to get him out of the picture?" The Senate majority leader nervously toyed with his cigar, his air of confidence shaken.

"And make Todd a martyr? That's just what the doctors need, a bona fide hero to turn their boycott into a full-fledged uprising." Carlisle got up from his chair and moved over to the window as if he would find some sort of revelation painted over the Washington landscape. "No, Bailey, I would trust the system. The doctors have slightly less than sixty days to comply. Hopefully, after they are through bitching and moaning, they will come around." The senator continued to look out over the gray edifices that surrounded the Senate Office Building. The image of Todd's line in the tablecloth that morning at the breakfast meeting was etched like a hot brand in his memory. A lump hung in his throat, his own trust in the system very much in doubt.

Forman's chair squeaked as he slid back from his desk. "And what if they don't come around, Ray? What do we do then?"

"Then I suppose we would have to look at Stokley's other option," Carlisle answered, holding on to the windowsill. The thought of what that might bring took the strength out of his knees.

Forman's eyes danced around the room as he appeared to be trying to recall the particulars of the attorney general's presentation. "What was that?"

"It's something I'd prayed we'd never be forced to do—not to the people we owe our very lives to," Carlisle said, the sadness in his words overwhelming. "Conscript them."

. . .

"I'm afraid you will have to speak with Mr. Bohannon about that," the director of admissions said. "But as long as your name is not on my list, you can't admit patients here at Community Hospitals of Longview."

Dr. Seldon Rogoff gripped the disturbing laboratory report of the patient in his examining room, his rage almost beyond control. "If I can't get her into the ICU quickly, there's going to be hell to ..." He stopped, unsure that maybe his ears might be playing tricks on him. "What did you just call the hospital?"

"Oh, didn't you know? This weekend, the board of directors completed the final merger with Mercy."

Rogoff was shocked. "What does that mean?" His question was loaded with suspicion. "Exactly."

"We've changed our name and ..." She paused. "You'll have to take that up with Mr. Bohannon too."

"I'm sending the patient over through the emergency room anyway," Rogoff said, his patience gone. "And you'd better have a bed for her." He slammed down the receiver and headed for the back door of his office, leaving instructions with his nurse to transfer his sick patient to the hospital and telling her where he would be.

The walk to the hospital took less than five minutes, since the professional building where Rogoff practiced was situated just down the street—a requirement if Rogoff wanted to be near his sickest patients. Just before entering the building, he looked up and noticed that the sign denoting Crosstown's name was covered with a canvas banner that said Community Hospitals of Longview.

"I'm afraid you'll have to wait," Bohannon's receptionist

said, signaling for Rogoff to take a seat in the far corner of the administrator's outer office. "With all the changes, he has been very busy."

Thinking about the patients who were scheduled to arrive in his office shortly, Rogoff started to object. But after looking at the oversized security guard who had taken up a position just outside the hospital administrator's suite, he decided to bide his time.

Just as Rogoff was about to take a seat, Bohannon appeared at his door. "Doctor," he said, his stare cold. "Did you have something you wanted to discuss with me?"

"Yes," Rogoff said, heading for the administrator's office without an invitation. "Why in the hell is your director of admissions telling me I can't admit my patients to Crosstown? Must be some sort of typo."

Bohannon recoiled slightly at Rogoff's approach but held up his hand to stop the security officer who had already rounded the corner in the administrator's defense. "I'm sure the doctor and I will be fine," he said to the guard. "But I'll keep the door open just in case."

Rogoff, fresh out of formalities, flopped down in the chair. "What the hell is this? You having trouble with the computers again?"

"They're working fine," Bohannon answered, circling his desk and coming to rest in his chair across from Rogoff. "As you may have heard, this past weekend the board of directors finalized a merger with the Mercy Hospital System. In terms you can understand, we have formed a new corporation." His tone was condescending, almost defiant. "Which means that Crosstown and Mercy no longer exist."

Rogoff wrinkled his brow, confused at how the merger would affect him. "I guess congratulations are in order, but I don't understand what that means to me or my patients."

"Because, Dr. Rogoff," Bohannon said with an evil smile,

"as of now, I'm afraid you don't have admitting privileges here at Community. If you would like one of our physicians to take care of your patient for you, I'm sure they would be glad to accommodate you."

Rogoff reeled back in shock. "You can't do that! The doctors have hospital bylaws to protect us from you and those scab*s* you hired to replace us."

"You did have bylaws, Dr. Rogoff, but that was when this institution was Crosstown," he answered as he rumbled through the top drawer of his desk, pulling out a document and sliding it across to Rogoff. "Here they are."

Rogoff snatched up the papers with the front cover labeled Medical Staff Bylaws of Crosstown Health Care System. "In here," he said, frantic with anger, "it says that if a physician's privileges are altered in any way that might adversely affect his or her ability to practice medicine, the affected party is afforded a due process appeal before a body of their duly elected peers." Rogoff sat back, his point made.

"Very good, Doctor." Bohannon's reply was smug. "Page 36 as I recall. And I thought you doctors didn't take time to bother with what you agree to. Now, Dr. Rogoff, since you seem to be such a scholar of the hospital's bylaws, would you please point out the part the to me that deals with the 'successor in interest' provision."

The look on Rogoff's face gave away his confusion. "The what provision?"

Bohannon leaned forward, resting his elbows on his desk. "I believe that is the provision some medical staffs put into their bylaws that protects them from the hospital doing away with previous bylaws and establishing new ones if the hospital is taken over by another entity or if there is a merger."

Rogoff nervously leafed through the forty-page document, stopping to review certain parts. He then went through it once again.

"Our legal people have checked it carefully," Bohannon said. "And it's not there."

"But the hospital's attorney drew this up. Wouldn't he have checked?" The answer to Rogoff's rhetorical question was apparent.

"As I said, the clause is not an automatic. He must have assumed the medical staff did not think the issue important enough; otherwise they would have requested its inclusion," the administrator said calmly. "At the time, you were given ample opportunity to have the document reviewed by outside counsel. It is not our fault your representatives did not choose to do so."

His shoulders dropped as Rogoff slumped back into the chair. "You sorry bastard."

"Doctor!" Crimson red flooded his face. "The next time you refer to me in terms like that, you will find yourself facing someone in a long black robe and holding a gavel." Bohannon stood up and pointed toward the door.

It was all Rogoff could do not to tear the smug administrator's head from his portly body. Behind him, he could hear footsteps as the security guard rushed to the door. Rogoff edged out of the chair, determined he was not going to give up without a fight. "I'll be back," he said, seething with anger as he sidestepped the oncoming guard. "And when I do, you'll regret the—"

"Oh, Doctor," Bohannon interrupted with a condescending glare. "You might want to pick up an application to our medical staff on your way out. Who knows? I might even put in a good word for you."

30

THE MEETING ROOM at the Dallas County Medical Society office was full to overflowing as the president, Dr. Ned Townsend, banged away on the gavel. "Ladies and gentlemen, please sit down and let's bring this meeting to order," he repeated. The physicians huddled in small enclaves, barely paying attention as they continued their heated conversations.

Bang! Bang! Townsend pounded his gavel on the podium once again. Heads from all parts of the room turned in his direction. Jordan Springer, sitting near the back, marveled at all the new faces in the audience—the most he had seen at a county society meeting since he couldn't remember when. Why weren't they here earlier when we needed them, so that maybe none of this would have happened? he thought.

"The recent events have turned our profession upside down," Townsend said, the furrows on his brow lined with perspiration. "Now, we face an ultimatum of whether to acquiesce or face loss of our ability to practice medicine. I, for one, am troubled."

"Say it like it is, Ned!" Dr. Dave Streeter shouted from his usual position in the back row. "It scares the crap out of you!"

First a collective laugh went up from the startled crowd, then scattered pockets of applause for the salty old family doctor's honest appraisal of the situation. Jordan Springer shot him a wink, but

Streeter didn't appear to notice, seemingly caught up in the gravity of the situation confronting them.

"That too," Townsend answered, apparently relieved that his longtime colleague had gotten to the heart of the matter. "Although we are probably facing the most difficult decision of our professional careers, just meeting here puts us at risk for prosecution if it is construed as collective action against a third party." He pulled out his handkerchief, blotting his sweaty brow, then continued. "That's why I have asked our attorney, who is sitting in the back of the room, to discuss our options."

There was a low rumble from the group as the middle-aged gentleman in a three-piece suit crisscrossed his way through the overflow crowd to the podium. "Your position with respect to the law leaves you with very few options," he said, adjusting the microphone to his shortened height. "If you defy the presidential order, not only will your state medical license be revoked, but you will also be facing a hefty fine and possible incarceration if you continue to practice medicine. My suggestion would be to comply initially and let the organizations that represent you work to overturn it through the courts." He reached down, removing some papers from his briefcase, then continued. "Since you are not working for a common employer, there is some concern that if a large number of you in any given area elect to continue this boycott and not to take our advice, this might be interpreted by the courts as collusion among interested parties, which is strictly prohibited under legislation that protects employed workers who go out on strike. As Dr. Townsend has mentioned, we are only discussing the options available to you without making suggestions, so to avoid the possibility of federal prosecution if—"

"That's a crock of shit, and you know it." This time, Streeter's tone was filled with anger. An uncomfortable hush engulfed the room as heads moved quickly back and forth between the two debaters. "For the last several weeks, I've been living out of my savings, because of some government screw-up. Then they tell me I can't bill my patients and let them collect. Finally, the feds are going to jerk my license if I don't bend over and let them put it to me one more time. And you tell me I'm going to get my ass thrown in jail if I ask the medical organizations I pay to represent me for help. Well, if that's all the advice you have to offer, you can count me out."

"It's not that, Dave. It's just that we can't—"

"I think we ought to tell the president to take his order and stick it where the sun don't shine." The cranky old physician cut Townsend, who had moved back to the microphone, off in midsentence. "Up to now, I haven't joined the boycott like a lot of other physicians, because I had hoped that the organizations I've trusted since going into medicine would bring reason to the debate without anyone getting hurt. But I see that they're as out of step as I was. We should stop fooling ourselves. The old system doesn't work. Those who have brought this upon our profession don't care about our patients or what is right or wrong, only the bottom line." He slumped back in his chair, a metamorphoses seeming to move over him. "I don't have much left to give, but if joining my younger colleagues is what it takes, then … I guess that's what I'll have to do." A tear glistened off his cheek as the anger faded from his face. "I think my patients would trust me to do what is best for them. Don't you?"

Silence flooded the room, as no one attempted to answer his question. Springer watched in disbelief as Streeter inched his feeble body to an upright position. Looking every bit his seventy-plus years, he reached out for his cane and battered briefcase, then slowly limped toward the rear exit. Suddenly, he stopped, braced himself on his cane, and turned around to the stunned crowd.

"I should have retired ten years ago, but my patients wouldn't let me," Streeter said, his voice now barely audible from the far back of the room. "Now I know why."

Initially, it started out as a single clap from a young female in the first row who stood up and turned around toward Streeter. Then she was followed by others throughout the room. At first it was the younger physicians, most of whom Springer had not seen before. But within thirty seconds, the room erupted, drowning out the speaker, who was once again trying to bring the meeting to order. Townsend could only step back and let the crowd pay its respects to someone who was willing to finally speak the truth.

. . .

"There is a reporter from the *Dallas Morning News* waiting for you back in your office," the receptionist said as Jordan Springer pushed through the ICU door.

Springer looked at his watch. It was a quarter till seven, just enough time to go over the stragglers left over from the night shift before he officially took over at seven. "What does he want?" he asked.

"He's a she," the receptionist said without looking up from one of her romance novels. "And she didn't say. With all the trouble you doctors are causing with the feds, no telling. I just know I don't want my name in the paper alongside yours in case they come looking for you," she said, grinning before turning the page.

Springer shrugged. "She doesn't …" He stopped, realizing the receptionist wouldn't be listening to him anyway, and headed toward his office at the far end of the corridor.

"Doctor," Traci Simms said, apparently startled by Springer's sudden entrance to what was loosely called his office when he was on duty. "My name is Traci Simms. I wonder if I might have a few minutes of your—"

"Ms. … Simms, did you say?" Springer said, throwing his jacket over on the sofa and reaching for his white coat on the back of the door. "I go on duty at seven, and there are a lot of patients out there whose problems become mine in twelve minutes that I don't know anything about so far. I don't have time to quibble with you, just so you can sell more newspapers." Springer's displeasure with the way the media almost universally came down on the opposite side of an issue from the doctors showed through.

"Would it matter if I told you my father is a doctor?" the reporter asked, fumbling with a small spiral notepad.

Springer looked up then continued to slip his arms through his laboratory coat. "Where?" he asked.

"Longview," she said. "Maybe I should rephrase it. He was a doctor. He says it's over the boycott and that the hospital changed its name or something, so they could kick him off the staff along with most of the other doctors in town."

Springer recalled hearing about some of the problems from John Terrell through his connections with the UMA but didn't realize it had gone that far. "What's he going to do?" he questioned.

"Temporarily, they've taken over a Days Inn and are staffing it with pool nurses," Simms answered, her face saddened. "But they're having to send the real sick patients to Tyler. I'm convinced it's only a matter of time, until the authorities shut them down and no telling what else for all the regulations they're violating." She sighed, tears welling in her eyes. "All he wants to do is take care of his patients. I thought maybe you could give me an idea why you doctors think this boycott is so important that my father is willing to sacrifice our family's security over it."

Springer looked at his watch, which now read one minute until seven. "Ms. Simms, I didn't go along with the ..." He hesitated, thinking back to last night's meeting and the gut-wrenching points Dr. Dave Streeter had so eloquently laid out. Clearing a catch in his throat, he continued. "I don't go along with what the hospital has done to your father. That's just another example of why the continuation of the boycott is so important, if we are going to gain back control of our profession." It was now obvious that he had made his decision about a lot of things. He paused, smiling at her, then reached for the door. "Why don't you let me go check out those patients. Then maybe we can have that interview."

. . .

"I think you'll want to take this one," Jerald Todd's secretary piped through. "It's that lady doctor from the American College of Surgeons you were on TV with, Dr. Tragus."

Todd, who was reviewing the latest membership statistics of the UMA, which had jumped over 25 percent since the news conference, reached for the phone, unsure what was in store for him. "Yes," he answered hesitantly.

"Have you gotten my application yet?" she asked then continued without waiting for a response. "You wouldn't know since you're the president, would you? But I've decided to join up. In fact, the trustees of the college are encouraging our members to come on board with you."

The sudden revelation caught Todd off guard. "Why the change of heart?" he asked as he slid the membership file off to the side of his desk.

"I don't think it was a change of heart, at least on my part. What you have been saying is something that every doctor has felt all along. There have been individual physicians who have spoken out, but by in large, they have been considered extremists. When you and the UMA came along, I think all of us who were supposed to be the leaders of traditional organized medicine wanted to put you in that same category, because, crazy as it sounds, you were in some ways a threat to us. It's like we weren't doing our job."

Todd leaned back in his chair, the receiver tucked under his chin, a sense of satisfaction sweeping over him. "I have felt a little like I was swimming upstream."

"It all goes back to our patients—not wanting them to get hurt by our problems," she said, her voice taking on a more somber tone. "That's the sad irony, isn't it? We've hurt them more by not standing up for what is right, no matter what the consequences. We've gone along with sending our patients home from the hospitals earlier than they should because some snotty-nosed bureaucrat says their time is up. Or we've allowed the third-party payers to dictate which drugs we prescribe even though we know there are better options available. Instead, until you came along, our solution was negotiate or throw ourselves on the mercy of our elected leaders, hoping they would do the dirty work for us." She smirked. "We doctors think we're so smart. Hell, by either passing legislation or allowing regulations to be put into place that have taken our health care system to where it is today, those same legislators are the reason for our problems in the first place."

Todd's mind raced as Arlene Tragus's thoughts so closely paralleled his, but he wasn't fully convinced of her sincerity. He had no intention of revealing the UMA's involvement in the boycott, at least not yet. "You know, our organizations can only act in an advisory role, and that's only if our members come to us as individuals or groups of physicians with a common employer," he said, testing out Dr. Tragus's seemingly unbridled enthusiasm. "Otherwise, we'll be sitting out the war as Uncle Sam's guests."

"You're not trying to tell me what you said the other day is all talk?" she asked, a note of reservation slipping in. "About being prepared to do whatever it takes to get our profession back. Look, the Department of Health and Human Resources is literally forcing many of the surgical subspecialties out of the hospitals and back into their offices. For many of the most common procedures, we get maybe a third of what we used to from the federal subsidy programs. Then it doesn't take long for the private insurers to follow suit. Surgeons have decreased the patients' risks by developing better ways to do these operations to make them safer and less invasive. And our reward is a pay cut. Then the feds put some of the risks back in by telling us we have to do these procedures as outpatients, no matter what other physical problems the patients might have that might complicate their recovery."

The young doctor had put him on the spot. Todd stammered, "The feds … well, they're just looking to nail a scapegoat to the wall for this. It's just that if we're seen as the instigators, then they'll—"

Dr. Tragus cut him off. "Did you say instigators, or was that saviors?"

. . .

A pall hung over the attendees like a shroud. No one spoke except in low tones and only when necessary as they waited nervously for the president to make his appearance. Senator Carlisle, already privileged to most of the information that would be presented to the select group, scanned the small White House conference room in hopes of judging the pulse of the leaders from both the House and Senate who were present. From the looks on their faces, it wasn't good, he thought. The attorney general, alone at the far end of the table, leafed through the briefing papers that he would rely on for the morning's presentation.

Suddenly, the president and his entourage composed of the vice president and the secretary of HSS flooded the doorway and took up places opposite the attorney general. "Gentlemen." The president nodded, without the usual formalities. "I believe Mr. Stokley has information that is of vital interest to this group." He then turned his attention to the far end of the table.

The attorney general moved uneasily in his chair as all eyes in the room fell on him. "Granted, we still have four days to go until the deadline," he said, clearing his throat, "but so far, there is no apparent large-scale move on the part of the physician community to comply with the president's order. In fact, except for pockets of physicians mostly associated with hospitals that have not participated in the boycott, the move has been in the other direction. The numbers had been holding steady at about 60 percent of the doctors not filing insurance. Then after that news conference with the AMA and the three other largest medical organizations, the numbers have gone through the roof."

"How bad is it?" the president questioned, his mood reflected in the long lines that furrowed his face.

"Over 85 percent of the doctors are involved, and now close to 60 percent of the hospitals," Stokley answered, picking through the papers strewn before him on the table.

Carlisle felt a tap on his shoulder as Lane Foster seated against the wall just behind him leaned forward. "The docs have him by the balls," the aide said with a note of apparent sarcasm. "With those numbers, the health care payment system is in a virtual gridlock."

"The president has got to make a move," the senator whispered over his shoulder. "But I don't think even he knows which way to go."

"If it were me, I'd lock their asses up until they complied," Foster sneered below his breath.

Carlisle shook his head. "Fortunately, Lane, it's not you." Then the senator's tone changed. "Sometimes I marvel why you still work for me …"

"Let's have only one conversation going," the president interjected, shooting a disgruntled look over in Carlisle's direction as Foster slithered back away from his boss. "Now, Mr. Stokley, it seems apparent we are headed for a showdown with the doctors. Would you lay out for the group the options you and I have discussed?"

"First, let me say, Mr. President," the attorney general said, "that we are not dealing with common criminals but some of our most respected citizens who passionately believe that what they are doing is in this country's best interest."

Bailey Forman cut in. "That's bullshit, if you don't mind me saying, Mr. President. It's about money. Those self-serving bastards just want more money."

"In the end, most disagreements are about money," Carlisle said, not able to let the Senate majority leader's remark go unanswered. "But not in the way you think. From what I've been able to tell, it's really about freedom to practice without constraints and quality of care, which, as you say, Bailey, takes money."

"You've turned into a damned poster child for the docs," Foreman said, shaking his head. "I should have never put you in charge of the Senate's health care task force."

The president clanked his glass on the table. "Gentlemen, let's not get personal," he said, calling for the group's attention once again. "Now, Mr. Stokley, please continue."

"Time is against both sides. For the most part, the doctors and the hospitals are living out of their reserves, and on the payer side, the longer this goes on, the further the paperwork backs up, which will already be a nightmare to straighten out." Stokley rearranged himself. "All that aside, I would still grant a two-week extension, Mr. President, to see if we can find a compromise. If nothing else, it plays well for you in the media. We'll let your press secretary tell the public you only want what's best for them and that you are trying to work out the differences with *their* doctors. That at least buys us some time."

"For what?" the president questioned, his face growing angry. "Has anybody in your department contacted the physician leaders in these organizations to see if we can come up with a solution?"

The attorney general shook his head. "No one is willing to step forward and act as their spokesman," he said. "We know it's not true, but on the surface, this boycott is made to appear as if individual doctors made the decision not to participate on their own, which, before your order was issued, was within their legal right."

"What about the organizations at the news conference?" the president asked. "Aren't they supposed to speak for the doctors?"

"We tried, and so have our people over at HSS, but their leadership all claim they don't support the boycott even though the vast majority of their members are now participants." The attorney general fixed his gaze on the president. "Remember, our predecessors made it illegal for volunteer medical organizations to participate in these type of activities. Because of that, we have no one to talk to."

Unwilling to share it with the group at this point, Carlisle knew if there was to be a negotiated solution where the answer would lie. He reluctantly raised his hand, then leaned forward in Stokley's direction. "What about the UMA?"

There was a long, uncomfortable pause as the group waited for the attorney general's response. "You really mean Dr. Jerald Todd, don't you, Senator? Well, he won't return our phone calls."

31

IT HAD NOT been easy to get all the states to comply with the president's plan. Arizona and Massachusetts were especially difficult. Arizona, because of its strong conservative leanings, did not want federal intervention into the issuing of medical licenses—always a state-controlled function up to now. Massachusetts, even with its liberal background, was also fiercely independent, not wanting the folks from Washington telling their doctors what to do. But with some arm twisting and a few well-placed calls from the president himself, everyone finally fell in line. The one consolation the states were able to get out of the deal was that all the accrued legal and document costs would be borne by the feds, which, considering any legal challenges, could be substantial.

Each state licensing board was to communicate with its membership by certified mail. They would be notified that for their medical licensees to remain valid, the physicians would have to agree to become participants in the federal subsidy programs that, because of the government's recent moves, included virtually every payer of health care services throughout the country. A contract was included with each communication that was to be signed, notarized, and returned before their licenses that allowed them to continue to practice medicine would be renewed. The staffs of both the secretary of HHS and the attorney general's office had been instrumental in drafting the document the physicians would be asked to sign, hoping to avoid any foul-ups if its legality was tested in court by members of the medical community.

Comparatively, the hospitals were much easier. Already strapped by lack of cash flow, they would be all too eager to get back on board, especially knowing their medical staffs had been backed into a corner. Since the president's extension was due to expire in a little over two weeks, time was of the essence with the documents ready to go out in tomorrow's mail.

. . .

His eyes growing heavy, John Terrell raised the remote and punched off the television screen. Although he had to be up early the next morning, he didn't want to miss anything related to the two-week extension the president had just granted, supposedly in hopes the medical community would abandon its boycott and comply with his order. Unfortunately, the White House press secretary had not expanded on the reasons for the delay other than the president was genuinely concerned with preserving what she referred to as the world's best health care delivery system. Although pressured by the press corps to divulge what the administration planned to do in case the doctors didn't fall in behind the president, the secretary held her ground, saying only that contacts were being sought throughout the medical community, hoping to elicit the physicians' help in working together to resolve the current problems with the system.

"It's like this whole thing is some sort of big mystery," Terrell said to Allison, who tried to snuggle up under his arm on the sofa. "If the president and his cronies over at HHS want our cooperation, all they have to do is climb down off our backs and quit telling us how to practice medicine."

Allison seemed to sense her husband's frustration. "John, that's just the spin doctors in Washington doing their job. They're just hoping that if they wait it out and make the public think they're trying to negotiate; the doctors will buckle under." She drew back, looking up at him. "And they may be right. We can probably make it another three weeks on what we've saved up, but if it doesn't turn around after that, one of us is going to have to look for something to supplement our income. I know you're standing on principle, but we've still got to pay the bills."

Terrell nodded. The whole ordeal was beginning to take its toll. With the failure of previous attempts to stem the tide of intrusions into the medical profession, he was now even more convinced that the boycott was the only way to get the attention of those who could make a difference. "Allison," he said, his voice settling down to just above a whisper, "Todd says if we give in now, it'll be even worse than before. Since the feds, for all practical purposes, have instituted a single-payer system, they would probably still pay us for what we do initially, just less. Then it's only a matter of time until we would be just like Canada, England, or ... Russia, and we all know where that leads." Terrell sighed, letting his mind wander. "I firmly believe our elected officials intentionally blind themselves to the truth, because if they go out on a limb and do what's really necessary to address the funding problems facing medicine today, it will cost them votes. That's the problem with the system in this country; everything is based on the next election cycle. If the president was sincere about preserving the world's best health care system, then the patients are going to have to cough up their fair share. It's the old Social Security syndrome."

Allison looked up at him. "What's that?"

"How many people do you know who give their Social Security checks back to Uncle Sam?" he asked. "Virtually no one. Even those who have so much money they couldn't hope of spending it all don't do it. It's the 'I've paid my dues, so I'm entitled to the reward whether I need it or not' point of view."

Allison pulled back, sitting up. "Sounds like you've put a lot of thought into this."

Terrell raised his head, acknowledging his wife's evaluation. "The next twenty-five years belong to our generation," he answered, rolling the remote control over in his hand. "What we do with it will not only determine how we live out the rest of our lives, but probably more important, it will become our legacy. As I see it, the biggest fault of today's generation is that they live for today, spending whatever is necessary to solve their immediate needs. Whether or not what they do holds up in the future is not the primary concern. Those problems are left for someone else to solve—that being the next generation."

"I'm sure you're going to tell me how all this applies to us making our next car payment," she said, now settled in on the other end of the sofa.

"It doesn't take a genius to know that there would come a day when the science in medicine would overcome our ability to pay for it. Prior to the 1960s, a lot of the advanced technology just wasn't available except in a few major medical centers. For whatever reasons, the majority of patients accepted that their doctor was doing everything possible and did not demand to be sent halfway across the country for the latest breakthroughs. But that's all different," Terrell said, looking over at Allison. "I don't know what caused the change—greater access, the thinking that health insurance means one is entitled to everything available, or a litigious society that expects everything should be done for them. But, whatever the reasons, there's not enough money to make all of medicine's resources available to everyone."

Terrell got up and moved into the kitchen. Several minutes later, he was back at the door to their den—a glass of ice water clasped in his hand. "I'd be afraid to say this outside of this room, Allison, for fear I would be strung up by the establishment. Fortunately, I have no plans to run for public office." Concern spread across his face. "The truth is the only new money, without jeopardizing other existing programs, that can be put into paying for health care services to cover more patients is out of the pockets of those who can afford it. That means funding through the entitlement programs goes to those who can't pay for it on their own."

"In your scenario, the wealthy have to give up their right to Social Security and Medicare?" she asked, pulling her legs underneath her.

"Maybe not totally but incrementally, depending on their financial status. In the nineties, it was referred to as a means test, which cratered in Congress faster than the *Titanic* because now they were talking about the velvet-lined pockets of their biggest contributors," Terrell continued as he moved back over to the sofa and sat down. "It even goes further. This country must accept the reality there will always be two levels of health care—a basic level of essential services for those without the means to purchase them on their own and one for those who can. Unless that day comes, there simply won't ever be enough money to go around to protect the millions of people who don't have some type of health care coverage." He paused, taking a sip of water, then set the glass down on the end table. "There are those who cry that everyone should have the same inalienable rights to medical care—the eternal struggle between the haves and the have-nots. We don't argue that everyone should drive a Cadillac or that every child should go to an Ivy League school."

"I don't think people see it that way when it comes to themselves or the ones they love," Allison said with a hint of defensiveness. "When they're sick or hurt, they want the very best. I know I do."

"And in most cases, that's what happens," Terrell answered. "Within the options that are available to them. The medical community and the health care payers finally came to that realization with managed care and the limits that exist within the different policies. It's probably the only thing we have ever agreed upon; if the patients want more than their coverage allows, the extra has to come out of their own pockets." He paused then looked over at his wife. "Allison, it's just as unethical to deny someone the right to buy a better level of health care as it is to deny someone else, who is less fortunate access, a basic level of health care services."

. . .

The air in Dr. Jerald Todd's crowded Washington office was heavy. Following the briefing by the White House press secretary saying that the president would be reaching out to key members of the medical community in search of a solution to their differences, the leadership of the UMA had been riding high. Now, with the news of the impending contracts tied to state licensure, the leadership of Todd's organization felt as if their legs had been cut out from under them.

Todd was staring blankly at a lithograph of sailboats on the Potomac that hung on the far wall when Dr. Anna Martinez finally broke the silence. "We've come too far for you to give up now," she said, her eyes sad. "You shared with us your dream of stopping the predatory business practices that were gutting this once-noble profession. You gave us hope that if we just worked hard enough, those who would legislate and regulate the doctors in this country into nothing more than high-priced technicians would fail. We believed in you, but more important, we believed in the same things you did. The difference was that until you came along, none of us in this room thought we could make a difference."

Todd turned toward Dr. Martinez. "Anna, sometimes when the odds are so heavily stacked against you, the better option is to accept defeat than to destroy those who have put their lives in your hands. With the government still controlling the purse strings, the doctors and hospitals that have joined us in this fight are running out of money. With the introduction of the contract, the physicians lose either way. Either they violate state law by practicing without a license if they don't sign, or they cave in, letting the government dictate how our health care system operates."

"Isn't what the feds are doing illegal?" Dr. Gene Broyle questioned.

"From what I can tell by talking to the attorneys with some of the state medical societies, the licensing boards are allowed to change the rules anytime they feel there is a perceived threat to the health of the public. Then it's up to the contesting party to question those changes through the legal system to prove them wrong. Usually, by the time the differences get worked out in the courts, it's months down the road." Todd shook his head then smiled. "Haven't you heard of the rule of law?"

Broyle was confused. "That's exactly what I was talking about—letting the law prevail."

"That's what I used to think too, Gene," Todd answered. "But I'm afraid our definition was wrong. In reality, what it seems to mean is that those who make the laws rule."

"Then we have to make a stand now," Anna Martinez said, her coal-black eyes fueled by the Latin blood that coursed through her veins. "I've fought the odds all my life to make it to where I am."

Todd raised his hand as if to protest. "If the UMA is seen as being behind all this, we will be fined out of existence, and most of us in this room will be stamping out license plates for the next ten years."

"But what if ..." Dr. Martinez stopped and smiled. "What were we before we gave up our practices to come to work for the UMA? Individual doctors who, the last time I checked, are still allowed to make some decisions on our own."

Broyle could sense a change in the mood of the occupants in the room. It was now Anna Martinez, a thirty-five-year-old Hispanic female who had crawled and scraped to make it to the top of her profession, who was giving them hope. If she was not going to give up, there was no way he would either.

All eyes in the room watched as the young doctor reached over and picked up a copy of the contract Todd had been able to obtain through his contacts at HHS. "I believe each of us will be getting one of these in the next day or so," she said, her voice paced. "If we're not allowed to lead, maybe each of us can set an example. The feds will still allow us to do that, won't they?"

Todd nodded without saying a word.

Dr. Martinez grasped the document with both hands. At first it was just a small tear at the top of the page, but quickly the ripping sounds confirmed the shredding of Todd's confiscated piece of paper. Within seconds, she laid the remnants of the contract back down in front of her superior.

The expression on Todd's face lifted as he looked around the room. "Maybe some our members who have the courage of Dr. Martinez might want to notify the media of their intentions."

. . .

"Where's Rogoff?" Martin Bohannon said as he leaned across the check-in counter at the Days Inn motel.

The nurse's eyes widened at the sudden appearance of the familiar but intimidating figure of the hospital administrator. "He's down the hall in … I believe room 12," she replied, uncertainty filling her voice. "Dr. Rogoff is currently with a patient. If you'll have a seat over there, I'll be glad be glad to tell him you're here." She quickly looked away, reaching anxiously for the telephone.

"No!" Bohannon shot back; his breath like a gust of hot wind barely eighteen inches from her face. "I'll get him myself." He turned abruptly, nearly knocking a stack of registration forms from the top of the counter, and headed toward the long hallway leading off the far end of the room. Suddenly, he stopped just before reaching the doorway, whipping his head around. "Don't I know you?" he asked, his unflinching eyes glaring back at her. "You're a nurse at …"

"Was," she answered hesitantly, drawing back from the reception desk as if in preparation for his onslaught. "I used to work in the intensive care unit at Crosstown."

Bohannon hesitated but didn't respond as he spun back around. With a look of disgust on his reddened face, he took off in the direction of room 12.

. . .

Dr. Seldon Rogoff looked around, his concentration broken as his former hospital administrator bolted into the room unannounced. "Would you mind waiting outside until I've finished?" he said, taking the stethoscope out of his ears and pointing toward the door.

"What in the hell?" Bohannon's eyes searched the room wildly as he continued to come closer. "You can't do this!" he screamed, pointing to the elderly lady now cowering beneath the sheet at the strange figure's unexpected interruption. "This is a motel, not a hospital."

Rogoff knotted up his fists—the anger welling up inside as he fought to not lose control in front of his patient. "For now, you're right, but that may change if our charter is approved," he said, moving rapidly toward Bohannon and the door to the corridor. "The four rooms I've rented on this floor are temporarily serving as an extension of my office. I believe doctors allowed to do that. Now, Mr. Bohannon, if you'll join me in the hall, we need to let Mrs. Kincaid get some rest."

Bohannon's jaw fell as he backed out of the room, at the same time trying to stay out of the angered doctor's way. "You're violating so many JCAH and Medicare regulations. This can't be legal for you ..." He stopped as Rogoff signaled him into the room just down from Kincaid's.

"Listen, you sorry-ass bastard," Rogoff said, his nose flaring as he slammed the door, then spun around. His fist was raised in a cocked position as all his restraint evaporated. "You come blasting in again on me again in front of a patient, and you won't need a judge to settle our differences, just a mortician."

Bohannon backed up in broken steps. The fumbling hospital administrator nearly tripped over the empty bed. "Maybe I overstepped my boundary just a little. But I was only trying to protect the patients you doctors have planted down here."

"Bullshit!" Rogoff reached out as if to grab Bohannon by the collar, but the administrator jerked back just in time. "All you want to protect is Crosstown … or Community or whatever the hell you call your damned hospital. So, don't give me any of your noble-ass crap about doing what's good for the community. We both know where your real priorities lie." Rogoff continued to move closer, crowding the administrator against the bed. "I hear your census over there is in the tank. What's it running now, Martin? About 20 percent?"

Trying to regain his composure, Bohannon skirted the bed, coming down with his full weight in the one chair next to the desk lined up against the far wall. "We're going through a transition, you might say." He coughed nervously, then grabbed for a handkerchief in his coat pocket, dabbing awkwardly about his puffy face. "The point is, despite what you think of me personally, we both want what's going to be the best for the citizens of Longview. If that benefits my institution in the process, all the better."

"I'm not sure what you're getting at." Rogoff stopped his advances then stepped back, relaxing his clenched fists. He still didn't trust Bohannon, but something had changed in the hospital administrator's demeanor from their last meeting. Bohannon was still the same old arrogant, demanding son of a bitch, at least until Rogoff had tried to tear his head off. There was more, but he couldn't quite put his finger on it. Rogoff's interest was piqued, so he decided to back off and see what turned out. "The patients we have in here are not the really sick ones. Those we transfer to the physicians in Tyler until we can expand our facilities here."

The administrator broke a sheepish grin. "And how long will that be, even if you can get a certificate of need approved by the state? Months? Years?" Bohannon did not wait for a reply. "Maybe we should both reconsider our positions. My new doctors, well, they haven't worked out as I'd expected. Seems the good folks here in Longview prefer that their doctors speak to them in English." Bohannon wadded up his dampened handkerchief and stuffed it back in his pocket. "And with the trouble with the feds, the docs and the hospitals need to stick together." His tone was almost apologetic.

He was shocked at Bohannon's apparent change of heart, but he wasn't about to let it show. "Now, that would be a first, wouldn't it?" Rogoff grinned, then reached for the door.

32

"WE NOW GO to Doug Pierpoint, who is on location for the latest on the physician boycott that has thrown this country's health care system into turmoil." The commentator's voice faded as the television screen lit up with the sign affixed to a large redbrick building, Georgetown Medical Center.

"The continuing saga of the doctors versus the health care payers has taken on a new twist. Tonight, we are here with a group of angry young physicians in training," the correspondent said, looking back at about the twenty or so assorted white coats lined up in the background. He motioned as one of the doctors moved up to join him in front of the camera. "Dr. Stenforth, could you bring us up to date on what has happened here today?"

"Yes, sir." The young resident's eyes cut back and forth, feeling the intimidation of appearing before a national television audience for the first time. "I received this contract in the mail demanding that if I don't sign up and accept what the government says they're going to pay the hospital for what I do, then my license to practice medicine is going to be taken away. The irony is I haven't even gone into practice yet, and the feds are already telling me what to do," he said, holding up what appeared to be a copy of the contract for the viewing audience to see.

"And what do you and your colleagues here at Georgetown think about this move by the federal government?" the correspondent said.

The pale look of stage fright faded from the young doctor's face as anger took over. "First, this contract was sent not just to us but evidently to all the doctors in this country. I would hope that the American people would see this for what it is—an attempt by the folks in Washington to take over the health care delivery system."

"Isn't part of the problem, Doctor," the correspondent intervened, showing an air of confidence bordering on cockiness, "that what you and your fellow doctors want most is more money, while our elected representatives in DC are just trying to control the inflated costs of health care spending?"

"It would be nice if it were that simple," Stenforth answered, his voice growing more forceful. "We have made great strides with the scientific discoveries, but these new tests and treatments cost more." The young doctor paused, then turned away from the camera and faced the inquisitive reporter, convinced that no answer along those lines would satisfy the correspondent's insatiable appetite to stir up controversy. "Mr. Pierpoint, I would imagine you've earned a college degree?"

The bewildered correspondent nodded slightly. "Well … almost."

"And I'm sure your network demands a great deal of your time for you to have advanced to where you are as a successful correspondent for such a prestigious television organization."

"Yes, they do," Pierpoint answered proudly, even though he was still reeling from the sudden change in roles. "Probably sixty hours a week. But, Doctor, I don't see how that information relates to the problems we're discussing here today."

Stenforth turned back toward the camera. "Well, sir, my friends and I put in eighty hours or more a week, and most of us are in our seventh to eighth year of training after graduating from college," he said, pointing to the assortment of young residents lined up behind them. "Now, I don't mind telling your audience what I was paid last year—that is, as long as you're willing to do the same."

Pierpoint's jaw dropped as a blast of foul language could be heard squawking out of the small receiver affixed behind his left ear. He recoiled, quickly putting his hand up to the side of his face in an attempt to block the stream of abuse from being picked up by the microphone that he was holding. "Dr. Stenforth, my director is telling me we are almost out of time." Ignoring the doctor's request to divulge his last year's salary, the reporter's face went flush with embarrassment. "So, before we have to break away, please tell us what you and your colleagues here at the hospital plan to do about these contracts."

The young doctor looked around to his fellow residents and nodded. Then almost as if directed by a higher force, Stenforth and the other residents held up their contracts and began to tear the controversial pieces of paper into shreds.

. . .

"What are you going to do about yours?" Cindy French, Springer's girlfriend, motioned toward the certified letter lying on the coffee table.

Springer, who had spent the greater part of the evening channel surfing for the latest information on the physicians' response to the president's ultimatum, shrugged his shoulders. "Looks like a snowstorm with all the physicians turning their contracts into confetti," he said, his face a mass of concern. "I'm afraid there is going to be a point of no return that neither side can step back from. Sort of like launching a nuclear attack with no way to call the missiles back in case there turned out to be a mistake."

Cindy placed her hand on his shoulder. "I think the president made that decision when he sent the physicians the contracts to sign."

Springer looked at her, then turned back to the television where another group of physicians demonstrating their decision to not comply with the presidential order flashed on the screen. He slowly leaned over, picking up his contract. "Pass me that ballpoint," he said, pointing toward the pen on the pad beside the telephone at the end of the couch.

"You're not going to …" she started.

Springer took the pen out of her hand and, along with the contract, held them up.

For a long moment, Springer just stared straight ahead, his thoughts a stream of contradictions. Then, without warning, he thrust the pointed end of the pen forward, opening up a giant tear though the middle of the page. His decision had been made.

. . .

The small group of Washington's elite huddled around the three large television screens lined up against the wall of the president's study. Atop them sat two smaller portable sets, which had been brought in recently, so the president could watch all five major news networks simultaneously. "Look up there," the Senate majority leader said, pointing to the smaller television on the right where physicians from somewhere in the Midwest were ceremoniously dumping their contracts into a flaming fifty-gallon oil drum. "Those sons of bitches are just throwing this contract business back in your face, Mr. President. It's one thing to not go along but another the way they're making a public spectacle out of it."

The president shook his head. "Obviously, we don't have any numbers in yet, but the way it's beginning to look, they're backing me into a corner. I've asked the attorney general to come over as soon as he gets through with a black-tie affair put on by the National Rifle Association. As labile as that relationship continues to be, we don't want to ruffle their feathers too," he said with only a slight smile.

For the moment, Senator Rayborn Carlisle sat silently, keeping mental notes since joining the president and Bailey Forman slightly over forty-five minutes ago. He had counted eight different stories showing doctors protesting. Each of the major networks had run the item as their lead, with ABC touting a segment on the subject later that evening. CNN was running a similar piece every half hour along with a headline summary on the quarter, while the subject had been the major focus on Fox since the senator started watching.

The physicians being interviewed seemed convinced that they had no choice but to protest the presidential mandate. That was to be expected, thought the senator. But it was their fervor that surprised and frightened Carlisle the most. Although he had come to respect the devotion most doctors held for their profession, he had not expected such a rebellious public demonstration of their dissatisfaction. He was frightened because the media, usually liberal in their slant when it came to differences between the fortunate and those that were not, seemed on average to be leaning toward the physicians' point of view. "I hope this plays better on the Sunday-morning talk shows," Carlisle said, knowing that, although small in numbers by comparison to the audiences that snoozed away their evenings in front of the boob tube during the week, it was on Sunday mornings that many of the so-called intelligent formulated their opinions. And it was this intelligent, silent minority who, through their vast resources, funded the political campaigns and determined what slants were put on stories appearing in the media.

The president nodded, his gaze still fixated on the images spewing out before him. "We've got to get our message out before the press makes a mockery out of this," he said with a sigh. "I hope the secretary and Stokley don't mind letting their wives go to church alone this Sunday."

"They knew what was expected when they signed on," Carlisle half-joked, knowing that they would have to lead the charge on the president's behalf.

Just then, an aide poked his head through the door. "Mr. President, the attorney general is downstairs seated outside the Oval Office. He seems a little out of sorts—something about being in two places at the same time."

The president signaled for his aide to find a nice way to tell Stokley to cool his heels until he got there. Then he turned back to Carlisle and Foreman. "I know that the two of you are on different sides about how to approach the doctors on this issue," he said, sounding troubled. "Just between us, Bailey, I'm closer to Ray's point of view than yours. It is very difficult to take on the individuals who have brought your children into the world and stood by you when you thought all hope was gone. Thirty years ago, I'd have said our side wouldn't have stood a chance—going up against the pillars of the community. Fortunately for us, in recent years, they have done a lot to tarnish their own image by introducing business practices into what they do. Although those tactics may pay off on the bottom line, each time physicians go on television or make radio commercials touting the benefits of what they do, the public as a whole loses a little more respect for the medical profession. It raises doubts about what they really care about most—the patient or the almighty dollar. Even though only a small group of doctors resort to those tactics, it spills over to the whole profession, and if our side is to win, we have to play off that growing distrust. Sometimes the public is smarter than we give them credit for. This is turning into a war that will not be won by the side who has the last standing but by which one of us the public believes is really acting in their best interests."

Foreman blinked. "Are you saying you're just going to step back and let the docs run over you, Mr. President?"

"Bailey," the president said as he reached over, flicking off the television screens one by one then rising from the sofa. "Which would you say was the most difficult war this country has ever fought?"

The Senate majority leader, following the president's lead, got up. "We suffered the most casualties in World War II, and in Vietnam, we got our asses handed to us."

The president headed for the door, then paused and turned back toward the two senators. "Neither," he said, his expression troubled. "It was the Civil War—brother against brother, sometimes father against son—fighting for a principle, the right to be free. If you think about it, Bailey, which side are we on?"

. . .

"Stokes," the president called out as he and the two senators approached the attorney general, who had taken up residence behind the receptionist's desk located just outside the Oval Office. "Let's go inside and see where we need to go on these physician protests." He flicked his head in the direction of the White House security officer, signaling for him to unlock the office. "I'm telling you it looks like we stirred up a hornet's nest from the way the media is playing this up."

"I'm afraid it could be a lot worse than that," the attorney general said solemnly as he got up from behind the desk and followed the president and his small contingency into the Oval Office. "We've put the states in the position of enforcement for the doctors who don't comply."

"Pretty slick idea," the Senate majority leader bragged, flopping down on the overstuffed sofa across the room.

"Respectfully, Senator, that could come back to bite us on the ass." Stokley shot Foreman a dirty look as he paced back and forth. "From the looks of what we're seeing, the number of physicians who aren't going to comply may well be in the hundreds of thousands. I've taken the liberty of contacting a number of my counterparts on the state level, and to the person, they aren't going to prosecute if there is more than just a smattering of resistance. First, many of the non-compliers might well be their own personal physician or that of an influential legislator. As they say, all politics is local. Well, in most cases, so is all health care delivery."

A look of despair crossed the president's face. "Stokes, you and the secretary need to pull this out for us," he said as he leaned forward on his desk. "If we can get you on with Wallace or *Face the Nation*, we can turn—"

"Mr. President," the attorney general interrupted, "those talk shows aren't going to change people's minds if it means closing their doctor's office down. And the states aren't going to go along if it means their voters are outraged either. There will literally be a housecleaning come the next election."

"What about the federal funding?" the president continued to question, a twinge of hope rising in his voice. "The states aren't about to let that money go."

Stokley looked around at Foreman and Carlisle, who had relinquished the floor to the president. "Senators, how long will it be until each of you has to run again for office?"

Carlisle sheepishly looked over at Forman, knowing that the attorney general was trying to tell them the best way to get back to port was not staying on board a sinking ship. "How do you think we should proceed?" the senator asked, deciding it was time for a fresh idea.

Stokley pulled up a chair and sat down halfway between the president and his confidants on the sofa. "Negotiation would be the first choice, but that should have started long ago, before we got to this point. Other than lobbying their elected representatives or the third-party payers, with an occasional lawsuit thrown in here and there, the way you and your predecessors have legislated, the doctors have their hands tied—which, I'm sad to say, comes back to haunt us when we need a party to negotiate with."

"So are you telling us we should create legislation that would allow them to collectively bargain?" the president said.

"Although there have been some moves in that direction, the situations where the principles have been allowed to apply have been limited in scope. No, I'm afraid it's too late—at least with what it looks like we are about to face now," Stokley answered. "The medical organizations that represent doctors are all at one another's throats, competing for the limited dues dollars that are available. And the AMA, the organization that should serve in that role, is not constituted such that it truly represents enough of the physicians in this country to be a viable voice when it comes to something of this magnitude. Hell, their membership numbers have fallen to less than one in six docs."

"I take it, Mr. Stokley, that you don't have an answer." The president's face was a pitiful shade of gray.

The attorney general nodded. "Except for Senator Carlisle's aide, Lane Foster, not one that you'd want to hear."

"With the options available," the president said, "I don't see how we have much choice."

"Put them under federal jurisdiction," Stokley answered, his response measured. "As we discussed before, Truman and Reagan used their presidential authority in this way when they felt there was a threat to the nation's best interest. That way, we don't have to rely on the states."

Carlisle, no longer able to hold back, spoke up. "And you think the public would allow that? Hell, at least one-on-one, the voters love their doctors." His anger resurfaced as the subject of conscripting one the most respected sectors of society came back up again.

"Senator, it's either that or giving in to their demands." Stokley's response was matter-of-fact. "I read a survey conducted several years ago that I think illustrates a very important point. When the managed care issue first came up, everyone was talking about the importance of physician loyalty versus the patients having their doctors selected for them. A group of patients were asked how much extra they would be willing to pay out of their own pockets, over and above what their insurance policy covered, in order to stay with the doctor they had previously been seeing. Do you know how much that turned out to be?"

Figures from the ridiculous to the not so ridiculous floated through Carlisle's mind as he and the other participants in the Oval Office waited anxiously for the attorney general's answer.

"Eight dollars."

. . .

On Dr. Jerald Todd's desk sat a bottle of champagne neatly tucked inside a bucket of crushed ice. A congratulatory card hung from the bright red ribbon adorning the still unopened cork. "How did this get here?" he called out, looking toward the doorway.

Gene Broyle's head poked around the corner. "I think Anna left it for you," he said. "Something about having the courage even though the odds were against you."

Embarrassed, Todd answered, "I think it's Dr. Martinez and all the young physicians around the country who are standing up and saying no to this virtual kidnapping of our profession who deserve this more than I do."

"I won't argue the point except to say our plan is working." Broyle handed his boss a sheet of papers with a column of numbers on it. "This is what we've been able to get so far."

Todd ran his finger down the row of figures. "This is more than we could have ever hoped for." His eyes darted back to Broyle, his look changing to one of concern. "Are you sure about these numbers?"

"Since there are still a few days before the deadline, they could change. But our mole over at Lou Harris is pretty comfortable with them. Why?"

Todd plopped his hip down on one corner of his desk, sliding the unopened bottle of champagne to the side. "I've looked forward to but at the same time dreaded what this day would bring for a long time. Both sides have now drawn their lines in the sand. Now, I guess we'll just have to wait to see who blinks first."

33

DR. JERALD TODD did not have long to wait.

"Since taking office, one of my primary goals has been to create a system that that would allow each and every citizen an affordable level of health care services. This has also been one of the top priorities of each the prior administrations here at the White House, starting with former president Bill Clinton, then Obamacare, unfortunately without much success. Today, even with the enactment of the Universal Health Care Protection Act along with the other federal- and state-supported subsidy programs, there are still millions of our citizens without any health care coverage and additional millions who are being forced to pay more than they can afford ..."

President Moore's televised address to the nation had now gone just past twenty minutes, and so far, he had yet to put forward any meaningful suggestions as to how to unlock the stalemate between the providers of health care services and those whose responsibility it was to pay for them. But if the experts were right, that was yet to come as millions of interested parties on both sides of the contentious issue clung to their television sets in anticipation of what he was about to propose.

"Today, this country spends almost 20 percent of its gross national product on health care. For our counterparts to the north, that number is closer to twelve. And even though we offer, unquestionably, the best level of health care in the world, we don't make it available to all our citizens. My administration has strived to establish relationships within the medical community in an effort to develop solutions to these problems, but I am sad to say, so far we have mostly met with resistance."

The tone of President Moore's voice began to change, taking on a harshness as he moved into the part of his speech where he would lay most of the blame on the medical community. The thrust, according to his advisors, was to paint the doctors not as culprits, which could incite a wave of backlash public support, but more as old-timers, out of step, still clinging to antiquated beliefs, and unwilling to go along with the sacrifices necessary in order to make health care affordable for everyone. That way, the folks in Washington could hold themselves up as paragons of virtue coming to the rescue, especially since they were willing to foot the bill.

"Several weeks ago, I signed a presidential order that would have afforded the citizens of this country some measure of protection until a long-term solution could be worked out. At that time, I asked the doctors and the other providers of health care services to join me in this effort. Regrettably, as most of you have witnessed through their public demonstrations, close to 75 percent have rejected our offer—creating a substantial threat to the best interests of this country. That is why tonight, as president of the United States and by the authority afforded me under the Constitution, I am federalizing our nation's health care delivery system."

A notable strain could be seen as the president's clasped fingers tightened into a firm ball. Fortunately, the television camera spared the nation that part of the president's pain by only projecting tight shots of his head. His eyes flicked slightly off-center as he began to list off his proposed changes as they scrolled down the teleprompter.

"To accomplish our goals of being able to offer each and every citizen an affordable package of health care services, it is imperative that those who would deliver these services be on board with us. That is why I am bringing the physicians and the other practitioners under the protective arm of the Department of Health and Human Services." The president paused, reaching over to take a sip of water, out of view as they showed images of protests from the leadership within the medical community. "That is to be expected. Change is not easy. We have one common goal—that is to allow our citizens protection from the ravages of problems that are beyond their control. Just like the other essentials afforded the people of this country, our citizens have the right to protection from those who would cause them physical harm, to an adequate education so they have the ability to find gainful employment, and to a safe food supply. Therefore, tonight my administration is adding to that list basic health care services. It will not be easy, but together, I feel confident the doctors and the other providers of health care will join us in this commitment."

. . .

Maggie Crawford turned away from the small television, set then threw the patient's chart, causing it to bounce across the counter of the triage desk before it scattered into separate pages on the ICU floor below. "That sorry son of a bitch," she said.

A veteran nurse of countless ICU wars in her days at Parkland Hospital before transferring to a relatively quieter life at Methodist last month, Maggie recoiled, then bent over, picking up the remnants of the patient's record. "I'll take care of this," she said, her voice sympathetic as the sound of the small television set on the counter still resonated in the background.

"I didn't put in all this time to spend the rest of my career under the thumb of the government." She was past angry as she regurgitated the words of the president. "Federalizing under the protective arm of the HHS ..." She felt betrayed and violated.

"Protective! Who in the hell is he trying to fool? Enslavement would be more like it—putting doctors on a paycheck. I wonder how hard he thinks they're going to work after that."

Still fumbling to reassemble the scattered pages, Maggie looked up. "Dr. Springer, could you really say you care more about these patients than I do?"

Springer flushed at her question. "I guess I never thought about it before."

She gently laid the reassembled chart back on the counter, and then her gaze locked on to Springer. "Before you answer, let me tell you that I've been on someone's payroll since the week after graduating from nursing school, over thirty-five years ago. So, welcome to my world. Now, why don't you go see that patient in eight with pneumonia," she said softly, nudging the chart back over in Springer's direction. "Right now, she doesn't care where your money is going to come from."

. . .

"I should get into the Dallas/Fort Worth Airport by about ten," Dr. Gene Broyle said. "Todd thinks we need to get back out in the field and check the pulse before we decide what our follow-up to the president should be."

John Terrell tucked the receiver under his chin as he scooted out of his white jacket. "I don't know about you, but the pulse of the physicians around here is weak and fading fast," he said, not sure with the mess they were already in that he was ready for any more of the UMA's suggestions. "Do you know any more about the particulars?"

"They're going to work off your tax existing ID number," Broyle answered. "We don't have all the finals in, but the White House has given the guys over at HHS three months to get the program fully implemented. From what we can tell, physicians won't be able to select whom they see based on coverage; it will be on time and space availability. If the feds pick up violations, there will be punitive repercussions to the physicians involved. What that will be we don't know yet."

Growing more agitated, Terrell asked, "How in the hell are they going to find out what we do?"

"The patients. That's one of the secrets to the federal plan—using our patients against us by rewarding them if they report an infraction. They first ran up that flag with suspected Medicare violators several years ago. It wasn't very successful then, but with the patient resentment over the boycott, their results will probably be a lot better this time around."

"Those bastards! Using the very ones we are doing all this for to bring us down."

Terrell, whose resolve to continue to fight back had paralleled his dwindling bank account, felt the burning in his chest grow once again. "If it wasn't so malicious, I'd call that a stroke of genius."

"There are a lot of good minds in the capital city. Unfortunately, many of them are misguided," Broyle said. "Since the feds have taken over as the intermediaries for all health care coverage, all the billing goes through them. And you know what that means: the folks over at HHS set the reimbursement rates for all covered services. With escalating health care costs and the feds controlling their cash flow, it won't take long until the private payers decide to go elsewhere, leaving our friends in Washington as the only game in town."

Terrell slung his jacket, barely missing the coat-rack in the far corner, and pulled up the stool that was parked just below the row of darkened view boxes. "Then why can't the doctors just continue the boycott and let the courts decide?"

"Because you've officially been conscripted into service by the federal government, which means the usual appeals through the judicial system afforded private citizens don't apply. It's the same as being drafted into the military, where justice is decided by a tribunal system. Only, instead of being under the control of the Department of Defense, all licensed physicians are under the Department of HHS."

His hopes dashed once again by Broyle's grim forecast, Terrell asked, "If the feds can tell us who we can see and pay us what they want, then they've won?"

"John, the physicians do have one thing left that the feds don't seem to be able to get around. The trump card none of us who took the Hippocratic oath ever thought we would have to play." Broyle's voice cracked, his pent-up emotion showing through. "They can't make us see our patients."

. . .

It was a far cry from the last time Dr. Jordan Springer had been there. Except for a scattering of long faces, the meeting room at the Dallas County Medical Society offices was barely half-full. He slid into his usual position in the back row, looking over to see if his older colleague, Dave Streeter, was also in attendance. To his disappointment, his usual spot was empty. The familiar banging of Ned Townsend's gavel brought Springer back to reality.

"Why don't those of you in the back move down front," Townsend said, then looked disappointed when no one took him up on his offer. "As you can see from tonight's turnout, we have plenty of room. I apologize for the short notice but didn't find out until yesterday that one of our former members, Gene Broyle, who as most of you know, is with the UMA, wanted to meet with us about the new ultimatum laid down by our former friend, the president of the United States." Townsend held out his hand as Broyle slowly ascended to the podium. "I might add, while he is coming up, that if I have any money left after the guys in Washington finish putting the screws to us, it won't be to fund Moore's reelection."

A forced chuckle arose, but the room fell back into a deadly silence as Broyle moved in front of the microphone. "I was sent here today to listen to your concerns," he said, his face showing signs of strain. "You know, it's good to be back. Dallas will always be home to me, and I—"

"Then listen to this. You gave your home up when you moved to DC," a voice from the center of the room thundered. "So, I would suggest that you take your lily-white ass back up east. You and your Unified Medical Association have brought enough pain on us already and are no longer welcome here."

Springer tightened at the unexpected outburst, straining to see who the respondent was. It was only then he recognized two familiar faces seated in the center of the front row—John Terrell and his old friend, Dr. Dave Streeter.

"I … I'm sorry you feel that way, but …" Gene Broyle appeared lost as he awkwardly searched for the right response.

"Mr. President," Streeter called out to Townsend as the salty old doctor struggled to get to his feet. "May I make a comment?" Without waiting for a response, he continued. "The doctor is correct in one sense. Dr. Broyle and his associates have brought pain on us today but only because they encouraged the doctors in this country to finally stand up for what is right." Streeter paused and turned around, facing the sparse audience. He took off his wire-rimmed glasses, his eyes dancing around the room as he appeared to be searching for the doctor who had made the caustic comments. "In case you haven't noticed, our profession is sick—suffering from a disease—a type of cancer that is squeezing the very life out of what it means to be a physician. Fueled by our own apathy and greed, this illness has not only taken away our freedom to practice medicine the way we feel is appropriate, but it has also robbed us of our own self-respect. So that in increasing numbers, many of our fellow physicians are either retiring early or resorting to selling their souls for a few extra dollars." He stopped, fixing his gaze on the participant who had made the malicious comment. "So, Doctor, if it takes going through some pain to rid ourselves of this malady, then I guess we have no other choice."

Springer shot John Terrell a grin that his young friend returned with a nod. They were both on the same page.

Bolstered by the elderly doctor's support, the anguish on Broyle's face evaporated as Streeter relinquished the floor. "As I had hoped to say, the role of any organization, medical or otherwise, is to speak for those it represents. To do that, we must first listen—not to just what is spoken but also to what is not spoken, to the heartbeat of our profession. That indescribable quality that is crying out for us to make whatever changes that are necessary, as the good doctor has so eloquently just put it, to nurse us back to good health." His face shifted to each side of the audience as he spoke to all those in attendance. "So, I come here tonight to ask you one question. Are you willing to make the sacrifices necessary to cure the disease that is sucking the very life out of our profession?"

. . .

Jordan Springer arrived early for his shift and headed over to radiology. After last night's meeting, he wanted some one-on-one with John Terrell before he had to take over. Terrell was just pouring his first cup of coffee when Springer poked his head around the corner. "Got a few minutes for the old man?" he asked, moving over to get himself a cup of java.

John Terrell nodded then picked up a plastic straw and propped himself up on a stool against the far wall. "Before long, that may be all I have," he said, his tone somber. "Time, that is."

"What about Broyle?" Springer questioned, picking up on his friend's negative tone but deciding not to bridge that problem at this time.

"He's got about ten stops to make before he heads back to

Washington at the end of the week. You know the UMA assigned him Texas, New Mexico, and Louisiana to cover."

Springer decided to get to the point. "About last night, after Streeter set that guy back on his ass. What happens after this?"

"I don't know for sure." Terrell shook his head. "Broyle tells me to hold tight. That if we're going to be conscripted, it puts the whole problem in a different light since we may not be able to turn to the courts for relief. Evidently, they're trying to put something together with the other national medical organizations, but he couldn't be more specific yet. Right now, they're just trying to get a feel of how far the physicians are willing to go with this."

"I know it was a small crowd last night, but judging by the response after Streeter's pep talk, there wasn't much question."

Terrell took a big gulp of coffee. "I'm not sure I can go along if it happens." His hands started to tremble, clasping tightly to the cup.

Springer bugged his eyes. "Hell, you're the one who convinced me the old way wasn't working—that to make the changes necessary, sacrifices were a given. And now you're backing down on me?"

"Jordan, I'm no different than thousands of other young doctors out there. When I went into practice, Allison and I had over $100,000 in debt that I'm still trying to pay off. Our only real security is in my 401(k), but if we dip into that, not only do I incur a 15 percent penalty unless I agree to pay it back, then we've got nothing to fall back on in case ..." Sadness spilled across his face. "It's not that I don't support doing everything possible. It's that we don't have the money to hold out much longer."

Jordan Springer knew his friend was not alone, and it wasn't just the younger doctors who were in a precarious financial position. He looked away, realizing for the first time that in this war between the payers and the health care providers, the payers didn't care how long it took because they were already holding the money. And if along the way they took out a little bit extra for their stockholders that was even better. "For the last forty years, we have offered this country the best level of health care in the world, and in return, the doctors been suckered into playing a waiting game with Washington and the large insurance carriers—fighting for crumbs as they dole out the least amount of their premium dollars they can legally get away with."

Springer paused, turning back toward his friend. "They've known all along that if they could just drag out paying us a little longer, not only would they get a greater return on our premium dollars, but we would be more willing to negotiate a compromise—a dollar here, then a dollar there. At the time, it doesn't seem like much, but over the long haul, those dollars add up. And in the end, they've won." He took a small swallow of his coffee then continued. "The sad irony is it's not the doctors who lose—not really; it's our patients. Because it's their money that is being siphoned off to line the pockets of the payers and their stockholders—money that was set aside for their health care."

John Terrell blew the steam off his cup, running his finger around the edge. "I'm not sure, knowing what I know now, that I would have done this all again … deciding to go into medicine as a career."

Springer flinched, the all too familiar statement by a growing number of doctors making Russell search his soul as to why he chose to become a physician. "John, the doctors didn't start this war, and I'm not sure the payers did either, at least, not intentionally. But now more than ever, I'm convinced it's ours to finish, whatever it takes. And your decision—next to marrying Allison, I hope it will turn out to be the best one you ever made."

...

"It just doesn't make sense," Lane Foster said as he rearranged the senator's briefing papers for the morning. "The docs make a public display of burning their contract notices in front of every television camera all over the country. Then the president conscripts them, and after that, not a word of protest. No public statements. Nothing! Other than a few trips by representatives from that United Medical Association, the people over at the AG's can't pick up that much else is going on," Foster boasted. "My guess is they finally decided not to fight city hall."

Rayborn Carlisle pulled off his glasses and slowly looked over at his aide, who was about to go through the morning's agenda. "I wouldn't count on it."

their lives to us." She looked around, her face flushed with anger. "Ask yourself why this is any different."

At first, it was just Todd who followed Tragus's move. Then, one by one, the other participants removed their headsets as her initial act of defiance spread like an epidemic throughout the room. The last to go along, but arguably the most important, was Dr. Leonard O'Bannon, now anointed by the AMA Board of Trustees to lead the giant organization in this contentious area. Looking around the room, Todd's heart jumped in his throat as the family of medicine had finally decided to start acting like one.

. . .

John Terrell's jaw hung low as he reread the email message from the UMA he had downloaded off the Internet several days before. "… must be quick and decisive in order to minimize our patients' suffering. … You will be informed of the exact time and date within the next twenty-four hours …"

Feeling Allison' touch on his shoulder, Terrell turned around. Their eyes then locked on the screen, with two long minutes passing before she said, "You can't," tears flooding her eyes. "It goes against everything you vowed to uphold when you went into medicine."

Terrell pulled Allison into his lap, resting his head against her chest. "As doctors, we don't just have a responsibility to our own patients," he said, looking up, his mind racing to bring order to this mass of contradictions being thrown at him. "We also are the doctors for the system that takes care of them, from the hospitals to the large insurance companies that pay for that care. Well, that system that all of us have depended on is sick … very sick. In fact, it has been sick since the first day the government started telling us how to take care of our patients. Up to now, the physicians of this country have not been willing to assume their role—retreating to their private agendas and hoping the problems would all go away."

Allison wrapped her arms tightly around her husband as if he were the only hope left. "But the very patients you say you're fighting for are going to get hurt."

"Unfortunately, some will," he answered, his voice cracking. "That's the sad irony—putting them through the pain to get the cure, but it's the only way the guys in Washington are going to listen." Terrell pulled away, his mind now clear about what he had to do. "One time when I was a kid, I had this terrible sore throat. So, my mother wrapped me up and took me down to the doctor. After he looked me over, he told my mother he had to give me a shot of Penicillin and that it was going to hurt. Well, I started screaming and trying everything I could think of to get out of having that injection. My mother was beside herself, so he sent her out of the room. I'll never forget what he did next. As soon as the door was closed, he turned to me and asked me one question. Did I want to get well?" Terrell sighed. "It's everything about being a doctor."

. . .

John Terrell had spent a restless night wondering what this day would bring. Terrell was almost a block away when he first noticed the long line of people spilling out the entrance to the emergency room while the big yellow Channel 5 helicopter hovered over Methodist. He eased by the jammed hospital parking lot, taking note of all the confusion, and pulled up to the turnstile that allowed him access to the employee garage alongside the medical complex. Just as he slipped his ID card through the slot, out of nowhere, a microphone was jammed through his open window.

"Doctor," the unnamed face called out breathlessly, "our viewers want to know why the medical community has abandoned them."

Terrell recoiled, realizing his green scrub top had given his identity away to the aggressive reporter. "I don't think we have ..."

He cut off his remarks when the correspondent's overweight assistant swung around to the other side of his car, aiming a shoulder-supported minicam in his direction. "No comment!"

The miffed reporter and his rotund assistant faded from view as Terrell's car rolled farther into the garage and away from all the commotion outside. Easing in through the employee entrance off the garage, Terrell knew it was only a matter of time until he would have to face those same questions again. Hopefully, the next time it would be under more controlled conditions. For now, he had ten minutes to get to his assigned position alongside Jordan Springer.

A secret meeting had been held early the previous morning by all the physicians who practiced in and around the medical complex. Since only emergency services were being offered, the consensus was to centralize them through Methodist's emergency room. Not only would it afford some level of protection to the physicians and their staff in case some disgruntled patient decided to seek retribution for the planned work slowdown, but it also added a measure of efficiency in what would surely become a chaotic situation. Additionally, with the spillover and in order to minimize patient suffering, all the physicians had to agree to share the added load by pulling shifts in the ICU, as the increased demands placed on Dr. Jordan Springer's department would quickly exceed its abilities.

"You look like crap," John Terrell whispered in Jordan Springer's ear as he edged around a group of patients propped up against the wall of the long corridor that made up the lifeline of Methodist's ICU.

"Thanks. That's just what I needed to get me through another twelve hours," Springer responded with a wink. "It's been like this since the news of the slowdown broke last night. They called me in to help out just after midnight. I already took over the cafeteria with another crew to help with the overload," he said, his voice turning solemn. "John, most of these folks are just scared and don't need to be here, but they don't know it—prescription refills, mild chest pains, upper respiratory problems. If their doctors hadn't closed their doors, most of these people would just have waited their problems out and, except for the medicine renewals, gotten well on their own. But with their support system gone, they panic."

"Can't say I blame them," Terrell said, leaning to the side as an orderly with an empty gurney passed by in the crowded hall. "What we're doing scares me too. I was accosted by this reporter coming in here, and the strange thing was when he tried to pin me down, I didn't have a thing to say—at least not what he wanted to hear."

"We've been trying to tell them for a long time," Springer said, signing a couple of prescriptions and handing them to one of the patients. "But they wouldn't listen. Unfortunately, the time for talking is over."

Terrell nodded and moved on, taking up his assigned position by the view boxes.

. . .

"Those sons of bitches really did it," Bailey Foreman bellowed as Rayborn Carlisle tried to slip into the Oval Office without creating an interruption. "I knew when they weren't bitching and moaning that they were up to something."

The president looked up, a grim stare covering his face. "Ray, we've got problems," he said, his massive desk littered with files and half-empty coffee cups. "Stokley here tells me that, except for a few scattered spots, mostly out in the rural areas, the doctors have shut down everything but emergency services."

"I thought that since they've been conscripted, that wasn't an option." Carlisle pulled up a chair next to the Senate majority leader. "Sets them up for treason or dereliction of duty or—"

The attorney general interrupted. "That's somewhat open to question at this point, Senator. The docs have filed for an injunction through the circuit court, trying to delay the presidential order. We are in a difficult position to act until we see if they're willing to hear the case." He paused and picked up one of the files. "It's a Constitutional thing—the checks and balances our forefathers created to protect democracy."

"Obviously, the physicians have set up some type of organizational structure to pull off an effort of this magnitude," Carlisle said, his eyes following the attorney general's every move. "Have you tried to make contact with them and see what they're willing to settle for?"

"We don't settle!" The president's forehead flushed with anger. "Damn, Ray, you're the expert. You know what they want—to go back to an indemnity insurance system and cut out the third-party payers. That concept died decades ago because it was not cost-effective."

"It died, Mr. President, because our predecessors here in DC felt they could do a better job of managing this country's health care delivery system than the doctors and their patients," Carlisle said, deciding it was time to get the facts straight.

"All that aside, my job is to carry out the presidential order." Stokley shook his head. "The doctors have shut us out completely. Even the AMA—they won't return our phone calls, no interviews, nothing. Through our contacts in the medical community, my office has obtained copies of email messages instructing the doctors how they should go about pulling off this slowdown." He dropped the file on the president's desk and picked up a small stack of papers. "They're anonymous of course, but my people in the intelligence section are pretty sure they came out of Dr. Jerald Todd's office right here in Washington."

Carlisle felt his chest tighten as reality of the dissident doctor's prediction at the early-morning breakfast had finally come to pass. "Why don't you send some of your people over there with a warrant and at least bring him in for questioning?"

"I'd just lock the bastard up if it were me," Bailey Foreman piped in, his voice filled with disgust. "If we cut out the heart, the animal dies, I believe the saying goes."

"Or becomes an icon," the president interjected. "Stokley's people have filed with the magistrate here in Washington for a search warrant of Todd's place. If we could get into his computers and prove he's behind all this, then we would have legal grounds to take him out of circulation if the circuit court ruled against our position."

"What happens if the court rules in your favor, Mr. President?" Carlisle asked, trying to look at all possible scenarios.

"That puts them under federal jurisdiction, and the president could be forced to call in the National Guard to protect the nation's best interest if the docs don't come to their senses," Stokley said, his tone sounding slightly amused. "And I'd personally take joy in locking Todd and all his cronies up in the brig myself."

Carlisle noticed the small grin on the attorney general's face as he continued to look over copies of the email messages. "May I ask what you find funny in all this?"

"Well, Senator, these guys are just not cut out to be solders," he answered, his smile remaining. "I guess that's why they're doctors. Every one of these messages keeps emphasizing the importance of not letting their patients get hurt in all this. Hell, don't they know that's what war is all about—hurting people until you get what you want. They may think they've got the upper hand, but their greatest asset is also their Achilles' heel."

A hush enveloped the room as all the occupants waited for what else the attorney general had to say. Even the president pushed back his chair in anticipation.

"And, gentlemen, make no mistake," Stokley continued, his resolve apparent in his eyes, "my people are all combat veterans and will have no qualms using the doctors' own weaknesses against them."

. . .

"Pneumothorax!" John Terrell called out, poking his head through the door to the trauma room, the chest x-ray in his hand. "Looks like she's only got a third of that left lung functioning."

Jordan Springer nodded, then quickly turned to the orderly standing by the wall. "Get me the chest set, STAT!"

Within ten minutes, the patient's color had pinked up, and her respirations were returning to normal. The small plastic tube exiting her left chest was the only visible sign of her near brush with death. Satisfied that his patient was stable, Springer stripped off his gloves and headed out to his next assignment, where he ran into Terrell.

"She do okay?" Terrell asked, shoving the next set of films up on the view boxes.

"Yeah, and thanks," Springer said. "Another couple of minutes, and we would have lost her. She's a very lucky la—"

Springer's remarks were cut short as Maggie tapped him on the shoulder, ramming a sheet of paper in his hand. "This just came in over the fax line for you," the nurse said. "I thought you'd want to know as soon as possible."

His eyes bugged as he read the emergency communication from the American Medical Association.

> At 10:45 a.m. today, the Supreme Court refused to act on the appeal submitted by the AMA and other medical organizations to issue a restraining order that would delay implementation of the presidential order to …

Springer handed the communication over to Terrell. "I guess this means you and I now work for Uncle Sam."

His hands trembling, Terrell looked up after reading the note. "This can't be it. We aren't going to just lie down and let them …" His voice trailed off to a whisper.

"I'm afraid it's over, John," Springer said, giving his young friend a reassuring pat on the shoulder. "Now, let's get back to doing what we're supposed to do—taking care of patients, at least as long as they let us."

Russell again turned to leave when a familiar voice stopped him.

"Dr. Springer," Britt Barkley, Methodist's chief executive officer, called out above the noise of the crowded emergency room. "Would you meet me in my office?"

Still reeling from his latest revelation, Springer pointed to throngs of patients still waiting to be seen. "I'm afraid it will have to wait," he said abruptly, his patience wearing thin. "Can't you see what's going on here?"

Barkley moved closer, his hands flared to his side. "Dr. Springer, I said *now*!"

. . .

"Come on in," Barkley said as Springer, still agitated by the administrator's interruption, moved into the office.

Reluctantly, Springer took a seat in front of the administrator's desk. "Let's not beat around, Barkley. I have a full house out there."

The administrator grinned, then shuffled in his chair. "I would guess that you have no idea how I spend my time when I am not here at Methodist," he said, picking up a memo from his desk.

"I don't see how that's relevant," Springer answered, wanting to say that not only did he not know, but he also didn't care.

Barkley laid the paper down, pushing it across his desk toward Springer. "The National Guard, where I hold the rank of full bird colonel." A broad smile broke out across his face. "Now, why don't you take a moment and read the memo from the attorney general of the United States."

Springer's mouth fell open as the words on the private communication shook him to his core.

Colonel Barkley:

It is my duty to inform you that you have been assigned to oversee the transfer of the physicians on the staff of Methodist Medical Center and the surrounding community as they transition from their civilian status and under the auspices of the Department of Health and Human Services … authority of the Justice Department of the United States of America.

Sincerely,
Carr P. Stokley
Attorney General

"So, Dr. Springer," Barkley said, leaning forward on his desk, his chest puffed with his newly acquired authority. "It seems fate has dealt us a different hand of cards to play. My first order of business will be to convene the medical staff so that we can inform the physicians as to the rapid reopening of their offices, allowing Methodist Hospital to return to normal operations."

"We!" Springer barked out in frustration.

Barkley leaned back in his chair, his hands now clasped behind his head. "Due to the respect the physicians around here hold for you, I have decided to appoint you as my liaison with the medical staff," he said, his tone smug. "I thought you would be honored."

"Bastard," Springer uttered under his breath, feeling he was being turned into a Judas goat.

Slam! Barkley brought his closed fist down on the desk with such force that Springer jerked back in shock. "From now on, it's Colonel to you, and don't forget it." Barkley jumped to his feet, pointing to the door. "Now, go on back to your ICU. I'll get in touch with you about the meeting."

Springer slowly raised himself from the chair and headed for the door, then stopped and turned around. "You do that … Colonel."

Springer had barely made it out the door to Barkley's office when he almost ran into John Terrell, who appeared out of nowhere and pulled him to the side. "I heard," Terrell whispered, slipping a folded sheet of paper in Springer's hand. "I just downloaded this from the consortium."

His mind still reeling, Springer said, "I never herd of them."

"I hadn't either," Terrell answered, smiling. "It's evidently a newly formed alliance of all the major medical organizations. Go on. Read." He pointed to the message in Springer's hand.

Springer silently mouthed the words printed on the confidential memo, his mind about to explode from shock. Dropping his hand to his side, he slowly looked up at his friend. "I hope that someday our patients will realize we did this for them."

. . .

"He wants to be taken to Methodist," Lou Bosser said, his voice almost drowned out by the roar of the siren. "Says his wife had her baby there, and he has a lot of confidence in their doctors."

Randy Sanchez flipped a quick look at his partner, who was holding a compression bandage on the patient's leg. "That's a good twelve minutes from here," he said, his eyes back on the road. "Do you think you can hold out?"

Bosser nodded, not that his fellow EMT could see, then readjusted the blood-soaked bandage to make sure the patient's severely lacerated femoral artery was still properly occluded. "I guess that's why I eat Wheaties," he said, knowing that with any slip on his part, the young man in his twenties would exsanguinate on the gurney before they could get help.

As the seconds grew into minutes, Lou Bosser's forearms began to take on the feeling of sacks of wet cement, growing heavier by the moment. "How much longer?" he called out.

"It's just up the next block," Sanchez answered as the ambulance continued to move quickly through the night.

Bosser heaved a sigh of relief, knowing help was just up ahead when, without warning, he was thrown forward as Sanchez brought the ambulance to a screeching halt. "What the hell is going on?" he asked, his hands still locked tightly around the patient's thigh.

"Hold on. Must be a power outage or something," Sanchez said. "There's a squad car in the parking lot. They'll know what's going on." He eased the ambulance on up alongside the idling vehicle and jumped out. "Be right back."

The fatigued EMT leaned back on his haunches, his arms and shoulders now knotted in pain. The sounds of his groaning patient were muffled as he waited anxiously for help. Suddenly, the rear door to the vehicle swung open as Bosser, his pain temporarily forgotten, broke into a dubious smile. Silhouetted only by the flashing lights of the police car, Sanchez stood silent in the darkness. A strange feeling engulfed Bosser as he said to his partner, "What's going on?"

"The hospital is closed."

AFTERWORD

IS IT PLAUSIBLE that, as the frustrations of just trying to care for patients continues to erode the morale of the physicians of this country, one day they would finally take matters into their own hands and say enough is enough? With growing frequency, we are seeing individual responses to that question with the increasing number of physicians who retire early or make career changes rather than continue the battles of reimbursement, liability threats, and the mounting number of federal, state, and third-party payer regulations that continually impede their ability to practice medicine. But what would happen if instead of individual actions by isolated physicians, that response was collective—physicians coming together and their resolve absolute that there would be no more compromises? Is that possible? Fortunately, the answer to that question has yet to be tested.

Three questionable assumptions, which are currently held by an alarming number of leaders in this country, make this plausibility more a possibility. The first is that no matter how much reimbursement for health care services are cut or how many regulations are forced upon those who deliver those health care services, somehow the quality of those health care services will not be adversely affected. Second, and the focus of this text, is that physicians will always be there for their patients, even under the worst of circumstances. Finally, it is the assumption that physicians, because of their dedication to a higher cause—protecting their patients' interests above all else—would never do anything that might endanger their well-being, even if it is for a greater good.

It has been said that humankind's strongest response is one of survival—the protection of one's own life. But couldn't that concept also apply to one's own way of life, as in the case of physicians? What if someday the physicians in this country decide that in order for the profession of medicine to survive, they must assume an overriding obligation not just to their own patients but to the doctors and their patients of future generations who will suffer from the injustices that our current generation has not been willing or able to adequately address?

If that day comes, the plausible becomes possible, and the possible could become reality.

01978695-02549082

Printed in the United States
By Bookmasters